# THE
# GOLDSTON
# CHRONICLES

# THE
# GOLDSTON
# CHRONICLES

*James D. Dailey*

*The Goldston Chronicles*

Published by Hats Off Books®
610 East Delano Street, Suite 104
Tucson, Arizona 85705 U.S.A.
www.hatsoffbooks.com

ISBN: 1-58736-369-0 (hardcover)
ISBN: 1-58736-449-2 (paperback)
LCCN: 2004109678

# CONTENTS

# FOREWORD

Although this story tells of a disaster, this story is about people—people who suffer great loss during global climate upheavals.

The whole world is thrown into darkness, in the twinkling of an eye. Everything—law and order, the everyday work place for most people, homes, shops, cities, and towns—is suddenly gone forever. They come through the turmoil by using common sense, their moral judgment, and a determination to recover and carry on with a new life and a new way of living.

During times of turmoil, when there is a power vacuum, there are those who will take advantage of a situation and try to take control as tyrannical leaders, such as the characters of Jason and his followers in the story. But people of good will and determination, with able leaders, can overcome those tyrants, as the people of three different locations come together in this story and succeed beyond their own expectations.

As time passes, and people find time to explore and move away from their immediate areas, they meet and greet new people, as did one of the main characters on such an exploration—meeting up with Big Nose Dushea and his boat crew, who in their turn had met many good people, but some bad, who they labeled "the Locust People."

This story relates the true axiom that there is always going to be the element of evil in and around human existence, but the human condition is one of goodness, and those elements that try hard to prove this wrong will be vanquished by the good that lives in all mankind, given enough time.

*Chapter 1*

# ZERO-THREE-ZERO

Sitting here on the hill, looking down on the small town below, my thoughts seem to drift back over the last few years since we settled in this valley. We have been through so much since the disaster that destroyed forever the world we knew in the twenty-first century.

I can see the first log houses going up, where the square is today. The storehouse, where we first put the precious few commodities with which we arrived, is now a huge warehouse, several times larger than the original. The whole valley is alive with people, old ones and new ones, all bent on one thing or another, some task to satisfy their needs or those of someone they are attached to by blood, marriage, or commercial endeavor.

Almost out of sight, the sawmill—completed just over five years ago—has changed the face of the town so much that expeditions returning from north or south are hard put to believe they're returning to New Virginia. But it was all to be expected—these people are pioneer stock. Colonists who took a virgin land and changed it in so many ways, over such a short period of time.

I would imagine the turning point in the life of the people and the town below was the day the dam on Elbow Creek was completed. From that day to this, there has been an ever-increasing flow of ideas and inventions to make life easier.

After the dam came the mill, where they grind all manner of grain. People from small villages, far and wide, came to see the ingenious operation, and to have their own grain milled. Now, even the sawmill has become such an everyday fixture that it's taken for granted. There's talk, now, of constructing a generator for electric power, something unheard of for over thirty years. What a benefit that will be to the people of this valley.

Someone's coming up the trail. It's not steep, but it winds quite a bit. I built it that way on purpose. If anyone from the town wants to see me, for some reason, he or she is going to get a good workout.

"Good even', Mr. Darby."

It was Rodney, the young man who has, in the past year or so, taken to writing a history of our times and travels since the great upheaval. He is well-suited to the job. His father was an excellent historian, and his mother has prepared him well to accomplish the job his father started years ago. But for Stephen, Rodney's father, the pressure of building a town and seeing to its administration has left precious little time for writing.

"Hi, Rodney. What brings you up here? Don't tell me you've taken your father's seat on the council and are looking for a couple votes."

"No, sir, nothing like that at all. I'm still working on the history of our times, and everyone's been telling me that you were with the band that settled the village. I thought that we could arrange for a few days of your time, to go over the past."

Rodney stopped, and with a smile, held his hands up, palms facing me, a gesture I took to mean, "Wait a minute, before replying. I have more to say."

"I know, I know—when you and the other old ones were voted off the council and retired, you stated that from that day forward you would never go near the town and that you didn't want anyone from town bothering you, unless it was a dire emergency. I believe your words were something to the effect that anyone venturing upon your land would most probably be thrown off the mountain?"

I had to chuckle at this revelation. I didn't know I was taken with such seriousness in the town.

The old ones, of which I was a member, were treated with great respect, and as our ranks thinned out, the ones left seemed almost mystical.

How could I say we were treated with great respect and have such a strong reaction to being retired? Well, I think the answer was twofold. First, the "new people," or those born after the great earth upheavals of thirty years before, have depended greatly on the ones now called the "old people," meaning those born before the catastrophe. Being called old had nothing to do with age, until recently, but was directed at those of the old society—a world long gone.

And second, I had seen this coming for a number of years. The young ones, now approaching middle age, wanted the old ones to move out of their way, let them show that they could do the work that needed to be done. As if to say, "thank you, but now it is our turn to run the show."

"Well, Rodney, I didn't mean to be so harsh in my last statement to the townspeople, but I was hurt that they would retire me against my will, just as they did your father, last year."

Rodney was busy writing a note on his scratch pad, so I continued.

"Susan and I have not completely cut ourselves off from you and the rest of the people below—she still goes down once or twice a week and helps your mother with school problems, if she can. She and I have a lot of friends, down there—some old people, some new. I don't mind her going down there so much as I mind the lecture I get when she returns and wants something done about straightening out the trail."

"Here's what I'm looking for. I want to let those that follow know how we got here, where their fathers and mothers came from, who started the first school, why a dam was built, by whom, for what purpose. I have a thousand questions that one day will be asked by a thousand children not yet born."

"I don't know, Rodney. I don't know if I can remember that far back."

"I'm sure you can. And if you can't remember some things, I can help you. My father knows a lot, and Mr. Foxworth and his wife were both from the original band."

"Sounds like a big project, but it may be fun. I don't have much to do, since being canned by the town committee." I tried to sound hurt, but winked to let him know not to take me entirely seriously.

"Do you think Mrs. Darby would like to help with the writing, with the history? I understand she and Mother were quite a pair."

"Susan? Sure! She was a history student, once, herself."

Thoughts of those days of long, long ago suddenly brought a mist to my eyes. I couldn't help it.

"When can we start?" he said. Now that negotiations had been opened, Rodney, with the exuberance of youth, was ready to write a history of the world before midnight.

"Let's wait until the weekend, so that I can get some chores done around the farm and have time to do some remembering."

"Sounds good to me. Gives me time to talk with my father and Mr. and Mrs. Foxworth. I'll take notes, and we can compare them when we get down to the actual writing."

"I think you're overlooking one of the best sources. Talk with Judy Burnside. She doesn't say much, now, and stays by herself out at the mill, since Johnny passed on, but she saw the same things the rest of us did. And she loves to talk with anybody about Johnny."

"I'd completely forgotten about her."

"I'll talk with Susan tonight, and by Saturday, we should be ready to sit with you for some serious history lessons."

Susan came out on the porch to announce supper and to see who would climb my crooked trail at this hour of the day.

"Rodney, how are you? I came to get J.J. for supper, and we'd enjoy your company at the table."

"Thanks, Mrs. Darby. I do appreciate the offer, but Mom's expecting me." Rodney turned to go, then stopped. "What time, Saturday, Mr. Darby?"

"Lets make it eight, so we can get a good start before my head gets clouded by the heat of the day."

"Okay, I'll see you Saturday."

"'Night, Rodney," we said in unison, as couples are apt to do after so many years of marriage.

As we walked to the supper table, Susan wanted to know about the visit of Rodney Adams. I told her about the history of the colony, which his father was going to write for so many years but had never started, and that young Rodney was finally going to get the project off the ground.

"He wants to talk with you, too. You know so many different aspects of our history that I don't know. Especially the year that I was away on the expedition to the east coast."

"I remember that year. First the flooding, followed by the miserable, dry summer, and wondering what trouble you and the rest might be in for."

"What an experience that was." For awhile, we were quiet with our own thoughts about the past.

My thoughts moved on to the chicken potpie that Susan had set before us. I still don't know the first thing about good cooking, but I do know that no more than five or six years ago the ingredients—chicken, carrots, potatoes, peas, onion, flour—weren't available. The big, old iron stove used to prepare the meal had been a relic, brought back out of necessity, and Susan had had to learn her cooking skills all over again. There were no such things as microwave, convection, gas, electric, or solar stoves to prepare meals. Those were all part of the past.

Susan broke the silence. "J.J., when did Rodney start on this project?"

"I don't really know, but I'm glad he has. There's so much that the new people don't know, and if we don't tell them, in a few years the past will cease to exist."

I thought about my last statement, and realized that a good deal of the past would be lost when we ceased to exist, if it was not written down by someone.

Susan brought me back to reality. "I'll give him my diary. It might come in handy for his story."

"Diary? What diary?" It occurred to me that, after forty years of marriage, there were still some things I didn't know about her.

"I meant to tell you about it, dear. I started the diary when you were off on the expedition—when was that, Year 18 or 19?"

I had to think for a few minutes. "We left in March of 18, and marched into the village on the 25th of May, 19."

"Anyhow, Beth Adams and I had nothing to do, and that hot, little cabin in the valley was just too dreadful to stay in. So one day, we sat outside in the shade, took some paper and pens, and started writing down our recollections."

"Just what we need! Maybe you could let me have a peek, before the boy comes back—bone up a little. Might jar something loose."

As I looked up, Susan was staring off into space.

"Penny for your thoughts," I said, "or a cookie, or whatever it is they're using for money, now."

She returned from far away. "I was just thinking how I have wished someone would write a history of our past, of our village, the people we knew before we came here, and all that could be remembered of the United States. I understand that some books have been recovered from the river near Old Norfolk, and that some of them contain historical material. Be sure to tell Rodney about that, in case he doesn't know."

I was looking forward to Saturday and getting started. The darkness was overtaking us rapidly, and it was time to light the lamps and get Susan enough water to be heated for the supper dishes.

My immediate problems having been taken care of, it was time to close up the farm. Anyone not living in the close confines of a village or large ranch still had to lock all doors and windows, if he wanted to be sure of a safe night's sleep. There were still raiders and marauders around. Not many, to be sure, and most of them old people, still angry in a new world they didn't want and couldn't understand.

The next morning was hot and sunny—a good day to take care of the garden. We'd had a garden up here since the first day we'd moved to the top of the mountain. Everyone over thirty years of age remembers the horrible time of hunger. We all grow gardens or plots, or have windowsills filled with tomatoes or some such thing, anytime, anywhere it's convenient, and even when it isn't convenient.

I was so proud of that year's crop. It was the finest I'd ever put together. In past years, I'd had help from friends, but they are mostly gone over to the other side, now.

"The other side." Where did I get such a phrase? From my boyhood, I would think. Some of the terms we old people use confound the youngsters. At times, they think we have a secret language that we haven't let them in on, yet.

No one wants to climb my crooked trail, to help some cranky, old man till his garden. I have to smile to myself, because they all complain, yet when they get up here, they look around, and I can see they are quite taken with the view.

We climbed many hills to get to that spot, and people will relate past experiences until dark, when it's time to head for their homes or back to the village. Every time, it's their last trip up that steep, crooked trail to help some cranky, old man till his garden, but I see the twinkle in the eye and the slight curve of the mouth into a grin that tell me they'll be back.

The important things are that we visit and help each other. Watching out for one another is something we have bred in ourselves, over the past years and through all of the miseries and good times.

It's time to stop all this daydreaming, and get on with the garden. The surrounding jungle is trying slowly to take over everything. It was determined, long ago, that after all the quakes, the land we now occupy is below and not above the equator, as it was once. We've inherited a tropical climate and rainfall.

But the advantage is that we can grow almost anything we want to, virtually anytime of the year, with the exception of early August through late September. A blessing, to be sure, when much of the world is still going through upheavals, and some of the people are still inclined to flee, as their land suddenly becomes part of a lake or the top of a mountain, as the earth continues to heave, shake, and rumble.

I must make it a point to be in the village when the next expedition returns. Timothy Engles will be returning with that one, and he is about the best when it comes to recording what he saw—the people's culture and the lay of the land.

When I go down, I have to stop in at the smithy—all of my blades for cutting or hoeing are about to fall apart, rust away, or both. My hand plow needs tightening up and a new wheel. And if I can bring myself to it, I might talk to the council and see if I can get a horse, next year. They're still in short supply, but just to bust the ground would be a great help.

"J.J."

It's Susan calling—must be time for lunch. I've wasted almost all morning daydreaming about the past, my friends, Rodney's book.

"J.J., lunch is ready. Can you hear me?"

"I can hear you. I'll be right there."

"I have a note from Rodney—he wants to come up tomorrow and start on the book. He wants to know if he should bring up extra clothing and spend a few days."

"I wonder why tomorrow, and not Saturday?"

"No one likes to tackle your crooked trail twice in one day, if they can help it, and Rodney will have papers, books, and lord-knows-what-all with him. As for tomorrow, he'd be up here right now, if he knew he could get away with it. He's so absorbed with this project that nothing else means anything to him, right now."

"Where's the messenger?"

"I sent him back. I told him to tell Rodney that I would bring your answer."

"You're going down to the village?"

"I told you about this weeks ago. Beth and I have organized a quilting bee. We're expecting at least two dozen women at her house, tomorrow morning. We want to get everything ready for the next expedition, and we don't have much time. The quilts are the only big project we have left."

"Now, I remember—the expedition to the south. I was wondering why the quilts, when we haven't had a use for them in years. How long will you be gone?"

"Through the weekend, at least. You and Rodney can manage. I've left plenty of ham, potato salad, freshly baked bread, and if you want to fix sweet potatoes, they're in the root cellar."

She kept on talking, as I followed her through the house, watching with great interest the precision she had for gathering and organizing herself and all the articles she planned to take with her.

"If we're not done by Monday, I'll have one of Harold's young-sters bring you word, so don't worry about me."

Easier said than done, and she knows it. I've been worrying about her since way before we married, in what was a small coastal village in what was the state of North Carolina. Don't worry, indeed. What would I do without her? She knows more about me than I know about myself. Just two kids, it seems like, on our first assignment for Past Explorations. *We present the past to you in the pres-ent*—that had been the slogan of the archaeology company we'd worked for, and we'd believed in it wholeheartedly.

She had just graduated from the university—the prettiest, smartest, most witty girl I'd ever known. Long, brown hair flowing everywhere. That was in nineteen seventy-eight. It had taken me almost a year to convince her that I was the best thing to come along in her life and would make her a wonderful mate. What a courtship—digging in the sand all day, on a small sand spit in the Atlantic Ocean, and scratching sand fleas half the night.

"I hear the Adams kids coming, now," she said. "Tell them to wait. I'll be ready just as soon as I get all these bags together. Would you send little Harold to the kitchen, to get the cookies I baked?"

"What cookies?"

"The cookies I baked this morning, and why didn't I tell you? Because if I had, I'd be baking more, now. I've left enough in the cupboard to last two hungry men for a week."

The children were climbing up the steps to the front porch. There were Harold, Jr. and his sister, Harriet—Stephen and Beth's grandkids.

"Come on in, youngsters. Susan will be ready in a minute. Harold, why don't you go on into the kitchen. There are some packages for you to take back to the village."

"Okay, Mr. Darby. Granddad said he sure wished you would come down more often, and come by and see him."

"I'll make a point to do that. How is your granddad?"

I couldn't wait for Harold's answer. Although he was only ten years old, he acted more like thirty and talked like a person of thirty. If I didn't know better, I would think he was a reincarnated old person.

"He's fine, still doing work for the council. He's resigned himself to letting the new people run the government and helping out when he can. I think that's why he misses you and the other old people so much. He says you all understand things so much better."

"I don't doubt that. Tell your granddad that I'll be down next week. I might need his influence when I go before the council, to ask for a horse for next year's planting."

I could see the women were ready to go, so Harold and I cut our conversation short, so that he could get the packages and cookies.

"Everything's ready," Susan said, as they gathered at the front door.

It looked to me like the expedition was starting out from here, by the amount of bundles the kids and Susan had.

"Be careful on the trail, dear," I said. "And if it's raining on Monday, please delay your trip back—you know how bad it can get when it's wet."

"You take care of yourself. Tell Rodney I think his book is a great idea, and I'm sorry I can't be here to help you two get started. I've left my diary on the kitchen table. You're both welcome to look through it and use what information may be useful. There's nothing personal in there, so tell Rodney not to be shy about reading it. See you Monday."

I escorted them to the place where the trail started its descent into the valley below, then I returned to the cabin to wait for Rodney. If I was a good judge of character, he would be here just about two hours from the time Susan and the kids got to his house with the message to come on up.

I filled the time gathering all of the notes we both had been making about our lives and adventures since coming into this valley. Then it struck me that Rodney was going to want to know more than the history of the valley—after all, he'd lived here most of his life. He'd want to go back much further than that, back before the disaster, back to the old United States and the world as it had existed. That would take shaking some cobwebs loose. Almost everyone who'd lived through that period wanted to forget it. This might not be as pleasurable a task as I'd once thought.

Everything was ready, so to occupy my time, I spent the last hour trimming vines and clearing out the lower part of the garden area for next year's crop. I sure would like to put in watermelon, next year. I thought the sunny end would be the perfect place for them.

I knew Rodney was coming a good fifteen minutes before he arrived. No one had yet figured out how I always knew. When I'd first laid out the route, I'd noticed that, with one more turn and a somewhat circular pattern, the trail would pass over a small knob visible from the cabin but not detected so easily by persons on the trail. If I was anywhere near the front of the cabin or in the garden, 99 percent of the time I would detect anyone coming up the trail when they passed over that small knob.

Since it was late afternoon when Rodney arrived, I suggested a supper of ham, potato salad, good hot bread, coffee, and, of course, freshly baked cookies for desert, which I had been sampling throughout the afternoon.

"Delicious meal, J.J. Can I help you with the cleanup?"

"No, you get your things put away. Susan has the front room all fixed up for you. Then, why don't you take it easy in the gazebo, until I bring out a good cup of coffee."

By the time I had the kitchen in a good and clean condition, the only way Susan would accept, Rodney was waiting in the gazebo, looking over some notes and papers that he'd brought up with him.

"Dad said to be sure and ask you about the expedition you led in 18 and 19. Seems it was the talk of the village for quite awhile, when you got back."

"I guess it was. What kind of a book are you going to make of this? How can I be of the greatest help to you?"

"I thought I'd make it a history of the people who settled this valley. We've been here fourteen years, now, and are growing and expanding every day. Within a few years, the children in school now will be taking over the council, the businesses, and leading the expeditions. I want them to know the history of the people—where you come from, Dad, Mom, and all the rest. I understand that you were from different areas of the old world, or 'old order,' if you will, but they won't know that unless there's a record left for them."

Sounded like what I would have done, if I'd known how to put it down on paper.

"I've a good piece of news for you. Susan kept a diary while I was away on the expedition, and she's been keeping notes and such since. She wants us to use it."

"That's great. You can't believe how much help I've been getting, since I started this project. Dad's turned over all his papers to me. The council opened up their files, and literally everyone who knows anything about the village or the past has been sending me letters, notes, and diaries. And do you know how many of those notes and letters mention you and Susan?"

I looked at him quizzically. It hadn't occurred to me that anyone, with the exception of my own wife, would keep a record of our lives and what we had done. Slowly, I shook my head from side to side, waiting to hear his answer.

"Everyone—well, almost everyone. You're written about everywhere, and many of the women who know Mrs. Darby say that, without her help and discipline, they wouldn't be here today."

"I'm very flattered, Rodney. I hope that I deserve whatever those good people have written." A little embarrassed, I changed the subject. "How about some more coffee and a cookie or two. I was led to understand there are enough cookies to last two good, strong men for at least a week. Let's see if there's any truth to that statement."

When I returned with what I determined was a good stack of cookies and enough coffee to last for awhile, Rodney was waiting with a question.

"Mr. Darby, about this small…I guess you could call it a house, or a room without walls—what did you call it?"

"A gazebo. Originally, the word meant 'gazing room,' and as you can see, as we sit here, we can gaze upon the whole surrounding countryside. These little rooms were quite common in the southern part of the United States. In fact, Susan and I built one when we were living in the state of Louisiana. Some were elaborate, with stone columns, concrete floors, some very large, some very small, to suit the taste of the builder or owner. We built ours to sit in during the hottest part of the summer, when remaining indoors would get too close for both of us. But we enjoyed it most during the spring, when we'd bring out our chairs after a cold winter and lounge around. Susan would read, or sew, or crochet. I thought about that little gazebo after my retirement, and decided to build another one here, overlooking the valley."

Rodney was writing all of this down.

"You're going to use something like that in your book?"

"Sure. It's part of your life, but it's also part of our heritage, especially now that we have one here."

He made a note.

"And when we uncover history books from before the disaster, as we surely will, and run across the word, we won't be taken by surprise. More importantly, when we uncover one of these little houses on an expedition, we'll know exactly what it is."

"Rodney, there's a lot more to history than I thought. This whole experience—the disaster, the moving from one place to another, the years of little food, bad crops—it has been truly like starting over again, without a blueprint but with just enough knowledge and understanding to keep us going from one year to the next.

"You sound like my father. He's told me all my life, 'learn from your mistakes, and don't make the same mistake twice.' Now that

I'm grown, I want to translate that to our village. If we learn from past mistakes, we won't make them ourselves."

"Good, but don't limit your quest for knowledge to this village. Reach out as far as you can; make friends with everyone and any village you come in contact with, whether you like their lifestyles or not. Remember, you can learn from them the same as from your own."

"It's all written down, Mr. Darby."

"'J.J.' will suffice," I said.

"All right, sir. 'J.J.' it will be. You know, not all of the new people believe some stories that are told about the past."

"What kind of stories?"

"Well, for instance, what my father calls 'television'—a window or a screen, something that everyone had in their homes that was used to tell stories, brief people on the days news anywhere in the world. It's said that the chief council member—I believe his title was 'president'—could talk to all of the people at the same time and never leave his home. It's hard to explain that such a thing doesn't seem possible to us, but the story about the television is told in much the same way by all the old people."

"Believe me, it's true. If we have time, I'll try to explain its use and how it worked. What else do the youngsters not believe?"

"It's not that we believe the stories are lies. I know my own father wouldn't embellish the past, but time does have a habit of making the good things seem better and the bad things fade."

"I'll give you that much. People do tend to highlight the best things in their lives, but I'm interested in what else they may believe we've exaggerated."

"Let me think." He was staring down into the valley, as if the landscape below had an answer to my question.

"There's the road system we hear about. A hard substance over which vehicles would pass at great speeds—those passageways through desert and forest would last for years. And that food or other goods could be transported from one part of the continent to the other, sometimes five or six hundred miles, in a matter of hours. We talk about this, and see that a good team of oxen takes a full day to go to the mill and back. The best and fastest horseman on a superb steed can't cover more than twenty miles in a single day."

"Listening to you, I can understand how you would doubt the existence of such things. It's hard to tell you about them, but they did exist, along with a host of other everyday miracles that we took for granted."

"Is it really true that you had instant food and machines that flew through the air faster than vehicles that crossed the ground? Or what about the instrument that let people in one village hear or speak to people in villages a world away?"

"The telephone or computer? Yes, we had them all. But it took man a long time to produce those wonders, and I have no doubt that he will again. As the expeditions return with more books and records of the past world, I'm sure more of these things will become known again. What say we call it a night, and get a fresh start in the morning?"

Rodney was closing the large writing tablet he had been using to take down our conversation. Written on the front:

*Conversations with J.J. Darby*
*At his home: Chesapeake Valley*
*Zero-Three-Zero, July 20*

"I couldn't help but notice what was written on the front of your notebook. When did we start using three-digit dates for the years?"

"Shortly after Dad left the council. Mr. Trammel, the miller, had been pushing for it for a long time, but while Dad was still chief councilor, he wouldn't let the proposal come up for a vote."

"So when your Dad left, he finally got it before the council?"

"It had been there for a long time, and everyone knew about it, but Dad had said it was not of earth-shattering proportions, and there was too much other business."

While Rodney was gathering up the last of his papers, I was staring down into the valley—at the meeting hall, where laws and regulations were now being made for all of the people within a fifty-mile radius, and very likely for all of the country within five hundred, some day. If our youngsters were up to it and were wise enough to govern such a large area.

Things must be getting better for our people and for the world, if they were now able to sit down and figure out that we needed three digits on our new calendars, to replace the present two. Democracy and its bureaucratic compartments were alive and well, and the year was 030.

NEW VIRGINIA VILLAGE
ZERO THREE ZERO

ABANDONED DEFENSE LINE

HOME OF
J.J & SUSAN DARBY

VILLAGE

WINTER FEED
GRAZING

SUMMER CROPS

SAW MILL
DAM

RESERVOIR

"T" FLOW

LIVESTOCK
GRAZING

NORTH

OLD LOOKOUT POINT
NOW HOMESTEAD

Drawn by J.J. Darby
For Rodney Adams
Ø3Ø

24

## Chapter 2

⁊

# THE TILT

The next morning, I was up with the sun, as usual. I didn't think Rodney would have arisen, so I started to the kitchen to get the old iron stove warmed up. The old, iron lady I call "Tin Lizzy" has been with us for a few years, now—ever since the day Susan rescued it from a pile of rusting rubble in what was to be our home, until the land there, one day, turned to jelly and we had to flee. We were quite lucky, then, as we had been during our long journey into this valley. She wouldn't leave Tin Lizzy, then, and we've taken it with us everywhere, since. I've sat on more than one occasion and wondered how old that stove might really be.

As I neared the kitchen, I smelled the coffee already brewing. Rodney wasn't a late sleeper, as I had thought.

"Good morning. Ready to get to it?" he asked.

"Just as soon as I have a cup of that coffee and some bread. My body needs the nourishment," I said. "Sleep good, or were you awake all night thinking about the book?"

"No, sir, slept very well."

"Should we work here in the kitchen or outside?"

Rodney thought for a minute. "I think I'd like the outdoors," he said.

"Okay. Let's get the coffee and bread, and go."

We had just settled in the little gazebo when the sun peeked up from behind the far ridge, across the valley.

"How do we start this?" I had never been interviewed in my whole life, so I wasn't sure just how this was to be done.

"Let's start with the time just before the first breakup. Where were you and the other members of the exploration—for instance, my father, mother, and anyone else who may come to mind? You tell your story, and when I have a question I'll stop you."

I sat staring at Rodney. He had no idea what he was asking of me. Or did he? After all, he was born soon after the breakup; his mother had been well into her fourth month, and had carried him through some very trying times. But he had been a very young boy, no more that a baby, when we'd almost starved to death during the terrible storms that had racked the planet for over a year, and he had been sheltered from some of the worst decisions that had been made by the council, during those trying times.

All of those bad times, all of those decisions, he now wanted me to recall for a book—a book that would tell others the things we old folks would just as soon forget ever happened. I was ready to back out. *I'm too old to remember. I've got some chores that need tending to. I'll talk it over with your father and some of the old people, first.* Nothing I could think of made any sense.

Then I thought of the old people, the old people of my youth—my parents, their parents—and the stories I had heard of the Depression, the horrible wars that racked the planet between 1917 and 1945, and the hundreds of brushfire wars that followed. They'd told us of their bad times, and had wanted the world to be a better place for future generations. Now it was time for me to make it better for my future generations, by letting them know about their parents' and grandparents' worst days. I found I was shaking, and wasn't sure if it was from the cool July breeze or from thinking of how scared I had been when the world had started falling apart around me.

"You all right?"

Rodney had been waiting for me to say something, anything, and I was sitting there like stone, staring into space.

"It still scares me to think of what happened that day. It scares me because I found out that the earth wasn't solid under my feet; that my world, the world I grew up in, doesn't exist anymore.

"It's like a dream. Did all of those things we discussed last night really exist? The television...I believe you called it 'the window'...computers, the telephone, the thousands of miles of concrete, hard-surface roadway—were they real? To me they were, but will never be again, except maybe many years in the future, your future. I don't believe I'll live to see such things again. But this isn't helping with the task at hand. I'm ready to go."

I leaned back and closed my eyes, trying to visualize the past. I could see the reservoir where we were working, that day, just as plain as if it had been yesterday.

We were still working for Past Explorations, the same company we had started out with shortly after our marriage, only now things were much different. Your father and mother had taken over control, and Susan and I had bought shares.

Everyone thought your father and I made perfect partners. He was tall and lanky; thinning blond hair, even in his twenties; the thinker of the two; calm, cool, and collected. I was his opposite; shorter; dark-brown hair, cropped short—I liked my crew cut; ruddy complexion; and at that time, I always wanted to go see what was another foot deeper in the ground or what was over the next ridge. Your father said it was my piercing blue eyes, combined with my dark complexion, that gave me an edge in any argument we ever had.

We were riding on the crest of a good life. The company was prospering with all of the federal business, and we had teams working in the Yucatan, the Greek isles, Alaska, and our dig in the Rocky Mountains. We always saved that one for ourselves.

We had been on it five years, by then, and the deeper we dug into the hill, southwest of the small village of Ioda, the more we were finding. We were sure that with just a couple more good seasons, we would expose a city perhaps more than ten thousand years old, covering better than fifty acres, which could have supported a population in excess of five thousand souls, at its peak.

With the excavation phase of the project over, there would be three to five years' work left—identifying objects, putting everything in its rightful place, seeing where the city fit in the scheme of things in and around the adjoining mountains.

Our digging season was shortened, due to the high altitude and the extremely cold temperatures up there, but once the basic lines of the city had been drawn up and uncovered, we had planned to winter over, right there in that ancient village. Of course, things didn't turn out that way.

Most members lived in a trailer camp we had set up outside Ioda, on the east side, along the only paved road into the town. There were three of our people living in Goldston, the largest town within fifty or sixty miles, and the Foxworth twins were going to school there. Over the years, many friendships had been made with the people of the town. Everyone shopped there for groceries and clothes and attended the annual rodeo.

There were also Judy Jones—you know her as Judy Burnside— and her roommate, Karen Valency; also, two students from Wayfore University, who had been on the dig before, but I can't remember their names, right now. All I can remember is one's first name was Aaron. He had long, brown hair that hung almost to his waist. We were always after him to get it cut, especially the women. He had the best-looking hair on the dig.

Let's see. Besides Goldston and Ioda, there was a small town across the reservoir that was virtually a ghost town in winter— Silverspoon, and another summer trailer park site on the north side of the reservoir, near the National Park headquarters.

The "parkies," as we called them, were forever bringing tourists over to the dig site for a look-see. We enjoyed talking about our work, and became good friends with the rangers.

On the last morning of the dig, Stephen, myself, George Foxworth, Johnny Burnside, and Tim Engles said goodbye to your mother and Susan. They and Nancy Foxworth were the only ones left in camp during the day. We started the mile walk to the dig site. Your father, George, and I were the only ones married, then. We had to head south and west, around Ioda and a small inlet, then head northwest to the dig site.

We left the trailer camp about 7:30, as we did every workday. Judy, her roommate, and the two college students were, as always, about ten minutes behind us. The three from town were always on site by eight, our usual starting time.

Your mother and Susan were working in a trailer we had purchased the year before, to hold all the artifacts until we were ready to go back to North Carolina. It was shortly after eight when I could have sworn I felt the earth move. It was almost as if I was having a dizzy spell; it reminded me of being lightheaded when at high altitudes for the very first time. It lasted no more than a second, and as I looked around, everyone was working away as if nothing had happened. I thought that I might have felt a slight tremor. There had been no shake-up of any consequence anywhere for six months or more.

As I look back now, there were a lot of warnings. California had been shaken by a quake that had started deep in the Gulf of California, traveled through San Francisco, and up the Pacific coast, terminating off the coast of Alaska. A quake had shaken the middle Mississippi Basin, from northern Louisiana and Arkansas across to eastern Tennessee and Kentucky. That hadn't happened in over one hundred years. Japan had suffered the most severe quakes ever recorded in modern times, Europe had felt quakes, and it was reported that new lands had risen in the Atlantic, along what was called the Mid-Atlantic Ridge. But there had never been any tremors to worry about in the Rockies, and we certainly didn't have a Mount St. Helens to put up with, there.

I forgot the incident, and was looking forward to the morning break. But by ten o'clock, I knew for sure that the earth had moved. I was in a pit by myself. The pit was our usual six-foot square, and I was just approaching three feet deep. I was taking a measurement of the west wall, by hanging a string from my horizontal line. The vertical string was marked off in centimeters, so I could get a quick reading for anything I found that might be in the wall. I was mapping in a beautiful projectile point—aqua blue in color, seven centimeters long. I had never seen anything like it. I was very excited, and was going to call your father over when I'd finished the mapping, have him take a picture, then remove it from the wall.

Without warning, the vertical line started to move from side to side. It was swaying no more than an inch, but I was fascinated. There was no wind.

The movement became more pronounced. Then, instead of moving from side to side, it started to tremble. I had to be going crazy. As I stared at the dancing string, I had the feeling that something or someone was pushing me toward the floor of the pit. I had been kneeling, and it was as if my arms wouldn't hold me up any longer, because of the pressure being put on me from above.

Then I heard the loudest, hardest hit that I think anyone has ever heard, as if someone had hit a baseball perfectly. The crack was so loud, it almost split my eardrums, and it came from below me. I looked down, and as if in a dream, I was being propelled upward out of the hole. I was flying through the air, as if by magic. Not only was I going up, I was traveling to the side, also. As I looked around, I could see other bodies being propelled through the air; then I hit the ground, hard. I couldn't move. The breath had been knocked out of me, and I was scared. I've never in my life been so frightened as I was at that moment. I knew we were all dead, the world had ended. My next thought was of Susan and what had happened to her, but I could only wonder. I couldn't make myself move—I was just too scared.

I turned over slowly. I had landed on my stomach, with my nose in the sand, and had remained that way for I don't know how long. Other people were moving around, and someone near me was groaning. I wheeled around without getting up, and lay there, looking up at the sky. I turned my head toward the sound of movement, when the sharp sound that had propelled me from my pit came again—and again, it came from the ground, but I wasn't flying through the air this time. Instead, the sun, which was over my right shoulder, disappeared across the western horizon. I closed my eyes and waited. This had to be the end. Someone was calling names, asking if anyone was there. I answered, but didn't get an answer in return.

Then, as suddenly as the sun had disappeared in the west, it reappeared again, but this time it was over my left shoulder. As it settled into place, the sound came back, followed by a rumble like a huge freight train traveling not more than two feet from my head. I could hear it coming, traveling from east to west, and the earth was trembling like so much jelly.

The wind above me was blowing from west to east—it had to have been in excess of many hundreds of miles per hour. Oxygen was being burned by the supersonic force of the wind and was leaving blue streaks all across the sky, with a sound like jungle cats screaming. With the ground rumbling below me and the wind screaming above me, my heart was pounding so hard that I actually put my hand over my chest to keep it from coming right out of my body.

The sun was again bouncing around in the sky. I had the sensation of being in my bunk with someone violently shaking it, trying to get me to wake up. Then, just as suddenly as it had all begun, the earth tremors stopped. The wind stopped. I heard waves crashing, waves in a violent sea, but there wasn't a sea or a large body of water within hundreds of miles.

Quiet. It was so quiet that my head seemed to hurt from the lack of any noise whatsoever. I looked around. George Foxworth was nearest me. He was struggling to get up off the ground.

"George, are you okay?" I asked. He seemed to be having great difficulty standing.

"I think so. My head is spinning," he said. "I can't seem to maintain my equilibrium."

I rolled over on my left side and started to rise. My shoulders hurt so badly when I put weight on my arms that I almost lay back down.

"I'll give you a hand," I said.

I managed to get him in a sitting position, and we both looked around, still stupefied. My first thought was that there was no water in the lake. The inlet that had been in front of us was dry. Ioda was gone, and so was our trailer park.

"The trailer park is gone," George said.

"I know. Take it easy; we'll find them." George looked reassured, but I knew we'd first have to get ourselves organized before we could hope to help anyone else.

Still kneeling by George, I looked to the right, where your dad and Johnny had been surveying, but I couldn't see them. There was a lot of sagebrush in the area, and if they were down in it, they would be hard to see.

Judy had been sketching the hill to the southwest, in preparation for more excavations. Your dad had everything sketched and photographed before we went into anything. I looked for her, and finally spotted her some thirty yards or so from where we were.

Beyond her and to the left had been the excavated city we had worked so hard on. It was gone, slid down into what had been a water reservoir that morning. If it had been destroyed, so had the people who had been working there. Judy's roommate and the two young college students had been on the ground level, mapping and marking artifacts for transfer to the trailer, in the morning. Two floors above had been our three workers who had lived in

Goldston. I can't remember their names or the ones that died in the rooms below. Your father can give you that information.

No one knew what had happened to Tim Engles. Later, I learned he'd been detailed to go to the very top of the mesa, above all of the excavations, and make a ground search. We had planned to put in some test pits, later on that summer, and he was to pick out some choice sites and map them in.

He had been standing up when the first shock hit. As the ground crumbled away under him, he had been hurled forward five hundred yards, and upon landing, slid with the rumbling earth all the way into what had been two hundred feet of water. Covered with mud and bleeding all over from scrapes and abrasions, he was then bounced across the ground, all the way to the north shore of the lake. We lost contact with him for that entire day and night, and it was not until the next afternoon, when he stumbled back into our camp, that we knew he had survived.

Once I had my composure back, I told George to go and see about Judy. I would try and find Steve and Johnny. They couldn't be far away, in the sagebrush or in the ravine that ran parallel to the inlet.

I found them in the ravine. Your father was trying to stop the bleeding around Johnny's head. He'd sustained quite a blow from a flying boulder or when he'd hit the ground. We got him up, and walked back to where George was trying to revive Judy. She was out cold, but breathing. More than likely, she'd had the wind knocked out of her when she'd hit the ground.

"You and Johnny stay here," I said. "Bring Judy around. Get one of the canteens and bathe her head, but don't move her until she comes around, in case she has broken bones. Search the excavation for any survivors, and look for Tim—he was on top of the mesa."

Your father and I headed for the trailer park. Our worst fear was that we'd find all the trailers had landed in one big pile at the bottom of the hill, and that no one would be alive. We both took off at a brisk trot, hoping that some miracle had saved our wives. I was conscious that the earth was still trembling below my feet, but it didn't make any difference anymore.

With the water drained from the inlet, Steve and I had a straight run to what had been Ioda and our trailer park. As we passed over the concrete boat ramp, on the far side of the inlet, I was amazed to see that the roadway was all crushed, as if some large sledgehammer had beaten the once-solid concrete road into powder and pebbles.

As we passed what had been the village, your father told me to continue on to our camp. He was going to detour through what was now a pile of lumber, tin, nuts, bolts, glass, and aluminum, and see if he could find anyone still alive. Until a few minutes before, that pile of rubble had been a general store and gas station; two different restaurants, catering to the summer trade; two rows of small cabins, rented to fishermen and their families; two very fine homes, belonging to some of the proprietors; a large meeting hall; and assorted sheds, store rooms, and the like. The season was still early, and most of the town was still closed up from the previous winter. No one lived there during the hard winters but the caretaker. But we thought there were three or four people there when the quake hit.

When I reached our vehicle parking lot, my heart sank. All the living trailers, the headquarters trailer, and our vehicles were strewn over the landscape for two hundred yards or more. Everything had shifted north, and as the trailers had reached the slope down to the water, it looked as though they had started tumbling over and over. The only thing that was anywhere near its original location was an equipment shed, torn to ribbons, with its contents all over the parking lot.

I started for the pile of ripped and torn trailers, calling names as I went.

"Susan, Susan," I said. "Beth, anybody, answer so we can find you."

No answer, so I called for Nancy, George's wife. Still nothing. As I approached to within ten feet, there came the call I had been straining my ears for. It was Nancy.

"Hurry, we're in here—the artifact room."

I started to climb the stack of rubble, with Steve right on my heels. He had just arrived, without finding anything in the village. The pile started to shift. Nancy was screaming for us to hurry, but we couldn't without shifting the whole mess around and possibly killing us all. I was wondering why only Nancy was able to call to us. What had happened to Susan and Beth?

We decided that the best thing to do would be to approach them from opposite directions, not putting too much weight at any one point on the pile of trailers and other debris. As I looked over the way the trailers were arranged, I yelled to your dad to try going up the south side and I would approach from and climb up the west side.

The trailers were torn up badly, and jagged metal edges were everywhere. I climbed slowly to the top, pulling myself up with great care, so as not to move anything around and to get there in one piece.

When I reached the door and looked in, the trailer was a shambles. The roof had been ripped away, and the only thing holding up the upper wall was the heavy oak table that we'd installed to hold some of the heavier artifacts.

Susan, bent almost double, and Nancy, in pretty much the same condition, were holding the oak table, wedged between the two walls, in place. Beth was wedged between floor and table, and if anything were to slip very much, the full weight of the upper wall would drop on the table, and all three would be crushed.

I knew the girls were worn out, and I kept saying over and over, "Hold on just a little longer, just a little longer."

I dropped into the room, carefully moved around Nancy, and slowly took some of the table weight from her. Steve appeared at the top, saw the situation, and, just as I had, slipped down and slowly started putting pressure on the table.

I asked Susan if she was okay. She nodded, too tired to answer and still too scared to move. I then called to Beth. She was all right, but was crying for us to get her from under the table. Nancy was now free, and I told her to get something to put under the table, so that we could get Susan and Beth out. She moved only a few feet, to where the two front legs of the table had fallen during the tumble down the slope. She passed one back; we wedged it between the lower wall and the table, then the other.

Now that the table would stand up by itself, I climbed back to the door and helped Nancy out, while Steve assisted Susan from under the table and up to the door, then I pulled her up and out. As they started down, I again dropped inside, to assist with Beth.

Johnny had arrived by that time, and had climbed to the top to help with the rescue. Within a few minutes, we were all climbing back up to the parking lot, shaken and tired. We had managed to get everyone out of the trailers without any further injuries.

Now, for the first time, as we sat where the parking lot had been, we tried to contemplate what had happened. If an alien space-craft had appeared out of the sky and landed right before our eyes, I don't think anyone would have been surprised. Nothing was beyond reason.

Of the fifteen on the site, only eight could be accounted for, and without a doubt, the other seven were dead. We were all in shock, and no one was willing to talk about anything. The married couples were holding their partners for support. Judy was hunched over, holding her knees to her chest. Johnny Burnside was lying on his stomach, face cradled in his arms, totally exhausted, and like the rest of us, still scared that at any moment the violent rocking and shaking might return.

The sun had reached its maximum zenith, and was now start-ing its daily journey across the western sky. We couldn't sit waiting for another upheaval, before long it was going to be dark. We had to do something, whether we felt like it or not.

"J.J., let's see what we can do about getting some shelter for tonight." Your father was coming out of the stupor first, and I was glad, because it brought the rest of us back from our withdrawal.

"Where are the tents we use for overnight? George, look through the remains of the equipment shed for the lanterns—gas or battery, it doesn't make any difference.

"Johnny, take a look through the trailers for something to eat. See if any of the water tanks are still intact. We're going to need drinking water, and that's going to be our best source for the pres-ent."

We were all bone-tired and sore from the pounding we had taken earlier, but everyone went to work. The tents were placed across the road from the former parking lot; there wasn't much sagebrush there, and the ground was soft and sandy.

Johnny had taken Judy with him, and they returned with soup, bread, a metal pot, and a five-gallon can of water. Susan and Beth dug a fire pit, and searched the surrounding area for enough fire-wood to brew up our meager supper and keep a small flame going through the night.

As we all assembled for the first food any of us had taken that day, Stephen asked the question we'd all been thinking. "Johnny," he said, "you know more about the geology of this area than the rest of us. What do you think happened?"

Johnny didn't answer for a few moments. As he stared deeply into the fire, his expression was that of a man trying to gather his thoughts before making a judgment call on such a profound question.

"I don't really know. My best guess, right now, is that this is not a localized thing. I don't believe we've suffered a severe quake in the Rockies alone, nor do I believe any of the extinct volcanoes scattered through northern New Mexico or Arizona have suddenly come to life."

"What would make the sun completely disappear?" I asked. "Was I the only one having that sensation?"

"It may have been a dust cloud," he said, "or something I'm afraid to even mention, because I don't think it could be possible or that we'd be alive."

"Don't keep us in suspense, Johnny. We've had enough of that." George's voice was strained to the breaking point, almost cracking under the pressure.

"Have you all either heard or read of the Continental Drift Theory or the Plate Theory?" We all indicated that we had.

Johnny continued, "What has crossed my mind several times today is that if a plate, say the Pacific plate, which completely surrounds the Pacific Ocean, slipped—not just a north-south pressure release, but an override, then the North American plate would either override or dive under the Pacific plate on a large scale—in this case, maybe from Alaska to Peru."

He stopped and looked around at our faces. We were all contemplating what would happen in such a case. "I think you get the same picture, all of you—worldwide destruction, a possible chain reaction affecting the whole globe."

I had a question. "If it's not tectonics, do you think what we're dealing with has been caused by nature or man?"

"If you're thinking war, I'd say with the shaking we observed today, only a nuclear blast in the thousands of megatons could have caused such destruction. Look at the hills around us—their contours have been completely changed. There's no water in the reservoir; the roadway and parking lot are dust. This is nature—pure, simple, total devastation."

Stephen interrupted the conversation. "We can talk about this tomorrow, but right now, I think we should start getting ourselves organized for what may lie ahead. J.J., you have all of the weapons in camp, and you and Susan are the only ones among us who have any military experience. I'd appreciate it if we all had a class on how to handle them, men and women. We may be hunting for our own food and protecting ourselves, before too long."

"Okay with me. When do you want to start instructions?"

"As soon as possible. But first, I want you to set up some type of watch list. I'll leave the details to you, but I want someone awake every hour of the night. We should have a continuous fire going, in case someone over at the park headquarters has survived. No matter who's on watch, if you feel that you need help from any one of us, don't hesitate to wake someone. No matter the reason. Understood?" We all indicated in the affirmative.

After supper, Johnny and I searched my trailer for the weapons and ammunition. Your father was right. We had no idea what tomorrow was going to bring. It was going to be a monumental task just to dig ourselves out, and then to see what was left of the rest of the world.

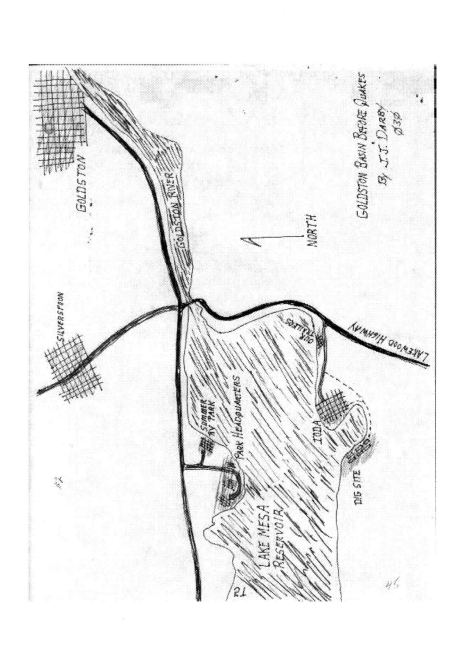

GOLDSTON BASIN BEFORE QUAKES
By J.J. DARBY
ø3ø

GOLDSTON

SILVERSPOON

GOLDSTON RIVER

NORTH

LAKEWOOD HIGHWAY

SUMMER RV PARK

PARK HEADQUARTERS

OUT TRAILERS

IODA

DIG SITE

LAKE MESA RESERVOIR

*Chapter 3*

❦

# DIG OUT

Day two of our ordeal began under bright, cloudless skies. I had the last watch, four to six, and had searched through the wrecked trailers and found enough coffee and bread for everyone when I awakened them.

No one was eager to get up and meet the new day. We were still worn out from the ordeal of the day before. Most were still smarting from bruises, scrapes, cuts, and wrenched bones. Our morning meal was eaten in silence.

Everyone was finishing the first cup of coffee when Judy brought up the subject of the moon.

"What about the moon?" Johnny asked.

"Well, it went down during my watch, and as I stood looking at it, I suddenly realized that it wasn't sitting in the right place. Only a couple of nights ago, we watched as it disappeared over there." She was pointing to a high ridge over the reservoir and almost due west of where we were then.

"I distinctly remember, because Marsha and I had been to a movie in Goldston, and we were in the parking lot talking about the movie at the same time the moon went down behind that ridge." She shifted her arm farther north.

"Early this morning, it disappeared just to the right of that small peak." She indicated a small peak at least twenty compass degrees north of the afore-mentioned ridge.

"Well, it's all related to yesterday's activity." Johnny was still trying to formulate in his mind some kind of explanation. "We've experienced some shift of the north-south axis or a big land shift—one or the other."

He was getting some quizzical stares, but continued. "Did anyone notice, yesterday afternoon, that it was decidedly warmer than on any previous day and the sun, like the moon, had shifted its orbit?"

Not waiting for an answer, and realizing that we were too busy to notice and were not as sensitive to these things as he, he continued. "I wasn't going to mention this, but Judy noticed it, too. I checked magnetic north this morning, with my compass, and found from where north was yesterday, it's shifted west almost forty-five degrees."

He paused and looked around at our faces. I couldn't believe it. I looked across the reservoir toward what I had believed to be north, then west where Johnny said it was now.

"Did you check with another compass?" I don't know why I asked such a question. Johnny was always sure of any statement or fact, when it was associated with geography or geology.

"Yes, I'm sure. I want to check the action of the sun and moon for the next few days, and check the position of the stars—one thing I completely forgot to do last night. It's my opinion, right now, that we are south of the equator."

"Impossible," someone said—I can't remember who.

We were still thinking about this revelation when I realized George was talking. "I have to find a way to Goldston, today. Nancy and I were up half the night, thinking of the boys. Lord only knows what might be happening there. J.J., can I get you to go with me?"

He caught me by surprise. I'd completely forgotten that the boys weren't around, but their parents hadn't.

"George," Steve said, "I'm sure you and Nancy are worried about the twins, but if you'll hear me out, I believe I have a plan that will help all of us." No one spoke, not even George.

"First, we have to make sure we can survive the next few days here, get ourselves organized, and then pack up and move out together. We don't want to split up, get lost, or make any move that will jeopardize what's left of our little band."

Everyone was still listening, but as he continued, his remarks were directed toward the parents of the children in Goldston. "If there's anyone left alive in Goldston, I'm sure they're banding together to figure out what to do, as we are, and I'm sure they'll take care of the children, just as we would.

"My plan—and if anyone has any suggestions, let's hear them now—is to dig ourselves out, find as much food as we can, try to get out one or two of the vehicles from the pile below, and bury our own dead. Then we can move to Goldston. Any questions or suggestions?"

George was looking toward Nancy for some indication of her feelings. As a mother, she wanted desperately to know about her children. She sat silently with her cup of coffee, looking at George.

"Okay, then, no questions. The first thing I'd like to do is search Ioda. If we find any bodies, we'll bury them right where we find them. Then we'll move on to the excavation and see about our own people.

"J.J., you and Johnny will give me a hand with that. In the meantime, I'd like for George, Nancy, and Judy to search the trailers and Ioda wreckage for anything that we can eat, drink, or stay warm with. Keep personal clothing to a minimum. We'll need blankets, sleeping bags, that sort of thing.

"Beth, you and Susan stay around the fire and weapons. Give a hand with the provisions as they're brought up. One of you should make a list of everything we have, especially food."

Your father had directed the first day's work for us. He didn't know it then, but he would be directing many days of work for hundreds of people, in the days to come.

Your father and I took shovels, Johnny brought along a pickaxe and a hand axe, and we moved out for Ioda, while George was getting his detail ready. Your mother and Susan were designating places for whatever was brought back to be stored and cataloged for our survival.

As we neared Ioda, we could see that most of our work would take place north of the town, all the way down into the reservoir. Where the town had originally stood, there was only some debris, so we fanned out and proceeded to search. The first to be found was the elderly couple who owned the general store and gas station. They were found in the wreckage, surrounded by supplies that had been delivered the day before. We surmised that they hadn't suffered, but had been crushed to death when the first powerful tremor threw everything into the air. We found the owner of the fast-food shop in much the same way. The other body we found in the wreckage belonged to a delivery man. We buried them not far from the wreckage where they were found. Neither of the three of us had ever had any formal religious training, so it was assumed that your father, being our leader, should say a few words over the new grave sites. Then we moved on to the excavations, knowing we would have to go through the same thing all over again.

We crossed the dry lake and came to the area that we'd fled in such haste, yesterday. As we faced the hill before us, I thought of the years of excavation we'd done on that mound of rock, sand, sagebrush, and cactus. During the peak year, as many as forty people had been working to clear away thousands of years of soil and vegetation. With the primary work over and the limits of the city established, we had been working with a small but efficient crew.

I could still visualize the four different levels that we had established as existing at the same time, over nine thousand years ago. We had built ladders to travel from one level to another, much as the cliff dwellers of the pueblos in New Mexico and Arizona had done. But these people hadn't lived as the pueblo dwellers had, perched on the side of a cliff with ladders retractable in case of attack. They had terraced the side of the hill on which they built their city. The dwellings we had found were oval-shaped, made out of poles driven into the ground and bent over and tied at the top with either twine or animal sinew. They had covered these with local vegetation and mud, to keep out the wind and rain. Although the area was now semi-arid, they had had a climate much as would be found farther south, in Central America.

There had been arguments between several universities and archaeological groups whether these people had been the forefathers of the cliff dwellers, and whether these huts might have been covered with hides, as well as with mud and straw. The arguments would never be answered, and seemed inconsequential now. Before me, now, was not a city, but a large pile of dirt and rock, which looked as if some large dump truck had deposited its contents there overnight.

"Does anyone know which level the college boys were working on?" I said.

Stephen pointed up towards the northern end. "Marsha was with them, just about here, on the first level. I sent Diane, Karen, and Mark to the fourth level."

We were of the opinion that, considering everything had moved north, they too would be found north of where they were last seen. "J.J., you and Johnny start digging where the first level should have been. If you come across anything recognizable, we'll stop and see what should be done next. I'm going to go to the extreme north end and see what I can find there. Then I'll go up to the top and try to find some trace of Tim."

With that statement, your father was off and we started digging. After a good half-hour of steady work, we decided it was time to take a break. We hadn't found a trace of anything that had been excavated—not one single clue as to what part of the dig we were trying to uncover. Boulders that had been buried until the day before were now visible. Top soil that should have been on the top of the mesa was now being uncovered more than two or three feet under the earth. Johnny and I discussed this and decided to split up and try a little higher up, in the vicinity of where level four should have been. We were still digging when Steve returned.

He called us over and asked what we'd found. "Not a thing," I said.

"We've tried on what should be level one," Johnny said, "level four, and two or three spots in between, but we haven't found a scrap of evidence to give us an indication of where we are. Nothing.'

"I hate to give up," Steve said, "but I'm sure they're buried under too much debris for us to uncover them. I can't find a trace of Tim, either. He shouldn't have been buried, unless he was caught in the slide northward, into the water. This afternoon, we'll fan out north and west and see if we can find him."

Steve turned back to look at the mound where at least six of our people were buried. "We can't find them, but we know they're there. Before we leave, I want to put up some kind of marker. If we do get out of here and find some of their relatives, we can at least tell them we marked the spot where they died."

We started back across the dry lake bed, and were nearing Ioda when we saw several people coming across the reservoir. We were overwhelmed at the prospect that someone had survived besides ourselves. We turned and headed for the group, which was now nearing what had been the shore of the reservoir. They saw our advance, and started yelling and throwing their hands into the air. There were nine persons in the group. Tim Engles was leading the way and running for all he was worth, screaming at the top of his lungs, followed by the national park employees.

Everyone in our camp had heard the commotion, and they were descending upon us as fast as their legs could carry them. We all came together right at the edge of the reservoir. Tim's group was tired and hungry, and they were all crying so much that within the space of a few minutes, with all the hugging and handshaking, we were all tearful and red-eyed.

We took our newly-found friends up to the campsite, and gave them water, coffee, and bread—all that we had at the time. It was evident that the people at the camp had been busy. There was a nice pile of canned goods to be inventoried, another pile of sleeping bags, blankets, coats, and an assortment of other types of clothing. We'd had a tiring morning ourselves, so while the new arrivals enjoyed their first food since the previous morning, we settled down for a cup of coffee and some bread.

"Tell us, Tim, where did you find all the rangers?" Beth said, pouring him some coffee.

"It was after I realized that I was on the north shore of the reservoir. I recall bending down, looking at a lithic scatter, when I heard a sound from below me. It was as though the earth had split open right below me. Out of the corner of my eye, I thought I saw the water in the reservoir jumping, as if loaded with thousands of fish. As I looked up and to the east, the landscape was rising. I mean, everything was rising—the mountains, the lake, the bridge, everything, and it was advancing towards me like a huge tidal wave."

Tim stopped, and with trembling hands, both around his cup, took a sip of coffee. "My first reaction was that this couldn't be happening. I didn't know what to do. I fell flat on the ground, and as I did, the wave hit me, throwing me into the air. I felt like I was flying. I landed about half-way down the hill and tumbled over and over, until I was in the old river bed. I tried to get up and run, but I was thrown down again. I was vibrated, literally vibrated, all the way to the north shore.

"When everything was quiet, I dared to get up and look around. That's when I realized that I was no more than fifty yards away from the park headquarters. The water that had been thrown from the reservoir was now coming back. I scrambled under a small cliff, in front of the administration building, as the water became a torrent. I had the feeling that I was sitting under a huge waterfall, and the fall was hundreds of yards long. The water didn't stay in the reservoir, but flowed on very rapidly to the west, indicating that the dams at the end of the lake were gone. I was thoroughly drenched and muddy beyond belief, when I came out and climbed to higher ground."

The whole group was transfixed, as Tim continued his harrowing story of survival. All work stopped; everyone was listening.

"I could see that the visitor center, the maintenance sheds, and the living quarters were all gone. Then I noticed that the top of the administration building was missing, but not the part that had been built below ground level. The west, north, and east walls were built below ground, using the new conservation-of-energy concept, with the south wall open as an entrance and exit. The tremors had destroyed the top level, and the water had wiped the rubble away, but the fact that some people worked below ground might have saved some of them.

"As I approached the building, there was a large amount of what had been the top floor filling the crevice of the south wall. The debris was filled with mud, shells, and rock left by the water. It was impossible for one person to get anywhere near a door. I climbed to the top, and found most of the roof was a shambles, had fallen in, and was also filled with debris, mud, and stones. I thought my only chance to find someone would be to find a window and dig it out."

Tim stopped long enough to catch his breath, take a bite of bread, a sip of coffee, and then continued. "I found a small hand shovel on the roof and started digging. I began to dig and listen for any sound of life. I kept saying to myself, *just a little deeper, there has to be a window.* One part of me kept saying, *you can't make it, quit, take a break, then go back to Ioda.* I was tired and sore.

"I took my break, but was determined to go just a little farther, when I heard a noise, thump. Someone had heard my digging and was banging a reply. Grabbing my shovel, I started at it once again. Finally, I struck something hard, part of the concrete wall, and to the left side was part of a window. I was only a foot off-center. Quickly, I dug over, and within a couple minutes had a window visible, but my troubles weren't over yet. The windows were installed not to be opened, and were at least an inch thick with wire mesh imbedded in the glass. They were not large, but very hard to break. I swung at the window with the shovel, but couldn't break it." Tim indicated with gestures how he had swung over and over at the window.

"By now, someone was on the other side, also trying in vain to break the window. I left the shovel, and ran to where the maintenance shed had stood, looking for anything heavy, but the ground was swept clean by the water. Returning to the top of the administration building, I saw a long, circular, metal bar in the debris and, with some pulling and tugging, was finally able to free it. It was a piece of cold-rolled steel, an inch in diameter and three feet long. It was a heavy rascal.

"When I got back, I indicated as best I could to get back, then ran that rod straight at the window. It didn't break, but it cracked. A few more good blows and I was through. A stale, musty odor was the first thing I received, then a great big grin from Mr. Fost, here."

"What a sight he was," Fost said, as he gave Tim a friendly slap on the back. "We had tried for hours to free ourselves, with no luck. Our last flashlight gave out, and we were all crowded against the north wall, with hardly any space to move. The air was growing stale and water was coming at us from all sides, when we heard Tim's shoveling. What a sound! I shall never hear one as sweet, if I live to be a hundred."

"We'd all be dead, if Tim hadn't found us," one of the rangers stated. Tim was turning quite red-faced, listening to himself being extolled as a hero.

It had taken Tim the rest of the afternoon to get all of the people out of the building. That included Jack Fost, senior maintenance officer for the park, two of his maintenance men who were in his office, one draftsman, two of the park's interpreters, and two secretaries. A total of eight people had been rescued, out of nineteen present when the quake had struck. Among those lost were the draftsman's wife and two small children, Jack Fost's wife, and the husband of one of the secretaries.

Once they were freed from the only structure left on the site, a search for others was made, with no success. Lack of water and food made it impossible for them to leave that night, so they decided to stay where they were until morning, when they would strike out for the closest place where they could get help—Ioda and the archaeological team.

A good rest and the opportunity to talk about their losses seemed to help our new acquaintances. We'd lost friends, but those people had lost very close loved ones, and they would feel the loss with a depth we couldn't understand. Work was the best cure of all of us, and no one knew this more than your father, so without delay, he put all of us to work.

Susan kept a tally of everything that was brought in from the trailer park and Ioda. Sorting and storing was going to be another big project. More tents were put up for the extra people, and we decided to try to bring up one of the trailers, for a storage shed. I had a four-wheel drive Jeep, with a winch on the front bumper. If we could bring it up first, we'd have a lot of horsepower to work with. I presented the idea to Steve, your father, and he concurred.

All available manpower was now turned to the vehicle, which was on its side and partially hidden by one of the trailers. The hard part would be to get it on all four wheels. We drove posts into the ground at the top of the hill, hitched a block and tackle to them and to the vehicle, and pulled. With the help of crowbars to hold the trailer off, we had it on its wheels more quickly than I had thought possible. The extra hands made things a lot easier.

Next, we put the winch in free-wheel, brought the cable to the top of the hill, and hooked it to the posts we'd driven into the ground and to the block and tackle. We put it in rewind, and, with the help of the rest of us pulling on the block and tackle, the Jeep climbed up the hill.

Should we try to bring another vehicle up, now, or a storage trailer? That was the first real controversy in our group. George Foxworth didn't want to bring up another vehicle, or a trailer, or anything. He wanted to take the Jeep, and try to make it into Goldston before dark and look for his children. We'd been working hard most of the day, and were pretty well exhausted. Steve called a break, then rose before the group, and addressed us in a slow and deliberate voice.

"All right," he said. "Before we start back to work, this afternoon, we need to have a plan and a leader to carry out that plan. I see no other way than to have some structure to the way we conduct ourselves, for the foreseeable future." Steve looked around the group. "Now, who has a plan to get us organized and safely through the next few weeks or months ahead, or at least until we find civilization?"

George stood up. "I don't have any plans. My wife and I are going to Goldston this afternoon, with or without anyone's help. Our children may be alive and starving, for all we know, and something has to be done."

"George, we're with you," Steve said. "But if we don't take care of ourselves first, we can't help anyone else."

"What has dragging a trailer up here, spending almost a full day getting a camp put together, got to do with our going to Goldston? I'll take the Jeep and go by myself."

Stephen's voice was still slow and deliberate, in answer to George's question. He wanted to answer him and, at the same time, let the rest of us know in no uncertain terms that, if we didn't plan right and be slow and cautious in our decisions, disaster could overtake us.

"There may be no city," he said. "We know from what we've seen already that everything north of the reservoir was destroyed. If, in fact, we do find someone there, we'll have this camp to come back to for food, shelter, and medical attention, if need be. We feel great sympathy for you, as we feel for the others in our group who have lost someone close. But we can't think only of ourselves, right now; we must think of the group.'

He was silent for a moment before continuing. "If we take the Jeep, go to Goldston, and you find your children alive but injured and other people alive but injured, how would you get them back? They'd need treatment before they could travel. What if you became lost? Look around you. The terrain has changed since yesterday. There's no direct road to Goldston, now. I'm asking you to be patient, just until we get our camp set up. Then we'll go to look for your children without delay."

George was silent. He knew that his emotions were getting the best of him, and that what Steve was telling him was the truth.

Steve then presented the group around him a plan to get us out safely and without any more casualties, if possible. Simple but direct—we would establish a base where we were. Next, we would send out parties to see if anyone else in the vicinity had survived. The first party would go to Goldston. Then we would send people west to the dam area and the city of Rosemont, and south to the community of Lakewood. When all of this was accomplished, we could make further plans for leaving the valley.

Before we broke up our meeting, that day, it was decided that Stephen Adams would be our leader. I was the second in command, followed by Jack Fost. Any decision that would involve the whole group would be voted on by the group, with a simple majority taking the day. Those simple rules were used for many months to come, even as we took new members into our group. They worked very well, indeed.

With that settled, we spent the rest of the day hauling one of the living trailers up to the top of the hill and repairing it with parts from other trailers. The trailer would hold all of our provisions and extra clothes and blankets. Beth and Susan would be in charge of keeping records and passing out food and bedding as it was needed.

It was also to be our guard shack. We'd decided that we would continue keeping the fire burning at night, with someone awake at all times. The guard would be armed.

We then turned our efforts to bringing up another vehicle. With two hours of light left, we gave it a try, and brought up one of the vans. It was only a two-wheel drive and bulky, but could hold a large amount of equipment or people, if needed.

Then we turned our attention to dinner—a good hot meal, the first in two full days. Good food brought everyone up out of the dumps and made us forget our hurts, scrapes, and bruises for awhile.

With the evening meal over and everyone preparing to turn in early, I sat down in the new guard shack to make a guard list for the coming night. With more people now, things would be easier—shorter hours and nights off. I made sure that everyone was familiar with the .38 caliber pistol and the shotgun that would be kept there. Then I was ready for a good night's sleep.

I awoke before dawn, to find rain beating down and the wind blowing with so much force that I was sure our tent would go at any minute. It occurred to me that I didn't have a raincoat or boots with me. I only hoped that someone had brought them from the wreckage.

I heard voices outside, and looked out the flap. Someone's tent had blown away. I couldn't tell whose, but I heard voices telling them to take refuge in the trailer.

Susan was awake, and I asked her about the foul weather equipment. She remembered writing down raincoats, boots, rain hats, and ponchos. The way the rain was coming down, I was sure that the wreckage at the bottom of the hill would be swept away in the flood that was sure to follow. I was thankful for two things, at that moment, that we had placed our tent on high ground and that we had decided to bring up that van the previous night.

By daybreak, it was evident that no work was going to be accomplished that day, so I dressed as best I could, and took off through the driving rain for the trailer. I could see that there was a lot of water in the lake, but it was moving westward at a rapid pace. Water was running down all the slopes. The ground wasn't absorbing any of the water, it was coming down so fast. It was strange weather for the area.

The storage trailer was the only really dry and warm place in our whole camp. The fire outside had been put out long before daybreak by the rain. The people standing watch had kept a fire going all night in the trailer, by putting charcoal in a bucket and putting it on the stove. A grate lying over the top of the bucket held a one-gallon can filled with good, hot coffee. The trailer was filling up rapidly with people whose tents were being flattened by wind and water.

We were forced to use the trailer and van for the ones who had lost their tents and not try to erect any shelters during the storm. The van wasn't comfortable, but neither were any of the other shelters, by that time. Water and mud had seeped into everything; the tents were soaked. The damp made everyone miserable. We felt sharp tremors during the day, but nothing to compare with what we'd been through on what we were calling the "Day of Destruction."

Deep gullies were being formed on all the hills around us, and tons of earth, in the form of mud, were filling up the reservoir at an unbelievable rate. The water was approaching the wreckage of Ioda, and our trailers and equipment that had not been brought up the hill were now being covered.

During the day, we saw wreckage—houses, trees, partially-submerged vehicles, and even human bodies—being swept along by the strong current. We couldn't help but believe that most, if not all, of the debris was coming from Goldston or Silverspoon, directly across the lake. Seeing that and knowing that the city where his children were may have been destroyed made George even more anxious to start a rescue mission.

The rain and gusting winds lasted for the next three days. We were all so miserable that no one moved when it wasn't absolutely necessary. Cold beans and canned meat were our meals, and the only warmth was the small charcoal fire that was constantly kept going in the trailer.

During the daylight hours, everyone made at least one trip to the trailer for a cup of hot coffee and just to stare at the fire. The fire became a symbol of hope; it was a rallying point. It seemed to say to all of us to hold out against the odds, never mind about the torrent outside. During the cold nights, everyone could see the glow of the coals—it was the only light visible until the rain stopped and the clouds disappeared.

On the third day of the rains, your father, Jack Fost, and I had a meeting in the trailer, to plan our departure after the rains and winds had subsided. We took everything into consideration, including geography, the makeup of our band, the easiest passage out of the mountains, food supplies, equipment, time of year, and the fact that we were sure that our position on the face of the globe was now south of the equator. We finally decided that east, or what had been east, would be the best way out, but before we left, all of the surrounding area should be checked to see if anyone else had survived.

Jack Fost, with two rangers, would go west—all the way to Rosemont, if he could get that far—checking both sides of the old lakeshore on the way. Tim, Johnny, and one ranger would go south to Lakewood City, and George, one ranger, and I would go into Goldston; on the way, we would detour north and see if anyone was still alive in Silverspoon. The remainder of our group would prepare all of our provisions, equipment, and vehicles for the move east, when all of the expeditions returned.

Those decisions made, we had another cup of coffee and watched the rain.

*Chapter 4: Early Exploration*

# MOVE TO GOLDSTON

On the sixth day after the destruction, the rain quit coming down. For three days and nights, twenty-four hours a day, it had not stopped raining. The only relief had been short periods of drizzle, which lasted for a few hours. During those times, the wind had stopped blowing and the whole world had been deathly quiet. Then, without warning, the wind would gust up to forty miles an hour and the rain would come in torrents. Between the downpours, we had tried to repair what tents were still standing, distribute food, and make ourselves as comfortable as possible before the next onslaught.

During one of the lulls, I think it was on the second day, one of the rangers and I had made a tour of the countryside. We had made our way down to Ioda, but there wasn't a thing left—not a stick, not a nail, not even any concrete foundations. Where the town had stood, there was now a deep gully, gushing forth thousands of gallons of water per minute, filled with mud. Where the debris of the town had piled up after the first earthquakes, there was nothing but water and mud.

We'd tried to get to the dig site, but it was impossible. Before returning to the campsite, we'd tried to climb the large hill that had been south of our camp and where, in earlier times, Susan and I had sat and watched both moon and sun rise, taking in the beauty of the surrounding mountains; from that perch, we'd watched fishermen and water-skiers on the lake that had been formed by the dams some distance to the west. But the climb was too rough. The rain had produced vast gullies, and the earthquake had thrown large boulders in our way. We gave up before reaching the halfway point, and it started raining before we reached camp.

The next two days we spent putting the camp back together, drying out all the equipment, and getting the exploration teams ready to go. We agreed to send Fost first; his team would have the roughest time, if in fact the rugged terrain still existed west of the first dam. He would take no sleeping bags or tents, but would sleep outside if shelter couldn't be found. He was to try and map the country as he went, and take an alternate route coming back. We all had maps, provided by the Forest Service, and they would be of great help; changes could be recorded as they were discovered. Food and water would be his main worries, and the three of them carried all they could muster. From our meager arsenal of weapons, they took the .38 pistol and the fifty rounds of ammunition. If game was available, they could augment the food they had with them.

Fost's team were to go west for a week. By that time, they should have been in Rosemont. They were to turn around there, pick an alternate route south of the one they'd taken going out, and start back. If they found survivors, the trip would take much longer and, depending on how many people they had with them and their condition, it might be advisable to return by the same route to save time. In any event, the base camp would move on to Goldston in two weeks, and if conditions were favorable, once the camp was set up there, someone would be sent back to Ioda to await their return.

On the ninth day after the disaster, we sent out our first expedition. There were handshakes all around, with very little talk. Your father told Jack to be careful, not to take any unnecessary chances, and they were off, across the deep ravine that had been Ioda. They climbed the short distance to the top of the mesa, above our former dig site, and disappeared.

We turned our efforts to outfitting Tim and Johnny for their trip south. The rest of the day was spent much as the previous day had been—getting an expedition ready, poring over our maps. There had been U.S. Route 117 into Lakewood City, and it would be used if at all possible.

The expedition was not expected to take more than a week to ten days, barring accidents or finding a large number of refugees. They, also, would not be taking any sleeping bags or tents, but would carry as much food and water as possible. Their armament was to be my twelve-gauge shotgun, with forty-eight rounds of ammunition.

By late that afternoon, we were ready to work on getting my expedition under way. George had been tense since the rain had stopped, and had wanted to get our trip on the way first. But Steve had decided to send ours out last, and George had not said anything.

Using the maps as much as possible, we were to follow the old shoreline east, to where the Lakewood City bridge had stood. We would cross over to the north shore and proceed to Silverspoon. The small village was only two miles north of the reservoir. We were quite sure that no one or thing could have survived the quakes or the volume of water that had been thrown out of the lake, but we were obliged to check into it, anyway.

Then, by the shortest route, we would go on to Goldston. The return trip would be devoted to finding the best route from our camp to Goldston, so that we could bring out our vehicles and equipment. If there were any survivors in Goldston, we would leave them there. We wouldn't have the trouble of traveling with a large number of people, as the others might. We were not expected to be gone more than seven to ten days, and the remainder of the camp would be packed and ready to go by the time we returned.

We were to take the last of my weapons—a World War II, .30 caliber, M-1 carbine. I had purchased it a couple of years earlier, had taken it everywhere we'd been, but hadn't fired the weapon, except once on a rifle range outside Shreveport, Louisiana. I had purchased sixty rounds of ammunition, and had fired thirty on the range. That left our camp without a weapon, but we thought the situation there was secure, for the time being.

We spent the evening sitting around the fire, discussing the expeditions, and enjoying a good, hot meal. We considered ourselves fortunate in that respect—food would be no problem for some time. Our trailers had been well stocked with food, and we had salvaged well: flour, cornmeal, sugar, coffee, tinned crackers, and a good number of canned goods from the wrecked store in Ioda. We had also salvaged and stored up about fifty gallons of gasoline from the wrecked vehicles, before they had been washed away. We hoped that would be enough to carry most of our provisions out of the valley and to Goldston, when the time came to move.

Everyone turned in early. It had been a hurried two days, getting everyone packed and ready to move, and Tim and I both wanted to get an early start the next morning. But the excitement of the days to come kept us all awake most of the night. Everyone was up and around the fire with coffee long before the sun came up.

Tim, Johnny, and one ranger left first, heading east then turning south where the roads split. It was still dark when they started, but they would be on well-traveled roadways for a good while, and our camp fire would put out enough glow to keep them headed in the right direction until the sun came up.

George and I were packed and ready to go, as they disappeared out of sight. I kissed Susan goodbye, with final instructions for her to take care until we could get back. She was more scared for my safety. Nancy wanted to go with us, because of the children, but George would hear none of her arguments. Susan finally took her away, and the last we saw of our wives, that day, they were standing quietly in the old parking lot, looking out across the Goldston River, their backs to us, crying profusely.

We followed Tim's trail for about half a mile, then turned northeast, away from his southerly trail. There had been a road running along the south shore of the lake, but it was completely obliterated, except for a few spots no longer than a hundred yards, in two or three locations. For the most part, we stayed on high ground to better keep track of our progress, and to stay away from the mud that had collected along the banks and, at times, extended in gullies away from the lake for hundreds of yards.

We kept a watch on the north bank as we progressed, but saw no movement, nor could we see the highway that had been on the shore there. It was early afternoon when we reached the old bridge. The bridge had been built where a long canyon, running generally eastward, ended and broadened into a large valley. There wasn't anything left of the original bridge, but there were huge trees, limbs, and debris that had wedged themselves into the mouth of the canyon so tightly that there was almost a solid wall of rotting timber and brush. That had held back some water, and it was still seeping through from the small lake that had formed on the other side. It was like a huge beaver dam.

George backtracked and climbed to the top of a rock face, in order to get a good view of the side of the jam where the water was being held back. From there, he hollered down that the water appeared to be ten to twelve feet deep and was full of debris for a quarter of a mile upstream.

We didn't have time to go looking for a crossing, so I decided to cross in front of the jam. We'd have to climb down to the river, which was now only thirty yards across, strap our gear to some floatable item, such as a tree limb, and swim across. As soon as George was back, we got underway, reaching the far side in a little over thirty minutes from the time we had reached the jam. As we were going across, I kept looking up at that wall of logs, and hoping that it wouldn't give way just as I was mid-stream.

Within another thirty minutes, we were in Silverspoon, but there was nothing there. It was no surprise to either George or me. The ground was swept clean by the heavy wind and rains of the past few days. The only things we found that showed anyone had lived in that place were a few buttons, a pair of eyeglasses, half-buried in the sand, and of all things, an umbrella.

It was getting late in the day, and it didn't seem wise to travel at night, so we made our way back to the log jam, and spent the night there. With an early start the next morning, we should be in Goldston around noon.

We were up before dawn. The small fire that we had kept going through the night now made our first cup of morning coffee. The second cup was used to wash down our hurried breakfast—a can of beans, with crackers.

The dimensions of the reservoir that had been the lake, at one time, were now covered in bright green grass. The Goldston River still flowed through the bottom of what had been Lake Mesa, and from the present river to the high water mark, the former lake was covered completely in that grass.

"Where in the world would all of the grass seed come from, to cover the lake bed like that?" I made a sweeping motion with my hand, as I was talking.

"I would guess the flooding up in the mountains carried a lot of it down," George said. "The old lake bed is probably covered all the way to the first dam and beyond."

The surrounding hills, which before the disaster were mostly brown, with patches of sagebrush and cactus, were themselves showing signs of green plants growing on their slopes. The whole atmosphere was different. The high humidity was evident in the air we breathed. The movement of the earth had brought us south of the equator, as Johnny had said. The previous week, we had been more than forty degrees north of the equator; now, we were seemingly in the tropics. What had happened to the rest of the world? I couldn't wait to get to Goldston, and see if they might still be in touch with someone outside our mountainous region.

Breakfast over, we packed up and started for Goldston. We tried to follow U.S. Route 8, which had been the main route through the mountains. Beginning in Denver, it had crossed the front range of mountains, followed along beside Little River until it reached Goldston, then followed the Goldston River all the way to Rosemont. There, it had turned to the northwest, and followed a series of mountain passes, through numerous small towns and villages, ending in Salt Lake City, Utah.

Now, all that remained of the road were short stretches that had been sheltered on the north side of the Goldston River by high bluffs. We used those stretches when possible, and made our way along the river itself when they ended. The going wasn't too difficult. By 10:30, we were approaching our destination.

We approached the town from the west. At the foot of South Butte was the junction of the Goldston and Little Rivers. Little River flowed away from the junction, to the east. The river was full of trees, mud, and other debris; water was still flowing, but underneath all of the wreckage. The face of the butte was littered with everything civilized man would have had in a town: clothing, cars, machinery, all manner of home furnishings, pieces and parts of buildings, iron girders, uprooted trees brought down from far upstream, glass, concrete, and other assorted possessions used in everyday life. Debris was strewn from the base of the cliff halfway to the top, around five hundred feet.

We couldn't see where the Goldston River turned north, as we approached. Our first impression was that the dams near Butte City, eighteen miles to the north, and a smaller dam in the mountains, only a few miles away to the northeast, had burst during the destruction. The waters had flooded down on the tiny town with great force, joined by the water that had been thrown out of the reservoir to the west. Together, they had flung the town, with its inhabitants, up against the butte. Our hearts fell, because it appeared that we would find no survivors there.

George especially was heartbroken. Tears were coming to his eyes, as we arrived at what had been the edge of town and saw the valley to the east and north of us swept clean of all signs of life.

"Stop where you are."

We all three jumped into the air. We'd been concentrating our attention to the front of our approach and toward South Butte, but the voice came from our left.

I glanced over and saw a man, middle-aged, sitting on the ground, clutching a meat cleaver. We started to approach, when he got to his feet.

"I said to stop where you are. Where are you guys from?"

I thought then, and I knew later, that he knew how to handle his weapon, so we stopped. "We're from the archaeological expedition that was working out at Ioda," I said.

"You ain't from Butte City?"

"No, George said.

"My name is Foxworth, George Foxworth, and I had two children in school here. Did any of the children survive?"

The threatening attitude of the man seemed to disappear; he even dropped the meat cleaver to his side. "Yeah, we have about a dozen or so. You have boys or girls?"

"Boys, two of them—twins." George was talking so fast that no one could understand him. "Are they alive?"

"Not so fast, Mr. George Foxworth. We have some children, but we ain't about to give them away to just anybody coming by looking. What's your boys' names?"

"Calib and Randy. Randy is the taller of the two; Calib has lighter hair," George said. He was getting impatient.

"You know where the school was?" the man said. George nodded. "Then go past the store yonder, and turn before you get to the wreckage of the schoolhouse. Climb up the bank to the first ledge you can walk on; follow it around to a large cave. The children are there. Everybody up there is pretty scared, so tell them Arthur said to let you pass."

George was gone before the last words were out of Arthur's mouth. The ranger and I then walked up to Arthur and introduced ourselves.

"Why the meat cleaver?" I said.

"We had some visitors here, yesterday; weren't friendly at all. They were from Butte City, about eighteen miles north of here. Two of them on foot; looked the place over, asked a lot of questions—how many of us, if we had weapons, and so forth. Well, after awhile of their poking around, I up and asked one just what they wanted, anyway. They grinned and said if help didn't come soon, they might come down here and take over this place."

We started to walk in the direction that George had taken, with Arthur telling us all about the visit of the two from Butte City. "They saw, or knew, that there'd been a grocery here." Arthur pointed ahead of us. "And the sporting goods store next door; both were built just a year ago. Well, anyway, before they left, they said they'd be back, and we better make progress in getting some of the food out from under all the rubble."

We reached the grocery store, and sat down to rest for a bit. Arthur continued with his story. "The school principal, Mr. Yates, gave them a hard time, and they showed him, by beating him pretty good. Then, they pointed a finger at me, saying, 'We hold you responsible,' and left. This morning, I took up a position where you found me, and one of my employees from the grocery store is north of town, watching."

After we'd rested for awhile and had a drink of water, Arthur took us up to the caves where the people that had survived had taken refuge. During lunch and the rest of the afternoon, he described to us what had happened from the time of the destruction until the present.

Most of the city had been destroyed during the first quakes. People hadn't had time to think what had happened, because they were swept away by water within minutes of the first shocks. The grocery store, the sporting goods store, and part of the school had survived, because they had been built on very high ground and were butted right up against a hill. When the main surge of water had come roaring down from the north, the town had been swept against South Butte.

Fourteen children, two teachers, four cafeteria workers, and the principal had survived. George Foxworth's children, Randy and Calib, were among the survivors. The principal had been in the cafeteria. He and the workers there had followed the teachers and children up the hill. Two of the workers had been pulled from the floodwaters twice, before they were safely away.

Mr. Arthur, four employees, and three customers had been trapped for awhile in the back of the grocery store. The roof had collapsed, trapping them in a small storage room. On the afternoon of the first day, the teachers and children had cleared away enough debris to free them. Together, they had been able to rescue two employees and one customer from the sporting goods store and a blacksmith from one of the large cattle ranches, before night fell that first day.

Since then, they'd taken refuge in the caves, where we found them, going down to the store below from time to time, for food. They felt sure help from somewhere outside the valley was only days away, and had prepared a large signal fire for aircraft or other rescuers. The rains had destroyed their signal fire, and they were in the process of repairing it when the visitors from Butte City had come around with their questions and insults.

With everyone gathered around, I explained our theory that the earth, one way or another—by land slippage, pole reversal, or even an impact on the surface somewhere by a huge meteorite, had undergone a radical change. We were sure that no help would come, we said.

The visit of the two brutes, the day before, had proven that other people had survived; how many, we didn't know. I assured Mr. Arthur and the rest that the group I was with had a plan for survival, and if they would join with us, we would all be much better off.

Everyone present was eager for the two groups to join. Now, our most important projects were, first, to get word back to Stephen and the rest about our findings and get our camp moved here, and, next, to set up a security system, much as the one that we'd planned for ourselves at Ioda. I thought it best to leave George there, to plan a defense in the event the brutes (everyone had quickly taken up the term "brutes," when referring to the unfriendly visitors) should happen to return.

I called over one of the clerks from the sporting goods store. "Can you tell me how many guns were in your store?"

He thought for a few seconds. "Between twenty-five and thirty handguns, thirty-eights and twenty-twos mostly; and one or two forty-five caliber. Not many rifles—we hadn't received any stock for the hunting season. I'd say five or six thirty caliber, lever-action Winchesters; plenty of twenty-twos, twenty or so; and an assortment of shotguns, all gauges, pump and semi-automatic."

"What about ammo?" I asked.

"Plenty for all the weapons, and if you want knives, we had a good two hundred in stock—small, medium, and large."

There was a good reason for the brutes to come back. They knew about the food store and about the weapons.

I seemed to be taking charge. No one objected; in fact, everyone seemed to want to do something, to have a plan. There were some good people in Goldston, but they'd never had to do anything like this. Their lives had revolved around a job, a home, and a vacation once a year. They seemed to appreciate my decisiveness, and I was more than glad to have their cooperation.

I was definitely worried about the weapons, so once again I turned to the clerk. "Do you know where the weapons might be, in the rubble?"

"Yeah. It's going to take some hard digging to get to them."

"Okay. How many weapons are there up here, right now?" I looked around the group. No one spoke up.

"None, except my meat cleaver," Arthur said. "I got it from the butcher shop, when we were digging our way out."

"What about the man you have on watch north of town?"

"The only thing he took with him was a piece of pipe. He was supposed to high tail it back here, if he saw anything; not try to fight."

I turned to George. "Tomorrow morning, you and I will make a reconnaissance around the surrounding hills; look for a good spot to defend these caves and the area below. If those two do come back, or if someone else like them should come around, stop them short of this place; don't let them get close enough to see how many of you there are or the condition of the food store. Might sound harsh, but we all had better be a little cautious, until we have a chance to go north and see how many people are in Butte City."

One of the teachers had a question. "Suppose it's someone who's hungry? Suppose it's a woman or a child?"

"George, you and Mr. Arthur make up your minds, one way or the other, if either of those situations should arise. I suggest bringing food out to them, and not inviting anyone into these caves until their motives are clear."

"What about weapons? All we have is your carbine."

"I'm going to leave you that. After our trip around, tomorrow morning, you and the store clerk search around and dig out enough weapons to defend yourselves until I get back. Four rifles maximum; leave the rest buried. Keep your guard north of town armed, and keep the rest of the rifles ready. Make sure the people you arm know how to fire the weapons, and keep them away from the kids. I haven't seen your kids, yet, George. Are they all right?"

"Just fine, absolutely fine." George looked ten years younger, now that the worry about the twins was taken off his shoulders.

"Mr. Arthur," I said.

"Yes?"

"After George gets his guard set up, I'd like for you to get everyone busy digging out the food store. I'm sure you know your business, but I'd bring perishables out first—potatoes and onions; find a good, cool place to bury them. As for the meat, the ham should be good; any beef that can still be eaten, boil it or dry it. Use your own judgment. We've been keeping a running total of our supplies, and I'd like for you to do the same. Pick out at least two people to distribute food, and let them keep the records. Is there anything I've forgotten, anything to add?" I looked around the group.

"Excuse me, but I have a suggestion." It was one of the women who had worked in the school cafeteria.

"Sure, go ahead."

"What about building a root cellar for the potatoes, onions, and so forth? Will we be here long enough for that to be practical?"

I hadn't thought of that, but it was a good idea. " Sure. We'll spend at least several weeks here, while we explore. Do you know anything about building one?"

"Oh yes. I was born and raised in the mountains of Virginia. I helped my father and brothers build more than a dozen, for ourselves and relatives."

"Outstanding, just what we need to get our group organized. Work with Mr. Arthur on that. Any more questions or suggestions?"

"Do you think I should actually use ammunition," George said, "or just dry fire the weapons, and save what we have?"

"I'd go ahead and fire at least ten rounds per man. That'll give them a feel for the weapon, and they'll know what to expect when it goes off. Set up your practice range somewhere to the south or west—as far away from here as possible, but not far enough that you can't get back quickly, in case of trouble.

"One more thing, George. Set up a watch here at the cave and one north of town. Our friends might come back at night, next time, and a lookout from here can intercept anyone, long before they get close. No fires at either location. A small fire somewhere back in a cave, perhaps, during the night, but nothing that can be used to pinpoint your location."

The store clerk seemed anxious. "I just remembered, Mr. Darby. There are hand-held radios in the store. We just started selling them this year. There must be at least twenty."

"Are there crystals and batteries for them?"

"Sure are. One model has a rechargeable battery." He thought about that for a minute, then smiled. "I don't guess that would be a useful selling point, right now." Everyone was able to get a small laugh out.

"Try to find a couple with batteries and get them working. Communications between the cave and a road guard would be the best thing we could have working for us. But don't spend too much time on that, after you get the weapons and ammunition. If you can't locate them, we can look again when we get better organized."

We had talked away most of the afternoon. Everything seemed to be pretty well set, for the time being. George was getting his watch schedule organized, and was going to take a walk with Mr. Arthur, north along the road, and find a place for a guard overnight, until a more suitable and permanent place could be found, the next day.

The evening meal was being prepared, and soon all the fires would be put out, except for a small watch fire, which we had decided could be placed in a deep ravine between two of the larger caves. You would have had to be practically touching the fire before you would have seen it.

The park ranger, Jim Goodman, and I spent the early evening scouting a route south of the Goldston River that would be suitable for bringing our vehicles back. The route north of the river was good for foot traffic, but not for the Jeep or van.

We had to travel east on old Route 8, then cut south, and come up in back of South Butte. Once on top, we had a good view of the valley where the town had stood, and could see up the valley almost two miles. It had been stripped bare by the floodwaters pouring down from Lake Butte. To the west and south, we could see quite a distance, and except for a few outcroppings and gullies, I thought we might find a suitable route back to Ioda, the next day.

We climbed back down, and retraced our steps to the caves, arriving well after dark. George had everything under control, so everyone, with the exception of the person on watch, turned in.

The next morning, George and I took off early to find our defensive locations. About three miles north of the caves, we found an area where the rocks and boulders formed a wedge, from the hills to the west almost to the road. There was a short, open stretch to the river, then a small bluff on the other side. Perfect for defense or ambush. That was the best place we'd found, so it would be the spot to guard.

We made our final plans. George would send three men per day to that location. There would be six men in camp all the time, until we returned. That would be enough to help the women and children, back at the cave.

As we walked back, I had one final word before I left. "George, I believe I'm correct in assuming these yo-yos from Butte City will follow the easiest trail between there and the caves. But just in case, in addition to the three men at the roadblock, send one man on a constant roving patrol out in back of the caves, to the north-west, and then have him come back on Route 8 into Goldston, and back to the caves. Two or three times a day should do it. I don't want to come back and find you all dead, taken captive, or beaten to within an inch of your lives."

"Don't worry about that. Those boys from the stores are good strong lads. Everyone was caught off guard, the first time, but it won't happen again."

Back at the cave area, I said good bye to Arthur and the rest. Jim Goodman was ready to go, and with a little luck, we'd be back at Ioda before nightfall. We followed our trail east and then south, crossing the Little River, and again coming up in back of South Butte. Then we struck out across country.

We encountered our first wildlife not an hour after we were on the trail. Two huge jack rabbits jumped up right in front of us and scurried off. Unfortunately, we had left the rifle with George.

We had to make a couple of detours around ravines that were too deep and wide for the vehicles to cross. By noon, when we took a break for lunch and a rest, we were just south of the old Lakewood bridge. According to our map, and with any luck, we would be able to eat a good, hot meal with the others that night. While we were sitting there, two elk walked not a hundred yards from us. I think we startled each other, but they didn't seem too concerned with us, and grazed off to the south.

Stretching out our pace the rest of the afternoon, we came to our camp just at sundown. We hadn't missed dinner, and everyone was overjoyed at our swift return. Susan and Nancy were the first to reach us, at a dead run. I could see the question in Nancy's eyes.

"They're alright, Nancy. George stayed with them."

She burst into tears of joy, and sat down right there in the middle of the road and had a good cry. We stayed with her for a few minutes, then lifted her up, and we all went into camp.

Steve was quite surprised that we were back so soon. "We figured you'd be out at least a week. I take it you found the children?"

"They're alive and well," I said.

I told him what we'd found in Goldston, and about the visitors from Butte City. "I don't think Mr. Arthur, the store manager, would exaggerate what happened," I said. "They were there the day before yesterday. That means they moved out from Butte City when the rains stopped, just as we did here."

"What's your suggestion?" Steve said.

"I'd like to move as soon as possible. Goldston would be a better base to work from than we have here. The food and other supplies in the grocery store could keep us alive until we either leave or grow crops of our own. Then there's the problem of the sporting goods store. If there are a bunch of ruffians in Butte City, out to run roughshod over the land. I'd prefer that we had control of all the weapons that are buried there."

"Who's in charge?"

"George. I had him get things organized, start a watch list, set up a roadblock, and so forth."

I was receiving some very questioning stares, and I had a hunch everyone was wondering why George was running the show. "Why is George in control—is that the question?" I said.

"You bet, J.J. That definitely is the question," Susan said.

"Those people need guidance. Their situation was different than ours. They still seem to be in shock, more so than we were the afternoon of the first day. And did George and I take control from someone there? The answer is definitely *no*. They seemed to be delighted to have someone to help. They're good people, but they've lived in a town all their lives. Then something like this comes along, and they're lost. They also have a dozen or so kids on their hands, with no parents. Mr. Arthur told us when we arrived that they thought for sure help would be arriving from outside the mountains any time."

"I think you've answered what we wanted to know," Steve said. "I wanted to be sure that those people weren't so scared they let you take over their lives."

"It wasn't that way at all, Steve."

"As you know, J.J., the other expeditions expect us to wait here at least two weeks for them to return. It wouldn't be right to leave here with all the food and equipment. They might be on their last legs when they get back."

I didn't know what to say to that. I was sure that if we didn't get back to Goldston first, with a good show of force, there might be trouble. It struck me as funny and sad, at the same time, that two groups of survivors were getting ready to do battle. If a leader like Steve were in Goldston when the confrontation took place, he just might be able to work out a compromise.

"At least we won't have a problem with food," Steve said. "We're sitting here with enough provisions, gathered from our trailers and Ioda, to feed a hundred people for six months, and you tell us there's that much or more in Goldston. Anyone would think we should be starving to death."

The conversation dropped off for awhile, as everyone was busy finishing off the evening meal. Jim Goodman was wolfing down his meal with the same zeal as I. Our two day trek had given us quite an appetite.

Stephen said he would make the final decision in the morning, whether to leave early or spend the full two weeks at Ioda, waiting for our people to return from Lakewood and Rosemont.

The next morning dawned with a clear sky and warm temperatures. The last night watch had the coffee ready on the fire, and Stephen had made up his mind. We would leave for Goldston as soon as everyone and everything was packed. The trailer would be left with enough provisions to provide for Tim and Fost, when they returned. In case they brought back survivors, allowance was made for that, too. A letter would be left, telling them where we were headed, with a map of our route.

Steve had been up half the night, writing that letter and a journal describing our group, where we were from, and what had happened to us during the destruction. He had described the area as it had been, and had told of our work. He had included maps and drawings. All of that material we would leave as a sort of time capsule, under the "Kings Chair."

The "Kings Chair" was a group of rock outcroppings that we'd worked around, our first year at Ioda. The natural formation of rocks resembled a chair, and it sat up quite high. It was not in the archaeological city we'd worked on for so long, but was located in back of our present tent city. Steve had chosen that spot so that if anyone should, in later years, come looking for the documents, the chair could be found with ease. At the same time, it did not stand out.

We got to work on packing up the van. I hoped the route we had chosen would allow us to drive back with little difficulty. The Jeep would be no trouble at all, with the four-wheel drive and double low. It could be used to drag the van, if necessary.

Within three hours, the vehicles were ready, chained together, and positioned. The tents were down and packed. Stephen and I had planted the documents under the Kings Chair, wrapped in two plastic bags. The trailer had been prepared with food and water, and the letters left inside, attached to the outside door. A letter left outside was also put in plastic, to protect it from the elements.

With a last look around, we started our move. The van proved to be quite heavy, but made good time, considering the terrain we were crossing. The chain between the two vehicles was left slack, except when the going got too rough for the van. Then the Jeep was put in four-wheel drive, and most obstacles were overcome. Dark caught us not quite halfway to our destination.

We would have been a lot farther along on our second day, but one hill was too steep and sandy for the van and Jeep together. We unhooked them, took the Jeep to the top, and winched the van up and over. It was rough going and slow, with the whole crew pushing at times, but it was well worth it for the provisions that were being saved. Sore and tired, we turned in early.

Our third day was much better than the second. We had learned from the previous day's experience. We crossed the Little River into Goldston in the early afternoon with all our people, vehicles, and provisions.

## Chapter 5

⁊⁊

# GOLDSTON, OUR NEW HOME

Once we had crossed the Goldston River and were parked near the site of the food store, we felt our journey from Ioda was over. It had been a very tiring three days, and we were all glad to be stopped. Trouble with flat tires on the van had cost us an extra few hours, but we were all there, and grateful for no broken bones and very few deep scratches.

As we rested and enjoyed either a good cup of coffee or a cold drink of water, George introduced everyone. He brought us up to date on what had happened since we'd left.

"Overall, it's been pretty quiet," he said. "The work on the food store has been going really well. We're using one of the caves for storage and the root cellar. It's a good start, although there's still a lot of work to be done. I'm sure glad you were able to bring the vehicles. We're going to need them to remove some of the biggest girders.

"We searched for some weapons; recovered four shotguns and ammunition. I've been leaving one at the outpost up the road, and keeping the other three up there in the cave. We found a good spot for observing the countryside north and to the west of here." He pointed to a spot high above the caves. "I sent out a patrol the first day, but the country is so open, up on top, that a person stationed in one location has a view of anything moving within five miles."

With a big grin on his face, he informed us that we had been seen yesterday, and tracked until we had disappeared behind South Butte, so our arrival had been predicted long before we'd got there. He was also happy that they had found a pair of binoculars and a couple of the radios. The binoculars and one of the radios were kept up top.

"Have you seen anyone?" I asked.

"Yes," he said, nodding his head. "This morning, I had gone up with the morning relief when I heard a Jeep coming from the north. I had everyone spread out along the boulders, then stood on the road, behind some logs we'd laid across the road. When the Jeep came into view of the roadblock, it stopped. Someone in the front seat stood up and looked around. There were four in the Jeep. I could tell they were talking, but they were too far away to understand. The one standing up kept pointing at me, then at the river, then back to the boulders. Trying to figure out a way around or how many we were, I would guess."

I was getting a little anxious. "Did they talk to you?" I asked.

"The one standing up told one of the back-seat passengers to go and talk to me. He walked up real slow, looking all around, as if someone was going to jump him. He was a little guy, about eighteen; couldn't have weighed much over one-ten, maybe one-twenty. Had on a pair of dirty blue jeans and a red, plaid shirt that hasn't seen a washing in a long time; blond hair and cocky.

"When he was at the log wall, about five feet from me, it dawned on him that I had a weapon, your M-1. He asked for the old man that he'd talked with before. I told him I had no idea who he was talking about. This didn't sit too well, and he was getting agitated real quick. He kept looking back at the Jeep for help or encouragement, or both. He heard the others moving around in the rocks, and turned and walked back to the Jeep."

Stephen joined me as George was relating his encounter at the roadblock. George acknowledged him and continued. "The guy in the front seat had to be their leader, because the little guy came back and said that Jason was going to come back in a week or so, and would bring his people. If the old man wasn't there when they got back, and if that roadblock was still up, there was going to be big trouble.

"He seemed to have more confidence since talking to Jason, and added on his own that he knew about the people hiding in the rocks, and that they didn't scare him or Jason one little bit. He walked back to the Jeep, got in, and they took off."

"What about Jason?" Steve said. "You say he was the boss?"

"Seemed to be. He was definitely making all the decisions. From that distance, I couldn't be sure, but he looked at least ten years older than the others I saw. He looked well over six feet tall, had a beard, and a big hat pulled hard down over his head."

Steve turned to Mr. Arthur. "Does that description fit the two that came here, talked to you, and beat up Mr. Yates?"

"The little guy, that's one of the two that worked me over," Mr. Yates said. "But the big one, I don't think he was here."

"I'll agree with that," Mr. Arthur said.

Steve thought for a minute. "Then, if Jason is leading these people, and he didn't make the first trip down here, but came this time to see for himself, we shouldn't assume he's a ruffian like the two that came first. He might be as cautious of us as we are of them."

"I don't know," George said. "Why didn't he come up to the roadblock and talk with me?"

Steve smiled. "Didn't you say they knew you weren't alone?" he said.

"Yes."

"And you were standing behind a barrier holding a rifle?"

Again, George had to answer yes.

"Then look at it from their point of view. You didn't seem any too friendly. You had a rifle and friends that were hidden. Did you offer to go and talk with Jason, or ask that he come have a cup of coffee and talk?"

George became somewhat defensive. "No, I didn't. But you weren't there, and from what I heard of their first visit, I wasn't going to be any more friendly that I had to."

Steve started to speak, but George held up his hands to indicate that he wasn't through. "But I see now what you mean. I can see that more diplomacy on my part could have helped matters a lot. And as you said, Jason may not have known about the beating."

"Okay, then. They should come next week, with more people. How many and what their attitudes will be remain to be seen," Steve said. "J.J., what's your view?"

I was listening to both sides of the conversation, and seeing myself doing what George had done at the roadblock. I'd seen how those men had beaten Mr. Yates, and I wouldn't have trusted them anywhere past that roadblock without knowing more about them. But your father put a new light on the situation. Jason could have been a decent man, and not known about the actions of the other two, and was scared off by George and his rifle. Still, I had to go along with George in that instance, and be mighty careful when it came to trusting that bunch of ruffians.

"Let's go and have a look at them," I said. "I could take two rangers, go up to Butte City, and check things out. Find out what they're up against, for food and shelter."

George was shaking his head. "Walking into Butte City might be walking right into a big mess of trouble," he said.

"Right," I said. "I thought the best thing to do would be to observe from a distance. According to the maps, there's a ranch west of Butte City—Highland. I'd like to see what's there, also."

Mr. Yates corrected me. "Highland *was* a ranch. Three years ago, the owners sold off acreage for home lots. Had a few takers, not many; most were retirees looking for a place to put a summer cottage. I don't think you'll find much. There was a caretaker for the old ranch house and to watch over a few head of cattle, but the summer people wouldn't have arrived."

We were getting ready to drift into an afternoon of idle conversation, but Steve was thinking ahead of us. "Seems that we have a lot to decide, and not much time to do it in. If we get rain in the next couple of days, we're going to be hard put to keep dry. Let's see about getting up some temporary shelter for ourselves."

We spent the rest of the afternoon putting up our tents and getting the Jeep and van unloaded. Our tents would have to be up pretty high, and away from the river. Without any dams upstream, we could be in for a flood every time it rained up-country.

The next few weeks were filled with all kinds of activity. And Jason, not being true to his word, didn't bother us during that time, although the roadblock was ready for his arrival at any time.

We were only forty-six persons strong when we started, but at any time of day, you could have sworn there were two hundred or more working around the camp. Steve and Mr. Yates worked hard at organizing our group, and everyone had an assigned task, and in some cases had more than one. It was decided that we would live as if there would be no rescue, and that we were on our own until such time as we could go in search of the rest of the world.

We would have to educate the children. Mr. Yates and the former school teachers would see to that. There were fourteen children, and twelve of them had no parents, now. The teachers would be their guardians, and care for them as their own. To that end, a school and dormitory to house the children would be built adjacent to the school, and serve as a meeting place.

The food store would be cleared and searched for anything still usable, especially food products, which would be stored in two of the caves. Mr. Arthur would be responsible for our food supplies, with help from Susan and Beth, who would continue to keep the records. Because of our situation, the food would be prepared by the cafeteria workers, and the kitchen would be left right where it was, for the time being, in the largest of the caves. Likewise, the sporting goods store would be searched, and all items would be put under the care of Mr. Arthur, and stored until such time as they might become useful.

Two people became indispensable in the process of setting up our new order and getting things accomplished. Mr. John Syminski, the blacksmith, had been in the sporting goods store at the destruction. He'd been a hired hand at one of the ranches south of Goldston. He was in his early fifties, and we were very lucky to have him around. In time, his shop became the birthplace of all our wagons and tools for farming; and, in general, he became our all-around handyman.

Mrs. Donley, the lady who had suggested the root cellar, became our second most important person. Raised on a farm in Virginia, she could build a house with the best, and became our principal farmer. With her knowledge of farming, and with Syminski's ability, they made and designed all our farm tools.

I was to organize a defense and protection force. We wanted to keep a watch at the roadblock and on top of the hill, above the caves. A twenty-four-hour watch was set up to protect against fire, wild animals, and in time of bad weather, to keep a particular watch on the rivers. The park rangers, the male grocery store and sporting goods employees, and George Foxworth would help me.

Susan was to augment our meager force of ten by training the women, as many as could be spared, to help with the watches. She was the only one among them who had ever handled any sort of weapon, and in that regard alone, she had her hands full.

Your father was left the task of putting everything into some kind of order. Priorities for building, for digging out the stores; assignments and detailing people to carry them out were his headaches.

The morning after our arrival, all those tasks were started, and everyone was more than eager to get to work. The food store was to be our first priority—clear away the wreckage, and haul everything useful up to the caves. The Jeep came in handy for pulling the heavier rubble away, and was used later to drag heavy timber into an area where it could be prepared for building material. The only thing restricting the use of our vehicles was the gasoline supply, which was dwindling.

John Syminski was busy with his crew, clearing an area below the caves and putting up our first building—the schoolhouse/community house combination. We were as proud of that building as any group of architects would have been of a skyscraper.

We worked hard all morning, starting at daybreak and going till noon. The afternoons were reserved for the least strenuous tasks, such as repairing equipment, recording supplies, making further plans for our building programs, or, in Susan's and my cases, training our paramilitary force.

Susan's main problem was to get the women to fire a weapon, much less hit anything. Her most reluctant pupil was Nancy Foxworth. Nancy had never fired a weapon, never seen one, and didn't want to be around one. She was all for carrying around a large stick.

For three days, she and Susan had been out on our makeshift range, firing the shotguns, and for three days Nancy kept firing in the dirt, not more than six feet in front of her. We were all afraid she was going to shoot herself before she hit a target.

Finally, Susan found out that when she would instruct Nancy without a round in the weapon, and would stand by her while she pulled the trigger, and it would fall with a click, everything was all right. But with a round, she shot into the dirt. She was closing her eyes as tight as she could, because of the loud bang she knew was coming.

Susan tricked her, by giving her a weapon fully-loaded and telling her to practice by aiming at the target. Nancy believed the shotgun to be empty and all that was going to happen when she pulled the trigger was a little click. She aimed at the target, pulled the trigger, and one large deer slug went completely through the center. You have never seen such a surprised, slack-jawed person in all your life. For a minute, she was so mad at Susan that I thought she was going to explode on the spot. Then she realized what she'd accomplished, and all was forgiven.

We were keeping a calendar by then, and were really proud of our progress after two weeks of hard work. All of our food and supplies were taken care of, for the foreseeable future. Our first building project was complete, and ground had been broken for planting some gardens, using seed we had salvaged from the store.

We hadn't been bothered by Jason or anyone else at the roadblock, and with any luck, Tim and Fost would be showing up any day. It was at that time that I approached Steve with the idea of going up to Butte City. I was curious as to why no one had shown up after the first week, and wanted to have a look myself. He talked me out of going right away, but approved my plan of sending someone back to Ioda, to intercept the expeditions as they returned and to lend help, if needed.

We sent Scott Allen and two other men out, the next morning. They were to take our southern route back to Ioda, check the trailer for the provisions we'd left, and if everything was in order, to wait there for a week. If no one showed up, they were to follow Tim's trail south for no more than one day, camp out, then return to Ioda. They would then follow Jack Fost's trail for the same amount of time. If no contact was made with either party, it was to be assumed that they were not going to return. We all hoped, of course, that Scott's team would return with all of the expedition members.

Once again, I was glad your father hadn't let me leave with a party to check out Butte City. We had completed our work with the food store, and were digging out the sporting goods store, when we ran across some very good luck. Not only did we recover the weapons that we were sure were there, but also a good number of radios and three one-kilowatt, gasoline generators. Hooking up a few light bulbs one night, in a cave; playing recordings; getting a real, honest-to-goodness haircut with electric clippers; or being able to use any one of the electrical appliances we had recovered would be a great help to our morale. More importantly, we could use the generators to recharge the batteries that had been recovered from wrecked vehicles up and down the Goldston River, and which had been powering what few bulbs we'd recovered. We would also be able to use the rechargeable batteries for some of our radios. Gasoline would be a problem, but we'd recovered close to one hundred gallons from vehicle tanks, in the previous couple of weeks. With good conservation, that would be able to last us a few months.

The morning after the detail left for Ioda, your father called me down to the old schoolhouse, which was now our village headquarters. He was becoming somewhat worried about what Jason might be up to, and felt it was time to send out a patrol.

"J.J., work is progressing at a normal pace, now, and with any luck, Tim and Fost will be back in a few days. I'm ready to hear what your ideas are on going up north and looking for survivors."

I walked over to the Forest Service map we had hanging on the wall, and looked at it for a second. I had looked at that map at least a hundred times, and knew by heart all of the markings on it, including the roadblock, observation post, our trail from Ioda marked in red pencil, and the new course of both the Goldston and Little Rivers. I wanted to present a good program, and wanted my facts and ideas straight before I got underway. Steve wasn't about to send me out to get into trouble, and even though we had known each other for a long time, I knew friendship wouldn't sway his thinking one way or the other.

"I'd like to take two men and head out across country," I said, indicating on the map a route about one-half mile west of the road to Butte City. "We'd be on fairly high ground, and could keep the road in view at least most of the time."

I looked at Steve, and he didn't seem to have any questions, so I turned back to the map. "If we don't see anyone on the way up, I'd establish a lookout post just about here, due south of the town. The map indicates this is about five hundred feet above the city, and we could observe from there for however long it might take to get a general idea of what the situation is, there."

"What about contact?"

"Depending on what it looked like, I'd do one of two things. First, I'd think about taking one man with me, circle around to the north, and approach the town from that direction. My observation post could keep us in view, and it would look like we came from somewhere else, other than Goldston. If things didn't look too friendly, it might be wiser to go in late at night and look around. We'd already have a good idea of where everything would be, by observing. I'd say a full day and night of observation, before making a move."

"How long would you think it would take to make contact, and bring whoever you find back here? Providing, of course, they want to come."

"Three to five days. We might find a hornet's nest up there, or then again, a bunch of lonely, starving people. We won't know until we go up."

"All right," Steve said. "Let's get the people you want to take with you in here, this afternoon, make some concrete plans, and kick off tomorrow morning."

I didn't care much for telling Susan that I'd be leaving in the morning, but we'd been discussing the problem for some time, so it really came as no surprise to her. My biggest problem was convincing her to stay there, and not volunteer to go with us.

The afternoon meeting was attended by the crew that was to go north: myself, Ranger Goodman and one other man, Mr. Yates, Mr. Arthur, and George Foxworth, who would take over my duties and act as my back-up, in case we ran into trouble. The final plan was to set up the observation post as we had discussed earlier, and make contact if possible. We would also check out Highland, depending on the situation at Butte City. We would take two radios, and keep Steve informed of our situation. Every man was to be armed with a rifle. Steve didn't much care for that idea, but I finally convinced him that it would be better to have weapons with us than having to call back for help, which might take hours getting to us. I promised him that when we made initial contact, weapons would be left at the observation post. If we found some friendly, honest folk, we would call back on the radio, and Steve and several of our group would come up there and meet the people. We also would advise if it would be better to bring the Jeep or van, depending on the condition of the road.

We wouldn't take more than three days' supplies, and if the situation called for a longer stay, George would re-supply us at a predetermined spot between the two villages.

With all questions finally answered, we broke up the meeting, satisfied that we had a good plan. I was happy that we were moving our horizons back, again. The next trip that we would be planning would take us over the mountains, either north or east. The trip planned for the next day might help determine which direction we would choose.

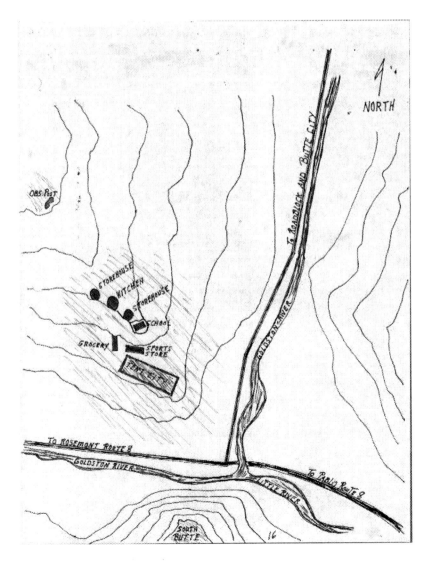

*Chapter 6*

# TROUBLE IN THE NEW WORLD

The next morning, we met at the village headquarters to get our equipment and to see if there were any final details to be worked out before we left. Steve was waiting for us. He was going to accompany us up to the roadblock, in the van. All of our provisions had been packed the night before, so the only things to work out were our radio call signs. We weren't sure if Jason's group had radios or not, but it was agreed that we should be on the safe side and not use proper names or places when talking on the air.

Radio had been in use at the roadblock for some weeks, by then, and at the headquarters. The two places used Blocker and Base as call signs, respectively. The position on top of the caves was called Looker. We would be known as Forward.

Persons working around or with the radios were given a code name or number. Your father became Big Base and Mr. Yates, who had routinely taken over as Steve's second-in-command at the headquarters, was known as Little Base. The rest of us used a simple number system. I was number ten, or as spoken on the air, One-Zero; George Foxworth was number One-One; and so forth. We found it worked rather well. If you called the roadblock, using the call sign Blocker, and you were answered by Block One-One, you knew immediately that you were talking to George.

A final radio check completed, we loaded aboard the van for the short trip up to the roadblock. I'd been pretty busy at the village, working with the cleanup of the two stores; the supervising and setting up of the watch system; weapons training; and lately, had started a program to reclaim what we could from the wreckage of the

city, which was still plastered up against South Butte. Therefore, I
hadn't visited the roadblock or the outpost on top of the hill. I was
in for a real surprise when the van stopped and I got out at the roadblock.

The last time I'd been there, a tent had been erected, so that
those not actually on watch could get some sleep or get out of the
rain. Huge tree trunks had lain across the old road, extending from
the boulders on the west side almost up to the river on the right. We
had continued to keep three people there, rotating them every
twenty-four hours. But I'd heard lately, from George, that there
were some who didn't like it at all, up there, and others who would
like to assume a permanent watch there. We'd discussed changing
the arrangement, but nothing had been worked out, one way or the
other. No one had told me about the building program that had
been going on up there.

What greeted my eyes was almost unbelievable. Where the tent
had been, there now stood a small, stone house. The north wall was
the boulders that formed a natural wall, running east and west.
Onto that had been built a house completely of stone, measuring
twenty-four feet, from east to west, with sides eight feet high. It had
been divided into three rooms. On the far left was the kitchen, the
middle was the sleeping room, and on the end was the guard
house—or watch room. The roof was made of rough, pine poles
that had been taken from the river bank, where they'd been
deposited during the most recent flood. A walkway had been constructed, running across the top of the roof, so that a man could see
over the top of the boulders, while at the same time be protected
from observation from the other side.

The tree trunks that had lain across the road and beyond had
been cut out, for a distance of approximately eight feet, and a neat-
ly-painted, red and white pole, balanced in such a way that it could
be raised, had been placed over the opening. In the area between the
road and river, south of the roadblock, a garden had been planted,
and was progressing quite well under the supervision of the personnel assigned to duty there. It was gratifying that the people up there,
who could have been living in a tent and sleeping, rather than doing
all that work, had chosen to be so industrious.

The last thing to catch my eye was the walkway that ran from
the roadblock to the house. Along that path had been built a circle

of stone, and placed in the middle was a flag pole, standing about fifteen feet high. Flying from the pole was one of the flags we had found in the sporting goods store. The flag of the United States of America, or I should say, the old United States. To top all of that off, a hand-hewn sign was at the base of the pole, reading *FORT DARBY*. You could have fired a cannon in my ear, at that moment, and I wouldn't have noticed.

Your father was standing at my side, with a big grin on his face. "Well, Mr. Darby, what do you think?"

"I think it's great." That's about all I could manage, at the time.

Several people then emerged from the building, among them Susan. She came up to me with all the formality of a woman who had never seen me before in her life.

"We would like to welcome you to Fort Darby, Mr. Darby. It is my privilege to present you with the key to the gate. May you have a pleasant stay with us." She gave me a big smack on the cheek and stepped away.

"You've put so much work into our small band," Steve said. "We thought it'd be nice to give you some recognition."

"The cook baked you a cake," Susan said, "to help celebrate the dedication of your brand new fort." The expedition to the north was forgotten while we all gathered around for coffee and cake.

After the festivities were over, all the guests piled into the van for the return to Goldston. Susan kissed me goodbye, with the admonition to be careful. It was exceedingly quiet, once the van rolled from view. A few minutes before, it had been so loud, with talking, laughing, and clowning around. Then it was back to the serious business of being a road guard or patrol leader.

A few parting words, handshakes, and we were on our way. We left the protection of the boulders, climbed up to the high ground, and proceeded north, paralleling the road, but far enough away and high enough that we couldn't be detected. The hillsides were covered with grass, and small trees were taking root. We couldn't see much to the west, as the hills rose in that direction, but the valley to our right and on the north was quite visible.

We were no more than thirty minutes away from the roadblock when I distinctly heard vehicle engines. I turned to one of the rangers, and without saying a word, he understood and was nodding his head, *We heard them, too.* We immediately dropped to the ground. We were on exposed ground, and could have easily been seen from the road, if anyone was looking.

My first thought was to alert the roadblock. "Blocker, this is Forward. We have vehicles on the road, coming your way."

"Roger, Forward. We can't hear them yet, but are on alert."

"Will keep you informed."

By the time I finished with the radio transmissions, they were upon us. I figured our position at about three miles away from the roadblock. They should hear them shortly, after they passed our location.

They came into view, traveling at a pretty good rate of speed, considering the condition of the road. In the lead was a motorcycle with two people aboard; following were three Jeeps. The lead Jeep had two people, and the other two were carrying three each. Following this procession was a very old pickup truck. I couldn't be sure, but it looked like two people in the front seat and four riding in the bed. Sixteen people were heading for our roadblock, which had only three defenders, assuming that it needed defending. They seemed to be in a festive mood, and that could be taken in many different ways.

About that time, the radio came alive. "Forward One-Zero, this is Base One-One."

It was George. He'd overheard my conversation with the roadblock.

"One-One, we might have a big problem brewing, in just a couple of minutes. We count five vehicles and sixteen people heading south, at a high rate of speed. Can you get moving?"

"That's affirmative. Heard your first call, and thought there might be trouble. Moving out now, by vehicle, with three people."

"Roger. Moving south myself, right now. Out."

If George could reach the roadblock before our visitors, he would have a total force of seven people. We couldn't get there without taking a big detour, but my force might do better by coming up either from the rear or to one side. If our visitors were up to any mischief, they were in for a really big surprise.

But first, I thought I'd better call and let our people know what to expect. "Blocker, this is Forward."

"Go ahead, Forward."

"Stand by for five vehicles: one bike, three Jeeps, and one pick-up. Should be at your location momentarily. Suspect about sixteen people aboard. We're on our way. Didn't see any weapons with this group, but don't take any chances. Over."

"Roger. We're on guard and standing by."

We ran down to the road, and started back. The going would be faster down there, and I wanted to get to the roadblock as fast as I could. We weren't halfway back to the roadblock when the first shots rang out. The firing sounded slow and deliberate, and I thought, from the sound, that all the rounds were traveling in one direction. Either our people were shooting or theirs, but not both sides. Not yet, anyway.

It was time for us to leave the road. We were getting pretty close, and I didn't want to come up on anyone from the back and scare them into shooting at us. We climbed up to the top of the ridge, and ran along there for about another ten minutes. All the time, shots were ringing out, slowly and from the same rifle, it seemed.

As we came abreast of their vehicles, we crouched down and took a position near an outcrop of rocks. We, as well as they, were about five hundred yards from the roadblock. Their vehicles were parked in a gully between the road and river, and the people were lying down on the south bank, facing the roadblock. One man had an M-16 rifle, quite capable of firing many rounds a minute, but at the time, he was taking careful aim and shooting at the roadblock pole, the one that had been painted red and white. Chips of wood would fly off when he made a hit, and it appeared he had made a score about one round in three. At that rate, if he was planning on cutting that pole in half, he would need a ton of ammunition.

I could see over the wall of rocks forming the back of the stone house, and saw that the van was there. George had arrived some minutes before, and I guessed he was trying to assess the situation. He would be as baffled as I was about the lone sniper.

I used the radio to find out how he was doing. "One-One, this is One-Zero. What's your situation? Over."

"Okay, I guess. All of my people are in place. We're receiving fire, but nothing serious. Are you in a position to see anything? Over."

"We just arrived. Can see everything. One man with a rifle firing at the roadblock. There seems to be a discussion. Wait.

Something's getting ready to happen, down there. Will call you back."

I broke off because the group that had been behind the man firing had started to move. Five people total—three were heading for one of the Jeeps and two for the cycle. The guy riding on the cycle pulled a large caliber weapon from his belt, checked it out, made some remark that drew lots of laughter, and got on. The guy getting into the back of the Jeep brought out a bolt-action rifle, gave it to the guy riding shotgun, up front, and they started for the roadblock.

I was on the radio fast. "You've got company coming, and fast— one bike, one Jeep."

"Roger."

As they hit the roadway, the bike was in the lead and moving out fast. It was about a five-hundred-yard dash to the roadblock, and they were flying. When they were no more than two hundred yards away, the guy on the back of the bike started waving the pistol around and looking back, a signal to the Jeep. The rifle carrier in the Jeep waved back, and the bike turned to the right and started heading across country. If I was correct, that course would take them up and over the top, just west of the rock barrier, and they could come down in back of the roadblock. But George knew that also, and wasn't about to let that happen.

As the bikers neared the wall, a line of rifle fire broke out that turned the bike's wheels into junk. The two men were thrown headlong into the dirt. One was lucky and rolled free; the other was hit by the bike twice, as it spun and tumbled its way down to the bottom of the hill.

The Jeep stopped instantly, on the road, and not more than a five-second drive from the barrier. The group not in on the attack were standing up, by then, and watching. The guy who had been doing the shooting had stopped. All was quiet for what seemed like a long time. One of the bikers was moaning, but nobody else moved. Then the guy in the Jeep, with the rifle, stepped out and walked to the front of the vehicle.

"What do you goofs think you're doing?" he yelled. "You probably killed those guys."

George answered from behind the roadblock. "I hope not, and if they're friends of yours, go have a look; see if they can be helped. But the first one of you that comes anywhere near this wall with a rifle, or fires another round at me or any of my people, will answer for it. Got that?"

"Yeah, wise guy, we got it."

He put the rifle in the Jeep, and started walking to where the bikers were lying. He approached the one who had been run over by the bike, knelt down, said something to him, then went over to the other. The second biker was able to get up with a little help, and together they went back over to the first man.

The guy from the Jeep looked toward George. "This guy's hurt pretty bad. I need to bring the Jeep over. He ain't never going to make it by himself."

George gave the okay, and they loaded him in and started back. I was sure I detected an air of dejection in the group, which now retreated. It was evident they had had enough and were ready to quit.

Back at their staging area, there was a big argument going on. The participants in the latest charge wanted to head back north, or so it seemed. The guy who was doing all the hollering to proceed had to be Jason. He fitted the description.

As that was going on, George called me on the radio. Steve had arrived at the roadblock, and wanted an update on what was going on at the other camp. I brought them up to date, and told them to wait; that they might either withdraw or make another try, I wasn't sure.

Finally, the Jeep with the hurt men started and left, heading north for Butte City. The rest were being directed by Jason, who sent the man with the M-16 and two others back to the position where they'd been before, when they were sniping. I immediately called the roadblock and told them to keep down.

The rest of Jason's crew took a heavy, metal sheet from the bed of the pickup, approximately four by six feet, and put it across one of the remaining Jeeps. It was situated with the long side across the bumper, short side leaning on the hood. They were making a shield for the Jeep, and they were going to try and break the roadblock with that imitation tank. The steel looked to be thick enough to deflect a bullet. They finished by tying it down with some heavy-duty rope.

Hurried plans were made, and Jason could be seen giving a mock demonstration of where everyone would be during the attack. He simulated the driver hunched over the wheel and the Jeep passengers crouched down. Apparently, there was going to be an infantry, as he demonstrated how to walk behind the Jeep, keeping as low as possible.

The people at the roadblock would have a hard time stopping the contraption before it got near, and if that were allowed to happen, someone would certainly be killed or seriously wounded. Those guys didn't want to talk, be friendly, or get along. I thought that my little detail could nip that thing in the bud. I took one of the rangers with me and got near the road. From ambush, we could knock out the Jeep. Then, with covering fire from the ranger left up top and from the roadblock, we could withdraw safely.

I called George on the radio, told him of my plan, and also gave him the exact position of the guy with the M-16. They couldn't see him, but enough rounds around and over his head would keep him down. I could hear the Jeep revving up, and it was straining pretty hard, with its load of passengers and its new steel shield. We made it to our new position and waited.

We didn't wait long. The Jeep was moving along really slowly; the driver hadn't taken it out of low gear. As they came nearer, I could see that not everyone was armed, and for the first time, I realized that there were women with this group. I looked at my partner, and pointed toward the walking troops.

"Women! Good grief," he said. "They've brought women to a battle."

My sentiments exactly. They were acting as if this were some kind of game, a way to amuse themselves until the world returned to normal.

"Okay, try not to hit anyone, if possible. Go for the Jeep's tires. When they go flat, fire away at the engine. I've got thirty rounds in my carbine, you've get seven; that should be sufficient to put out them out of commission."

As they came abreast of us, all I said was, "You front tire, me rear," and we started blasting away. The tires went down right away, all four, then I turned to the hood and fired away. That Jeep was dead before I had got half of my rounds into it. Just to be safe, I kept five in my magazine, because I wasn't any too sure what those nuts might do next. I didn't look up, but I could hear firing coming from the roadblock. They were undoubtedly firing at the unseen target in the rear.

I didn't have to worry about a counterattack. The enemy infantry was running for all it was worth, back to the safety of the other vehicles and the small ravine. The people in the Jeep were crouched down so low that we couldn't see anyone at all. I found out later that the guy with the M-16 had thrown it away and run for the river, with his two companions on his heels.

I stood up, and hollered toward the Jeep. "Jason, you in there?"

A figure on the passenger side slowly emerged. "Yeah, I'm here," he said.

"I've got some questions for you. Why are you and your friends acting like fools? Why the action with the bikers and this contraption?"

"Man, you don't know nothing. Just wait until the Feds get here—you and your friends over there are going to jail. Look at my Jeep." Jason was becoming more emotional as he spoke. "Who's going to pay for my Jeep? Who's going to pay?"

I wasn't going to say anything else to this nut. It was obvious he was insane. But why had the others taken up with him? I wouldn't have to ask him any more questions, and I was glad. I saw Steve, George, and two others approaching from the fort. But I wasn't going to take any chances. If I knew Steve, he wouldn't be armed.

"The rest of you, out of the Jeep." I didn't get any response. "I'm not going to repeat myself. You get out now or you get pulled out."

They started to move. Soft words and asking please weren't in their vocabulary.

"Jason, you stay where you are. The rest of you, get back there with the rest of your friends."

As Steve came up, he looked at Jason, held out his hand, and smiled. "My name is Stephen Adams," he said. "I'm sorry we had to meet like this, but surely we can settle our differences without resorting to shooting."

Jason didn't say a word. He stared right through Steve. He clenched and unclenched his hands in a slow, steady motion.

Steve looked at me. I shrugged my shoulders. I had tried to talk to him, and I knew George had tried. Now, Steve was finding out what we knew—the man was not rational.

Steve asked Jason what his last name was, where was he from, what did he want. No reply. Steve was perplexed. I don't think he had ever run into such a person. I know I never had.

"Jason," Steve said, "We're going to have a big supper in town, tonight. Why don't you bring all of your friends and join us. Everyone's welcome."

He stood looking at Jason for a full minute. Jason was still staring right through him. Steve turned and started walking away.

Jason came alive. "Let me tell you something, big man. You can take your town, your supper, and go straight to hell. Because just like I told your stooge, here, when help comes, I'm going to have all you people thrown in jail. I'll get the best lawyers. Just you wait, you're all going to be sorry." Steve tried to speak, but Jason cut him off. "I told you what's going to happen, and I mean it. You think you're so smart, with your roadblock and your big talk. Just wait, you just wait."

Jason had talked himself into such a frenzy, he was about to explode. His pale complexion had turned beet-red, and his fists were clenched so tightly that his knuckles were white. He turned to leave, and ran right into the Jeep. He took some of his anger out by kicking the Jeep a half-dozen times, as he passed.

He was still screaming as he walked away. "You just wait. It's going to be my turn, one of these days. You keep your stooges away from Butte City. You ain't seen trouble, yet. You keep away."

He was still talking, mostly to himself. We couldn't hear anything, anymore—just mumbling. The others had loaded into the remaining Jeep and truck. They wanted to get out of there. But Jason wasn't through, yet.

He reached into the Jeep and threw someone out, then a second person. He was so mad that he started hitting and kicking and screaming. They ran to the pickup and got in, still smarting from the hits they'd received. Jason got into the Jeep, and both vehicles were gone.

We stood in the road, not quite knowing what to do. The air was still filled with the smell of gunpowder, as we watched the vehicles disappear up the road. Somehow, the whole experience didn't seem real.

I motioned for the ranger on top of the ridge to come down, and we all started back to the roadblock. We were too tired to head out for Butte City that day. I talked with Steve as we walked back, and it was determined that we should stay there overnight and leave in the morning.

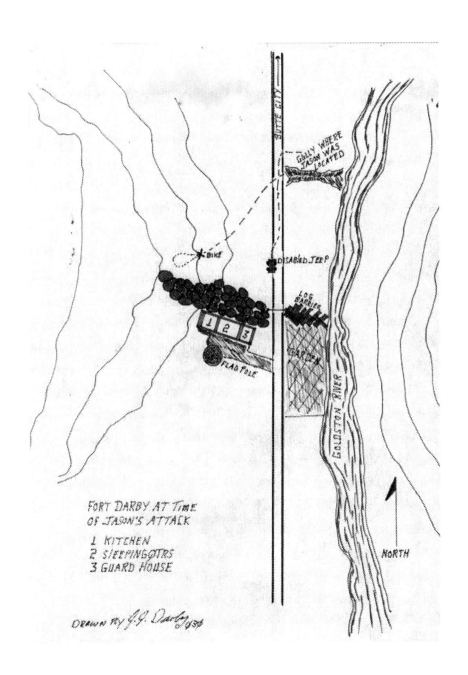

BUTTE CITY

GULLY WHERE JASON WAS LOCATED

DISABLED JEEP

BIKE

LOG BARRIER

GARDEN

1 2 3

FLAG POLE

GOLDSTON RIVER

NORTH

FORT DARBY AT TIME
OF JASON'S ATTACK

1 KITCHEN
2 SLEEPINGQTRS
3 GUARD HOUSE

DRAWN BY J.J. Darby 1938

# Chapter 7

⟨∾⟩

# BUTTE CITY

The next day, we spent the morning clearing the battlefield of the wrecked motorcycle and imitation tank. There wasn't any trouble with the bike, but the Jeep was a different matter. First, we had to remove the shield that Jason and his men had tied to the front. We loaded it into the van, with other parts that we could remove with hand tools; then brought my Jeep up from Goldston, to drag the frame and shot-up engine back behind the roadblock.

John Syminski, the blacksmith, was more than happy to see that pile of junk. It was more raw material for him to work with, in his shop. Anything from the two vehicles that could be used for repairs of our own would be kept, and John would use whatever remained for making farm implements.

Steve was back in the afternoon, and for the first time, we discussed the possibility that there might be people in Butte City being held against their will. Some kind of a rescue would have to be worked out.

Steve didn't want anyone hurt, and he was very explicit in his instructions. "We are not the law of the land, here, any more than Jason and his bunch. If and when help or rescue does come, everyone is going to have to account for their actions. For our part, there have been two men hurt, here. I know we were just protecting ourselves, but I'd like to see that be the last of it, if possible."

He thought for a minute then continued. "That doesn't mean that you and your men shouldn't protect yourselves. But if it's at all possible, stay out of a shootout. We'll continue with the rest of the plan, just as we talked about before. When will you be ready to leave?"

"This afternoon. We might be expected, now, and it might be best to approach them after dark. If we leave around 2:00 or 2:30, we should be in the vicinity shortly after dark. If we can find a good observation spot, we should be able to get settled in during the night, and by dawn of the next day, get a pretty good look at them."

"All right, then. I'm going to head back for Goldston. Have a good trip, and be careful."

I assured him that we would. We shook hands, and he climbed back in the van for the short trip to Goldston. I informed the other two men going with me of the plans that Steve and I had worked out, and that we would shove off by 2:00 that afternoon—just enough time to get an hour's rest.

When we left the roadblock, that afternoon, everything was back to normal. The regular watch had been reestablished, and with the exception of John and some others working on the wrecked Jeep, it was quiet.

We retraced our steps of the day before, passed the place where Jason had been set up with his people, turned west, climbed back up to high ground, and headed north. The terrain wasn't bad. A few small gullies to navigate around, but the going was easy. We could have made better time on the road below, but the tables could always be turned, and we could be ambushed taking the easy route.

The grass was now knee-high, and there were small trees taking root on what had, until recently, been barren ground. We had easy cover if we did encounter anyone, as long as we stayed off the sky-line. The grass was the right height to fall down in, lie flat, and disappear.

The weather, which had been nice, began to turn for the worse. There were rumblings of thunder to our west, and the sky was rapidly turning dark. It would surely rain before we reached our destination, but that might work to our advantage. At the speed we were going, we would have reached Butte City way before dark, so we slowed our pace and planned to stop short, about two miles away, prepare our evening meal, then proceed in the dark.

We were interrupted before we could get to our meal stop. The lead man spotted two people sitting on some rocks, slightly off the road, not more than three miles from Butte City. They weren't trying to hide, although their vehicle, a vintage Harley Davidson, was more or less hidden some distance from them, in a ravine. They were keeping up a steady stream of conversation and horseplay, almost as if they wanted to be seen by anyone approaching from the south. If that was Jason's only outpost or roadblock then we didn't have too much to worry about.

Those two kept a nervous eye on the road all the time, and I would think they were supposed to head out if they saw anyone coming. Well, if I could help it, they wouldn't see anyone this day, so I motioned for the lead man to keep going, slowly and quietly.

We kept a steady pace for another half-hour, before we found a nice secluded spot to stop, have our evening meal, and wait for dark. Our meals on that trip weren't anything special. For our supper that night, we dined on canned meat, crackers, and canned peaches for dessert. Our beverage, as it was for most of the trip, was water. We saved our small coffee supply for the mornings.

According to the map I had with me, Butte City was no more than a half-mile due north, just over one or two small rises of land not big enough to be called hills. On the last one, south of the city, we might find a good place, secluded and high enough to observe from for a few days. We made our supper spot the permanent camp, set up a tent in order to stay reasonably dry when it started raining, and had a small fire when possible, to heat our food and make coffee.

After the tent was up and all of our gear stowed, two of us went forward to look for our observation spot, while the third man stayed in camp. After only ten minutes, we could hear voices and the rush of water over rocks, or so it seemed at the time. It was very dark by then, and we proceeded as slowly and soundlessly as we could. One mistake and our whole observation game would be over.

We came to the last hill south of town, crossed over the top, and took up a position on the forward slope—a perfect place to observe. There were boulders strewn across in front and all around us. About one hundred yards below us was a natural wall of timber and all matter of debris, which had been washed down from upstream. A little digging and moving of some rocks, and we had a perfect, two-man position.

Using the binoculars, I took my first look at Butte City in over a year. Susan and I had gone up there the previous year on a sight-seeing tour and to buy souvenirs. We had only stayed one after-noon, but I could see that things had tragically changed.

Lead Creek, which ran east to west and formed the southern boundary of the city, was filled with large boulders, and the bridge that should have been directly in front of our position had been completely destroyed. The highway coming up from the south now disappeared into sand, two hundred yards before reaching the river.

The old pickup truck that had been in on the attack at the road-block was now sitting where the macadam stopped, apparently abandoned. To our right should have been Lake Butte, but the earthen dam at the south end of the lake was gone, and so was the lake's water. The mud and rock from the dam and the water from the lake had helped to wipe Goldston off the face of the earth.

I remembered that there had been a large pavilion next to the lake, and it seemed to still be there. I could see people moving around it, and there were two Jeeps parked in front, along with one motorcycle.

As I was looking over the pavilion, the bikers that we had observed earlier appeared. They rode up next to the truck, stopped, and left the bike there, then swam across the river. As they approached the pavilion, they were joined by other members of their group, no doubt anxious to see if they had any news. The pavilion was lit with several candles, and from what I could see, seemed to be in reasonably good shape. It was a wood structure, and had either withstood the quakes or had been rebuilt recently.

Across the street and to the west was the main part of the busi-ness district. There were several old buildings left over from the days when Butte City had been a big boom town, riding high on the silver strikes of one hundred years before. Most of those buildings had been brick, and had been reduced to rubble. I could see some low walls still standing, but nothing else.

Looking still farther west, to the residential part of the town, I could see a few small fires going. What had been mostly wood-frame houses were now twisted piles of wood and plaster, and were more than likely supplying fuel for the fires burning around them.

The northern part of the town was buried under tons and tons of rock. The streets that had run north disappeared into what was now the side of a mountain. I tried to follow the main road, as it wound north between the old brick buildings and frame houses, but it disappeared. What I was looking for were the ski lodges. Without a doubt, they were gone.

I had seen enough. I instructed the ranger to keep a watch on the town for a couple of hours and get some idea of what time they went to sleep, what sentries they had, if any, and then to get some rest. I would be back before first light, and we could take a daytime look.

It started raining before I got back to camp, and I was thankful we had a tent to keep ourselves and the supplies dry, over the coming days. I talked to Steve on the radio, and told him of our findings, then turned in early.

I was back at the observation post before first light. It was still raining, just as it had all night—a slow, soaking rain. The ranger had made a shelter out of his poncho, but it couldn't keep out the cold, and he looked really miserable. I told him to go back to the base camp, get some breakfast, and turn in for a few hours. I would stay most of the day, and he could come back early in the evening.

He told me that not much had happened the previous night. The people in the pavilion had been up pretty late. They had secured beer or whisky from somewhere, and they seemed to be really drunk before the last one turned in. Other than that, nothing had moved anywhere.

After he left, I took the binoculars and made a sweep of the town, starting with the pavilion. I could see several people sprawled out in several locations and one person in a Jeep, sleeping off a drunk no doubt. That had to be Jason and his group.

As I looked to the west, the binoculars came to rest on a lean-to in the rubble of the brick buildings. The small fire outside the lean-to had gone out during the night, put out by the persistent rain. I could see people in the building adjacent to the lean-to. One person, a woman, was moving around in the small space that had been created when the roof had collapsed. She was looking over and talking to several people. They seemed to have been injured in one way or another. That was their hospital, such as it was.

As I watched, two other women came up to the building. One had picked up wood from somewhere and was trying to get the fire going again. They were joined by the woman from within the building. A few words were exchanged, and two of the women started walking in the direction of the pavilion, while the third was left to tend the fire.

The rain stopped as the sun came up, and the sky was clearing of clouds, although the air was still damp and heavy from the previous night's rain. Looking farther to the west, I could see more people stirring in and around the remains of the town. Some had built what appeared to be good-sized and sturdy shelters, while others were living almost out in the open. Several people were walking toward the pavilion, along the road that ran next to Lead Creek.

People were gathering at the south end of the pavilion and standing around. After a few minutes of what seemed to be idle talk, some of the group seemed restless, and one member yelled into the pavilion. Someone from Jason's group appeared, looked around, and went back inside.

Jason appeared a few minutes later, looked the group over, paced up and down in front of them, then began talking. I couldn't hear what he was saying, but he seemed to be angry about something, and the more he talked, the wilder he became. Before he came to the end of his speech, his arms were cutting through the air wildly, and he was stamping his feet to emphasize his point. As he finished his wild and furious attack on those gathered in front of him, food was being brought out from the building and placed before them. As each person approached and picked up a few cans or boxes, he or she would bow to Jason, turn, and leave. The ritual was repeated until everyone had received his allotment of food and departed. The two women from the hospital were the last to leave. They were accompanied on their way back by two of Jason's men, carrying some of the boxes.

Well, there was some organization within this group, I thought. I didn't like the looks of the distribution system, and wanted to find out how Jason and his mob had taken over.

I spent the rest of the day trying to get an accurate count of the people in the town. I made a crude map, and had everyone placed where it appeared they were living.

By mid-morning, all the cooking fires were once again burning, and some life had returned to the little town. There was some building going on, mostly to improve the structures already there, but I didn't see any indication of group unity between the people of the town and Jason's group in the pavilion. There were no gardens, so the food they had on hand must have come from whatever was found after the destruction.

Jason appeared on the south porch of the pavilion again, with what appeared to be most of his people. I was able to count seventeen. He was spinning around in a chair as he talked, giving orders for whatever he wanted accomplished that day. When he finished, the group broke up. Some went back inside the building, and others wandered around.

Two men came out of the pavilion with shotguns, joined two other men, and the four proceeded west, along the road leading to Highland Village. The two bikers that we'd encountered the day before crossed the river once again, got the motorcycle running, and left for their observation spot.

The rest of the day passed peaceably. The people in and around the pavilion either slept or listened to Jason, who got a lot of pleasure out of sitting in a big wicker chair on the south porch, giving orders, and telling stories.

The women at the hospital were busy feeding and otherwise taking care of the patients in the hospital. The patients were behind a brick wall, and I couldn't see how many there were, but guessing from the size of the structure and bowls of food taken to them, I thought there were at least five people in there. I had seen several young children during the day, in and around some of the structures, and put their total at ten.

Around noon, several of Jason's people left the pavilion, and went through the city gathering up some of the men into a working party. When a sufficient number had been gathered, they walked up the road leading to where all of the ski lodges had been located. They disappeared from my view after they left the town proper, and I speculated that they were still digging around the ski lodges, trying to find supplies. There had been a small shopping center up there, and that might be one place they were getting their food and other provisions.

I had gathered all the information needed. The next step was to go down into the town and talk to someone. The woman at the hospital seemed to be the best bet.

I left the observation post in the early afternoon, and joined the rangers at the base camp. I brought them up to date on what I had seen and my plans for the next night. We would stay in camp for the rest of the day. All three of us would move up to the observation post before dark, take another look around, and make final plans. Then, Ranger Goodman and myself would move down the hill and into the town. The man left behind would keep track of us as best he could, and if we were discovered and got into any trouble, he would report at once to Steve and have George bring up whatever force would be necessary to get us out.

Before we left base camp, I radioed Steve and told him what we had learned so far, from our observation of Butte City. I informed him of my plan for going into the town. We put out the fire, stowed all of our extra equipment in the tent, and left for the observation post, arriving there shortly after sunset.

Not much had changed since I had been there, a few hours earlier. The bike was once again parked next to the pickup, on our side of the river, so the watch was back. But what about the four who I had seen going toward Highland Village? I would have hated to swim across the river and be caught on the road, before we got to the town.

There was no reason to worry. We had been in position no more than five minutes when we heard someone approaching from the direction of Highland Village. The four men were pushing along a wheelbarrow full of fresh meat.

I looked at my companions. "Now, where do you suppose anyone could go and kill an animal with shotguns?" I said.

Ranger Goodman held out his hand. "Let me see your binoculars," he said.

I handed them over. He looked at the four men and the wheelbarrow for a long time.

"I'm not sure," he said, "but I'd swear they have regular old cow there."

I took the binoculars back and had another look. "What makes you think it's a cow?" I asked.

"Several things. First, they aren't the best butchers in the world, and second, what I can see of the hide makes me think it's cow and not deer or elk. Plus, they used a shotgun. I'd be willing to bet they walked right up to old Bossie and let her have it with both barrels."

They passed by a great majority of the townspeople, on their way to the pavilion, and by the time they got there, half of the town was following them. That was probably the first fresh meat they'd seen in awhile, judging from the crowd's reaction.

Jason was there with most of his mob to meet them. The whole bunch did a lot of hollering and jumping around, like a bunch of savages.

The townspeople stood back, observing. All they wanted was some fresh meat, but I was betting they'd get very little, if any at all.

Once things settled down a little, Jason started giving instructions. It appeared he wanted a big fire started, and had dispatched a wood detail. Someone not of his group asked him a question, and he laughed, pushed the guy away, and continued giving orders.

The lady from the hospital pushed her way up to him, and was really letting him have a tongue-lashing. I could tell that he was mad. He was staring at her just as he had at Steve the day before, at the roadblock. But whatever it was she was saying finally had an effect. He gave some instructions, and the townspeople lined up at the wheelbarrow for a piece of the meat. The portion given was small, but no one complained. The lady from the hospital stood there, when her turn came, and waited until she was satisfied that she had an ample amount for the patients, then withdrew.

Jason stared at her the whole time, as she was walking away. I had a feeling he was trying to think of some way to do that lady harm. She was definitely a thorn in his side, and she was the only person whom I had seen stand up to him.

Before long, Jason's crowd had a huge fire going on the east side of the giant pavilion. Someone had made up two spits, and the cow was being roasted. Cans of beer now appeared, and Jason's barbarians were off to a good start on a party that might last all night.

Goodman and I waited until the party was really going well and most of the fires in the other part of the town had died down, indicating that most of the sane people down there were going to sleep for the night. Then we started down the hill. We made our way down the forward slope of the hill and over to the two vehicles that had been left on the south side of the river.

I wanted to raise the hood, take out the spark plug wires or distributor cap, and disable the truck. But there was a lot of light from the bonfire, and it was too risky. We opted to flatten the tires on both the truck and bike. No one was likely to go very far with them in that condition. It was a gamble letting them know we'd been there, but I felt better knowing they'd have to follow us on foot, if they were going to follow at all.

We proceeded back up the south side of Lead Creek, looking for a good ford. If we were to bring people out, I didn't want to be swimming, with Jason and his gang in hot pursuit.

The creek was running very high, and we had to travel some distance to find a crossing. I was wondering where Jason had brought the Jeeps and truck across. We were about three-quarters of a mile from the old bridge site when we came across a huge sand-bar in the middle of the creek. The water was swift and deep on the south side, but with ropes, we should be able to bring everyone over without too much trouble. From the sandbar to the north bank, everyone would be able to wade, with the exception of some of the smaller children, and if the level of the creek dropped about two feet, this side would be no trouble at all.

Once across, we made our way slowly back into town. I didn't want anyone to see us as we came in. The fewer people who knew about our presence, the better. Things looked a bit different from that side of the river. There didn't seem to be any of the original structures standing, as it had appeared through the binoculars. Smoke from the numerous fires still hung in the air, along with the smell of the meat that had been roasted, earlier that night. Their sanitary conditions weren't the best, and there was an awful stink coming from the space between the road and the creek.

We approached the downtown section very cautiously. The big fire at the pavilion was illuminating most of the area, all the way to the washed-out bridge site. We turned left and started north, along what had been the main street.

Goodman spotted the lean-to first and pointed. The fire out front was almost out; small, glowing coals were all that remained. As we approached, I could hear someone in the brick building moaning and a woman answering with comforting words. The nurse or doctor, whichever she was, had to be in there with the patients, but there wasn't any light.

We waited outside the lean-to for approximately fifteen minutes before she finally came out. When she saw us, she was understand-ably startled. I put my finger up to my lips, then motioned for her to follow us away from the hospital. She was reluctant at first, then realized we were strangers. Her eyes sparkled; she was thinking, *Rescue at last.* I hoped we didn't have to disappoint her.

When we were far enough from the hospital not to be heard I spoke. "My name is J.J. Darby, and my friend here is Park Service Ranger Goodman. We've come to see if you need any help."

She didn't answer at first. I could see she was so overcome by our being there that she couldn't speak. She started to cry, and we had to sit down by one of the wrecked buildings until we could get her to stop.

When she was somewhat calm and composed, I told her that we'd been watching the town from across the river, and pointed to the hill. From our position, I couldn't see the top of the hill, as it was in darkness, but I hoped we were being monitored by our sentry.

"From what we can make out, a man that we know as 'Jason' is running things around here, and not doing a very good job of it."

It seemed to startle her that we knew Jason, then a large smile came over her face. "Then, it was you that gave him and his mob the whipping down to Goldston."

"We had a run in, yes."

"You shook him up quite a bit. They just knew you'd be up here to get them. They waited all day when they came in, with their tails tucked between their legs. Put barricades up around the pavilion, talking big about how some skunks down to Goldston had jumped them when they were looking for food, and how they were going to get even. Said you stole one of the bikes and their best Jeep. Is any of that true?"

"The only truth is that they came looking for trouble and they found it," I said. "We thought it best to come up here and see for ourselves how they lived, and if anyone here might need our help."

"Do we ever. They've terrorized this town. Things weren't bad at first; everyone was in a daze and didn't know which way to turn. Then, three days after the worst, Jason and his bunch came upon us from the north." She turned and pointed toward the north, where the ski lodges had been located. "They'd been out four-wheeling, and had managed to come out of that hell in one piece. Beats me how, but they did.

"Anyhow, they came up, telling everyone that no one should worry. Help would be here pretty soon, or they'd go find it. We were all for that. Here was a young man telling us not to worry. He seemed to be a leader, knowledgeable, sure of himself; we were all taken in."

She stopped talking. The long days, little food, and worry were taking a toll on that courageous lady. She took a long, deep breath, then continued.

"He set himself up in the pavilion, had all the food stored there, and set up a distribution system. Set about getting shelter for everyone, and went so far as having his bunch act as hunters. Some hunters—all they can kill are cows and pigs so old they couldn't run if they wanted to."

I interrupted, and told her we'd seen the hunters bring the meat into town earlier, and that we'd watched when she'd given Jason a good tongue-lashing.

She smiled.

"I have him buffaloed, right now, but he scares the devil out of me. So you've seen how he treats us, like we were his property."

"But you said he did so much for the town, at first," I said. "What happened to change things?"

She stared at me, then shifted her gaze toward the hills across the river. "It wasn't anything you could put your finger on. The change came on real gradual, to a point. Then Jason went crazy. One morning, he was real nice, trying to help people; then, the next, crazy.

"The trouble started when he tried to take one of the local girls for his own," she said. "The girl was only sixteen. Her name was Cristine Tibbs, and her father went down to the pavilion to have a talk with Jason. His daughter hadn't been home in two nights, and he was sick with worry."

She stopped talking. There was a noise in the shadows, but no one appeared. She then continued, her voice slightly above a whisper.

"The other thing that changed the way we were living was the beer and whiskey that Jason and his gang had brought with them, plus what they found in the pavilion. Two days before the quake, over three hundred cases had been delivered. The summer season wasn't far off, and the manager was getting stocked up. They also found I don't know how many barrels of whiskey, some at the pavilion, but most at the ski lodges. Most of the glass bottles had been destroyed, but the cans and the barrels had survived—some of them, anyway. Enough for them to be drunk every night.

"The night Tibbs went to see Jason, a party was in full swing. Well, the next thing we all knew, Jason had beat poor Joe to a pulp, then kicked his daughter out, too. But the thing that really set Jason on his ear was two nights later, when Joe took his family and some others and left town." She pointed west, toward Highland Village, indicating the direction the group had taken.

"Jason didn't know this, of course, but Joe had been planning on leaving and trying to find help since the quake. Jason and his antics helped Joe to get out a little sooner. Joe asked me to go with his group, but I couldn't leave the people that are hurt. I didn't know what Jason would do, if he found out I'd left. I was afraid he might kill them out of spite."

"How many people did Joe Tibbs take with him, when he left?" I asked.

"Let's see. About thirty people, including himself and his family. Some were children."

"How many are left?" I asked.

She seemed to look around and count at the same time. "The best I can make out is thirty-four. Then, I have four of my own here in the hospital, and one of Jason's crowd that you put out of action, the other day."

During the next hour, we found out a lot about her and the little town of Butte City. Her name was Thelma Brown. She and her husband had retired there five years before. She had left the nursing profession and he a monotonous factory job, to open a small gift and curio shop, catering to the skiers in the winter and fishermen, boaters, hikers, and four-wheelers during the summer. She hadn't seen her husband since the destruction. He'd gone up to the ski lodge to sell some merchandise to the shop there, and had never returned.

Her description of the day of destruction was much the same as ours had been. She estimated that about a third of the town's population of 117 had been killed outright. Of the people remaining, there were many sprains, bruises, and broken bones. She still had four bad cases in her hospital. One man had two broken legs, one had head and back injuries, and two had fever and nausea. Her fifth patient was the biker who had been in the scrape down at the roadblock. He'd broken some ribs and was covered with scratches and bruises.

There had been ample food in the town, but now it was all under Jason's control. For awhile, everyone had tried to improve their lives by building shelters, digging out the main part of the town, and rebuilding the pavilion. A plan to leave if help didn't come had been discussed, and town meetings had kept everyone's morale up.

But after Tibbs left, Jason had gone on a rampage. All of the dwellings that had been abandoned by Tibbs's party were burned. Jason forbade anyone to leave town without his permission, and sent his goons out at least once a day to beat up on someone, burn a house, or solely to harass everyone. But they had been somewhat subdued since their encounter at the roadblock, and had left the townspeople alone.

I asked her what she knew about Highland Village. She said it had been a very large cattle ranch, at one time, but lately, they'd been shutting down and selling parcels for home sites. There had been a caretaker and a few ranch hands. No one from there had been down since the destruction, and that's where Tibbs was heading when he and his party had left.

She said that Jason had sent people out in every direction to find Tibbs and his party, but with no luck. The first two men who had shown up at Goldston had been looking for those people.

We'd been in town well over two hours, and Jason's party at the pavilion was still going strong. Thelma said it often went on all night and into the next day, especially when a hunting party had been successful.

Before we left, I told her not to tell anyone of our visit. I wanted time to make a plan for getting everyone away safely, and if Jason and his crew heard about it, they might wind up killing someone. She seemed worried, as we prepared to leave, but I assured her that we would be back. I asked her if she could swim, and she said yes. I told her how to find the island in the river, and where to find our observation post, if anything happened and she had to get out of the town.

We devised a signal system. If she had news that we should know, or if the town's situation changed, she would wear a red shawl all day, and that night one of us would come into town. I told her that I would tell our people to expect some new arrivals, and in the meantime, we'd check out Highland Village to see if anyone was up there. If so, we would take everyone south at the same time.

After saying our goodbyes, we made our way back down to Lead Creek, crossed the sandbar, and climbed back up to the observation post. There wasn't any use keeping a sentry up all night, so we all three made our way back to the base camp for a bite to eat and some sleep. The next day and the few days that followed were going to be long ones indeed.

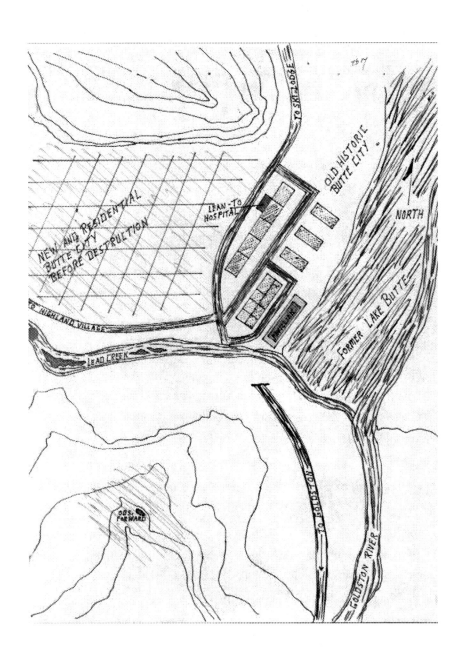

# Chapter 8

⟨෴⟩

# EXPLORING HIGHLAND VILLAGE

We were up bright and early, the next morning. Ranger Goodman made the coffee, I fried up the canned bacon, and our remaining ranger cut bread and made toast. After breakfast, I wrote a letter explaining to Steve exactly what we had found in Butte City and what we'd been told by Thelma Brown. I informed him that there would be about forty people to rescue, not all in good health, and that I would work out a plan as soon as possible to get them all out. Along with the letter, I enclosed the map I had drawn of Butte City, noting where Jason and Thelma Brown were located. The first thing I wanted to do was check out Highland Village for survivors, any tools and equipment that might be useful to us, and to see if there were any cattle there that Jason's men hadn't found.

While I was writing the letter, Goodman was at the observation post, checking on the town. He reported back that all was peaceful; no one in the pavilion was moving. Some of the townspeople were up and cooking breakfast. Even the motorcycle was still parked next to the truck. That meant Jason didn't have his lookout posted today.

As the ranger was leaving, I called by radio and let Steve know he was on the way with the letter and map. I told him we'd be leaving shortly for Highland, to check it out, and that I'd call him by radio when we got there and let him know the situation. Before the ranger left, I told him to take his time, spend the night at Goldston, and return tomorrow with whatever instructions Steve might have. We would be at Highland, so he could wait there, making periodic checks of Butte City until we returned.

Ranger Goodman and I packed rations for two days, and stowed all the other gear in the tent. We left shortly thereafter, proceeding due west for a mile, before turning north and descending to Lead Creek. We didn't want to be seen by anyone in the town, friendly or unfriendly. We crossed the creek without any trouble, and proceeded alongside the road, so as not to leave any prints that would give away our passage.

Before we had seen any buildings, we came to a large sign over the road, welcoming us to Highland Village. The two very stout poles on either side of the road looked as though they'd taken a real beating from the quakes, but the sign between them was still hanging over the road—although, judging from its tilt and sway, it might not be there much longer.

I spotted the rubble of some large structures off to the right. I told Goodman that we'd go very slowly from that point on. If there were survivors, they were probably hiding, especially if they had seen Jason's men.

We left the road, and cut across country toward the wrecked buildings. As we came near, it was evident that one of the buildings had been a barn, a well-built barn—cinder block walls reinforced with steel rods and cement, with a good, strong, wooden roof. But now it was a big heap of concrete, wood, and metal rods.

Someone, recently, had been digging around in both barns. It could have been the Tibbs party, but more than likely, it was Jason's boys.

Directly to our front, there had been a large house. Either someone had set fire to it or it had burned when it was wrecked by the quakes. The east wall was supported by a large tree it was leaning upon. About five hundred yards farther to the west, there had stood another house, but it too had been burned; but not during the quakes, because we could see some of its contents strewn around near it—furniture, clothing, and so forth—and none of it had been touched by the fire.

We had been walking most of the morning and were ready for a break, so before we explored any further, we decided to eat lunch. I had just opened a can of fruit when I thought I heard hammering. I looked up at Goodman, and it was evident he had heard it also, but neither of us could pinpoint from which direction it came.

We'd sat down between the two destroyed barns, and the two burned-out houses were directly between us and another group of buildings to the west. I believed that was where the hammering was coming from. I motioned to Goodman that we should move slowly in that direction.

We took a path that would carry us to the north of the two houses, and keep us out of sight of the next group of buildings. As we came up on the north side of the second house, I took a position beside what had been a tin shed and listened. The hammering continued, so I guessed that we had not been detected. I told Goodman to stay hidden while I tried to get closer. The next building I could get to was to the southwest and back along the main road we had come in on, but to get there, I'd have to cover two hundred yards of open ground, either running or crawling. I didn't like the latter, as it would take too much time, so I made a dash for the building.

I waited until the hammering was loud and clear, then ran as fast as I could for the building. It seemed to take an eternity to cross that open ground. Shortly before I reached the safety of the building, the hammering stopped, but I continued to run as fast as my legs would carry me, and I dove behind the building. I lay there panting, waiting for the hammering to resume, but it didn't.

It was very still, nothing moved, only my hard breathing was audible, and I could have sworn it could be heard for a mile or more. I lay there a good five minutes before I moved, so that I could see around the building concealing me. To my immediate left was the main road, with a road branching off to the south. Along the branch road was a house, still partially standing, about two hundred yards away. Beyond that house, the road turned back to the east, and within two hundred yards was another house, which seemed to be in remarkable shape compared to the other structures. At the far end of that loop, where the road again turned north and rejoined the main road, was the foundation of yet another house, with a trailer home, presently on its side, parked not far away. The area was undoubtedly the portion of the ranch that had been sold off as home sites.

Returning my gaze to the north, where until recently the hammering had been coming from, I saw a dozen or so small structures, probably cabins, on the north side of the road. They were in bad shape and some had been burned. The structure I was hiding behind had been the local store and gas station. The concrete apron between the store and the dirt road still had the built up island for gas pumps, but the pumps were gone. The store had been gone through thoroughly, and I couldn't see anything left behind that wasn't broken, rotted, or burnt.

I saw movement around the cabins. A man, moving very cautiously with a hammer in his hand, was moving from cabin to cabin in my direction. As he reached the last cabin, he stopped and looked for a long time in my direction. It was evident that he could not see me, although from my vantage point, I could see him clearly. He was very thin; I would guess he was in his sixties, probably the caretaker from the ranch, although he may have been an owner of one of the houses or perhaps of the station and store.

It was a standoff. He wasn't going to come any closer until he was sure of my location, so I made the first move. I stepped out into the street slowly, and stood there in full view of the gentleman with the hammer. He didn't move a muscle, didn't say a word.

"Good afternoon, sir. My name is J.J. Darby."

I didn't receive an answer for what seemed like a very long time, so I started to move in his direction.

"Mr. Darby, I wouldn't come any closer just yet," he said. "There's a rifle pointed at you, right now, and I suggest that you tell me a little more about yourself, or turn around and head back to Butte City. That is where you are from, I take it?"

"No, sir, it's not. Myself and my friends have established a new town at Goldston. We've been checking for survivors and happened upon your ranch."

"Did you come through Butte City to get here?"

"Not directly, no. You see we had a run-in with some of the people there, and we aren't on speaking terms."

"I see. Are you alone?"

"No, there's a park ranger with me. We were both working on Mesa Reservoir when the destruction came."

"Well, you don't seem like a bad sort. You and the ranger come on up, and let's talk."

I turned and hollered for Ranger Goodman. He waved and started in my direction. When I turned again, I saw, standing beside the first man, another of approximately the same age but a bit shorter, with a long, flowing beard and mustache, carrying the Winchester I had been told about. At his side was a woman, carrying another hammer.

As Goodman and I approached the trio, we could see a flood of relief on their faces and very broad and friendly smiles. We all went back to the cabin they'd been working on. They weren't building one; they were tearing it down. The first thing they wanted to know about was Butte City and the people there, and about Jason and his crew, although they didn't know Jason by name until we told them.

We told them about the town we were building, and about the clash with Jason, which seemed to really bring out the warrior in Samuel Burns, the ranch caretaker, the first man we had encountered. There had been no burnt buildings until after Jason and his people had made a few trips up there. The large house next to the concrete buildings had been the main ranch house; the other house, burnt and with furniture lying around it, had been Sam's house.

The quakes had destroyed or damaged most of the dwellings on the ranch, but Sam's house was still in reasonably good shape. He and two ranch hands, along with Ronald and Miriam Lancaster, the owners of the unfinished house and overturned trailer, had planned to fix up the house to live in until help arrived.

They had been rebuilding the house and clearing out the store when Jason and four or five others had come up to look around. Jason had immediately had his followers start looting the store, taking everything that could be carried and loaded into one of the Jeeps. Sam had got the best of them that time, by bringing out the Winchester and the two ranch hands.

He said Jason seemed nice enough, at the time. Said he needed all the food and other supplies that he could get for his people in Butte City, and was sorry that his kindred had been so bold and acted so nastily towards him and the Lancasters.

"He even asked us to pack up and move down to Butte City, and be looked after proper, down there," he said, "seeing as we weren't any too young, anymore. Well, let me tell you, we were sorely tempted to go with them—to someplace that would be safe and secure." Sam's demeanor turned from pleasantness to stern concern, as he continued telling us about his first encounter with Jason.

"Then I made a very bad mistake," he said. "I told him that we would have to stay and take care of the livestock—cattle, hogs, and some chickens. 'Course, I didn't know that loco weed would come back and try to kill off all the cattle and hogs."

"How much time did you have between Jason's first and second visits?" I asked.

"About a week, I believe it was. My two boys were over yonder, working on salvage from the store. The Lancasters were helping me with some work around the house, and we were to the point of plowing up a garden.

"It was the wildest, gosh-darn sight you could ever see. There were four on motorcycles, two abreast, followed by a Jeep-load of hollering banshees. In the next Jeep was this guy you call Jason, standing up in the front seat like the conquering hero come home." Sam Burns puffed out his chest, putting one hand on his hip, the other extended forward, in a mock pose of Jason.

"There was one more Jeep behind his, loaded with the meanest, dirtiest lot of the group. I was tempted to laugh—looked like a parade of crazies come to town to show off."

Sam's Jason pose turned to a frown with clenched fists, as he continued his story. "But I didn't laugh for long. The Jeeps took the loop by the main house and come up to my house. The cycles went on down to the store. Before we could get a word of greeting out, the crazies in the last Jeep drove right on by and stopped at the hog pen, over there, and started shooting the pigs. I mean, pumping slugs into them, one and all. The bikers went wild, and beat my two poor ranch hands within an inch of their lives. I went for my gun, but Jason grabbed me before I got turned around good, and I never will forget his words: 'Old man, you so much as move and I'll break your scrawny neck. Then I'll break every bone in your tired, old body.'

"The Lancasters were standing like stone, not moving a bit. One of Jason's women went up to Miriam, looked her square in the eye, and started hitting her about the head. Miriam fell to the ground and balled-up, without saying a word. The girl looked around at Jason, laughed and moved away. I thought they'd go after Ronald just for the fun of it, but they left him alone."

Sam was really wound up by then, and he became very animated and would gesture and point as he continued his story. "They set fire to the store and the main house, and drove around and around hollering and yelling, while they burned. One of them caught sight of some cattle further up the road, and the cycles and one Jeep took off after them. But the cattle were pretty well spooked by the fire and all the yelling, and got away—all but one old heifer. They killed her, drug her back up here, told me to butcher it. I did.

"Shortly before they left, Jason told me he wouldn't hesitate to kill us if we gave him or any of his people any trouble. Then they left just like they'd come—cycles in front, Jason standing up in his Jeep, and the rest yelling their fool heads off.

"We managed to get the fires out, but not before they had spread to some of the cabins. Three of them were burned to the ground. The main house and the store were a total loss. Jason took most of what we'd salvaged from the store, but he didn't know that the first barn over there had been a storehouse. We saved all that."

Sam had to stop. His emotions were such, by then, that he had to take time to blow his nose and wipe his eyes before he could continue. "The hogs were a total loss, almost. After they did all that shooting, they didn't bother to take any meat, other than the cow. We managed to butcher and smoke some of the ham, but we lost a lot. The two boys were laid up most of the following week. Both were too sore and bruised to do much, although I don't think neither one had any broken bones."

"Where are your ranch hands?" I asked, looking around. I saw that Sam's house had been ransacked and burnt to the ground, but he hadn't mentioned how that had happened. "What about your house?"

"Well, we knew we weren't a match for that bunch, so that afternoon, we started moving. Over there, down that branch road, you'll see a house still partially standing. There's a trail from there leading down to a small valley, not more than a half-mile away. We took all we could carry, and set up down there.

"We saved one of the old sows that was shot up. She gave birth to a dozen piglets, and we have some chickens. The cattle we drove over to the mesa, which is south of here, about three miles. Once in awhile, a cow or two will drift down from the north country, and we'll round them up and drive them down to the mesa. Jason's boys were here when a couple came down, and they got to one and killed her before we could chase her off."

That would have been the one we'd seen brought into Butte City by wheelbarrow, the other day. I told Sam that we'd seen them bring the carcass into town.

"About the two boys that worked for me, a fellow by the name of Tibbs came through here with a group, not too long ago. They were from Butte City, running away from that gang."

I told Sam that we knew Tibbs had left town with a group and had probably come through here. He looked at me, clearly startled that I would know something like that, then continued.

"You know about his troubles, then. I tried to get him to set up here, so we could fight that bunch together, but he thought they were too mean and wanted to keep going. All he wanted was enough food and whatever else we could spare to get out of the mountains. He thought there might be someone left in Rosemont. If not, he was going to keep heading west until he found someone or hit the ocean, whichever came first."

Thinking about Tibbs and his group brought a smile to Sam's face. "He did say that if he ever did find any law, his first priority was to see to it that Jason and his crowd were put away proper. Tibbs had at least two dozen people with him, and my boys didn't want any more trouble, so they went too. I didn't say much about it. I would have gone too, but I'm too ornery to give up so easily."

"How long did his group stay with you?" I asked.

"They were in here before daylight and gone within a few hours. He figured if they stayed any longer, there'd be trouble. Sure hope he makes it. He's a good man, but that trip he's on is a little different than running a ski lodge or a store.

"Didn't have to wait long for trouble, either. About mid-morning, two longhairs come blazing through here on cycles. They stopped at the store, looked around; it wasn't hard to see all the tracks in the road. I was hidden back across the road over there, watching those two. They went up to my house first, hollered for me, then went tearing out of here, back toward Butte City."

"Then they came back later with Jason and burnt your house," I said.

"Pulled right up to the front steps. I can see Jason on the porch, right now, just like it was yesterday, hollering for me. Two bikers took off up the road; the others scattered out, looking. Jason was still on the porch, pacing up and down, when the bikers came back.

I wasn't close enough to hear, but I knew they were telling him which direction Tibbs had gone.

"Jason turned around and gave orders to tear the house apart. They were throwing furniture out the windows, then jumping on it, and ripping and tearing it apart with knives. They broke everything in sight, then started ripping off the doors. When I saw them take dry grass inside, I knew they were going to burn it down. I couldn't take anymore. I ran back to the valley, got my Winchester, and came back shooting. By the time I came back, the house was already ablaze and they were running around it, hopping and hollering like Comanches on the war path.

"They didn't realize I was shooting at them until I put two bullets through Jason's Jeep. Two of them shot back at me with shotguns, but I was so mad I didn't care. I kept on walking and shooting. I was trying to kill that louse Jason, but he ducked into one of the Jeeps and took off. When the rest saw that, they all high-tailed it down the road."

"Do you think you hit anyone?"

"No, I was too mad to hit anything. I did hit the Jeep, and I believe I winged one of the bikes as they were leaving."

"And your house, a total loss," I said.

"Yeah, but that little demonstration of mine has kept them away, for the most part. They do sneak around once in awhile, to kill a cow or something, but they don't parade through here anymore with their bikes and Jeeps."

Sam then told me about the present project they were working on. They were tearing down the cabin for the boards and nails, to improve the little cabins they had built in the valley, away from the prying eyes of Jason's people. We helped them gather up the lumber, and walked to their new home in the valley.

Once we left the road and proceeded down to Lead Creek, there wasn't any trail visible at all. Sam and the others never took the same route twice, so that no trail would be beaten down for someone to follow. The ford was no more than waist deep and rocky on the bottom. Therefore, even though the stream was swift, there was no worry of falling down.

There were two small dwellings in the valley, one for Sam and the other for the Lancasters. A pigpen had been built for the sow and her litter, and there were a few chickens running around. From the valley, a pathway climbed in a zigzag pattern to the top of the mesa, where Sam had taken the cattle. They had enough supplies to last quite awhile, and were already planning on reaping a good harvest from the garden they'd been working so hard on.

I asked Sam about the cinder block barns. He said they were built originally as barns, but one was a storehouse. Extra supplies had been kept there for the gas station and store. Most of the goods were still buried under the fallen roof. There were plenty of food-stuffs also—sacks of sugar, flour, cornmeal, salt, and the like. I asked how Jason hadn't found out about it. He said that he'd made a mistake one time with Jason, but when asked about the barns, he'd told the truth about the one being full of machinery and so forth, but he'd lied about the other. He'd told Jason it was filled with sacks of feed for the horses and cattle, along with a few hundred bales of hay, and Jason had been gullible enough to believe him and never went to see for himself.

Sam invited Goodman and me to spend the night there, before starting back to our observation post. We quickly accepted. I wanted to ask Sam and the Lancasters to join up with us and move to Goldston, but didn't know how to go about it.

They were perfectly well off here in their little valley, even with the threat from Jason. They had cattle, pigs, chickens, and a good vegetable garden. I thought if they didn't want to go to Goldston, maybe I could make him a deal for the farm machinery he'd mentioned. He had said there was vegetable seed still buried in the barn, but wasn't sure what kind, variety, or quantity.

Before I had a chance to ask him about going to Goldston with us or about a deal for the machinery, he wanted to know all of our actions since the destruction, and especially about our run-in with Jason at the roadblock.

By the time I had run through our story about the dig and the reservoir, about the expeditions to Lakewood and Rosemont, the fight at the roadblock, and my conversations with Thelma Brown in Butte City, we had finished supper and a cup of coffee, and everyone was ready to turn in for the night. I figured it was just as well. By morning, I could have a good speech planned in my mind, a speech designed to get Sam to move to Goldston.

I awoke to the sound of a very loud motorcycle, accompanied by one or more other machines. It was a few minutes before sun-

rise. Sam was already awake, and motioned for me to get up and follow him. We took off running for the creek, forded it, then lay in
the grass. Sam had brought his Winchester, and looked mad enough
to use it. I had my carbine, but hoped I wouldn't have to fire at
those locos.

As we watched, the bike riders left the main road and took the
loop past the main ranch house, and stopped at Sam's old house.
The people in the Jeep proceeded along the main road, and stopped
at the burned-out store. The bikers searched around Sam's house,
yelling for him to come out. They kept saying no one wanted to do
him any harm.

Sam looked over at me. "I believe that about as much as I
believe they're all Harvard graduates come to rescue me."

"What do you think they want now?" I said. They'd stolen
everything worth carrying off, except for what was underneath the
barn, and they didn't know about that.

"What they want is me," Sam said. "They know I'm still around,
and they know I have food. They do this every so often, trying to
make me mad, so that I'll reveal my location. I circled around one
time and took a couple shots at them from behind the cabins. They
left for awhile and came back later, searched all over the cabins for
me, but of course found nothing."

The people in the Jeep disembarked, and proceeded to once
again go through the old store and station. Not finding anything of
any importance, they searched through the cabins once more.

While they were in the cabins, Sam motioned for me to follow
him, and we took off at a trot. What he wanted to do was circle
around to the north and observe from there. If we were discovered,
we could exchange a few shots with those hooligans, then disappear
in the timberline to the north. They would be none the wiser as to
the true location of where we were living.

But it didn't work that way. The bikers left Sam's house and
came on down to where the Jeep was parked, while we were still
moving. We dove for cover not more than twenty feet from where
they eventually parked.

"I don't care what Jason says, that crazy old man and the others
took off with Tibbs. They're more than a hundred miles from here,
now," one of the bikers said.

"You know that ain't so," another said. "That old buzzard shot at us from over at the cabins not more than a week ago. I say Jason's right—he's here and watching us right now."

They looked around, but no one looked anywhere near where we were hiding. There were five of them and two of us. I thought for a second that if we had brought Goodman and Lancaster, we could have taken that bunch. Then I thought of the possible cost in lives, not only to them. One of us might get hurt, so I decided not to even think of such a plan. Those guys would kill somebody before it was over, if we confronted them now.

They continued looking and talking, as their companions from the cabins joined them. "I tell you what we can do to draw the old man out," one said. "Let's start a fire. He hates to see his precious farm burn."

Sam was raising his Winchester, but I reached over and gently pressed it down.

"What you gonna burn? We burnt his house, barn, store, and what's left of those cabins ain't worth the effort."

"What about those houses over there?" They were now looking in our direction, more specifically at the house over our shoulders, not more than fifty feet away.

I looked over at Sam. He wasn't going to let them burn that house, or what was left of it, without a fight. There was no way we could leave our position and get Goodman or Lancaster up here. Consequently, if they did carry through with their threat, someone was going to be either dead or dying within the next few minutes. There would be no use in trying to stop Sam. I slowly raised my carbine and, like Sam, waited for them to come forward.

"Now, y'all wait a minute. You know Jason said to leave those places alone."

"What for? They gonna burn up real nice. Look how dry they are. What's he want to keep them for, anyway?"

"'Cause he said when he gets tired of Butte City, he's gonna burn it to the ground and move up here. There's more game and cows up here, and he's gonna start a garden and make everybody move up here with him."

"I ain't going to start no garden, not me. I ain't no slave. I say let's burn those houses, then we can't move up here."

Big Mouth started in our direction, but the other guy prevailed. "You dumb sucker, you get in that Jeep right now. You start a fire and I'll live to see the day Jason skins you alive."

They stood looking at each other for a minute, then the one called "dumb sucker" took the M-16 out of the Jeep and shot a full magazine of ammo into the house. Sam and I were hugging the ground for all we were worth, as round after round passed over our heads. When target practice was over, they piled into the Jeep, the bikers mounted, and they took off in the direction of Butte City.

What I had overheard about Jason planning to burn down Butte City scared me. I knew there would be several of the townspeople who would resist, and that meant trouble.

Sam and I stood up, and with a great sigh of relief, started back to the cabins in the valley. I thought that would be as good a time as any to see if Sam would go to Goldston and leave the ranch.

"Sam, what would you think about moving to Goldston, at least for awhile. Until we can get this thing cleared up with Jason."

He didn't answer my question. But I knew he was giving it some thought. We crossed the creek and met Goodman. As we returned to the cabin, I told him about the encounter.

The Lancasters were waiting when we got back, and Sam told them the same story I had told to Goodman. Sam sat down by the fire and poured a cup of coffee. He was ready to talk now.

"Son, I can't see leaving here and going back to Goldston with you. Now, if the Lancasters want to go, it's perfectly all right with me. But I have a responsibility to the owners to save as much of this place as I can, and if I was gone, there's no telling what that bunch will do.

"But I tell you what I will do. You bring some of your people up here to help me dig out that supply barn and you can have all that we find. I've got plenty here, and you can even take all the cattle, bull and all. I'll keep the pig and horses."

"Horses?"

"Had quite a few at one time. Some died when everything went haywire. The ones that could run took off in every direction. I've got four mares and a stallion up on the mesa with the cattle. Good workhorses, too, not those thin, high-strung things you find on a race track."

I sipped my coffee and stared into the fire. I was thinking of all the equipment, horses, cattle, and everything else that was located right there at the ranch. I was tempted to ask Sam about moving everyone up there, from Goldston.

"I think I have a plan that can help all of us," I said.

"Let's hear it," he said.

"How far would you say it is from here to Goldston? If we had to go across country, I mean. With Jason in Butte City, we couldn't go by road."

"Well, there's a couple trails," he said. "Haven't walked any of them in many years, and with all the shaking up, I don't know if they're still there, but at a good pace, a man could walk the distance in about five, maybe six, hours."

"What about cattle and horses, could they make it?"

He laughed. "Son, if a man can make it, there's no doubt in my mind that horses and cattle could."

During the rest of the morning and afternoon, I told him about my plan for saving his ranch and helping the people of Goldston really get a handle on the new life they were living. First of all, I needed him to draw a map of the country between there and Goldston, at least as best as he could remember it. I was going to send Goodman back with instructions to bring up enough of our people to move everything worth keeping from this ranch down to Goldston.

"Sam, here's what I'd like to do, with your permission, of course. We'll move what machinery we can use in Goldston for farming, using the horses for power. Anything too big to take down or that we can't use, we'll take from the storage barn and hide. Same thing for all the food supplies in the other barn. Anything you want to keep, we could bring here for your use, although I wish you'd come with us, for awhile anyway."

"What about Jason?" he said. "You're talking about a couple weeks' work, and he won't let you alone once he finds out you're taking something he's been searching for."

"We won't have to worry about Jason. I'll ask George Foxworth to come up and set up a roadblock, out by your old entrance sign. Believe me, George won't let Jason or any of his crowd get near this place."

"We might have to talk a little about the machinery," he said. "As I said before, the food, your welcome to it; even the seed, you can have it all. But the machinery, there's my obligation to the owners, you know."

"Tell you what I'll do," I said. "I'll ask Stephen Adams to come up and sign for everything we take away from here. He's our leader, down in Goldston—a good man. I was working for him on the dig, was with his company many years. I know you'll like him. If and when this world ever gets straightened out, I'm sure we can arrange to pay you for the use of everything we take, including the food and seeds."

Sam still didn't look like he was convinced, so I kept on talking. "Sam, for all you know, this may be your ranch. There may be no owners left; there may be nothing outside this mountain range. If there is and if the owner ever comes back, I can assure you he'll say you're doing the right thing. If I could get you to go to Goldston, see the people there, talk to them, I'm sure you'd agree."

"I'll tell you what, son," he said, "I'll go with Goodman, here, and see these people of yours for myself. If I like what I see, I'll turn the whole ranch over to this boss of yours—on a lease basis, of course. Deal?"

"Deal." I couldn't have asked for anything better.

Sam took the time to draw up a map of the surrounding area, including the ranch, the road to Butte City, and the hills and small valleys between there and Goldston. I was surprised that the route he drew for him and Goodman to follow would take them less than a mile south of the outpost we'd established south of Butte City. I told Goodman to swing up to the look-out and see if anything had changed, to see that the ranger there was all right, and to tell him that we'd been detained for a longer time than we'd originally planned. Sam wanted to leave right away, but it would have been dark long before they reached their destination. I convinced him that, with all of the mudslides, terrain changes, and so forth, it would be better to wait and start early in the morning.

"I'll call in on the radio and let them know, back there, you're coming," I said. "From the route you've planned, you'll be coming out of the foothills near the roadblock."

"Radio—that reminds me," Sam said. "There should be an old radio somewhere under the main ranch house. Old Man Winters was a radio buff."

"Do you know what kind of a radio it was? I mean, small like the one I have here, large, what?"

"It was pretty big, green; he bought it from Army Surplus. Had all kinds of parts, a microphone, earphones, and I remember you didn't have to use house power to operate it, in a pinch. It had a little generator with it that a man could sit on a little seat and crank away—always reminded me of a coffee grinding machine."

"How about its power or range? Could he talk to people who were very far away from here? Say, in another state?"

"He said he could talk around the world, if he could get enough power and the right antenna. He had wire strung all around the ranch, once. Spent many a winter night down there in the basement, talking to people like they were the best of friends."

"Sam, when you get back, I'd like to find that radio," I said. "It might be our chance to talk to someone outside these valleys."

We were all up bright and early, the next morning. Sam and Goodman were on the trail before the sun had had a chance to peek over the top of the mesa. I knew Sam would like what he would find, and that within a couple days, we would be moving a lot of supplies down to Goldston. I hoped we would be left alone to make the move.

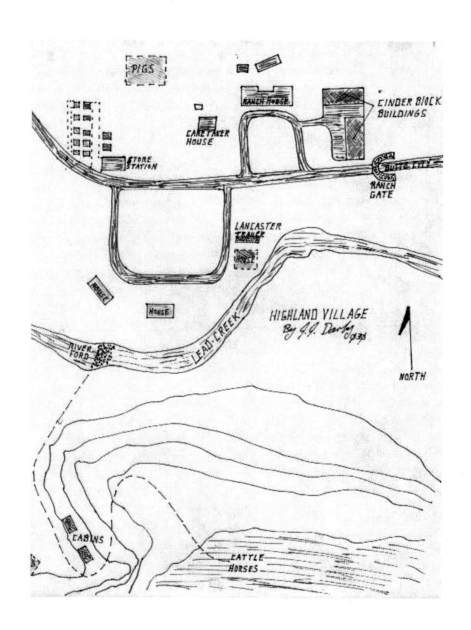

HIGHLAND VILLAGE
By G. G. Darby 1938

*Chapter 9*

❧

# HIGHLAND AS A FORWARD BASE

After Sam and Goodman left, Ronald Lancaster took me on a tour of the ranch. First, we followed the same trail taken earlier in the morning by Sam, up to the top of the mesa, and looked over the acreage for awhile. That was the first chance I'd had to see the horses and cattle that had been hidden there.

During the afternoon, we toured the rest of the ranch. First, we poked around what was left of the main house and, with a little digging, we discovered that the basement of the house was still intact. We couldn't tell without more digging how much fire damage there had been, but I was hoping that the radio was still useable.

The cinder block barns were full of seed, dry stores, and farm implements, but we wouldn't touch them until help arrived from Goldston. I didn't want to be caught by Jason or his gang digging around them, until we could remove what had been buried there.

We checked through the old store and gas station, but as Ronald had said, we didn't find anything there. Jason had made sure everything useful had been removed before he'd had his hoods torch it.

As we stood on the road facing the store, Ronald told me about the day it was burned. "When I saw them start the fire in there, I knew right then and there that those two gas pumps out front would get caught up real good and we were going to see an explosion."

Ronald was shaking his head from side to side. "But Sam had drained down the pumps earlier in the year, so there was no gas in them or the lines."

"Any idea of how much gas is still down there?" I asked.

"I believe there's better than two thousand gallons, unless the tanks were ruptured during the shake up."

"And Jason didn't take any of the gas before he set the store afire?"

"Those boys didn't seem to know much about pumping gas. The pumps are electric. No electricity, no gas, as far as they're concerned. They kicked the ground, stomped, and looked for a way to get at it, but couldn't.

"Right over there, about fifty feet from the store, are the caps where gas was put into the underground tanks. You can't see them now, because with all the mud that was flowing through here for a couple days, they got buried."

"How deep are the caps, do you think?"

"Oh I don't know, no more than a foot, I would think," he said. "Want to try and find out?"

I sure did. We walked over to where the caps should have been and started digging around. Without shovels, and not knowing the exact location, I was sure we'd be in for a long afternoon of fruitless searching, but Ronald had a good memory. Taking a bead from the store and the nearest cabin, he found the first cap within a half-hour. He was wrong about the depth, however; the mud and dirt were no more than three inches deep. With the first cap found, it wasn't long before we had the last one uncovered.

I removed the second cap, and out came a good, strong gasoline odor. I took a small pebble, and with my ear close to the opening, dropped it in. It was nice to hear the splashing sound, as the pebble fell. We were not as lucky with the other tank—either it was dry or had been ruptured. There was a smell of gasoline, but my pebble only produced a large clunk as it hit bottom.

"How would you suggest we get the gas out?" I asked.

I knew he was waiting for that question. A big smile came over his face, and I guessed he was thinking of me as being just as dumb about such things as those others.

"No problem," he said. "Somewhere on this ranch, more than likely in one of those barns, is a hand pump, or maybe two or three. Ain't no ranch that would be without a hand pump. With that and a good, long hose, I dare say we can take most every drop."

With the gasoline problem solved and Ronald quite satisfied that he had the answer for its extraction, we explored what was left of the cabins and the old hog pens. As we were walking, I asked Ronald about any wagons that might be available for hauling. He wasn't sure, but there had been two or three big hay wagons there, the previous year, when he'd first looked over the property that he was going to buy.

We arrived back at the log cabin around sundown, having looked over most of what had been a very big ranch. We hadn't found much outside of the main ranch area. All of the line houses and corrals that were located a couple miles west of the cabins had been wrecked and burned, more than likely by Jason and his men. We had found one wagon alongside the road. It was in pretty bad shape, but if the blacksmith were to come back with Sam, he could repair the wheels and tongue.

After supper, I called Steve on the radio to make sure that Sam and Goodman had arrived. He said they had. He didn't want to give me all of the details over the radio, but wanted me to know that he'd be coming back with the party. I asked about John the blacksmith being able to come along. I told him about the wagon. Steve was reluctant, because John was so busy there, but he had an apprentice who could take care of things while they were gone, so in the end, I won my case and it was agreed that a blacksmith would be useful. I had the impression that Steve was bringing up a big group, and that we'd be there for quite awhile. That meant that Sam had agreed to let us take what we needed.

The next morning, I was up before the sun or Mr. and Mrs. Lancaster. I knew it would be late in the afternoon before the party from Goldston would arrive, but like a child waiting for a new toy to arrive, I couldn't be patient. I only hoped that Jason wouldn't send one of his hunting parties up, that day, and see us before we had time to make plans, get settled in, or have the roadblock in place.

After lunch, Ronald and I walked up to the mesa to await the arrival of the party from Goldston. It was quiet and peaceful up there, no sign of man or his civilization. Even the quakes had not disturbed that piece of ground—not so that you could see, anyway. The horses were grazing to the east, away from us, and the cows were taking an afternoon break along the trail, chewing cud and looking content, as usual.

We walked around awhile, talking about things that came to mind. Ronald told me about his move to Colorado, when he'd retired and sold his business in Pennsylvania. He had owned a small company that had specialized in home computers. The company was started by one of the large corporations to make computer chips, but after a year, it was found to be more economical to buy the chips, rather than produce them. He had stepped in, bought the company, kept on all the employees, and within a year, had been turning a good profit—not only making computer chips but also producing a small, compact, lightweight computer. His health had turned sour, and his sons hadn't wanted the responsibility of running a company, so he'd sold out and headed west.

It was just by chance that he had crossed the continental divide, and being too tired to go on, he and Miriam had stopped in Goldston, where they'd heard about Highland Village. They'd checked out the place the next day, and had liked it so much that, within a week, they had purchased a trailer to live in and a piece of property on which to build a home. That had been seven months before the destruction. As I had seen earlier, the house had not yet been completed.

The horses sensed that someone was coming long before Ronald or I knew. I saw them raise their heads, one after the other, all ears pointed toward the front and to the east, down the trail. Not two minutes later, I heard noises—men moving down a trail, not being overly noisy, but not moving with stealth either. When I saw the lead ranger come around the bend and move into the clearing, it was as if I had been rescued. I don't know why I felt that way, but it was as if Ronald and I had been on that mesa for days, waiting.

George Foxworth was next, a big smile on his face, waving his arm over his head. As I waved back, I saw that there was quite a crowd of people. Steve had come prepared for anything and everything. He'd brought George and four rangers for the guard, the blacksmith, ten other people to act as workers, and of course Sam Burns, walking along in his big bush hat, as if he'd just returned from the Far East with all the spices in the world.

We shook hands all around. Ronald was introduced to everyone, and we all moved down to the cabin to meet Miriam and to rest for awhile. I couldn't wait to ask George who was running the guard, since he and most of the rangers were there and at the outpost overlooking Butte City.

He had anticipated my question. "J.J. you look like a man with a question to ask, and I'd bet that question is, who's looking out after the store, so to speak."

"Who's at the roadblock?" I asked.

"Either you haven't had your radio on today, or you haven't been listening. If you'd been listening, you'd have heard Susan barking orders."

I realized that I had left my radio at the cabins. What a dumb move on my part.

"You know," George said, "She knows more about running that guard than I do, and those girls of hers are trained just as good as the rangers I have with me—she saw to that. If Jason's crew tries to give her troops a rough time, they're in for a rude awakening. Here's a little care package she sent up for you."

I took the package, and while everyone was coming in and getting settled down, I opened it. She had sent me some socks, underwear, a pair of jeans, a clean shirt, and a short letter telling me that she missed me and loved me very much. Before I'd had time to finish reading my note, Sam was slapping me on the back.

"My boy," he said, "I've never ran across a nicer bunch of people. I met your wife, a real nice lady, and Stephen Adams was just as nice as you said he'd be. Got a good head for leading, too—real nice feller."

Steve was coming towards us. "All I can say is, real nice job," he said. "Mister Burns has agreed to let us move as much as we want down to Goldston. How about you and Sam showing me around the place? This is the first time I've had a chance to get out and do any real walking, since we got to Goldston."

I called to George, and the four of us left on a grand tour of the ranch, while everyone else got something to eat and found a good place to sack out for the night. We covered much the same ground as Ronald and I had the day before, and I showed Steve the wagon that I thought John could get back into shape. Sam and Steve were both tired, and after the tour, they headed back to the log cabin. Before George and I returned, I took him out to the main gate.

"This looks like a good spot for us to set up a roadblock," I said. "You can't see the barns from here, and if we stop Jason or his men here, they can't see what we're up to."

By the time we returned to the cabins, everyone had pretty well set in for the night. In place of the one fire that the Lancasters and Sam had kept going since they'd moved to that spot, there were now a half-dozen burning. People were preparing an evening meal or building shelters. The place was taking on the air of a small community. Steve and Sam invited George and me to join them for a bowl of stew. Miriam had been looking forward to the arrival of the relief party, and had spent most of her day in its preparation.

During the meal, Steve told me that the party had stopped long enough to have a look at Butte City. "Just as soon as we get organized here, I want you to make plans to get the people out of that town," he said to me. "The ranger you left there gave me a pretty good idea of the daily routine, and even pointed out Thelma Brown to me. She still seems to have some control over Jason, as far as the townspeople are concerned, but if he ever calls her bluff, the situation could turn ugly."

"I know. I think the best way to bring them out would be from Butte City through here. We could rest and feed the people behind the protection of George's roadblock, then proceed to Goldston along the road you came up."

"Why not take the short route from Butte City straight through our roadblock, north of Goldston?" he asked. "It would take half the time."

"My first thoughts were on that line," I said. "But after visiting with Thelma and seeing some of the people firsthand, I think it'd be difficult to get everyone out in the dead of night without making noise. If we were to cross the river near Jason's people, turn east, and skirt close to where they are before turning south, they'd have a good chance of catching us before we could get to our roadblock."

Stephen seemed to be willing to let me talk, so I continued. "Two advantages of coming here would be, first, we don't have any rivers to cross before reaching this position, and when we do cross, we'll be behind George's roadblock. Second, we'll be moving west, directly away from Jason's position, and there'll be less chance of being detected.

"If indeed we do get away free and clear," I said, "and are not reported missing until dawn, my guess is that Jason will come to the conclusion that we moved due south, on the short route, but the only thing he'll find is Susan and some of her rangers waiting for him."

George couldn't help but let out a loud chuckle, as he pictured Jason coming up to the roadblock and confronting our people there. But Steve thought the situation serious enough to give George a very disapproving stare. George returned to his bowl of stew, but with the grin still on his face.

"Okay," Steve said, "I see your logic. How soon do you think you can get them out, and how many people will you need?"

"Only Goodman and myself. The smaller our crew, the better. As soon as George gets the roadblock in place, we'll go back and make contact with Thelma and a couple of key personnel to help move everyone out. The number of people we contact before the actual move will depend on what Thelma can tell us. The smaller the number of people who know about the move beforehand, the better it will be for all of us."

"Can we make the move in the next six or seven days?"

"Without a doubt. Maybe even sooner."

"Now, to another pressing problem," Steve said. "George, when can you have a roadblock in place and a patrol out to watch for Jason, if you think one is needed?"

George looked into the fire as he arranged his thoughts. The way his fingers were flipping up and down, I knew he was counting his people mentally and deciding where to place them.

"There's no trouble with the roadblock itself; there's plenty of material around for that. I'm more concerned with protection of the person on watch. If Jason holds true to form, he'll have his people fire on our man first, then ask what he's doing there.

"I was thinking of making some kind of strong point behind the roadblock itself, where a watch can see the road and surrounding area, but be protected at the same time. If we have to stay, say, for longer than two weeks, I'd like to set up a better fortification."

"I'm sure that within two weeks we can be out of here," Steve said.

Sam nodded. George grabbed a stick. To illustrate his point better, he drew a diagram of his plans in the dirt.

"One man or two located at the strong point could see the road-block and all the territory to the river, on the right. To the left are open fields, where Jason could make a run around and head for the barns. But we'll be working there, and he'd really run into trouble.

"We don't have to worry about him coming at us from south of the river, because the only place he could cross would be right under the nose of our observer at Butte City. My only concern is the tree line, about five hundred yards up the road."

"No need to worry," Sam said. "Trees are packed in too tight, too many big boulders, and the angle going up the side of the mountain would make it impossible to get any kind of vehicle through there. But he could put out someone to stay in there and spy on us."

"That's what I thought," George said. "I'd like to put out a patrol in those trees, two or three times a day."

Satisfied that he had a good plan, George put down his pointer, brushed the sand from his hands, and sat back, waiting for Steve's reaction. You could tell Steve was pleased with the plan.

"Sam," Steve said, "how long do you estimate it will take to dig out the storage barns?"

"Digging out won't be the problem. With the size of your crew, we can have everything ready to move within four to five days. But transportation, that's going to be our big problem."

"How many wagons are up here?" Steve was asking the same question that had been on my mind, the previous couple of days.

"I'd estimate three to five, depending upon how good a smithy you have with you."

"John's the best, providing of course that he has some sort of wheels to work with—parts, if nothing else."

"I'll give you the wheels, wagons, and horses to work with," Sam said. "I sure wish I'd thought sooner to ask you to bring that Jeep. With its pulling power, we could string up two or three of these wagons and move them all at one time."

Steve looked at me. "What do you think, J.J.? It's your Jeep."

"All right with me," I said.

"Send Goodman back for the Jeep first thing tomorrow morning," Steve said. "You two won't be heading back to Butte City for a day or two, anyway."

Everything seemed to be settled, and although it wasn't very late, everyone was tired from the march and the excitement of the work to come. We all said good night and turned in.

I awoke to the smell of freshly brewed coffee. George handed me a cup before I was fully awake.

"'Morning," he said. "We have about three hours before sunrise. How about you and I walking out to where we're going to set up the roadblock, just to make sure we have all our signals straight?"

"All right," I said. "I've got to get Goodman headed back for the Jeep. See you in a few minutes."

Goodman heard all the racket George was making, getting people up, and was wide awake when I found him. I told him to get back to Goldston as fast as possible and bring back the Jeep. I thought of the gasoline tank we had found the previous day, and told him to bring back as many gas cans as he could find. I was sure that we'd taken some out of the sporting goods store.

By the time I got back to the fire and the coffee pot, Sam and Steve were up and ready to go. George returned, and we told Steve that we were going to survey the roadblock site, and mark an exact location for it and a protective place for the sentry to stay.

There was a thin ribbon of light in the eastern sky as we stood on the road, surveying the line of trees and the cinder block barns we had discussed the night before. The final spot we chose was at the old gate site for the ranch.

George and I were talking about the foot patrols into the trees when the other rangers arrived, with picks, shovels, and axes. I left George in charge, and returned to the cabins. John was getting a place set up for a forge, and was trying to find the best spot for the large anvil that he and Sam had brought from the burnt caretaker's house, the night before. You could see from the way the two worked that they were going to be good friends. Sam had promised John that, by sunrise, he'd have more wagon parts spread around him than he could fix in a lifetime—or a week, at least.

With everything and everybody ready, we headed for the location to be cleared first. Sam said all the farm machinery, parts and supplies, tools, and harness equipment would be found in the big cinder block building nearest the old ranch house. While one crew started clearing the rubble away, Sam and another crew scoured the

ranch for wagons and wagon parts. Iron to be used for raw material was found, and John had a set of billows working when the first
wagon parts arrived.

By noon, all of our hopes of clearing away and building the
roadblock were dashed by heavy wind and rain. The storm came up
suddenly from the south, and everyone was drenched by the time
they could get back to the cabin and tent locale. We were lucky that
not enough rubble had been cleared away to get anything wet
underneath. The downed buildings were still acting as an umbrella, covering the contents below.

A shelter of questionable sturdiness was completed at the roadblock, and two people were left there, in case we had visitors. They
also had a good view of the warehouses, which we couldn't see
from across the river.

The way it was raining, I was sure we'd be stuck in our tents for
at least two days—three, counting the time it would take for the
ground to dry up enough for us to start work again. I thought about
the ranger we had left at the outpost, overlooking Butte City. He
didn't have a radio, and couldn't report to us what Jason might be
doing. Being there the better part of a week by himself might have
been draining his resolve, by then.

I talked to Stephen about sending another ranger from our
group back to the outpost with food and my radio. He agreed, and
even though it was still raining heavily, I sent the ranger back with
the radio and food.

I called Goldston on Steve's radio and found out Goodman was
there. He had arrived drenched and cold, but in good shape, and he
was out looking for gas cans, despite the rain. I left a message for
him to bring back food for the rangers at the Butte City outpost and
another radio.

I asked about Susan. She had been caught at the roadblock
when the heavy rain had started and had stayed there. She heard my
conversation with Goldston, and broke in to answer my question
about her whereabouts. It was good to hear her voice, seemed like
we had been apart for months.

All we could do, then, was wait for the rain to stop.

*Chapter 10*

◈

# HARD WORK/BIG REWARDS

For the next two days, the rain kept coming, with some short breaks lasting an hour or two, but never any longer. All we could do was drink coffee, try to keep warm and dry, and wait. We were able to keep our spirits up by making plans.

Steve and I talked for hours about the rescue of everyone from Butte City. We started referring to them as the refugees. I told Steve about the people in the hospital, and we were agreed that, if at all possible, they would be brought out. The broken leg case could be handled, but moving the last one, with the head and back injury, would be a problem. Steve and I thought about it for a minute.

"I'd better make one more reconnoiter to Butte City, before we pull everyone out," I said. "What do you say?"

"Good idea," Steve said. "You going alone or taking Goodman with you?"

"I'll make this trip alone, just as soon as the rain lifts and I make a check with the observation post and see how things are there."

Sam and George came over and wanted to talk about preparations for excavations in the barns, so our discussion of Butte City was over for the time being.

The next day, our sixth in Highland Village, the sun came up, bright, hot, and very welcome. The ground was too wet to move anything heavy, and the stream was running extremely high and was very hard to cross, so we spent the day hunting up wagon parts for the blacksmith. He had the forge fired up and was working hard, by the time we started back with wheels, tongues, struts, and various pieces of iron that had been found around the farm.

Everyone was full of energy, after the two-day break, and eager to get out and do something, anything. George took two of the rangers and checked the road in the direction of Butte City. He came back through the grove of trees north of the road, and reported numerous mud slides and broken and damaged trees, not there before the latest storm. He said the road was in pretty bad shape, and he was sure Jason couldn't bring a vehicle down that road for at least three days. Even then, he'd have to remove several downed trees within a mile of our roadblock before he could get through.

With the high energy of the early morning expended, the afternoon was somewhat settled down. The roadblock was improved, all the tenting and bedding was dried out, and we were ready to get started on a normal work routine.

One wagon was on its wheels and ready to roll, by early afternoon. John, our blacksmith, was as proud of his accomplishment as Henry Ford had been of his first Model T. In any case, as soon as we retrieved some tack from the barn and hooked up the horses, we would be in business. While John and two helpers sorted through a mountain of parts for his next enterprise, the rest of the crew spent the afternoon and early evening uncovering the equipment barn.

It was slow going, at first. The heavy, steel-girded roof fell straight down, and our first thoughts were that everything below had been crushed. But Sam told us that the roof had been put up as one large, curved piece, and therefore, the only parts touching the ground were the ends. With that piece of good news, we started again.

It was getting dark when we'd uncovered enough of the barn to start removing items, but we came to the conclusion that it would be better to wait until the next day, when everyone would be fresh. We did, however, send two people down into the structure, between the uncovered girders, to have a look around.

"What do you see, son?" Sam shouted down to one of the workers.

A loud voice came back. "There's a lot of rough-cut lumber just below where you're standing. Looks like it may have been a wall, before the roof came down."

"I do believe you're either in the tack room or just outside," Sam said. "Do you see any leather straps, buckles, saddles, or anything like that?"

"There's a lot of straw. It's more of a dirt floor than concrete."

"Okay, son. You're in the horse stall. Best to watch as you step around." Sam gave me a big grin and a wink.

"What should I be looking for?"

Everyone was grinning, now. We certainly had us a city slicker down that hole.

Steve thought we'd done enough hard work and called it quits for the night. Sam was sure that, by moving around a few of the boards from the fallen wall, we could have harnesses and gear for the wagon out without any trouble, and could start removing some of the farm equipment. With the horses in harness, we could move along much faster, especially moving the heavier objects that took the whole crew to budge. But Steve said he'd rather lose an hour now than a man, down in the darkened building.

"Sam, I appreciate what you are doing for us," he said, "but it's best to wait. Tomorrow, we'll all be stronger and not so tired."

Sam agreed, and we started back across the river to a good night's rest. But Steve had other plans for me. While we had been working during the day, the observation post at Butte City had called, wanting to talk with either myself or Steve. As soon as we could get to the radio, Steve returned the call.

"Forward, this is Big Base, do you have a message for me?"

We all listened, but nothing came back for a minute or so. Steve tried again.

"Forward, this is Big Base."

Again, we waited. Finally, the ranger responded.

"This is Forward. We have big trouble. The people from the pavilion are burning sections of the town—some occupied, some not."

"What about the townspeople, what are they doing?"

"Nothing, at present. At first, they tried to put out the fires, but that just made Jason's men mad and they set another fire, and another, until the townspeople gave up. They're doing nothing, now—or that was the situation as dark fell. The fires are pretty well burnt out. I can't see the town too well, but the pavilion is lit and a party's in progress."

"Two more questions. Were any persons hurt on either side, and do you have any idea what started the trouble?"

"There are some townspeople hurt. I estimate at least three or four men, I don't know how serious. I saw the nurse tending to them. As to what started the trouble, I don't know. A hunting party left this morning, heading down the road in your direction. But before I had a chance to warn you on the radio, they came back. They were quarreling, but I couldn't hear or tell what was the matter. They went to the pavilion to talk with their leader, and came out a few minutes later still arguing."

The ranger unkeyed his handset, and all we heard was background noise. Either he was giving his voice and the radio battery a break or something had happened to make him stop.

Presently, he came back on the air. "The next thing I knew, some of the houses were burning. The squabbling and burning went on all day. Finally, Jason came out into the town, yelling and screaming. Somehow, he put a stop to it."

Once again, the voice on the radio stopped and the background noise came back. We stood staring at one another; everyone was trying to make some sense of what had happened in the town or what was going to happen.

Steve broke the silence. "Forward, thank you for your report. I'll get back to you in a few minutes."

Steve looked at me. "What do you make of it?" he said.

"I'm afraid that Jason may be getting tired of waiting in Butte City for rescue, and is getting ready to move here. If that's the case, then he might destroy the town before he leaves."

"I hate to ask you," he said, "but I need you to go there, talk to Thelma Brown, find out what's going on, and make plans to get those people out of there, and fast."

I agreed. After packing some food and medical items for Thelma and grabbing a bite for myself, I took off for Butte City. The rangers at the roadblock wished me luck as I passed through their position, then I was on my own. The night was positively dark—plenty of stars, but no moon. It was rough going, at first, because the road had been washed out at one point and, not far from the washout, there was a huge tree over the road. I could see why George had said we wouldn't have to worry about Jason. With the road in such bad shape, it would be hard to evacuate the townspeople, as well. It took over three hours to cover the eight miles between the two locations, but I was slowed on several occasions, while trying to find alternate, more easily traversed routes to be used later.

Long before I reached the town, I could smell smoke from the fires. As I drew near the hospital, I could see that all was quiet, with the exception of a fire burning near the pavilion and one small fire that Thelma was tending at the hospital. I was surprised to find her awake. She was startled as I approached, but her apparent apprehension turned into a huge smile when she realized it was me. I told her that we'd heard about the trouble, and I'd come to investigate and make plans to get everyone out.

She was emphatic. "If you were to get us all out of here tonight, it wouldn't be any too soon."

"Jason's getting harder to get along with?"

"He's gone from just plain mean to outright brutal."

"What caused the trouble today?"

"A number of things. He's confused, for one thing; doesn't know what to do anymore. They've run out of supplies from the ski lodges. He sent out a hunting party up north, the other day, and had two of the local men go along to act as bearers. Well, one of the men escaped, even though Jason's goons fired several shots at him. I believe he's afraid to go south; he knows your people are down there. He's scared to death that at any time you'll show up and force him into a showdown, which would be a disaster. I know he'd sacrifice any number of us before giving up his little kingdom, here. He's cut rations. He gives out canned goods once a week, and meat and flour whenever he thinks it's to his advantage."

"What about the trouble today?" I said. "What sparked that?"

"His goons are tired of hunting. It was fun, at first; now it's work. They wanted some of our men to go along and carry the game, but Jason said no, after what happened last week. I guess they had enough of it and, instead of going hunting, they came into town and started fights with anyone who got in their way. When that wasn't enough, they started burning houses, saying those lazy bums weren't going to lay around while they were hunting. The men fought back, but lack of food has taken its toll and they were no match. When the men would fight, Jason's goons would torture and burn just that much more."

I was very worried about all she was telling me, and wished I was there to get everyone out. "How many know about our existence and that we're trying to get you all out of here?"

"Only a couple of the men who I'll need, when it comes time. Why?" she asked.

"I don't want Jason to get wind of this."

I thought for a minute, trying to formulate some plan for evacuation that would be both safe and secure. "How many do you have under your care, right now?" I asked.

"Only Paul, the young man with the injured back. I don't know what the trouble might be, without proper x-rays and tests, but he won't be able to walk for quite awhile, if ever."

"What about the biker with the broken leg and ribs?"

"He didn't like it here; raised Cain until they moved him to the pavilion. I go to see him whenever he's sober enough to know I'm there."

She looked into the hospital. "I do have burn victims," she said, "and a few broken bones, but nothing that would hamper us moving. The two men who got burned will be a long time healing, but they aren't serious."

"Let's plan for a move two nights from now," I said. "That will give me time to get back and get things set. That gives you two days to line up things here. What I want you to do is have two men here to move Paul. You don't have to tell them you're leaving, just that you might need help. Have the two men you trust meet me at the west end of town, at 2 a.m. We'll evacuate the town west to east, so you'll be the last to move. If everything goes smoothly, you won't know we're here until we get to you. Any questions?"

"Why not let everyone in on the move, tell them the afternoon before?"

"It's not that I don't trust these people," I said. "But if someone, for any reason, lets on that something's about to happen then everyone might be lost."

I could see she didn't like all the secrecy and was scared something would go wrong with the plan. "We have a man keeping a watch on you," I said. "He'll know what we're doing, and can let us know if your situation should change."

"Lord, I hope nothing happens," she said. "I'm about to have a nervous breakdown myself."

"Hold on for two more days. I'd better get out of here before someone comes around, and we both have plenty to do."

She grabbed my arm, as if to say something else, or maybe just to keep a friend around for one more minute. Then she nodded.

"If you aren't back in two days, I'm going to organize these people myself and meet you in Goldston," she said.

"Understood. See you in two days."

Before I left, I couldn't help but take a walk down near the pavilion, to see if anyone was awake. Surely Jason would post a sentry to keep a watch over his domain. I approached to within twenty feet of the fire and stopped. I was taking a chance, but I figured if I could get that close then there wouldn't be any problem on the night of the move. The whole place smelled of rot, and there were cans everywhere. Torn-up paper, used for packing and boxes, was strewn all around. It was a wonder they weren't all dead from some dread disease spread by the pure filth. Animal bones littered the place, where they had been butchered, and someone had tried in a very amateurish way to stretch hides.

Having seen enough, I retraced my steps to Highland Village, making notes about the best possible route to be used in the evacuation. I reached our roadblock about daybreak. Our sentries were wide awake and alert, and knew of my approach long before I arrived. It made me proud to know I was part of a group of good people who thought about and helped each other.

Everyone was up and ready to go. That was the day to load the wagons and start moving everything down to Goldston, and everyone was eager to get started. Steve and George saw me enter the camp, and were anxious to hear about my trip. I told them everything about the fighting, the man who had escaped, and about the plans for evacuating everyone.

"Why two nights?" Steve asked. "You could go back tonight and get them out. Seems like the sooner the better."

"I'd like to have one more night for things to settle down," I said. "One more day will give a little more time for the injured to heal, and I want Jason to be completely off guard."

"Okay," he said. "Get some rest. You've been going at it for the past twenty-four hours, and we don't need you sick or exhausted at a time like this."

I was glad to hear Steve say that. The fatigue was starting to close in on me, beginning from my legs up. After they'd left, I sat by the fire, had a cup of coffee, then curled up in my sleeping bag and fell asleep.

I awoke some time in the afternoon, to the rumble of a wagon. A wagon was going up the valley, with a four-horse team pulling and four very excited people pushing. The wagon was piled high with a little bit of everything—sacks of grain, bales of hay, pieces of farming equipment. I saw a hay rake and a one-horse turning plow bouncing around on the top. As it disappeared around the corner, I realized Steve was sitting by the fire writing.

"Seems like the work is moving right along," I said, from my make-shift bedroom.

Steve looked around. "We're doing real good," he said. "Goodman is back with your Jeep, and as soon as we get that load of equipment up to the top, Jefferson is going to start back, pulling a two-wagon load. We have three operational, now. We'll use the one remaining to keep hauling.

"I figure Jefferson can get into Goldston tonight, unload, and be back here by morning with the empties. With any luck, John will have another wagon online by this afternoon, but I'm sure that's as far as he can go. He's about run out of parts."

"Four wagons, that's not bad," I said. "Where did all the wheels, axles, and beds come from?"

"All over the farm, plus we found one in building number two, this morning; a gasoline tractor, too, but it'll take some more digging to get it."

"Did Goodman bring back any gas cans?"

"A whole Jeep load. He and Lancaster are filling the cans now. As soon as we can get to that tractor and get some gas into it, we can relieve the poor horses."

I got the last bit of sleep out of my eyes, had a cup of coffee and some of Mrs. Lancaster's delicious biscuits, then went to work, helping Lancaster and Goodman pump the gasoline. By early afternoon, the tractor was freed, fueled, and hauling. We decided, with Sam's permission, to send a couple of the horses down the next day, for Mrs. Donley to use in her farming. I could picture the look of pure love when she saw those two beauties arrive.

The first full day of excavations was going really well. Building number two was well on its way to being cleared of all the equipment that could be used, and the grain that had been stored in building number one was already on its way to Goldston. By the end of the day, we'd have a pretty good idea of when we could end the work there and move everyone back to Goldston.

We pumped over two hundred gallons of gasoline from the one good, remaining tank. Through good luck, Lancaster had come up with two fifty-five-gallon drums, which we placed near the river ford, to be used as our local station for filling up the Jeep on its daily runs and the tractor when needed. There was still gasoline in the underground tank, but we had no idea how much. All of our containers were filled; pumping would have to continue when we had either emptied the containers on hand or found more.

Everyone was working full steam ahead; you could feel the electricity in the air. Morale was sky-high; everything was going so well. The buildings were providing more supplies than imagined, and almost nothing had been destroyed. We had figured, at first, that at least two weeks would be needed to clear the building and get everything moved, but as the day was coming to an end, it was evident that, with things working so well and with the cooperation of the weather, the job could be finished in a week.

I was anxious to get to the radio equipment that Sam had said was in the basement of the main house, but a more pressing problem was the condition of the people who I'd be bringing back the next night. I called the outpost above Butte City.

"Forward, this is One-Zero. Over."

No answer for a couple seconds. I was hoping they were near the radio, and above all, I was hoping it was turned on.

"Forward, this is One-Zero. Over."

"This is Forward. Over."

"Can you give me a report of activity in Butte City? Over."

"Quiet today. Very little movement since yesterday's activity—no hunting details, no nothing. Over."

"Good. Keep a sharp lookout for trouble and movement, especially in our direction or south toward the roadblock. We have vehicles on the road that should be alerted, if it looks like they might be discovered."

"Understood. From our position, we can hear vehicle movement, but it didn't disturb the people below us one bit. Over."

I was glad to hear that. We had completely forgotten that the Jeep might be heard in Butte City.

"New item," I said. "The evacuation is set for tomorrow night. Make sure anything out of the ordinary is radioed back to this location immediately. Will keep you informed and up to date, so that you can keep track of our movements when we kick this thing off. I'll have someone monitor this radio continually, for the next two days. Is there anything you need, up there?"

"Nothing, at this time. Good luck on the move. We'll be watching for you. Over."

"Nothing else, for now. Out." I was glad to know our movements were not being detected, but I thought I had better talk to Steve about stopping the supply train to Goldston after the evacuation, until we saw Jason's reaction.

Everyone was coming in for the evening meal, when I finished the radio conversation with Forward Base. I told Steve about the conversation, and briefed Goodman on the plan that he and I would execute the next night.

"Did Thelma give you a firm count of how many people?" Steve asked. "How long will it take?" Steve had a concerned look on his face.

"We can make the trip in three to four hours," I said. "If we're on the road by two, we can be in here before dawn. As to their number, I would figure between thirty-five and forty."

"If they get wind of what's going on, they may shoot at you."

"I don't know about that, but I'd like to go armed; Goodman also."

"Do you want to take anyone else?"

"No. If we need extra help, I can call the observation post. That should really confuse them, to get hit not only from our position but also from across the river."

"Okay, and what happens when you get them here?"

"Settle in the valley for a day or so. Let them get some rest, see what that mob will do, then make plans from there."

I had brought a smile back to Steve's face. "That sounds fine to me," he said. He looked around. "Sam, will you and George come over here?"

After they joined our group, Steve continued. "I don't think I'm needed here, anymore," he said. "George can handle security, Sam and Lancaster know where all of the goods are located, and Sam knows what he'll let us haul away and what he wants to keep. Besides, these youngsters are working me to death. So I'll be going back to Goldston, tomorrow. I know I can do a better job as an administrator there than I can as a laborer here. Anything we need to discuss?"

Steve again looked around the group. "Good. Let's get a good night's rest. Sam, I'd like to talk you into coming with us, before I leave. We can use, you down there."

"Let me think it over," Sam said. "Maybe I'll get tired of this place and want a change."

After the meeting broke up and everyone was having supper and getting settled in for the night, I couldn't help but think about Susan and what she must be doing. That was the longest time we had been parted since being married. I started to call her on the radio, just to hear her voice and to make sure she was all right, but I decided not to. Everyone on the radio net would be sitting glued to their receivers, with great big grins on their faces. She was probably making plans and rosters for the guard detail, anyway, but I determined it might be nice to tell her how much I loved her when we got back together. I decided to turn in for the night.

I could have sworn I'd just laid my head down when I heard George getting everyone up for the day.

"George," I said, "could you spare Goodman and myself from the work detail, today?"

"Sure, J.J. Want to get ready for the trip tonight?"

"No, I'd like to get into the basement of the main house and find that radio. I'm anxious to see if it'll work. Is that okay with you, Steve?"

"Sure, as long as Sam has no objection," he said. "I'd like to know if there's anyone out there."

Sam had been listening to our conversation. "Son," he said, "you get that radio working and I will personally grind that generator for you."

Within an hour, everyone was busy at one task or another. The two wagons were loaded and positioned on the mesa, awaiting the

Jeep's return. Steve and Sam were going over an inventory of what
had been loaded aboard the wagons and taken to Goldston. Steve
wanted Sam to keep the list up to date, after he left. Some of the
equipment and parts were of great value, and he didn't want them
lost in the shuffle.

George wanted to keep a patrol constantly on the move in front
of the roadblock, that day. If they were to find any of Jason's men
snooping around between then and the time we brought the townspeople out, he thought it would be best to keep them hostage until
the move was completed. He could then let them go, and it would-
n't matter what they told Jason.

Ranger Goodman and I looked the main house over, and tried
to figure out the best plan of attack. The east wall was still leaning
over on a large tree, but shouldn't be any danger to us. Sam had said
the radio equipment was located in the southwest corner of the
house. The fire had destroyed most of the superstructure, but the
hard oak floor was still intact. With any luck, anything in the basement would have been spared.

The stairs on the north side, leading down to the basement,
were gone, probably destroyed in the quakes. It appeared that
someone had been chopping away at the floor in the vicinity of
where the stairs had been. It might have been Jason's people, in
their frenzy to destroy and loot everything in sight. We finally
decided to go in through the west basement wall. There was too
much debris around the stairwell, and we wanted to stay away from
the east and south walls, which we wanted to protect.

First, we dug out the dirt at the basement level, where the basement wall joined with the floor supports. Then, with some well-
directed blows of a sledgehammer delivered by Goodman, we tore
a man-sized hole in the basement wall. With a flashlight, I looked
through the hole, but everything in the basement was in such a
jumbled mess that I couldn't really make out anything. I could see
the huge furnace, and where the stairs had been. Along the south
and west walls, I could make out a row of cabinets. They were a
mess. The ones that had been attached to the walls above what had
been a work bench, loaded with small appliances, had come down
and broken apart, spreading their contents everywhere.

Goodman was the smaller of the two of us, so we procured a
rope, put it around his waist, and lowered him down into the base-

ment. He disappeared only for a moment, then promptly popped up in the opening.

"We have a small problem," he said. "There must be at least two feet of water down there."

All the rain since the shakeup had added another problem to our finding the radio and equipment. I was fearful, now, that it might be ruined by water damage. I helped Goodman out, and we went looking for the hand pump that we had used to get the gasoline out of the service station tanks. For the next two hours, we took turns pumping water from the basement. The Jeep had returned, and Steve came over to see how we were doing and to wish us well, before he left for Goldston.

"Don't tire yourselves out," Steve said. "The two of you are going to have a busy night."

I appreciated his concern. "Keeps us both busy," I said, "and not counting the minutes until it's time to leave. If we quit a couple hours before sunset, we can get enough rest."

"Good luck," he said. "See you back in Goldston, in a few days."

After Steve had gone, we continued the pumping, taking turns and checking the water depth every fifteen minutes or so. I was taking my break when the pump started sucking air. Goodman called me over, and together, we checked for water. The floor looked fairly dry.

I helped him down, once again, and although he found some wet spots with standing water, it wasn't enough to hamper our operations. He moved a heavy metal desk under the opening, and I crawled in. Together, we moved enough rubbish away from the south wall that we could start searching for the radio.

The cabinets that had been above the long bench had fallen in such a way that we had to move them before we could search the cabinets below. Working space was small, at first, and with limited light, the going was slow. We had almost gotten them moved behind and away from us when Goodman made our first discovery.

"I've got something, here. Looks like a log book, and here are some papers. I believe they're messages."

"Let's see. Take them over to the desk by the opening."

The log was more than ten years old and covered a three-day period. What was interesting to me was that he had left for us a lot of frequencies and names of people and stations. Places and people that we could contact, if we could find enough equipment and if the equipment would work.

It appeared that he had transmitted in both voice and CW or Morse Code, which meant the equipment had many capabilities and a good range. Although most of the traffic in the logs appeared to be local or within a short range, there was one entry from Nova Scotia, two from England, and according to the notes, a call from Brazil, but the message had been only partially received, due to poor atmospheric conditions at the time.

The last entry had either been received phonetically or by Morse Code, according to the way it had been written in the log. The messages were mostly items of interest between friends who had never seen each other, more than likely. One in particular caught my eye. The first part of the message and who it had been sent to or received from had been obliterated by the water, but the readable part had to do with disasters: "...AND IT IS MY THOUGHT THAT WE SHOULD THINK ABOUT A RADIO NETWORK BETWEEN OUR-SELVES DESIGNED TO HELP ONE ANOTHER IN TIMES OF CRISIS OR DIS-ASTER. IF WE ACT NOW..." If someone on the radio circuit had sur-vived, we might be able to contact them.

Now, to find the equipment. There were a number of drawers below the counter, but they had items found in every shop—pen-cils, paper, one was filled with sandpaper, another with different sizes of screws and bolts. In the far corner, where the south and west walls came together, we found evidence of antenna switches and some wire leads coming up through the floor below.

In a small corner cabinet, we found a large, green bag contain-ing headsets, microphones, a CW key, a wide selection of wires and cables that we didn't know what to do with yet, and two wire anten-na systems, neatly folded and preserved in oiled paper. An excep-tional find, indeed, but we still needed the transmitter and receiver.

I was beginning to become worried about time. The sun was start-ing its slow decline, and soon, what little light we were receiving from the sun and our flashlight would be gone.

As we were taking the bag of accessories to the desk, to be taken out, I ran squarely into a small, green cabinet, not more than three feet high. The door was knocked open, and inside were two metal shelves. On the top were two very well-preserved transceivers, extra log books, a sheaf of paper, and a box of sharpened pencils. The second shelf had a small, portable generator, along with an attachable seat that could be used to power the radio. In the bottom of the cabinet was a power transformer, neatly stored with all of its assorted cables. The transformer, I surmised, had been used to convert the house current into DC, to operate the radio, and the hand-cranked generator could be used in emergencies.

Goodman and I were so pleased with ourselves that we couldn't help but let out some very loud howls or yells. We were talking loudly and fast, when some faces appeared at the entrance point.

"Hey, you guys all right down there?"

"Great," I yelled back.

"We found ourselves a radio station."

"You found a what?"

"Radio equipment. How many people up there?"

"Two. You need some help?"

"You two will do. We're going to hand this equipment up to you. See about getting a couple more hands, and take it over to the Lancaster cabin."

Getting the radio equipment out wasn't difficult, until we came to the transformer. It had been sitting in water and didn't look worth saving, but one never knew, so we pushed, pulled, and with a rope and help from the people on the ground above us, we finally got it out. There were a large number of items still in the basement that could be used, but their removal had to be left for another day.

Both Goodman and myself were quite happy with ourselves when we came out of the basement. All of the radio apparatus we had passed up had been taken across the ford and stored. But we had no time to look at it, now. Goodman and I needed to get something to eat, get a little rest, and prepare for the upcoming trip to Butte City.

# Chapter 11

⟨∾⟩

# ESCAPE FROM BUTTE CITY

Ranger Goodman and I were both too keyed up to get much rest. After supper, I retrieved two pistols from my knapsack, along with holsters and twenty rounds of ammunition each. Goodman looked very surprised when I handed him one of the pistols.

"I don't care to carry one of those," he said. "I'd just as soon leave mine here, if it's all right."

"It's not all right, Goodman. I've seen Jason and his people in action. All I'm asking you to do is protect yourself and whatever people may be in your charge. Nothing more—no attack on his position, no taunting to try and draw him out. We'll get the towns-people out with the least amount of trouble."

All arrangements at our valley encampment had been complet-ed. Enough tents or tarpaulins had been put up to temporarily house the people we'd be bringing out, and Mrs. Lancaster would be up and would have a big breakfast ready when we arrived. I had a suspicion that our guests-to-be would have the most lavish meal they had seen for some time, and as a matter of fact, that we had seen in awhile. There had been a strange absence of eggs and milk products around, for the past few days, and my guess was the Lancasters had turned a large amount of that into cheese and but-ter.

I called the observation post on the radio to find out how things were going in Butte City, but they had nothing to report. The pavil-ion had been quiet; some of the men had gone with two of Jason's people up to the ski resort area, and had returned a few hours later, but that was about all.

145

For several days, they had been coming over to the south side of Lead Creek to work on the old truck. They didn't really work very hard; most of the time, they would lie around, smoke, drink, and chase each other, until it seemed time to go back to the pavilion. The bike was still running and, once in awhile, they'd play around with it, do some stunts. It would run out of gas, and they'd park it right where it had quit running. Whenever they got too loud, Jason would make an appearance and scream a little, until they calmed down.

That was good news. I asked about the hunting parties, but they said no one had been out since the trouble of a few days before. I told them we'd be in their area around midnight or so and to watch for us, then signed off.

We spent the remainder of the evening trying to rest. A thousand things were going through my mind. What, if anything, had I forgotten? I worried about Susan. What if Jason was so mad that he attacked Susan's roadblock in force?

Goodman broke my chain of thought. "Wake up, J.J. It's almost 9:30. I think we'd better get on the road."

"Okay, let's get going."

We said our goodbyes all around, packed up our light packs that carried water, some first aid gear, a knife, and a flashlight, and we were on our way. I knew the people we were leaving behind wouldn't get any sleep that night. We passed by the roadblock that George had set up, and he was there to wish us well.

Having already traveled the road, I pointed out the pitfalls that Goodman should bypass on the way back. We made excellent progress, and reached the outskirts of town right at midnight. My heart really sank when there was no one there to meet us. We stopped in the middle of the road and knelt down.

"What do you think," Goodman said, "something go wrong?"

"I don't know."

I looked up toward the observation post. It was dark and quiet there. The town seemed to be asleep, nothing other than Goodman and myself seemed to be moving.

"We'll wait here for a few minutes," I said. "If no one shows up, I'll go ahead to see if everything is all right."

I had just finished that statement when I heard my name called. "Your name Darby?"

My heart ran very fast for the next few seconds. "Yes. Who are you?"

As I made myself known, I slowly reached for my holster, in case Jason had a roadblock we knew nothing about. Two men seemed to rise right out of the ground, not more than ten feet from us, slightly off the road.

"Thelma sent us." They didn't come toward us, but stood their ground.

"Outstanding," I said. That's all I could think of to say, I was so relieved.

We shook hands all around. Dave White, the older of the two, had been owner and operator of the pavilion, before Jason took it over. Jimmy Wills, a youngster in his early twenties, had operated a ski lift before the quakes.

I told them of my plans to bring out families with children first, and get them on the road as soon as possible. If we were going to have a noise problem, I thought it might be with the small ones. They agreed. Both knew exactly where everyone was located, so without any further discussion, both men disappeared down the road.

Before too long, we heard voices coming towards us. We couldn't have the noise, so Goodman went to meet them and act as a guide. When they got to me, they looked very confused. I told them not to worry, that we had come to take them to Highland Village and, ultimately, on to Goldston. The children were waking up, by then, and becoming very excited, and it was all the adults and I could do to keep them still.

Dave White returned with the next group, and told me all the children were there and ready to go. We only had eighteen people, so I told him to wait for another group before moving on. Goodman came back with four more people, and he took the lead and started down the road. Everything was going well; it was just past one o'clock, and the first group was moving away, very quietly.

More people showed up over the next few minutes, just as confused and bewildered as the first group had been. I could see the relief and amazement on their faces when we told them what was happening.

I took White aside for a final briefing. "I want you to stay here until everyone in town has been accounted for. I'm going up to the hospital, to see if Thelma needs any help moving the back injury patient."

"Jimmy Wills and one other man should be there by now," he said.

"Okay, hold everyone here. I'll be back."

I moved down the road at a trot. The evacuation was going much faster than I'd thought possible. Before I turned to go to the hospital, I thought it might be a good idea to look in on the pavilion, to see that all was quiet there. There were two men sitting by the bonfire, playing cards. Their voices were carrying far into the night, and it made me aware of how far a voice or any noise could be heard during the dead of night. But we had almost everyone out; just a few more minutes and it would be all over. I retraced my steps to the hospital, and arrived as two men were bringing Thelma's last patient out.

"I'm glad you're here," she said. "Everything's ready. Just the one patient, and these two seem capable of carrying him on the litter."

"You seem anxious to go."

"You know I've been ready to leave since your first visit," she said.

"One small problem," I said. "There are two wide-awake people sitting around the fire, down there, so we're going to work our way back through town, rather than run the risk of going down to the main road. A stumble or a moan from the patient might ruin our whole night."

"Jimmy, can you get us back through town without too much trouble?" Thelma asked.

He didn't speak, indicated yes with a gesture, picked up the litter with the help of his friend, and we started off. We threaded our way through the town, reaching the others a little after two o'clock. We were still on schedule. We changed litter bearers, I took the lead, and we were on our way out of Butte City.

Going back was somewhat slower than the trip Goodman and I had made, a few hours before. Lack of a proper diet was really showing. We made frequent stops, so everyone could catch their breath and to change the litter bearers. But everyone made it, and by the time dawn was breaking, we were in sight of Highland Village.

George and two of his rangers were out looking for us, and were a great help getting over the last mile or so. By the time we had crossed the ford and had everyone in the valley, the sun was about to rise.

The first group was still awake, even though they'd been fed a wonderful meal by Mrs. Lancaster and had been give a place to sleep. They said they couldn't rest until we arrived. You would have thought they hadn't seen each other in months, they were so happy and relieved. They were shaking our hands and hugging each other for a long time. When things settled down a bit, my group gathered around the table Mrs. Lancaster had set, gave thanks for the blessing that had been bestowed upon them that day, and began eating.

The rangers and workers from Goldston were up and ready to go back to work. The new arrivals were being taken care of, so I thought I'd head for the observation post, to see what Jason's reaction would be when he discovered everyone gone.

As I was leaving, George caught up with me. "J.J., don't you think you'd better have some breakfast and a little rest before you go?"

"Not now. I'll get something to eat up there."

"Take one of the horses," George said. "Sam can have it saddled and ready to go in a couple of minutes."

He was right, I was slowing down. Fatigue was setting in. By the time I'd had a cup of coffee and got up to the pasture, my mount was ready. I'd never been much of a horseman, but was assured that my steed was old and slow, but reliable. I certainly hoped so; I didn't want to go galloping head over heels down the nearest embankment.

When I approached the nearest point to the observation post before the road turned south, I left the horse and walked the remaining few hundred yards. There was one ranger in camp, waving to me as I came in; the other was up at the forward position, keeping an eye on Jason.

"Anything happening down there?" I asked.

"No, not a thing. We were up all night."

It was at least two hours since the sun had come up. "You mean, they don't know the town has been evacuated?"

"No, they don't. They usually don't get up until around now, anyway. Want to take a look?"

I sure did. But before we left, I had a cup of coffee and a large chunk of bread with gobs of jam on it, then I was ready to go. When we reached the other ranger in the forward position, he had the binoculars up and was looking over the town.

He greeted me with a big smile. "We didn't even know you'd been down there," he said, "until we looked the town over this morning and saw no movement anywhere. Except for the dog."

"Dog?" I hadn't thought of pets.

"He's right over there, by the big lean-to. Let's see…one, two, three streets from the hospital."

He gave me the binoculars. A big, red Irish Setter.

"Did he belong to one of the kids?"

"No kids lived there, but they'd come over and play with him. Seems to be a real gentle dog. Had to belong to the middle-aged couple that lived there, along with an elderly gentleman."

Undoubtedly, they'd thought I wouldn't have let the dog go, the previous night, but I'd have rather they had brought him. He was lying with his head on his paws, but I couldn't tell if he was sleeping.

I turned my attention toward the pavilion. The two who had been playing cards the previous night were still sleeping, right where they had been that night. Someone was moving around in the pavilion, but I couldn't see who or how many.

"What's the usual morning routine?"

"Usually, one of the women will come out, get the guard up, and have whoever it is help with getting something ready for breakfast. Sometimes they cook inside, sometimes outside over the fire. Jason should be out pretty soon. He usually swims before breakfast; one of the few I've seen take a bath. Then they all gather for breakfast. That's when Jason tells them to go hunting, check for supplies, or whatever."

"I'm going to sleep a little. Wake me if anything happens down there." In about ten seconds, I was fast asleep, but not for long.

"Wake up. J.J., wake up."

"What is it?" I asked.

"Jason. He was going to take a swim, but he stopped. There he is, right where the old bridge washed out."

I took the binoculars. I hadn't seem him in awhile, but he looked as mean as ever. He looked all around him, as if he were listening for something. He looked up to the top of the hill, and I could have sworn he was looking me right in the eye.

He suddenly turned and started back for the pavilion. He was yelling something, but I couldn't make it out. A couple of guys came toward him, and he motioned toward the town. They took off at a fast pace. Jason stood there, a towel thrown over his shoulder, hands on hips. More of his group were gathering around him.

I watched as the two dispatched couriers started to search the town. One looked into the hospital, then into Thelma's lean-to, then took off after his companion. They were running through houses yelling, but they weren't getting any answers, until they got near the dog and he started to bark. They ignored him, at first, and continued the search, but when they found nothing, they picked up the dog on the way back to report to Jason.

As they were making their report, I could see their arms flailing in all directions. Jason was looking at the dog. He must have been thinking the same thing I was: turn the dog loose and see which way he goes. Without delay, Jason took the rope off the dog, and with a wave of Jason's hand, the dog was running down the road, straight for Highland Village.

Now Jason knew, but what was he going to do about it? It appeared, at first, that he would do nothing. He and the rest of his gang stood there and watched, as the dog disappeared down the road. Finally, he reacted. He tore the towel from around his neck and walked toward the pavilion, calling for everyone to follow, or so it seemed.

I told the ranger to get on the radio, and tell George that the dog was coming and to take care of him when he arrived. He belonged to someone in our group. I wished Jason had not called everyone inside, because it was difficult to see what was going on. I could see Jason pacing back and forth and talking. He would stop every so often, point to someone, then continue his pacing.

Before long, some of them came out. They had bags, sacks, and some empty boxes with them. They hitched a trailer, about twelve feet long with no sides, to one of the Jeeps and proceeded to go through the town site, picking up anything that was useable—food, clothing, and metal items. It took the better part of the day, and when they finally came back, they had quite a haul.

In the meantime, Jason had some of the others go up to the ski lodge sites and retrieve whatever was left up there. The remainder seemed to be packing up all the goods at the pavilion.

I slept most of the day away, while that was going on. By early afternoon, I felt good enough to take a turn on the binoculars and let the two rangers go back for a meal and a little rest.

It was evident that Jason was getting ready to leave, but he seemed to be taking last night's event calmer than I had imagined. I wondered if this was the calm before the storm.

Just before dark, he sent two people over to the south bank of Lead Creek, to retrieve the motorcycle. They stripped all useable parts and wiring from the old truck while there. That indicated that they were not going south.

East was definitely out—there were nothing but towering peaks in that direction, and no roads. North was where Jason and some of his bunch had originally come from, but the country in that direction was almost as rugged as that to the east. That left west.

I called Highland Village to speak with George, but he was out helping load wagons for the trip to Goldston. I was told that the dog had arrived, and had been happily reunited with his owner and all the kids who loved him very much. I also learned that his name was Sir Von Reginald La Rouge, but everyone called him Red or Big Red. I left word for George to get back to me as soon as he could.

The people below me, in Butte City, had put in a full day's work. Darkness had arrived, and a huge bonfire was burning in front of the pavilion. The three Jeeps were lined up on the road heading west. All were heavily loaded. The lead Jeep had no trailer, but was packed so heavily that the only space available was for the driver. The second had a regular one-quarter-ton trailer, which is usually associated with the vehicle. Both were loaded way above their maximums. The third Jeep had the twelve-foot trailer attached. Like the first two vehicles, both were heavily loaded.

They still had two motorcycles. One had been lost when they had tried the end around run at our roadblock, but the remaining ones were loaded as much as possible; one even had a small trailer attached. They were packed and ready to leave, but I didn't think they would leave so late in the day. If they were heading west, it was going to be a heck of a trip with those vehicles loaded as they were.

I was surprised that Jason hadn't tried to chase down the people we'd taken out of the city. Maybe he was more level-headed than I had given him credit for being. Right then, it seemed as though there was going to be a big party. I saw a few cases of beer brought out to the waiting group, along with a couple fifths of whiskey. I'd have thought that, by then, all of their alcohol stock would have been depleted.

I also saw some weapons brought out, and that disturbed me more than the beer or whiskey ever could. I saw at least three rifles, and several of the men were carrying pistols, either in their belts or in holsters. For the first time, I was able to get an accurate count of Jason's group. A total of twenty-one people—seventeen men and four women. I had never thought they were more than ten or twelve strong.

Nothing was going to happen that night. I thought I might head back to Goldston and see Susan, get a good meal, and come back in the morning, but the nagging thought stayed with me that anything could happen. The best thing to do was to stay put.

George had never returned my call, so I got on the radio again. He came right on the air and apologized for the delay, saying it had been a hectic day. I asked what had gone wrong, and he said nothing. The work was going smoothly and the Jeep had returned before nightfall, so they were all ready to start hauling the next morning, if I thought it would be safe. The only real trouble was that the new people wanted to help and there were too many on a task, so he'd made it mandatory for all newcomers to rest, whether they wanted to or not.

"Let's do this," I said. "I'm not sure of Jason's motives, yet, but I'm sure he won't go south of Lead Creek. I'm almost certain he'll head in your direction, probably tomorrow morning. I suggest you let anyone of the newcomers who are strong enough to make the trip back to Goldston go with the Jeep and trailers, but I'd keep their numbers to less than a dozen."

"Sounds good to me. You coming back here soon?"

"When Jason makes his move, I'll let you know. If there's nothing more, I'm going to call Steve and tell him what we've decided."

"Okay, see you. Highland Village out."

Before I could get on the radio again, I received a call. "This is Big Base, One-Zero. I've been monitoring your traffic. We'll be waiting for the goods and people to arrive. What's going on in Butte City? Over."

"All of the vehicles are packed and ready to move. They're having a real party tonight, but I haven't heard any war cries, so it may be a calm one. Over."

"Nothing further, Base out."

By the time I left the radio and got back to watching the party below, things had changed quite a bit. I did hear war whoops, now, and people were making torches. I knew exactly what they were going to do, before the first house was burning.

They lit the torches from the big fire and started off through the deserted town, yelling and screaming. Within a few minutes, fires were starting. They were burning all the shanties, shacks, and lean-tos left by the previous tenants. Then I heard the first explosion. The old hospital built by Thelma was blown to bits. I tried to locate, with the binoculars, who it was who had the explosives, but there was another explosion farther up into the town before I could locate them.

I finally found them; there were three. Two were carrying a wooden box about three feet long by one wide. The other one was running ahead with something in his hand, probably an explosive, but I didn't know what or where they'd got it. They hadn't used it against the townspeople or us, so they might have found it recently. One thing was sure, we didn't want them anywhere near our roadblocks or our people.

Another explosion. If we were lucky, they'd use all of it up that night. The whole place was lit up, by then. Some of them had been trapped by the fires; while they were torching the center of town, others were starting fires around them. The town was a complete mad house. Some people were burning and screaming, while others continued to set fires. The three with the explosives were trying to find something worth blowing up, and Jason was back at the pavilion, strumming a guitar and watching some of the others dance. I had the feeling that I knew what Rome must have looked like when Nero watched the city burn to the ground.

One of the rangers came up from the tent. "What in the world is going on?" he said. "George called on the radio; they can hear those explosions all the way over there."

"Tell them that Jason has some kind of explosive, I don't know what kind or how much. I'll get back to him as soon as I can."

The crazy scene below went on for hours. The burn victims were returning to the pavilion and one of the women was taking care of them. From my position, the burns didn't seem very bad.

One more loud explosion, and I saw the long box being thrown into the fire. I hoped that all of the explosives were used up.

The party settled down after there wasn't any town left to burn, and as people passed out, one by one, the night seemed to become quieter and calmer. One of the rangers came up to relieve me, and I retired to the tent to get some rest.

"J.J., wake up. Jason is on the move."

It was the ranger who had relieved me the night before. It was nearly sunrise.

"Are you sure, after that party last night?"

"I'm sure. He's already thrown two of them in the creek, and he's down there now kicking sleeping bags."

By the time I got up to the front, almost everyone was up and milling around. Some seemed to be mighty groggy. I could smell the coffee brewing, and one lush was downing a can of beer. A few of the night's fires were still smoldering, but no one seemed to give them a thought, as they prepared to leave. They were throwing a great deal of items into the fire ring outside the pavilion, most of it clothing. It appeared that what they couldn't carry with them, they would burn.

A few more belongings, cases of food, and some other odds and ends were put on the already overloaded vehicles, and Jason called a meeting. I couldn't hear him, but by his gestures and the reaction of the crowd, it was a good old pep rally. When it broke up, people started putting on packs, gathering up canteens, and piling on the Jeeps' hoods, side-rails, whatever was available. The lead Jeep started moving, and the other two fell in behind. The two bikes, fully loaded, brought up the rear. Anyone who could not hitch a ride was walking.

When they were leaving, I glanced back at the pavilion. They'd left it intact. I thought, when they were far enough away, I'd take a ranger with me, put out the fire, and check out what was left of the town. As I continued to watch them wind down the road, I saw that everyone kept looking back. I looked back at the pavilion and before I heard the explosion, I saw the walls splintering into millions of pieces. The roof was rising skyward, as the sound reached us. A great shout went up from Jason's crowd.

I got back to the radio, and told George that they were on the way. I warned him, again, that Jason might have explosives with him, and told what had happened to the pavilion. He assured me he was ready.

I signed off, and took one of the rangers with me, down to what was left of Butte City. We didn't have to look long to know Jason hadn't left a thing there. We put out the biggest of the fires that was still burning. The building that had been Jason's headquarters didn't exist anymore. We didn't find a clue as to what kind of explosive they had used.

The ranger and I climbed back up to the observation post, and I prepared to go back to Highland. I left instructions for the two rangers to stay for a few days, until I had time to see what Steve might want to do about keeping a permanent observation post there. I assured them that, either way, we'd have a relief up within two days.

My old mare had found her way back home a long time before, so I took off down the trail at a slow trot. Jason would be in Highland before I arrived, but not by much. I was wondering what he planned to do when he got there. Then it dawned on me that he didn't know we were there. He might believe that the townspeople left on their own and he would catch up with them. If that was what he believed, then he was in for a big surprise. I slowed to a walk. If Jason wasn't going to be in a rush, then neither was I.

When I reached the pasture above Sam's valley hideout, I found my mare enjoying an afternoon drink and a little romp with the other horses. She looked my way, acknowledged my arrival, and shook her head up and down several times, as if to say, "I see you can get around on your two legs just as well as I can on my four," and with that, she took off on another jaunt.

As I descended into the valley, I had the distinct feeling that not all was right. It was too quiet. As I came near the Lancaster's cabin, I could see some children playing in the new tent area, but there wasn't anyone else around. I gave a quick hello, the children looked up, and Mrs. Lancaster came out of the cabin. Some of the other women came out of the tents.

"Where is everyone, Mrs. Lancaster?"

"Up at the roadblock," she said. "George took most everyone up there; said he wanted what he called a 'show of force' when that crazy bunch showed up."

As she was talking, I heard someone splashing through the ford, coming that way. It was Sam and some of the other people coming back.

"How's it going up there?" I asked.

He broke into a big grin. "Son, you missed a good showdown."

"Not with weapons, I hope."

"Nope, Jason ain't that crazy," he said.

Sam couldn't wait to tell the story. "Well, after you called this morning, George got us all together and told us he needed our help."

Sam poured a cup of coffee and sat down next to me. By now, everyone else had gathered around to hear the story.

"We all go up to the roadblock, and he tells us to spread out along a line from the barns, down through where the gate fell, and on down to the river.

"Lancaster and I have our rifles, but most of the men don't have anything but sticks, so George tells us that, once Jason arrives, he wants us to go up and down the line, giving our rifles to some. Let him get up, strut around with the rifle for awhile, sit down, then we give the rifle to someone else. Said he wanted a lot of movement, like we had two hundred people—even had us practice. That boy knows what he's doing, let me tell you."

Sam took a break to get a sip of coffee to wet his tongue. "George took some of the rangers and went into the tree line, way up from where we were, and waited. It was a long wait, but finally we heard the sound of motors; couldn't see anything for awhile, then a gunshot. We had been getting a little restless, but that perked us up real quick.

"Pretty soon, the motors stop, but we still haven't seen the vehicles. A long time passes. Finally, we see Jason and George come walking down the road. George waves his rifle over his head—that was the signal for us to act busy, pass the rifles up and down the road, make noise, and show off in general."

Sam was laughing so hard, he had to stop his story long enough to compose himself, take another sip of coffee, and continue. "Well, it worked, because Jason turns to George, and we could all see he was white as a sheet. He was pounding one fist into the other and telling George something. But George was shaking his head.

"Jason turned to us and shook his fist, then turned and headed back for the tree line. About this same time, George called in the rangers he'd stationed out there, and they passed Jason going that-a-way, when they was coming this-a-way. Boy, was he mad. Anyway, George comes to the line, gets everyone down, and we wait."

Sam was enjoying himself immensely. He took another break, had a long drink of his coffee then continued. "Wasn't long before a guy came streaking, hell-bent for leather, out of the trees on a motorcycle. Let me tell you, he was flying. He had something in his left hand, looked like a small box trailing a sparkler. George figured out what it was just about the same time I did. He and two of the rangers starting shooting. They were trying for the bike, using the same strategy employed at your roadblock, earlier, and they got it— both tires flat just like that.

"Somebody hit the front axle, because the whole bike came apart, all at once. The guy goes skidding all over the road and drops the explosive. By the time he got up and figured out what happened, he didn't have time to look for what he dropped, and he took off for the trees as fast as he could go. He had a lot of people yelling to help him along. His bomb went off a few feet from the bike, but I don't think he wanted it back, anyway."

"Was there any more trouble after that?" I asked.

"No, not a bit. They're still out there, but George said to go back to work. They'd proved their point and we'd proved ours. Some people are over at the barns working, and we came down to get something to eat. Then, we go back and relieve the people George kept on the line."

I thanked Sam for his story, and took the opportunity to go up and see how George was doing. As I crossed the creek, I could hear the tractor working and people shouting, shouts you hear on any job. That seemed to be normal, anyway.

I continued past the barns and up near the small house George had constructed behind the roadblock. Two rangers were there. One was resting, while the other had binoculars and was watching the road and the tree line, out ahead. I asked about George, but before they could answer, he was tapping me on the back.

"Saw you coming," he said. "I was up at the barns. What do you think? Did Sam tell you what happened?"

"He did. What do you think Jason will do now?"

"I don't know. I told him that as soon as you or Steve arrived, he could speak to you; that I had nothing to say to him."

"Did he have any idea we were here?"

"None whatsoever. He was totally surprised."

"That's what I thought."

"The guy is really bonkers," George said. "He thinks this is his territory, and that we have no business here."

"What do you mean?" I asked.

"He said that all lands north of Lead Creek were under his jurisdiction, that we'd have three days to clear out, and furthermore, that he knew we were holding the people of Butte City and Highland Village hostage. If we didn't comply with his request, he had no alternative but to attack us, and when order was finally restored to the federal and state governments, he'd see that we were either shot or hanged."

I didn't know exactly what to say. How in the world were we ever going to deal with a man like that?

"Why did you bring him out to see the lines?" I said. "Didn't he believe you had protection set up here?"

"Nope. After he finished his little speech, he noted that there wasn't but four of us total and that we were not going to stand in the way of his authority. I asked him to walk down the road with me, by himself.

"He didn't trust me at first, but he's so cocksure, he couldn't resist. I guess Sam told you about the signal, and passing the rifles, and all."

I nodded in the affirmative.

"Let me tell you, from out there, it looked like a hundred well-armed individuals itching for a fight. He screamed at me for awhile, telling me to clear out before it was too late. I said no, and he stomped off.

"I called the rangers in, and you know about the one motorcycle attack. It's still out there. I don't think anyone could put that one back together. That fool biker is lucky he didn't blow himself to kingdom come."

I looked over at the place where the bike had landed, and told George how Jason had destroyed the pavilion back at Butte City. I was sure he wouldn't hesitate to use that explosive on us, if he got the chance—not in an open bike attack, but at night, if he thought he could get away with it. We would have to be careful, until we could solve our problem with him.

I thought about giving Steve a call on the radio, to see if he wanted to come up and deal with him, when I noticed a Jeep on the far edge of the field. A man was standing on the hood. I asked the ranger for the binoculars.

"What do you make of it?" George said.

"It's Jason. He's looking over at the work around the barns. Now he's looking over this way. He passed us; he's looking at the creek. Maybe he's trying to figure a way to get around us."

"He won't do it by way of the creek; it would suck up those Jeeps before they were halfway across."

"He's panning back this way, now. He's looking right at me. I'd swear he's looking right down my binoculars."

"Well, stare right back," George said. "Don't let him get the upper hand at anything."

I held really steady and stared back. Jason finally took the binoculars from his eyes and stared at me. I thought the polite thing to do would be to do the same thing, so I took mine down.

"What's he up to now?" George asked.

I handed the binoculars to him, and he stared at Jason. One of us had to take the initiative. I walked out to the roadblock, stood on top, and waved my arms above my head, in Jason's direction. He looked at me for awhile, and finally started waving back. I walked out into the road and motioned for Jason to join me. To my surprise, he jumped off the Jeep and began to walk slowly toward the roadblock. I waited in place.

I had taken some wild chances in my past, but that was one of the wildest. I was sure I could reason with Jason, if I could talk to him one on one, so he wouldn't have to show off for anyone. I was certain that, even though he acted off-balanced at times, he was really quite smart. Mean, perhaps, but smart. I was trying to think of something, anything I could talk about to get him in a talking mood, and not one of confrontation. When we were no more than five feet apart, we stopped and stared at each other.

"I'd like to talk with you," I said. "Just you and I, one on one."

His expression didn't change, but finally he did respond. "What do you think we have to talk about?"

"Our situation here. Hell, I don't know, about anything."

"Where and when do you propose we talk?"

"Right now, in the middle of the road," I said. "Sit down."

I pointed to the ground and waited. He sat down, and I followed suit, thinking all the time, *what in the world am I doing here?* We were both quiet for some time, and I figured it was up to me to speak first.

"Jason, you see what we're doing here; you've seen what we've been doing in Goldston. I'm asking you point blank, do you want to join with us or keep going?" I thought for a second he was going to get up and leave, but he didn't.

"Where do you think I'm going?"

"We believe that the quakes have destroyed a great part of the world," I said. "Look around you. We're in the mountains of Colorado—is it cold or even cool? Look at the position of the sun and moon, as they cross the sky. Check the stars at night. The world has turned upside down." I knew both of our parties were watching this discussion, so I put as much animation and arm movement into my recitation as possible.

"If anyone was going to come, they'd have been here by now. Have you seen any aircraft of any type? There may be people out there, but they're looking out for themselves."

Jason was motionless, as he let me continue without interruption.

"Now, you and the people you have with you can join with our group or you can continue on down the road. We'll let you through, if you want to go. You may find other people west of here, in Utah or further west, provided anything further west still exists. But I saw what you did in Butte City, last night and this morning before you left, and I can tell you nothing like that will be tolerated here."

My last statement was too much for him. He jumped to his feet. "You think you can dictate to me?" He was furious. "I've made it this far without your help, and I can live without your help now. Understood?"

"Sit down. You agreed to talk; let's talk."

I was mad, now, and he knew it. He sat, but it was his turn to talk. "I'll tell you something you don't know," he said. "I've had my way all my life, and it's going to stay that way. I won't take orders from you or any of your lousy crew, and you're not going to make a prisoner of me, because I'll kill first."

"What about the people with you, what about their wants and needs?"

"They want what I want," he said. "They get exactly what I give them. You won't mess with that, either. I won't let you, and that you also better understand."

We were both silent. I realized that Jason wasn't going to join with our group under any circumstances, and he wasn't about to let any of us try to talk some sense into any of his people. I think I had him convinced that we were as strong-minded as he and wouldn't put up with his wildness.

"We've been playing cat and mouse long enough," I said. "You understand our position, and now, I think I understand yours. If we let you through Highland Village, will you promise to keep going? I'll talk to the others, and we'll give you supplies, if you need them—food, fuel, or water. We won't follow or harass your group in any way, provided you don't come back."

He didn't answer, but at least he wasn't staring at me anymore. He was looking past me, toward the roadblock.

"I'll have to talk it over with the others," he said.

"Jason, I know you're the leader. Give me an answer or come back with a counterproposal."

He stood up abruptly. So did I.

"I'll think it over," he said.

"Good."

I held out my hand. He looked at it, then up at me, turned, and walked away. He disappeared into the trees. I turned and walked back to our roadblock.

George was waiting, and I told him what had happened as we walked back to our camp. It was dark already. I was hoping tomorrow was going to be a better day.

After supper, I called Steve on the radio. He thought he might come up and talk with Jason, but I said he was so antisocial that I didn't think he could ever be part of a society he couldn't control. I asked him about the observation post at Butte City, whether he wanted to keep it or close it down. Nothing was decided, so we signed off for the night. It had definitely been a tiring forty-eight hours, and I was ready for a good night's sleep.

George sent a ranger for me right at daybreak. Jason was at the road-block and wanted to see me; he wouldn't talk to anyone else. I dressed quickly and went to see what was on his mind.

Jason was about a hundred yards down the road, pacing back and forth. I went out to meet him. As I approached, he held out his hand for me to stop.

"You make that deal with your people?" he asked.

"You mean about the supplies?"

"No, I don't want anything you have. I want to go west, and the only road leads right through that town." He was pointing through Highland Village.

"Absolutely. You can go through if I have your word you won't make any trouble once you get past the roadblock, and that you won't come back and make any trouble."

"I want your word that there won't be any tricks on your side," he said. "You won't try to stop or talk to any of my people."

"You have my word," I said.

"Then open the road."

I walked back to the roadblock and signaled for George. He came running.

"George, let's open up the road. Jason as agreed to come through."

"Can you be sure he won't change his mind and charge this position, once we open up?"

"I can't be sure. We'll open it up and stand back. Get some rifle-men up in the barn area, but don't bring them out into the open, unless Jason tries some sort of trick. Once he's through, I want two people to shadow him, for at least two days."

While George was getting the riflemen placed and two more people ready to track Jason and his people, the rest of us got busy opening up the road. It took almost an hour, but everything was finally ready. Everyone withdrew to the valley or up to near the barns, except myself and one ranger. We stood by the block house and waited.

In a few minutes, we heard the Jeep motors roar to life, followed by the popping of the remaining motorcycle. When the group came out of the trees, Jason was in the lead, followed by several of his group. They were walking at a pretty good clip and were to the roadblock in a very short time. Jason didn't acknowledge I was there, but looked straight ahead.

True to his word, he kept going right on through the compound. He didn't look from side to side, but his followers did. As they passed me, one even waved. I politely waved, then put my hands behind my back. I didn't want anything to go wrong at a time like that.

They had just passed out of sight when I saw the two men George had assigned to follow fall in behind them, at a discreet distance. I let out a huge sigh of relief. George came up, and together, we stood there watching the road.

"What do you say we get busy moving some supplies?" I said. "What needs doing?"

"Let's go drive a tractor," he said, grinning.

*Chapter 12*

❧

# COMMUNICATIONS ESTABLISHED

The rest of the morning, we moved supplies from the barns, across the creek, through the valley, and left them on the plateau, so they could be reloaded and moved on down to Goldston when the Jeep came back. If we'd had more transport, it would have saved a considerable amount of manpower and time, but the blacksmith was having trouble keeping our meager hauling equipment on the road. I got a kick out of operating the old tractor, and was getting very proficient by the time we took a lunch break.

"To be perfectly honest," George said, "I was sure Jason would be back by now."

"I think he's had enough," I said. "Jason's getting to the point where he's afraid of losing the few people he has under his control. He made me promise that no one would talk to his people as they passed through, this morning, but if anyone in that group wants out, they'll find a way."

"Then, you don't think they'll be back."

"Not anytime in the near future, anyway. He knows we'll be on our guard."

"I hope so. I'm scared of a crazy man like him, especially when I know he has explosives. If he should go off the deep end, he might try to blow us up while we sleep."

"We'll have to wait and see," I said. "Our people should be back in a couple days; we should know more then.

"In the meantime, I'm going to take the afternoon off, if you can spare Goodman and me. I want to break out the radio equipment and set up a radio watch. We have some old radio logs and frequencies that were with the equipment. We might get lucky and find someone who can tell us a little about the outside world."

For the remainder of the afternoon, Goodman and I carried the radio and assorted wires, antennae, and accessories up to the animal pasture. The ground was pretty high there, and would be better for transmitting and receiving.

For the next two days, all the work at Highland Village went at a smooth clip. The majority of the people we had brought from Butte City were now throwing all their energy into whatever task they were assigned. Some had been evacuated to Goldston, among them were the children. Steve had thought it best to get them back in school. The contribution they could make now would be small compared to the role they would be required to fill in the years to come, with proper training and learning techniques applied.

The barns were completely free of all useable commodities, so attention was shifted to digging out the main house, Sam's house, and the old store and filling station, as well as the cabins that had escaped Jason's scorched earth policy. A large amount of building materials was extracted from the barns, and that had been stacked near the cabins, to be used by Sam and the Lancasters to help rebuild the farm. They had decided not to move to Goldston with our party, when we left.

The two men who had helped us the night we brought everyone out would also stay. Dave White and his wife were willing, for the time being, to let their two children reside in Goldston, in order to go to school. Jimmy Wills was not married, but had hopes of being able to woo one of the single girls, when things settled down a bit.

On the afternoon of the second day after Jason had headed west, we completed everything we had wanted to accomplish there. Sam had been good enough to let us take an enormous amount of food stuffs, equipment, grain, and other materials from the farm to Goldston. Now, it was our turn to help him. There were enough cinder blocks recovered from the two equipment barns to build a fairly large house and barn in the valley, for Sam and the Lancasters. Wood for framing and other building materials were also taken from the old houses and used in the new buildings. Sam did not want to build in the old town site, for fear that more visitors like Jason might come down the road. He'd be much better off in the little sheltered valley.

Dave and his family would move into the vacated Lancaster cabin, temporarily. They wanted, eventually, to build a house up on the plateau and farm there. Likewise, Jimmy would move into the small cabin Sam would vacate.

By now, the radio watch had been set up and was running smoothly. A lean-to was constructed for the equipment and a transmitting schedule of four times a day incorporated. We were lucky to have found so much of the equipment in operational order and that all of the operating manuals were also with it. The only thing that we were really missing was a battery to use when we wanted to receive, dial around, or leave the radio on and listen to some particular frequency that had been listed in the logs. In our present situation, someone had to hand-crank the small generator found with the equipment all the time, in order to keep the radio operational.

The generator was an easy setup. There was a small seat provided, like on a child's rocking horse, but instead of a head, there was a generator, and instead of ears for the horse, there were two handles to turn. It wasn't hard work, but became boring and tiring, if you had to crank for any length of time.

A wet cell battery, such as in the Jeep or tractor, could be used to power both the transmitter and receiver, and when we had time, something was going to be rigged up with one of the vehicles. We had extra wet cell batteries at Goldston, but I didn't want to bring one up there, then, when we planned to shift the radio watch down there, in a few days.

We had found two very good, long wire antennae with the equipment, but were only incorporating one in that location. Although the equipment would have been considered antique a month before, it was very well built, rugged, and would receive and transmit on most of the standard radio frequencies. If we could talk to just one other person outside our immediate area, we'd be much relieved. We were getting more anxious every day to find out about the rest of the world.

The introductory information had given instructions on sending and receiving Morse Code, and included a partial list of what were called "Q signals," an arrangement of any three letters of the alphabet beginning with a Q, which could represent a group of words or a complete sentence. For instance, you could send QRK, and the receiving station would know you wanted to know how you were being received at their station. The receiving station would only have to reply QRKS 5, very well, down to QRK 1, very poor. The only trouble would be if the other station operator didn't know how to read Q signals.

We were making one call using voice and one in Morse Code, both within a thirty-minute period. We'd decided to use Morse Code because the range was much farther, required less power, and might catch someone's attention through all the other static on the radio, where they might not hear a very weak voice signal.

The first call went out at 8 a.m., in voice, and would be transmitted for five minutes; then we would listen on that frequency for ten minutes. We would then switch over to Morse Code and transmit for five minutes; then listen again for ten minutes. We would repeat the calls again at noon, 6 p.m., and 10 p.m. All the messages were the same: "Any station on this frequency, this is Five Kilo Yankee Three Three (the call sign used by the original owner at Highland Village). We are calling to establish communications. If you cannot transmit at this time, we will be on the air again at noon, this date, or four hours from now."

After the ten minute listening period, we would send out our Morse Code call: "AA DE 5KY33 INT QSA QRK VVV VVV VVV." What we were saying in effect was, "Any station, this is 5KY33. What is the strength of my signal? What is the readability of my signal?" Following were the Vs, which were transmitted so that the receiving station could tune into our call. We would stay on the same frequency for the four calls, then consulting the logs, change frequencies the next day.

I had completed the 8 a.m. call in Morse Code, when both the ranger cranking the generator and I realized that the usual noises from down in the valley had suddenly stopped. Most of the crew had been working on Sam's new house, and we could usually hear hammering, sawing, or voices calling for one reason or another. Now, nothing—almost total silence. There were voices, but they didn't sound exactly right.

We secured the generator, and started working our way down the path into the valley. Long before we reached the housing area, I could see a big crowd forming, as if they were listening to someone in the center of the crowd. I heard someone say, "Here comes J.J.," and the speaker came from the crowd toward me. It was one of the men we had sent out to track Jason. My first thought was that we were about to have trouble with him, all over again.

Sam was right behind him, and as they approached he broke into a big smile. "You think Jason has come back," Sam said.

"I saw our tracker," I said.

"Well, it ain't all that bad. Go ahead, boy, and tell him."

By this time, everyone had gathered around us to hear the rest of the story.

The tracker began.

"As I was coming back into the village, I saw George over at the barns, and he told me to come over here and get Mrs. Brown and a couple of other people, to help bring in one of Jason's people."

"You brought one back here?" I asked.

"Well, not exactly. He's back down the road a couple miles. He's in pretty bad shape. Last night, Jason or one of his thugs shot him. He told us a story, but it was real confused. We found him this morning, about daybreak, on the road. He was trying to get back here."

"Why'd they shoot him?" Sam asked.

"The night before, there'd been a big argument over which road to take, a lot of shouting. We were so close, they could have seen us if they hadn't been fighting so much. It got so bad, Jason finally fired into the air to get order. From what we could hear after that, some guy wanted to take his girl and come back and join us. Jason said there was no way. He got real nasty, and beat the troublemaker real bad, while two other guys held him."

"Is that when they shot him?"

"No, things settled down after that, so we withdrew about a mile, so that we could make a fire and get something to eat. There were shots fired during the night, but there'd been shots the night before, so we didn't think anything about it."

Someone handed our storyteller a cup of water and a biscuit. He took a sip and a bite, then continued.

"It was our day to start back. We'd planned to check the place where they'd stopped, make sure they were still heading west, and start for home. Well, this morning, before we had time to check, we found this guy on the road, bleeding real bad. He'd been shot in the stomach."

I looked at Sam. "Has Thelma Brown been told about this?" I asked.

"She and two young fellows are already on the way to see about him."

"She didn't mind making the trip?"

"Not at all. She gathered up some medical supplies and was ready to go before her escort."

"How about Jason, is he still going west?"

"Yes, not real fast, though," the ranger said. "There's a whole bunch of tension in his group. I think some of them thought Jason was going to stop here and join with our group.

"Some, the real mean ones, wanted to come back the first night and attack. They were mad Jason made the deal in the first place; thought they could have taken us coming in."

George came up at that time, and the story was retold for him. We were all trying to digest what the courier had told us when Thelma returned with the wounded man. He was white as a sheet, and it looked like blood covered him from head to foot.

As Thelma neared, I stopped her. "Will he live?"

"He's lost a lot of blood, but from what I can see, no major organ has been damaged. If not, he'll pull through. What I need to do now is find out his blood type and get some donors. Without a transfusion, he's too weak to make it."

"Let us know when you're ready. I'm sure we can get enough donors."

She left to attend to her patient, while we broke up and started to get back to work. I held George back for a minute.

"George, I think it might be a good idea to send out another two men to watch Jason for awhile."

"Already taken care of. The same two men that just returned have volunteered to track him for at least a week, or until he's too far away from us to matter very much."

The Jeep returned with two empty wagons and the two men who had been the watch at Butte City. Steve had given instructions to pick them up and bring them to us. Nothing had moved down in the town after Jason left, and a patrol once a week through the area seemed sufficient, for the time being.

It was good to see the two men. Everyone we could get would make it that much easier to finish the work and move. George suspended the continuous watch at our roadblock and that gave us a little more manpower.

As soon as the workday was over, I went up to the radio shack to see how things were going. The Jeep wasn't staying with us at night, but would be hooked to two new loaded trailers and start back for Goldston every afternoon. Otherwise, we could have used the battery for power to the radio. Then it dawned on me, why not use the old tractor? There might be a slight problem getting it up to the shack, but it might be worth that trouble.

I went back down to the tent area, told George what I planned to do, and with the help of Goodman, we finally got the tractor to the top of the hill and hooked up to the radio by nightfall. To keep from using the tractor's fuel, we didn't run it while receiving. The operation did not draw much power from the battery if we left it on for only a few hours, and it gave our little hand-cranked generator a much needed rest.

We hooked up the tractor for the 10 p.m. call. Then, at 10:30, we put the battery on the receiver to listen for awhile. We picked four of the frequencies listed in the log book and listened to them, but with no luck. Around midnight, I decided to get some rest, and left Goodman and another ranger at the radio. They wanted to dial around and try some more of the frequencies in the log book. I said goodnight and headed for my tent.

Around 4 a.m., I was aware that I was being shaken, and very vigorously. It was Goodman. I hadn't had a chance to open my eyes before he was talking.

"J.J., we have them."

"What are you talking about?"

"The radio! We can hear someone—not very good, but we can understand some words."

I sat straight up, wanting to believe he was really there and that I wasn't dreaming. "Are you sure? You heard a voice?"

"No mistake. We were about to shut down for the night, and made one more run through the list of frequencies. The third one on the list was where we heard the voice. I don't know the frequency, but I remember it was the third one."

"Did you answer? Did they hear you?"

"We answered. I don't know if they heard us or not. I didn't want to take the time to unhook the tractor and hook up the generator, so I started the tractor and we answered as fast as possible."

I got dressed as fast as I could. I told Goodman to get George up and have him meet us at the radio. As I was heading up the hill, I could hear Goodman trying to explain to a very sleepy George Foxworth about the radio contact.

When I arrived at the radio site, the ranger was sitting with the earphones on, his hands pressed against them as if trying very hard to hear. The tractor was parked pretty close to the radio, and now that it was running, the only way you could hear was through a pair of phones.

I didn't say anything for fear that I would interrupt what he might be receiving, but I did notice some writing on the pad in front of him. He was still trying to hear, so I reached over and took a look at what he'd written—all kinds of notes, with words here and there, and the frequencies we'd been transmitting on. One of the frequencies had been circled. 11.775 megacycles, or megahertz, depending on how up-to-date your reference material might be. That was where the contact had been made.

I continued to wait, while he tried his best to figure out what was coming over the airwaves. Finally, he stopped and picked up the microphone.

"This is Five Kilo Yankee Three Three. Can't understand you. Please stay on the air. Will be back to you in a few minutes. Please stay on the air." With that, he dropped the mike and threw off the earphones.

"What have you got?" I asked.

"Not too much. Can we turn off that tractor? I can't hear a thing."

I got up and turned off the tractor. I didn't realize how loud it had been until it was shut off.

"Okay, now what have we got?"

He picked up his notes. "Not really very much we can use," he said.

"Did you get any conversation at all?"

"I think it was English. But the noise coming over the headphones and the tractor almost drowned him out. He kept fading in and out, which isn't unusual with these old sets and the long-wave propagation we're using. Maybe he's almost out of power, still able to receive but not transmit. I'm not sure of anything. We might have better contact in the morning."

"That may be true," I said. "But then again, our morning may be his night. If he's anywhere near us, why would he come up at four in the morning? But on the East Coast, it'd be about daybreak."

"If he's in Europe, it'd be the afternoon," the ranger said. "And we could guess like this for days, if we wanted."

George, Goodman, and a dozen other people who had been awakened by Goodman's journey through the camp joined us, and the excitement was running high. Another voice had joined our own. We didn't know where or who, but it was comforting to know there was someone out there.

We tried to make some sense of the notes that had been scribbled down, and the best we could come up with was: "NO POE ROW, MUSCLE NO SHOULDER, TELEPHONE BELLS." None of it made too much sense. ""NO POE ROW" could have been "no power." He was running out of power. That would have explained the weak signal. The rest of the notes were a complete mystery, especially the "TELEPHONE BELLS."

We were determined to make contact again. The same ranger was put back on the phones. We used the hand generator, this time, to keep down some of the noise. We were finally ready.

"Any station, any station, this is Five Kilo Yankee Three Three. Over."

We waited for a minute and tried again. "Any station, any station, this is Five Kilo Yankee Three Three. Over."

While we were waiting for an answer, we went through the logs and records to see who might possibly be on 11.755 megacycles, but the frequency was not one listed in the log. Goodman had written down the frequency when he'd heard someone there, and had circled it in case the receiver should be moved, so that he'd know where to go back to on the dial.

We tried again and again. Finally, we heard a reply—very weak. It was intermingled with so much atmospheric noise that no one who was in range of the radio speaker could make any sense of what was being said. I looked at the ranger with the headset. He shook his head. I looked at my watch. It was a quarter after five; the sun would be up soon.

"Tell him this and repeat it twice: Closing down now, will be back on the air in three hours."

He sent the message, and we waited. Something did come back, but still it was incomprehensible.

"Everybody take a break," I said. I figured everyone was keyed up and no one was going back to bed. "Let's get something to eat. The sun'll be up soon, and we still have plenty of hauling to do and buildings to build."

The crowd was slowly breaking up and heading back down into the valley for a little rest, a cup of coffee, or breakfast, before the workday was to start. George and I moved right along with it, talking about our situation and our new-found radio contact. We left the radio station unmanned. The tractor would be needed more down in the valley than at the radio site, so it was brought down with us.

Shortly before 8:00, Jefferson, the ranger who had made the radio contact earlier and who was our best code operator, Goodman, and myself were back at the radio site and ready to try contact again. We had taken the speaker off and patched in two pairs of earphones. If the signal was weak, we might pick out more of the signal with two people listening intently. The third person would power the generator.

Precisely at 8:15, we sent out our first call. Jefferson had been doing the voice transmissions, so he continued.

"Any station, any station, this is Five Kilo Yankee Three Three. Over."

Jefferson and I, with the earphones, were tense as we waited for an answer. There was no response for two minutes, so we sent out the call again. That time, we received an answer.

"This is Fred DeFreese. I hear you. Can you hear me?"

Jefferson and I yelled "Yes!" in unison. Poor Goodman, on the generator, couldn't hear a thing.

"We hear him, Goodman, and he hears us," Jefferson said.

"Says his name is Fred DeFreese."

"Jefferson, get back to him," I said. "Go down this list of questions."

He took my list and pressed the transmit button. "Fred, we'd like to know where you're located and a little about your situation. Over."

"I…we are at the Alexander Graham Bell Home and Museum. We are fine. Have survived tremors and tidal waves. We have some food, but not much. Plenty fresh water, much rain."

We were both writing down everything we heard. Goodman was looking over my shoulder while he cranked.

"J.J., where's the Bell Home and Museum?" Goodman asked.

"In Nova Scotia, I think. Jefferson, ask him if that's correct."

"Fred, are you in Nova Scotia?"

"Yes, where are you?"

"In the mountains of Colorado. We too have been through a great upheaval, here. We're doing very well, so far, but you are our first contact outside the valley in which we're located. Over."

Fred came right back. "I'm having problems with my power supply. If I lose you, will meet you back here in twelve hours. Before we lose contact, I'd like to know name of person to whom I'm speaking."

"My name is Thomas Jefferson. With me at the radio site are J.J. Darby and Berl Goodman. We're about a hundred strong, at present, but believe there are more people around; it's just a matter of finding each other. Our food supply is good, and we've found animals and seed for next year's harvest. We believe most of the world was destroyed."

I had to break in and stop Jefferson. He was very fast wearing Goodman out on the generator. "Jefferson, cut it off. We have to take a break; get Goodman off the generator."

I took off the headset and moved to take Goodman's place. Jefferson finished up his conversation. "I'll have to stop transmitting for awhile. Before I go, can you give us some idea of your situation? Over."

Fred, our new radio partner, was very slow and deliberate in his speech. It was evident by his pronunciation that he wanted to make sure we understood everything he said to us.

"There are over one hundred of us. Have had much sickness due to exposure and lack of proper care after tidal waves. We are very short on medication, especially need first aid items. Have heard code two or three times, but no one here can understand. You might try to contact them."

Now that Jefferson was not transmitting, I was able to stop the generator and take a break for a few minutes. We had a good, reliable contact out there, and he had, moments before, told us that he'd received code from somewhere. After my arms regained some of the strength that had been expended during the long transmitting session, I thought we'd better get back on the air.

"Jefferson, get back with two questions. First, a frequency on the code, and second, what's wrong with his power supply?" As I powered up the generator, a low, steady hum came back to the radio set.

"Fred, can you give us a frequency on the code, and what's wrong with your power supply? Over."

"I am not a radio operator and don't know too much about these sets, but the code comes in on band three and is somewhere between 4.5 and 4.7. Does that help any?"

I was hoping he was referring to 4.5 or 4.7 megacycles. If I was right, we might be able to raise that station, also.

"Ask him about the power supply," I said.

"What about your power? Anything we might help you with? Over."

"We have worked that out. We are now using batteries from an electric golf cart, but right now, we have no way to recharge. We had to change batteries to talk to you. My helper here is putting the batteries in parallel, so they will last longer."

"Understand. Will call you back in a few minutes."

Jefferson took off the headphones and let out a loud sigh. "He's weaker, again," he said. "I think his batteries are going."

I had not heard the last conversation, being on the generator, but as I read the message he'd received, I could understand why. They were operating on wet cell batteries, but had no way to recharge, and were trying to extend the life by operating with more than one battery at a time. I wished there were some way to help, but the distance between us was better than two thousand miles. What really hurt was that we had a very good store of medical supplies and he had next to nothing, and there wasn't a thing we could do to help their situation.

I told Jefferson to call Fred, again, and tell him we'd try to get through to the code station and see where they were located. We might be lucky and find they were a great deal closer than we were. Jefferson also told Fred that we would sign off for then and call back the same time, the next morning.

Fred was glad to be in contact with someone else, and said our call had given everyone there renewed hope. We assured him that he had done plenty for our morale, as well. With that, we shut down our radio station.

We finally unscrambled the first message received from Fred. "NO POE ROW": no power. "ALEXANDER SCRAMBLE": Alexander Graham Bell. "MUSCLE NO SHOULDER": museum, Nova Scotia. "TELEPHONE BELLS": he was trying to tell us "the inventor of the telephone."

*Chapter 13*

⟨๛⟩

# HIGHLAND VILLAGE/REBUILT

When we made our way to Sam's new house, we were swamped with questions about the contact. It took awhile, but we finally answered questions to everyone's satisfaction. We created another stir when we told the group that we had another station to contact, later on in the morning. We told them that we didn't know much about the other station, except that Fred had said all their transmissions were in Morse Code.

The Jeep arrived about ten o'clock, and we quickly confiscated it to use in our radio operations. It would be a great improvement over the tractor we had tried to use, and we all were grateful that we would not have to use the hand-cranked generator, at least for awhile.

The tractor would be used to transport the loaded wagons to Goldston. Now that all the goods were stacked and waiting for shipment, on the plateau, there would be no need for a vehicle to bring supplies over from the old town site, anymore. On its last trip, the tractor would stay in Goldston, and Mrs. Donley would use it in her farming operations. Sam did not want to keep it, due to the repairs that would have to be made from time to time and the gasoline shortage that would develop in the near future. He said a horse and plow would do just fine for the farming he had planned.

We had the Jeep set up and hooked to the radio by noon, the next scheduled time to start our radio calls. We ran through our regular schedule, and added another fifteen minutes to try contact on the 4 to 5 megacycle range. Jefferson was again our primary operator, because he was now more experienced with our radio and he

179

could operate in Morse Code. We would be able to listen for hours without having to start the Jeep, and cover more of the frequency band. The Jeep's battery was strong enough that we could transmit for a limited period of time, if the need arose.

With everything running smoothly at the radio site and with the building of Sam's new residence nearing completion, there wasn't much left to do up there. The tractor had been hitched to two fully-loaded wagons, and was ready to start back for Goldston in the afternoon. About half of our work crew were to leave, taking with them five of the cows, one bull, one more horse, and four of the piglets.

We'd wanted to build a stockyard and barn for the remaining animals, but Sam said that was a project he wanted to work on with the Lancasters and the others who had decided to stay there.

"Something like that will keep us out of trouble for awhile," he said. "Then we can come down there and pester you folks, when we finish."

There was no radio contact during the noontime calls. After the tractor, wagons, and people were on the trail, George, Sam, and I walked over to the old town site for one more look around. It seemed so tranquil, hushed, and deserted, after all of the hustle and bustle of the previous weeks. The barn and ground around it looked rather neat, considering all the destruction when we'd first arrived. Stacked on what had been the parking lot were huge stacks of cinder block, brick, lumber, and even a couple of kegs of nails.

"You know, it looks like we were going to build here," Sam said. "The people you brought up and those from Butte City are a hard-working crew. Look how neat all the stuff is stacked. But it won't be there long. We plan on using some up on the plateau, for animal shelters and barns, and I'm hoping from time to time some of the folks down in Goldston might want to come up here and build. We'll probably need more than this in a year or so."

"Are you going to put something up here, or build everything in the valley?" I asked.

"Oh, everything in the valley. Not here, not again. Not unless things get back to some kind of normal." Sam was shaking his head from side to side and looking down the road toward Butte City. "I'm afraid someone like Jason might come down that road one day and, we'd have to go through this mess all over again."

I was looking down the road as he talked, and realized that the Highland Village sign had been taken down. The road was completely clear where the roadblock had been. George's cinder block house, which he called his strong point, had been disassembled. As we were walking back toward the river, I'm sure George and I were thinking the same—that that might be the last time we would see the place.

"I think, after we get back to Goldston and things settle down, I'm going to bring Nancy and the boys up here for awhile," George said. "It's amazing how much different this place is than down there. The trees alone are worth the trip."

The trees were much more plentiful, and it seemed to be cooler, even though both locations were at about the same elevation. Highland seemed to reflect a mountain valley more so than did Goldston.

"George, you've talked me into it. Susan would fall in love with this valley. After a week, I might never get her back to Goldston."

"You boys do that," Sam said. "Get the ladies and kids and come on back. Not more than two miles west and a little south, there's a valley—I hope it's still there—that you'd both love."

He looked from one to the other of us. "Well, what do you say?" he asked.

"You're too fast for us," George said. George was looking to me for encouragement.

"We still have a lot to get accomplished down south."

"Well, I like you both, and the invitation will stand. Whenever you want to come back, let me know, and I'll come get you and take you there."

"You know that our invitation to you still stands," I said. "You're welcome in Goldston. We could use your expertise down there."

"Well, I thought about it some." He paused for a minute. "You know, Mrs. Donley wanted me to come back," he said. "Said she was tired of being the only real old person around. I thought about it some, thought we might team up and become everybody's grandpa and grandma. So you youngsters might see me come courting down that way, before long. Only thing is I would take away the only person who really knows farming."

"You wouldn't have to take her away. Stay with us. The Lancasters could look after this place for you, and it's not far."

"Looks to me, what we have," Sam said, "is me trying to talk you into coming up here and you trying to get me to come down there."

"Yes, Sam, but we have the advantage," George said, without smiling.

"What advantage? I got the best looking country, best farmland, trees, and water. What do you have?"

Now George had a smile on his face. "We have Mrs. Donley."

We were all in good spirits as we crossed the creek and headed to the valley. It came to me that we ought to build a bridge of some type across the creek. Every time we came back and forth, we ended up with wet feet.

"Did anyone ever ask you about a bridge across the creek?" I said. "At least a foot bridge?"

Sam was way ahead of me. "I thought about it, especially when so many people were working on the other side, but then I thought that a bridge or even stepping stones were an arrow pointing the way to the valley, so I thought the best thing to do would be to leave it as is. We won't be crossing the creek again, anytime soon, now that all the work over there is finished."

When we got back, the crew was on a break. The building was almost completed, at least the part we were going to do. Sam thought that was as good a time as any to thank everyone for their help, and wanted us to convey to the people who had left already how he felt. Everyone assured him they felt the same way.

The end of the workday was sad, in a way. It was time to pack up and head for home. Not that everyone wasn't anxious to get back to Goldston, but there was a genuine family feeling between the people who had come up there to work. As we sat around the fire, that night, the talk wasn't of things that had happened at other times and places, but stories of what had taken place there, at Highland, in the past couple of weeks.

I went to the radio shack for the 6 p.m. calls, and stayed there until we completed the 10 p.m. calls. No signals were received. We stayed in and around where we thought the code station would be, but with no luck. The next day, we would try to reach Fred in Nova Scotia, to see if he had more information for us that could more closely pinpoint the station.

By daybreak, everyone was up, as usual. The morning fires were going, and breakfast was being prepared. The difference, that day, was that instead of everyone getting ready to go to his or her specific job, everyone was packing for the trip.

As soon as I'd washed and dressed, I went up on the plateau to get the radio ready for the morning calls. Jefferson was going to take a well-deserved morning off from the headphones. He said that, all the previous night, he'd kept hearing static coming through the air, long after the radio was closed down and he was away from the set.

There wasn't really much to do for a morning setup. I started the Jeep about 7:45, to make sure I had a fully-charged battery when I tried to call Fred. I then made a list of questions I wanted to ask, and waited.

At 8 a.m. sharp, I started making the planned calls. No signals were received by either voice or Morse Code. My code wasn't anywhere as speedy or accurate as Jefferson's, but I didn't think I would be receiving a speed demon, trying to burn up the airwaves.

I didn't want to spend too much time elsewhere, before talking to Fred. With no contact by 8:30 on any of the frequencies, I put the transmitter on the Nova Scotia frequency, tuned the receiver to the same, and pressed the mike.

"Nova Scotia, this is Colorado. Over."

I was sure that if Fred were listening, he would know who we were without going through the formality of proper call signs. I waited for over a minute, and was just about ready to give another call.

"Colorado, this is Nova Scotia. You have a good, strong signal. Can you hear me?"

"Fred, this is J.J. You're coming in loud and clear, this morning. What have you done to your transmitter?"

"We have some new batteries for transmitting and some not-so-new to listen. Also, we found another antenna—what is called a directional—and set it up to transmit in your direction."

"Outstanding. I don't want to keep you on the air too long, today, but have a couple things. First, we will be moving our radio station to another location, either this afternoon or early this evening. If you don't hear from us tomorrow morning, at the regularly scheduled time, please listen for us at noon and again at 6 p.m. Disregard that...wait. I'll be back to you in a minute."

I'd almost blown that. They weren't on our time, and I wasn't sure what time zone they were in, or if they even had any way to tell accurate time.

"Fred, this is J.J., again. I'm not sure of the difference in our time, so if you don't hear from us at the scheduled morning call, listen for us every four hours, until we establish contact again. We might have to move our antenna, or even the whole station, once we get to our new location. Over."

"Understand that. Anything else?"

"Do you have any more you can tell us about the code station you referred to yesterday? Over."

There was a very long pause. I didn't call, because I figured they were putting their heads together to see if they could come up with anything else. I waited for what was at least five minutes.

"We have heard the Morse Code several times, have tried to make contact, but cannot communicate. We do not have anyone here who can understand. We hear them mostly at night, no special time."

"Thanks, Fred. We're going to try and contact them again. Can you pinpoint your location for me, in case we do make contact with someone close to you? Over."

"We are confined to an island. Most of the land has been covered with water. Before the tidal waves, we would have been located in the northern part of the province, approximately twenty-five miles south of Port Sydney."

"Have you seen any boats or ships? Is there any kind of useable vehicle there?"

"Nothing that will run. Have seen no ships. We are busy building a craft to see if anyone is left on nearby islands."

"All right, my friend, no more questions for now. Hope to hear from you in the morning. We'll use call sign Goldston, tomorrow. That is the name of the town where we'll set up the equipment. In fact, it'll be our home for awhile."

"Good luck, Goldston. Will talk to you tomorrow."

After shutting everything down, I thought about packing the equipment up for the trip to Goldston, but thought I'd wait and make the noon calls, first. I had a lot of company, now. Everyone was packing and moving up to the staging area, next to the last of the loaded wagons. The two empty wagons that would be brought back that morning by the tractor would stay there, and we'd keep the two now packed and ready to go.

George and Jefferson came up with Sam, wanting to know how the communications with Nova Scotia were going. I told them about the morning call, and showed them the notes I had written.

"If only we could contact the code station," I said. "They seem to hear it quite often, so I'm inclined to think it must be in their vicinity."

"But if it's a Morse station and on a low frequency, they could be bouncing the signal off the ionosphere for greater distance," Jefferson said. He had a point. "A station with no voice capabilities couldn't be too sophisticated, not in this day and age."

It was hard to imagine that we had gone from a world of instant communication, using television, radio, telephone, computers, satellites of very description, microwaves, and instant transportation from one place to another to worrying about contact with one small radio station that couldn't even transmit a voice conversation.

We heard the popping engine of the old tractor. It was a mile or more away, but that distinctive sound could be heard for a long distance. Everyone was up and on their feet, anticipating the arrival of their transportation home. More were arriving from the valley, and Miriam and Ronald Lancaster had come up to tell everyone good-bye.

As the tractor and wagons came into view, I saw that the lead wagon was loaded with a cargo of people. I saw Steve wave to the group nearest the waiting wagons. Also aboard were a couple of the rangers and some of the people from Butte City, who had been sent down the trail only a couple days before. There were also some of Susan's rangers, Mrs. Donley, and finally, I spotted the one person I'd been looking for, Susan. She had been searching the crowd for me, but I saw her first. As I started for the wagon, she finally found me and a bright, big, beautiful smile came over here face.

The tractor driver brought his cargo up to the staging area, and stopped next to the equipment that was to be loaded. Everyone was relieved when he shut down the noisy engine. I rushed up to the wagon, and helped Susan down. I was so glad to see her, so surprised, that I began to cry. I hugged her tighter, trying to hide my tears.

"J.J., when was the last time you had a meal? You look absolutely famished. It's a good thing I talked Steve into letting me come up here. I bet right now you'd be telling him that you have to stay a couple more days to finish up some work. Am I right?"

"Well, there might be a chance of a radio contact that would be lost if we moved. I was thinking of keeping the radio equipment up here for a day or so."

"You need a rest. I want you to come back with us. Couldn't someone else stay?"

"Let's go talk to Steve. Have you heard about the radio contact?"

"We've kept up with everything."

As we were nearing the group gathering around Steve, I noticed that Nancy Foxworth had also come up, and remarked to Susan that I hadn't noticed her until then.

"She wanted to make the trip as bad as I did. She knows George is a lot like you. And just look at him, thin as a rail; his shirt looks like its hanging on a metal coat hanger."

"Now, come on. We don't look that bad."

"When was the last time you looked in a mirror?" She had me there, we didn't have a mirror.

George and I took Susan and Nancy on a grand tour of the valley, across the creek, and through the old town site. They were more enthusiastic about the work we'd done than I'd thought they would have been. They would have a question answered and come right back with another.

The time came for the noon radio calls, and Susan wanted to be there to see the operation, so we left old Highland Village and went back up to the plateau. When we got there, Jefferson was already setting up for the next contact. He was reading the notes I had taken from that morning's calls.

I had left the radio on Fred's frequency when I'd shut down that morning, and that's where it was when Jefferson had turned the receiver on. We were in no way prepared for what we heard. It was CW—continuous wave transmission. We first heard the letter v being transmitted over and over, three vs at a time, with a short break in between. That was standard radio procedure.

Jefferson and I both scrambled for a paper and pencil. Neither one of us could read each letter, if the station should start transmitting something other than the letter v, and that might happen at any time. Very shortly, he should send his call letters, the letters of the station, and the frequency he was transmitting on, but we were surprised again.

VVV GOLDSTON CAN YOU HEAR ME. We wrote out the message as it came over the air.

"Unbelievable," Jefferson said.

"He had to be listening to me when I was talking to Fred," I said. "I told him we were going to move to Goldston. Get back to him quick; let him know we're here."

Jefferson picked up the key, put the earphones on, and started tapping a reply. HEAR YOU 5 BY. STAND BY FOR MESSAGE.

While he was transmitting, I was writing out a list of questions. I passed the questions to Jefferson, and he started transmitting. CAN YOU COME UP IN VOICE. WHAT IS YOUR LOCATION. TELL US SOMETHING ABOUT YOUR SITUATION. OVER.

Jefferson did not transmit the letters OVER, but sent the correct letter for the word, K. We waited for a reply.

I could see that this type of communication was going to be awfully slow. The other station was undoubtedly writing down a message to us before transmitting, which of course was the easiest thing to do.

About four minutes passed before we heard a faint signal start and get stronger. He had his key depressed, as if to load his antenna, trying to get the maximum transmitting distance from his equipment for this particular frequency. Then he started transmitting.

NO VOICE FOR TRANSMITTING. ONLY SMALL SET FOR PRACTICING CW OPERATIONS. WE ARE AT SITE OF NAVY BASE, NEW LONDON, CONNECTICUT. HEARD YOUR TRANSMISSION TO CANADA. WILL HELP WITH SUPPLIES. CAN UNDERSTAND HIS TRANSMISSION. K.

We were delighted with that piece of news. I told Jefferson to have him wait while I drafted another message.

Nobody else knew what was being said. They could hear the code coming over, but no one else could read the signals. I handed the message we'd just received to Steve, and he passed it back to the anxiously awaiting crowd.

I finished the message and gave it to Jefferson. He read it over, to familiarize himself with its contents, then started the transmission.

WILL TELL CANADA THAT YOU CAN HELP. WHAT ARE YOUR PLANS. WE WILL PASS ON INFORMATION. TELL US ABOUT YOUR AREA. WERE YOU HEAVILY DAMAGED IN QUAKES. HOW STRONG ARE YOU IN PERSONNEL AND SUPPLIES. WILL DRAFT MESSAGE TELLING YOU ABOUT US. PLEASE STANDBY. K.

While Jefferson was transmitting, I was busy drafting another message telling them where we were located, our situation, and that we were doing quite well, for the time being.

The station came back. WAIT. DRAFTING LONG MESSAGE. AR.

The fact that he sent the letters AR meant that he knew something about Morse Code. Those two letters were the international sign for "out," or "no further transmissions at this time."

Excitement was running quite high in our group. The first message had been handed around and read and reread numerous times. Everyone was anxious to hear more. Many in our number had relatives in and around the Atlantic coastal area. We waited an extremely long time before the station finally came back on the air. Even though no one could understand the code, I could hear a sigh of relief when the signal began coming through.

GOLDSTON, THIS IS JERRY. WE ARE IN BUNKER ON NAVY BASE. BASE DESTROYED. QUAKES DESTROYED OUR HOMES, MANY KILLED, BUT TIDAL WAVES MUCH WORSE. WATER COVERED LAND FOR 24 HOURS. VERY LITTLE LEFT. WE ARE IN MOUNTAINS NOT SEA SHORE, NOW. NO CITIES AROUND. HAVE EXPLORED A LITTLE. SEEN SOME PEOPLE. MANY NOT FRIENDLY. WAIT. MUST STOP NOW.

Jefferson sent back, UNDERSTAND AND WAITING. AR.

The message made a noticeable stir, as it was passed around. Jefferson and I were both copying, as we were both very rusty on code and didn't want to miss anything. Jerry was sending slowly. I didn't know if he could go any faster or not, but we were delighted with the speed, which we believed to be between eight and ten words per minute. Not the fastest transmission in the world, but we were communicating, and that was the important thing.

While waiting, we discussed what had been received already. It appeared the East Coast had been wiped off the face of the earth. We already knew that eastern Canada had become a series of islands.

Jerry was coming back on the air. We could hear him depress his key before he started to transmit. That accomplished two things: first, he knew his transmitter was working, and second, it gave us time to pick up our pencils and get ready to copy.

TROUBLE WITH POWER SUPPLY. HAD TO REPAIR. HAVE ONE KW GENERATOR FOR LIGHTS AND TO USE ON RADIO. FOOD LIMIT, BUT HAVE PLENTY HOSPITAL EQUIPMENT. FOUND MANY BANDAGES AND OTHER MEDICAL SUPPLIES SEALED IN METAL CONTAINERS. WILL LEAVE TOMORROW FOR CANADA WITH SAME. TELL THEM TO WATCH FOR US. THREE MEN. WILL TAKE A FEW DAYS. HAVE TO FIND AND REPAIR BOAT. THOUGHT CANADA UNDERWATER UNTIL HEARD SIGNAL. NO OTHER CONTACTS BUT YOU AND CANADA. WE CAME HERE FROM NEW LON-DON TOWN. FOUND RADIO WITH OTHER EQUIPMENT. SMALL SET USED FOR TRAINING. WE WOULD LIKE TO KNOW YOUR SITUATION. K.

As soon as Jefferson and I compared notes, he started sending our reply, as requested. I took the message just received to Steve. He read it over, and passed it along to the waiting crowd.

"What do you think?" I asked.

"I think our worst dreams about this disaster are coming true. Here's proof that this thing was widespread."

I was trying to visualize what the East Coast might look like, now. "I wonder if any of our people on the dig in Mexico survived?"

"I'm beginning to think that there are plenty of small pockets of people around the earth. I'm curious about Jerry meeting people and some not being friendly," Steve said.

I went back to the radio to get another message ready. I also started the Jeep; the battery would be pretty well drained with so much transmitting. The Jeep wasn't very loud when running, and headphones would drown out the sound.

I had not quite finished drafting the new message when I was suddenly aware that the crowd around the radio was dispersing and everyone was busily loading the wagons with their belongings, as well as the few remaining items of equipment. The tractor was started and hitched to the two wagons, and put in position for the return trip to Goldston. Steve came over to me and said he was going to get started back before it was too late, so they wouldn't have to travel after dark.

"I'd appreciate it if you and Jefferson would stay here and complete the traffic with the Connecticut station. If it's too late in the afternoon to start back, wait until morning."

"Sure. I'll stay up all night, if he wants."

"We'll shove off, now. See you tomorrow."

Steve turned to walk away, as Susan was approaching. "We're about ready to leave," he said to her. "You're just about to miss your ride."

"I don't have anything important to do in Goldston, so I'm going to spend the night up here, with J.J."

I was delighted. "You want to stay up here, or wait down in the valley until we get through with traffic?" I asked.

"In the valley. Mrs. Lancaster said she could use some company, so I'll be down there."

She turned and started toward the valley. Jefferson was still transmitting, and the tractor was pulling the wagons slowly down the road and out of sight. I could scarcely hear the popping, as it departed. The plateau began to grow quiet.

As soon as Jefferson was through with our return traffic, I told him I'd take over. There was a lull on the air for awhile, as the people in Connecticut read over our last message. While waiting, I looked over the message I intended to transmit when Jerry came back up again. We still wanted to know how many persons were at their location and if they planned on staying there or moving on. If possible, I was hoping for information about the people they had met and how they had survived the tidal waves and the long period of being under the water.

The radio once again came to life. Jerry said they understood our message, and did we have any further traffic? I transmitted the message I had prepared, and waited for a reply.

UNDERSTAND. PLEASE WAIT. SHUT DOWN ONE HOUR. GENERATOR NEEDS REST. K.

I transmitted back that I understood, and closed down. After shutting down the equipment, I decided to go down in the valley and have some lunch, rather than sit by the radio. As luck would have it, I met Susan as I descended the trail. She was bringing me something to eat, as though she'd been reading my mind.

We turned around and went back up to the radio site. It was the first time we'd been alone together since the quakes, and we spent the next hour telling each other what had been happening in our independent lives, during the separation. After an hour, I turned the receiver on to await the message I was expecting from Jerry.

"I was worried about you," she said. "We felt helpless, down there, knowing those people were trapped in Butte City."

"I know. I was scared that Jason might head for your roadblock, once they were rescued."

Our conversation was interrupted by a call from Jerry. GOLD-STON. HAVE MESSAGE. CAN YOU COPY.

I told him to wait. Jefferson hadn't returned, and I wanted to get him up there. With two of us copying, there'd be less chance of missing something and making Jerry transmit again.

Within five minutes, I was back and told Jerry to go ahead and transmit. He was on the air for almost an hour—not constantly, because he had to rest his generator every so often—but once he'd finished, and Jefferson and I had put our notes together, we had a pretty good idea of the situation at Jerry's location.

He and the rest of his family, a total of seven people, had taken refuge in an old storage shelter. It had been built originally in the 1950s, as a bomb shelter, made to withstand the shock of heavy bombs, and was well equipped to take the shock from the quakes, which hit first. It had been buried in the earth, and then wave action had actually drawn the shelter out of the ground. The shelter was constructed of plastic, foam, and rubber, and had started bobbing around like a cork, in the floods. They'd managed to stay nearly upright by huddling in the middle of the floor.

They didn't have any windows, so they couldn't see anything that was going on outside, but could hear the waves hitting the shelter, from time to time. When they did run aground, Jerry's father had opened the hatch and found they were near the naval base.

The floods had devastated what had been left by the quakes and tidal waves. Huge mountains surrounded them. The country was harsh; not a living tree stood, as far as they could see, not a building was intact. Not a living soul was to be seen for many days.

Their number had reached a total of twenty-seven by the time they had contacted us. They had seen many more while out exploring the countryside, but many were not friendly. Some were trying to protect a food supply, or had met others and been treated harshly. Jerry's father had become the head of the group, although all members were usually in on decisions.

They planned on a move to a valley to the south, but wanted to search their location for anything useful before leaving. They would delay the move until the three they were sending by boat to Canada returned.

Their power for lights and the radio was provided by some small, one-kilowatt generators they had found. The gasoline was procured from wrecked vehicles they uncovered, whose tanks hadn't been contaminated by the floods.

Food was in short supply, but many plants were starting to grow. Trees were sprouting everywhere, and they were quite sure that, before very long, they would be in a dense forest.

The weather in general was very hot, much more so than prior to the upheavals. It had rained for days, and many shocks had been felt in the area until recently. They were overjoyed to have made contact on the radio, and hoped that someday we would meet.

Without anything else to transmit, we told Jerry that we would close down for the time being, and would call him again as soon as we were set up in Goldston. He acknowledged our transmission, and we shut down the equipment. Together, Jefferson and I wrote out a report of our transmissions with Jerry. We added verbs and adjectives to his account, because he transmitted a shortened text, to save time and transmitting power, but we didn't change the text of his message. Quite a story, and undoubtedly, we didn't know it all, yet. We seemed to be in good shape, compared to what they had gone through and would have to endure during the weeks, months, and years to come.

It was getting late, too late to pack up and move to Goldston that afternoon, so we shut down everything for the night. We decided not to make the evening calls, but wait and try calling Fred in the morning, to tell him about our contact, before we packed up and moved to Goldston.

We passed an enjoyable evening with the people remaining at Highland Village. Sam was interested in our conversation on the radio. We talked long into the night about what had happened to us in the previous few weeks. We were all becoming more aware of our isolation.

"It's strange," Sam said. "We're in our valley, and two thousand miles away, more or less, are people in another valley who we can talk with but can't get to or help. It's a bad situation. I thought I'd seen a lot of things in my life, but this is beyond my comprehension."

He was looking into the cooking fire outside the old Lancaster house and shaking his head. "No, sir. If you'd told me this was going to happen, I'd have sent you packing. This destruction is hard to believe."

We were all lost in our own thoughts about the catastrophe we'd been through, had seen, and what we imagined the rest of the world had undergone.

"But that's all behind us," Sam said. "I suggest we break up this wake, get some rest, and make the best of what little world we have left to us. J.J., you promise me that you'll bring Susan back up here and stay with us for awhile. And you, young feller." He looked over at Jefferson. "You come back up here and teach this old dog how to send that Morse Code."

We both assured Sam that we would return to see him, from time to time, then we all retired to get some rest. We still had a very busy day ahead of us, the next day.

Shortly after daybreak, we were up, dressed, and ready to go. Sam, the Lancasters, Dave White and his family, and Jimmy Wills were all up at the radio site to hear the final radio broadcast with Canada, and to see us on our way.

We loaded all of our belongings aboard the Jeep, and prepared the radio. Shortly before 8 a.m., we turned on the receiver and went through our list of frequencies, but found no one there. At 8:30, we set both transmitter and receiver on 11.775 and gave Fred a call. He came right back to us, almost before we were finished with our transmission.

"Hi, Goldston. Heard some of your transmissions with code station, yesterday. How are they doing, and where are they? Over."

"Good news, Fred, They're located on what was the Connecticut coast. They tell us the terrain has changed a bit. They were under the impression that all land up your way was underwater. Over." I stopped there, to give the transmitter a breather and to make sure Fred was receiving my transmission.

"You told them different, of course," Fred said. "Glad to hear there are more people surviving. Are they doing all right?"

"Quite so. They've been monitoring your transmissions, and are aware of your need for medical supplies. They're located at or near either a hospital or where medical supplies were stored and have an overabundance. Therefore, they are going to send a three-man party your way with these type items, and want you to watch out for them. Over."

Fred didn't come right back that time. There was a very long pause.

"My friend, you have made this group of people very happy with your last transmission. If my code friends are listening, we thank you very much for your kindness, and will be eagerly awaiting your party's arrival. If we can be of any service to either of you in the future, please don't hesitate to ask. We are so pleased to find that there are caring people still left in this wounded world of ours. Again, thank you both very much. Over."

"Don't have any more, for now. We delayed our departure for Goldston until we could send you the news. If you have nothing further, we'll close down for now, and call you tomorrow morning from Goldston."

"Nothing else, now. Have a good trip. Hope to talk to you again tomorrow. Fred out."

We immediately began to take the radio apart and pack it for shipment. The antennae were brought down and packed, and we were soon ready to leave. All the villagers from Highland said their goodbyes.

Sam came up to me, a big smile upon his face. "Son, don't be a stranger. You take some time off and bring Susan up here and visit, from time to time. Now, don't forget."

"I won't forget, Sam. You have done so much for us, we can't forget you."

"Didn't do nothing but what was right and proper."

"We appreciate your letting us take the radio equipment, along with everything else you gave up."

"I couldn't operate it, anyway," he said. "I'd appreciate it if you kept us informed of any news."

"We'll sure do that, even if we have to send a special courier up to you."

We pointed the Jeep towards Goldston and left. We were closing another chapter in our lives. What had been an operation to get rid of Jason and his group, and to rescue a whole town's population from his control, had turned out very well, and we'd made some very good friends.

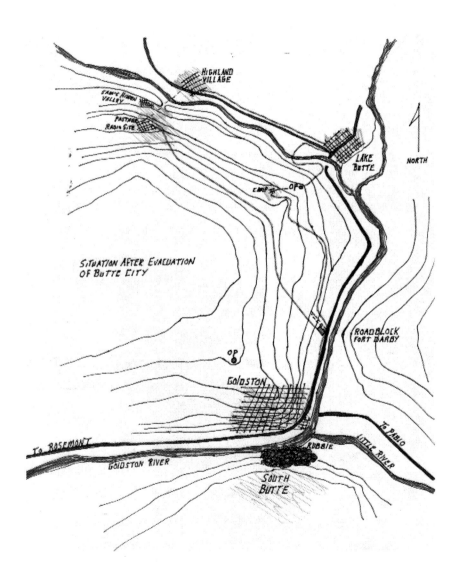

HIGHLAND VILLAGE

CRANE RIVER VALLEY

PASTURE RADIO SITE

LAKE BUTTE

NORTH

CMP OP

SITUATION AFTER EVACUATION OF BUTTE CITY

OP

ROADBLOCK FORT DARBY

GOLDSTON

To ROSEMONT

RUBBLE

To PABLO

LITTLE RIVER

GOLDSTON RIVER

SOUTH BUTTE

*Chapter 14*

❧

# RETURN TO GOLDSTON

The trip to Butte City took no time at all. We reached the turn south for Goldston almost before I knew it. Jefferson and Susan had never seen Butte City, so I stopped the Jeep about where I had left my old gray mare, a few days before, and we walked the distance to where the observation post had been for the previous few weeks. The rangers had long gone and taken everything with them, but as with any place that had been occupied for a period of time, it wasn't hard to find.

We hadn't had rain for awhile, and the town looked dry and dusty. There was a slight breeze blowing from the northwest. I pointed out where Thelma's hospital had been located and the pavilion where Jason had stayed with his henchmen. The fires and explosions had completely destroyed all of the habitable buildings. There were plenty of foundations, but not much else.

"He didn't leave too much for the next guy," Susan said.

"Not much at all. If he'd just left the pavilion," I pointed to a large hole in the ground, with pieces of wood, plaster, and brick lying all around, "we could have used it as a starting point for rebuilding the town," I said.

Susan seemed somewhat shocked. "What do you mean?"

"If we grow too much, down at Goldston, this would be a good place to start another town. I've about made up my mind that the world as we knew it is gone, and we're going to have to make it the best way we can."

"I was thinking the same thing," Jefferson said. "That could be a nice little town, all cleaned up and rebuilt."

"This is so depressing," Susan said. "Let's get going."

We turned and started to leave, when Jefferson noticed the truck parked on the south side of the creek.

"Look at the old truck down there. Do you think we could get it running?"

Sam's old truck. Jason had brought it back from one of his raids on Highland. They'd had it on the south side of Lead Creek when the heavy rains had come. After that, it had been impossible to get it back to the northern bank.

"I'd bet that, with some work, we could. We'll have to talk it over with Syminski when we get back; see what he says."

We were all quiet as we walked back to the Jeep. I wasn't in any big hurry, so we took it easy as we followed what, by then, was the well-worn path from Highland Village to Goldston. The trail was almost a highway, packed down very well, which would make it useable in case of bad weather.

As we drove along, I realized how much the countryside was changing. The high plateau we were driving along had been dry, sandy, and covered mostly with sage, cactus, and rocks. With the huge amount of rain we'd had and other changes in atmospheric conditions, the area was undergoing a complete revision. Small trees were now growing in a few places, and grass covered a large amount of the ground. There were tropical flowers growing in and around the rocks.

We drove slowly down off the high ground, and as we descended to the valley floor, we came in south of the oblong stone structure that had been dubbed Fort Darby. But what I saw was in no way the same as when I last was there.

There were people busy at one task or another everywhere. The old, small, stone fort was crammed full of supplies, and there were new houses being built south of the fort and on both sides of what was now the main road to Butte City. I saw that, across the river, the ground was being broken up for crops to be planted.

I stopped the Jeep and looked around in amazement. Where had all the people come from? I saw Rich Arthur seated at a desk, in what was the guard room. He looked up at that moment, and for an instant, was as stunned to see us as we were to see him. All at once, he jumped up from his chair and came running toward the Jeep. I stepped out to meet him. We shook hands.

"J.J., it's so good to see you," he said. "And Susan, I'm glad you're back. I need your help with the accounting something awful. You're Jefferson, I believe."

Jefferson nodded that he was, still somewhat bewildered by all the commotion.

"What's happening here?" I asked. "I mean, where did all of these people come from?"

"Things are moving so fast," he said. "Come into my office."

He indicated the open door to the old guard shack. Once we were all seated, and Mr. Arthur had given his lists and some instruction to his assistant, he began to explain.

"For the past couple of weeks, as you know, we've been busy with all the supplies that were coming in from Highland Village. We kept up, but it was tough at times to keep track of everything."

He stopped now and looked over at Susan. "And let me tell you, Susan, Beth can't wait for you to get back. Poor girl has worked herself ragged. She says you're the only person in the world who has the methodical mind needed at a time like this. Fair warning, you'll be pressed into service as soon as you get back.

"But back to my story. Let's see, it was two days ago that Tim Engles, Johnny Burnside, and another ranger returned, just after Steve had left on his trip to Highland Village."

"What did they find?" I asked.

"Well, as I said, Tim came in two days ago. They had about thirty-five people with them."

The three of us didn't say anything, but looked from one to the other.

"A most bedraggled bunch of people," he said. "Really worn out from one thing and another. We took care of them, of course. We were worried about their health, especially the children.

"No sooner had we gotten them settled in temporary shelter than Jack Fost came down the road from the old reservoir, with another whole group of people. I'd thought Engles's group was in bad shape, but these people were on their last legs. He had better than forty people in his band, and they needed more help than the first group, especially a few lead by a man named Tibbs."

"Tibbs?" I said.

"The same group that left Butte City," he said. "But let me finish first, then we can talk about other things."

"I'm sorry, Rich. Go ahead."

"Well, things were getting pretty crowded, as you can well imagine. But we were able to get everyone fed, clothed, and housed somewhere. Steven called a meeting yesterday, as soon as he returned from Highland Village. You should have seen the crowd.

"He had us all take a seat on the ground in front of the old schoolhouse, and told everyone what had been happening there, up here, and at Highland Village. He didn't have to tell Tibbs about Butte City. Anyway, he put it on the line that everyone couldn't stay all crowded up in Goldston, and asked for volunteers to come up here and build up this place. As you can see, he got a good response."

"How long have you been up here?"

"I brought the last group up here yesterday."

"But all the supplies and the building I saw going on, you couldn't have done all that since yesterday. I can even see plowed ground on the other side of the river."

He nodded. "Quite correct. But Steve is a very perceptive man. He knew people were coming from Butte City, and that the expeditions sent out from Ioda might bring back more, so he'd had people up here getting prepared. He'd even had some of the supplies being brought down from Highland Village stopped here, rather than hauling them all the way to Goldston."

"How many people volunteered to come up here?"

"Let's see," he said, looking over a roster on his desk. "Counting the people who've been up here since the roadblock was set up, we have right at fifty, now."

"That's quite a few. Are you going to stay up here?"

"No. Most of those staying here were with the Tibbs group, and he'll come up and take over administration as soon as he feels better. He was in bad shape, and Steve demanded he stay in bed for a few days. He knew better than to let Tibbs come up here now; he would have worked himself to death."

"That's a lot of good news," I said. "But we better get moving on down the trail to Goldston."

He rose from his chair and shook my hand again. "It's good to have you back, and you, too, Susan."

We said our goodbyes to Rich, and got back in the Jeep to complete our journey. After we had traveled around four miles, I could smell freshly turned earth. I mentioned this to Susan, and she told me about the farming project Steve had set up.

"Mrs. Donley was having a fit, watching all that seed and farm equipment coming in from Highland Village, every day; and Steve was having it inventoried and stored. When the horses and cattle came down, it was too much for her to bear. She took Steve by the ear, and bent it pretty good for the better part of a day. Steve was trying to tell her that we weren't even sure of a growing season, yet. He was trying to be rational, or so he thought, but in the end, she won out and started a big operation on the east side of Goldston River. She has plenty of volunteers, and she works them from sun up to sun down."

"Have the small gardens been dropped," I asked, "the ones we started when we first got here?"

"Oh no, they're going strong. Now that some of the vegetables are ripening, the food in the mess hall tastes much better."

"So we're still eating cafeteria style, not in individual houses, yet."

"Best way to get all hands fed, with the least number of personnel—and we get by on less food, that way."

She gave me a long stare. "You'd rather have me fix our meals than eat in the mess hall?" she asked.

I thought I'd better think that over before I answered. We came near the river, and I could see the fields being worked on the other side. To our immediate left and at the north end of the plowed ground were two new buildings, built entirely of wood.

"Those are the first buildings she put up over there to house the animals," Susan said. "The second one is for farm implements."

The buildings were quite impressive. "Where did she get all the lumber?"

"She and Steve sent working parties over to South Butte, where almost all of the debris from the floods had come to rest. They retrieved enough lumber, nails, tools, and other materials to build several houses.

"As we get near the turn-off to the old schoolhouse, look closely at the south end of the fields. You can see some of the houses she's building for the people who've volunteered to help farm."

When we neared the point in the road where we would turn right and proceed toward the command post, I could indeed see the houses. I stopped the Jeep to take a look.

The farm area had been swept clean by the floods, and nothing had been left standing. In addition to the fields that now occupied most of that area, there were also equipment and animals, barns, and housing for those who had to work the land and take care of the equipment. Trees had been planted at strategic points around the fields, and even as we sat in the Jeep and watched, work was continuing.

Susan pointed out that a ford had been constructed about two hundred yards above where the Little and Goldston Rivers met. We didn't have the expertise to build a good, heavy-duty bridge, so everyone had helped construct a rock bed across the river, so that the animals and equipment wouldn't get stuck.

Having seen enough, I started the Jeep, turned right, and proceeded up to the command post. Even that building had changed. It had been painted, and the place now reminded me of any number of government buildings I had seen. The southeast side was used for gatherings—you could tell by the number of benches and chairs that were located there, plus the ground had seen a world of use in the previous few weeks and the grass was well trampled.

As we left the Jeep, I had the impression that I was in the wrong town. So much had changed. People were coming and going from the headquarters, and I didn't recognize anyone. I turned to Susan.

"Are you sure this is Goldston?"

"Of course it is," she said. "While you talk with Steve, I'm going up to our house and clean up. I feel like I have a pound of dirt and dust on my face alone."

"Our house?"

"I didn't want to tell you until we got back," she said. "You go ahead and met with Steve. I'll get the house opened up, and meet you there."

She turned and left, and I could see there wasn't going to be a discussion. About fifteen steps away, she turned back, and with a cute little grin on her face, gave me a small wave and proceeded on her way.

"J.J., where are we going to set up the radio equipment?" Jefferson asked.

"I don't know, yet. Let me see what Steve says. Why don't you go get something to eat, and take a break. I'll meet you back here in about an hour."

As Jefferson ambled off in the direction of the kitchens, I walked the short distance to the headquarters. Steve and several other men were gathered around a table in the old principal's office, which Steve had adopted as his own. Steve looked up and saw me, before I had a chance to turn and leave. I'd thought I could do some more looking around while they were busy.

"There you are," he said. "We've been waiting for you."

"Oh, I'm sorry. I didn't know I was expected."

"Come on over here. I want you to meet some people."

As we neared the table, everyone rose to meet us. Steve took care of the introductions. There was Mr. Yates, the school principal; John Syminski, the blacksmith, and two of his helpers; and lastly, Mr. Tibbs, the tall, lean man who had escaped from Jason at Butte City.

"Mr. Tibbs, I am truly glad to meet you," I said. "I've heard so much about you from Thelma Brown."

Tibbs was a very tall, angular man. He stood well over six feet, and I imagined he'd weighed well over two hundred pounds, once. But due to the long trip and harsh living conditions of the previous month, he was down to, at most, 140 pounds.

"J. J. Darby. You're the man who brought Thelma and the rest out of Butte City. I don't see how you and the rest remained so cool, when that crowd came through Highland. I have never hated any-one in my life, until I met that man, Jason."

Steve broke in on our conversation. "Tibbs, I think we should complete our discussion on personnel and supplies for Fort Darby. It's getting late. J.J., could you wait half an hour? I need to talk with you."

"Sure. I want to look around. Susan said we have a house."

"I know you're anxious to get home, but when I said to wait, I meant here. We'd appreciate it if you'd join us for the rest of this discussion."

"Be glad to, Steve."

Someone found me a chair, and we all regrouped around the table. I saw stacks of paper being passed from one to the other, and hadn't realized until then how much of an undertaking running of the settlement had become. The stacks of paper turned out to be rosters of people, where they had come from, what they were suited to do, what they wanted to do, and where they would live. I noticed that the paper we were using came from the supplies we had brought from Highland; most of the paper supplies that had been in Goldston had been destroyed in the floods.

Then there were the unending lists of supplies on hand, supplies to be taken to Fort Darby. After that, there were plans for expansion. Personnel were to move over the river to the farm site. Still more people were to move to Fort Darby, to start a dam up there. Steve wanted, eventually, to build a mill in that vicinity. With so much activity going on, I was beginning to feel that I'd been taking it easy, running around the countryside.

As I sat there listening, I was also amazed at the facts and figures that Steve had at his fingertips, and also that he could recall from memory, when needed. His leadership abilities had been direly needed after the catastrophe, and I could see they'd been sharpened and expanded since.

His confidence seemed to be transmitted to everyone in the room. As they progressed through the business at hand, I could see that Steve's ideas were paying off immensely, and that, because of the intense desire on everyone's part to make the community work, a great deal was accomplished in a relatively short time.

I was beginning to feel the afternoon wearing on me when the meeting finally broke up, with everyone satisfied with the plan for the next few days. I once again shook hands with everyone, as they left, and made Mr. Tibbs a promise to tell him all about the rescue from Butte City, the first chance I had.

Steve turned to me, when everyone had gone. "I'm sorry to keep you waiting," he said.

"I understand. I don't have much to tell you that you don't already know. You've been getting my reports. Did George fill you in on the radio contacts?"

I gave him the copies of the radio traffic with both Nova Scotia and New London. He looked them over hurriedly.

"I hope we'll be able to keep the contacts. You know that both Fost and Tim are back from their missions?"

"That's the first thing Rich Arthur told us about, when we got to the roadblock."

"I think it would sound better if you said 'Fort Darby,' rather than 'the roadblock,'" Steve said. "You may not realize, but everyone catches 'roadblock,' when you say it."

"'Fort Darby' it is."

"Good. What I'd like to do is get everyone together, let's say, in two days. Have one great, big meeting out there on the lawn. I've already instructed both Tim and Fost to have a report ready to give to the community as a whole. We've grown considerably, and I think it's to everyone's advantage to get to know each other a little better, what they have gone through to get here.

"Then, I'd like to tell them where I think we should go. I'd like a report from you and George on the operation at Highland Village. I've asked Mr. Tibbs to tell us about his trip, and that will be included in Jack Fost's presentation."

He paused for a minute and shuffled some papers on the table. "Conditions haven't been the best, but the willingness of these people to work together and to survive has been fantastic. Survival—that's the name of the game, right now."

"What about the future?" I asked. "Are you planning on staying here and running the show, or somewhere down the road, had you planned to leave?"

"What do you think? Should we go looking for the rest of the world, or wait until it comes to us?"

I had to think about that for awhile. I had presented a question to Steve that I hadn't given much thought to myself. Our families—what had happened to them? I had a sister living in Mississippi, if the state still existed. Susan had relatives in the Northeast that she thought about, but getting there, now, would require a major undertaking.

"What are you trying to decide, J.J.?"

"The answer to my own question. Should we leave or stay?"

"I agree it's a hard one. Let's not decide anything now. We have plenty of work here to complete. Let the future take care of itself, for the time being."

Our meeting over, I got up to leave. Steve accompanied me to the front door.

"I'd like to get the radio equipment set up and ready to operate by morning," I said. "I'm hoping we can still reach our two contacts from here. I'd like to keep Jefferson as chief radio operator, and get one more man, or woman, to help him operate the set."

"That's perfectly fine with me. Have you had time to look for a location?"

"No, but the best spot would be up at the observation post, overlooking the kitchens and storehouses. It's about the highest piece of real estate around. I'll work that piece of ground over, first. Then, if that doesn't pan out, if we can't get contact, we'll try something else."

As Steve and I neared the front door, it opened, and there was Mrs. Donley. We exchanged greetings without much chitchat. She seemed to be in a hurry, something to do with the farming operation. I said goodbye and left.

My walk took me by the old sports store. All that was left was the concrete slab, stacked high now with machinery and supplies sent down from Highland. Everything was neatly stacked and tarped down. The same with the old grocery store, nothing but a concrete slab piled with supplies.

As I turned west and headed for my house, it dawned on me that I didn't know where my house was. I came first to the gardens. They were flourishing, now, well taken care of and watered—some of Mrs. Donley's hard work, no doubt. The new housing area was just ahead of me. Off to my right, I could see the meeting hall that had been constructed earlier; and farther up the hill, I could see people busily working around the kitchens and storehouses, preparing the evening meal.

I was standing at the eastern end of the houses and tents when I saw Susan waving at me from the farthest and most northern house. I waved back in acknowledgement, and walked towards her. She met me at the door with a big hug and kiss.

"How did the meeting go?"

"I don't really know, yet. He's got so much on his mind. We only talked for a few minutes. I'll go back and talk to him after we get the radio set up and operating."

She grabbed me by the hand. "Want to show you the house. It's not much, yet, but it sure beats that tent."

Before I could answer or respond, she had taken me through the door. My first impression, as I looked around the room, was how tidy it was. Susan had always kept a clean and neat house. On the left wall was a fireplace and hearth; to its left, a wood box, full. In front of the hearth, she had placed two chairs, with a small stand between them. To my right, under the only window in the room, was a small, roll-top desk. I wondered where she could have found it.

Across the room was a table, surrounded by four chairs. Two chairs matched; the other two were from another set. Behind the table was a long cabinet, with two sinks set into the cabinet top. The room was quite impressive.

As my eyes came to rest back on Susan, she was looking up at me with a big smile on her face. "What do you think?" she asked.

"It's great. Where'd you get the desk?"

"Later. Right now, I want a big hug and welcome-home kiss from you."

We stood in the entrance, holding each other and kissing, until I became aware that the door was still open, and that anyone walking by would think we were two newlyweds, not yet over the honeymoon. I mentioned this to Susan, but instead of pulling away, she closed the door with a free hand and put her arms back around my neck for one last, long kiss.

"I've missed you so much," she said.

She again grabbed my hand. "Come on. I want to show you the rest of the house."

"There's more?"

"Sure."

We went through a curtain hung between the rooms, and came out into the bedroom. It was the same as the other one for size, but had two windows, whereas the other had only one. The bed was flanked by two nightstands. In the far corner, Susan had put a dresser and placed a wash basin on top. To my right was a huge closet.

"Susan, this is impossible. Where did you get all the furnishings?"

"Much of it came from over on South Butte. When the wreckage was cleared away, underneath we found a lot of good furniture. John Syminski had a working party bring all the usable things over, then everyone picked what they wanted."

"Are all of the houses fixed up like this?"

"No. Some of the youngsters are still living in tents. They aren't ready for a house, yet. There were twenty-one housing sites laid out, here, and twelve of them have been completed. Steve wanted to build some over on the east side of the river and some up in Fort Darby, to get everyone spread out a little."

As we were coming back through the curtain into the living room, Jefferson knocked at the door. I told him to come in and take a look at the mansion Susan had built. He was very impressed. He had already had supper up at the kitchens, so I sent him back to get the Jeep and drive it up to the observation post, while Susan and I went to get something to eat.

After supper, Susan and I joined Jefferson at the new radio site. The observation post was still manned during the day by a spotter. From there, we could see all of the terrain to the north and west, for a distance of at least five miles. To the south and east, the spotter was able to see all of the present town, plus the new fields and the road leading to the east. The new town of Fort Darby could also be seen, by walking a short distance north on the ridge.

Our small observation post, which had been built when we'd first arrived, was big enough to hold all of the radio equipment and leave the spotter room to maneuver. It was getting late, so once the Jeep was unloaded, I told Jefferson to drive it back down the hill. We would meet up there at 7 a.m. and get everything set up for the morning's calls.

"Jefferson, I talked with Steve about keeping you as radio operator."

He seemed pleased. "Thanks. I enjoy the work."

He said good night, and left with the Jeep. Susan and I looked over the country for a few minutes, before walking back down the hill to our new house. It had been a very rewarding but tiring trip up north. I was glad to be back home. Sitting in front of the fireplace, taking life easy that night, would be very enjoyable.

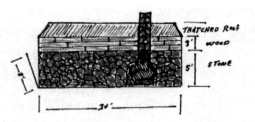

THATCHED ROOF
3' WOOD
5' STONE

24'

**GOLDSTON HOUSING**
**DARBY'S RESIDENCE**

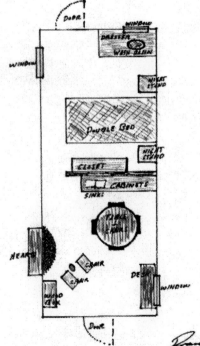

DOOR

WINDOW

DRESSER
WASH BASIN

WINDOW

NIGHT STAND

DOUBLE BED

NIGHT STAND

CLOSET

CABINETS
SINKS

TABLE & CHAIR

HEARTH

CHAIR
CHAIR

DESK
WINDOW

WOOD PILE

DOOR

# Chapter 15

༺❧༻

# A TIME OF ADVERSITY

I was up the next morning before the sun. Very surprising, considering how tired I had been the night before. I contributed my early rising to having slept in a real bed for a change. During my stay at both Butte City observation post and Highland, sleep was taken where one could find it—on the ground, in a tent, or with any luck at all, inside a sleeping bag.

My morning routine was somewhat different on my first day back. Susan had banked the fire on the hearth, the previous night, and had made the fire glowing hot with little effort. She warmed water for both of us, and it was pure delight to be able to shave using warm water.

Jefferson was at the set when I got there. He was always prompt—the first thing I'd noticed about him at both Butte City and Highland. And always cheerful, as he was on this morning.

"'Morning," he said. "Looks like another beautiful day."

"Yes, indeed."

As I came into the lookout post, I noticed that Jefferson had hooked up another piece of equipment that we'd brought out from the house at Highland, but had never used before.

"Jefferson, what do we have here?" I pointed to the oblong green box that was now connected to the radio.

"It's a power converter. The radio will only operate on DC current, and our generators, the small gasoline ones, operate only on 115 volts and 220 volts AC. This converter will change the AC to DC, and we can operate without running the Jeep or cranking all the time."

"Now, that is an improvement. What made you think of using it?"

"I was lying in my tent, last night, and I kept thinking that the guy that owned the equipment operated from inside his house, and the house current was 115 volts AC. So how did he do it? I broke out the manuals, went out to the equipment dump, found this old green oblong box, and sure enough, it was what we've been needing all this time."

There was a power cable from the radio to the converter, and another one ran outside. The one outside was connected, at some distance from the shelter, to a small generator. He'd been very busy.

"Did you do all of this by yourself?"

"Some of the guys gave me a hand, before they took off to their jobs."

I also noticed that he had connected a storage battery by a smaller cable to the receiver. The one battery should last for days before we would have to recharge. He had put a great deal of work into the arrangement. I hoped we could get contact from that location without having to move.

"Good work, Jefferson. Let's see about stringing some antennae, before it's time to call Fred."

We found the direction in which we wanted the antenna to run, and put some poles in the ground to support it. The type of antenna that we were using was called a "long wire," and ran parallel to the ground for however many feet we needed, according to what frequency we wanted. We were using 11.7 megacycles, so the formula used indicated that we needed an antenna of around forty feet. The poles supporting the antenna were around twenty feet long; that made it high enough in the air that no one would run into it, day or night.

At 8 a.m., we were ready to go on the air. Jefferson started the generator, turned on the power converter and the radio, and sent out his first voice call. We went through the same routine we had used at Highland—first a voice call, then calls in Morse Code. We kept it up on the frequencies we'd been using until 8:30, when it was time to call Fred.

"Nova Scotia, this is Goldston. Over."

We waited almost two minutes before trying again, but the results were the same—no answer. After fifteen minutes of silence to our calls, we started to check out the equipment. The generator was operating normally, as was the power converter, transmitter, and receiver. The only thing to do was to take down the antenna, put it back up on a different azimuth, and try again.

Still, we hadn't had any luck by 9 a.m. We switched to Morse Code, and started our calls to Jerry. Jefferson sent the usual call, but this time, he transmitted the call three times before stopping.

No answer. We transmitted in code as usual for fifteen minutes, then unhooked the power converter and switched to the battery to listen, just in case one of them might come up late. We even tried using the reliable hand-crank generator, but for nothing.

"I don't know," I said. "All of our equipment seems to be fine. We've checked every connection at least a dozen times."

"I don't think it's the location," Jefferson said. "We're actually higher than we were at Highland, there are no obstructions. It has to be trouble on their end."

"I'm inclined to agree with you, although it does seem strange that both stations would go down at the same time."

For the next hour or so, we checked and rechecked everything we could think of that might be loose, dirty, corroded, or worn out. Susan came up before lunch to see how we were doing. She could tell right away, from our actions, that something had not gone right that morning.

"What's wrong," she said.

"We couldn't contact anyone, this morning," I said. "What brings you up to the top of the hill? Ready to go to lunch?"

"That and to tell you that both George and Steve want to see you, sometime today."

"Do you know what they want?"

"George wants to talk with you about this presentation that Steve wants. I don't know about Steve, he didn't say."

"Okay. We'll make the noon calls, then we can shut down and go to lunch. It's going to be awhile. Are you going to stick around?"

"I think I will. Beth went home to lie down for a bit. The baby's due in about a month and she tires easily these days."

We spent the remainder of the morning talking and looking the countryside over. Susan and I walked north on the ridge for some distance. It was good to have a day where we could relax, even if everything wasn't going right.

Precisely at noon, we started our calls again. At 12:30, we came up on Fred's frequency and started the voice calls again. We called and listened for the better part of an hour. Nothing. The same with the code. Jefferson sent fast, then slow; he sent a series of Vs, over and over. Still nothing. After an hour and forty-five minutes, I thought we had tried enough.

"Looks like nothing's going to happen," I said. "Let's close down and get something to eat, before they close the kitchens."

"I'm baffled," Jefferson said. "Do you think we might have to change our location?"

"I don't know. Let's not panic just yet. We have the evening calls, and then the calls tomorrow morning. If we don't have anything by then, we'll think of looking for a new location, although I really hate to think about moving, especially across the river."

After lunch, Jefferson went back to the radio site, while I went to see Steve. He wanted to string another antenna that afternoon, when we tried again, one that would use more of a sky wave configuration and give us better distance.

As Susan and I were walking back down to the command post, which in reality was more or less a town headquarters building or town hall, she brought up the subject of another radio operator to help Jefferson. "Have you given much thought as to who you might pick to help Jefferson with the radio?"

I could tell from Susan's tone of voice that she had already picked someone for me. "Someone who would be compatible," she said. "Who could get along with him."

"What's her name?" I asked.

"Ruth Ashberry. She's a bright, intelligent girl, just right for the job. And she has a crush on Jefferson."

"Do you think this girl can become a good radio operator, or are you playing matchmaker?"

It was silent for a minute, as we continued our walk.

"Let's put it this way. I'm doing you a favor, Ruth a favor, and Jefferson a favor. How about that?"

"All right. Where is she assigned now?"

"For the past few days, she's been helping control the inventory account for Fort Darby. She counts everything, then likely as not, takes it up there herself. I'm telling you, the girl is a real worker."

"Why don't you find Ruth," I said, "take her up to the radio, and tell Jefferson that she'll be his new assistant?"

"And where will you be?"

"With George or Stephen, whoever I find first."

Susan stopped and gave me a big salute, then turned and started toward the housing area. "As you command, sir. I will look up the young lady in question and deliver her, as requested." With a little wave over her shoulder she was gone.

When I reached the old school house, there was no one to be found. I waited around for a few minutes in Steve's office. There were some plans pinned to a bulletin board, and someone had left a bunch of papers on one of the chairs, but other than that, nothing indicated the hustle and bustle that usually took place in that room.

After more than half an hour of walking around and looking, I finally spotted George coming down the road from the Goldston River. I went outside to meet him.

"George, I've been waiting for you," I said. "Susan said you wanted to see me."

"It's about this presentation Steve wants. Do you have any notes or anything made up?"

"No, not yet. I was up at the radio all morning. We're having trouble making contact."

"You can't get through or they can't get back?" he asked.

"We aren't sure, yet. Seems like everything is working, but we can't receive anything. Jefferson is up there, now, working on a new antenna."

George indicated that we should go inside and talk there. "Let's use these desks," he said. "I believe there's paper and pencil in that drawer."

He indicated a large drawer that was located in the middle of the large table that now served as the conference room's main piece of furniture. It was the one everyone gathered around during those long discussions. Having retrieved enough materials to jot down some notes, I joined George at a nearby desk.

"I like to keep my talking as short as possible," I said. "How about you taking everything that took place at Highland, once you arrived, and I'll take care of my first trip up there, all of the arrangements that were made to get everyone out of Butte City, and the radio contacts."

"You mean that I should talk about all of the excavations, that sort of thing?"

"That and the supplies, some about the tonnage recovered, the recovery operation itself, how many people you had working, the conditions you had to work with. Your guard should be mentioned and the people who tracked Jason."

"Sounds good to me. By the way, we won't be having the meeting tomorrow, as planned. It's been delayed."

"Why?"

"Steve's having some problems bringing everyone together."

"He wanted to see me this afternoon. Do you know where he might be, right now?"

"Up at Fort Darby, working on one of the problems that's holding up this presentation," George said. "People, projects, food, and now that the shock is wearing off, people are returning to their same old habits of 'me first and to hell with the rest of the world.'"

Steve had said something about grumbling, I thought. George saw my perplexed look.

"Don't get me wrong. Things aren't falling apart at a rapid rate or anything. There are a couple of hotheads who don't want to take orders from anyone, don't like where they've being assigned, that sort of thing."

"That's why Steve is up at Fort Darby?"

"Rich was having some trouble with people telling him what to do, instead of the other way around. He called Steve this morning, angry, said he was ready to pack up and come home."

"Is the trouble with Tibbs?"

"I don't think so. He only left yesterday, to go up and look around. He's still not a well man, but he wanted something to do."

"Why, George, you sound angry," I said.

He looked surprised, at first. "Seeing how much we've all put into keeping us going, and then to see people come in who want to live off that hard work makes me mad, yeah.

"Take Mrs. Donley, for instance. She works from before sun up to after sun down every day to get a farm program going, and one or two people are constantly fighting her every move."

"Wouldn't you agree that people have always been pretty much that way?"

"It still makes me mad. Now Steve is up at Fort Darby, trying to settle some kind of disturbance, which, if everyone was doing his job, would more than likely never have taken place to begin with."

"Steve will get it straightened out."

"Oh, I don't doubt that, not for a minute," George said.

"Has he said anything to you about our leaving here?"

"Not to me, he hasn't. Why, do you want to leave?"

"Not right now, but somewhere down the road. I guess I'm more curious than most. I want to know what's outside these mountains. We know by the radio contacts that the East Coast is changed, but what about in between? What about Mexico? What about the rest of the world?"

We were both silent for a few moments, running a scenario in our minds of what the physical world might look like after all the storms, quakes, and atmospheric phenomena that had taken place recently.

"Wouldn't that be something if our hemisphere were destroyed and nothing had happened on the other side of the Atlantic or Pacific," I said. "Or if the destruction was confined to North America. I have to find out, but I'm not about to take off on my own. I know we all have a job to do here, first."

"The way I feel today, if you wait an hour while I pack, we can be on our way."

We were silent again, both writing notes of what had happened at Butte City and Highland Village. From time to time, George would ask me a question, or I one of him.

Around 4 p.m. or so, we heard voices, someone was coming up the walk. It was Steve, Tibbs, and one other man I hadn't met. They came into the building and stopped right inside the door to talk. I thought they might want to use the room we were in, so I gathered up my notes and prepared to leave. George was busily doing the same thing.

Just as we were going out, the three men were coming into the room. We greeted each other. Steve walked back to the building's entrance with us, for a short discussion.

"J.J., has George told you that I want to put off the meeting?"

"He did."

"There are some problems to be worked out. How's the radio business? Were you able to establish contact from up there?"

"Not yet. I've sent Ruth Ashberry up to the site, to work with Jefferson."

"Good. You'll have to excuse me now. I'll see you two later."

Steve turned and left. George and I walked outside the building.

"What do you think?" I said. "Steve seemed in a good mood; there must be something good going on at Fort Darby."

"Not necessarily. I don't think I've ever seen the man lose his temper."

"I guess you're right. No sense in worrying about a problem when I don't know what it is."

George laughed.

"What are you doing now?" I asked. "How are you filling your days?"

"I check on the guard post, once in awhile. I've been doing some work with Syminski and his crew on the houses. What about yourself?"

"I haven't really thought much about it. The radio has taken up a large part of my time, but Jefferson is more than capable there, and with Ruth working with him, I guess I'm going to be unemployed. You don't know of anyone looking for an old archaeologist?"

We both laughed. The whole world had become an archaeologist's dream, but there weren't any colleges, universities, museums, or anyone looking for our services.

We parted company before reaching the meeting hall. George wanted to go by the blacksmith shop and see Syminski, and I wanted to get back to the top of the hill and see how Jefferson was getting along.

As I climbed the hill, I looked down over the housing area and saw the gardens. Susan was there with some other women. They were all grouped around, taking a break from weeding and cultivating. She saw me as I climbed, and waved. I acknowledged her wave, and she returned to her conversation.

Ruth and Jefferson were going through one of the technical manuals when I arrived. Both looked exceedingly happy with themselves. Susan was right, as usual; she had undoubtedly made a good match.

"How's everything going? Think we can make contact this afternoon?"

"I sure hope so," he said. "I've been over everything, and there's absolutely no reason why we shouldn't."

"Looks like you have a new antenna. What's this one called?"

"A doublet; it should increase our range. But just in case, I left up our original long wire, as well."

I passed a few minutes with Ruth, asking her how she thought she'd like her new job and if she was finding anything difficult. She said that Thomas was a good instructor, and he thought she would be able to go on the air immediately in voice and in two weeks using code.

We waited until 6 p.m., then started our calls as usual. Nothing from Fred. Nothing from Jerry. At 7 p.m., we transferred over to battery; and Jefferson and Ruth worked the dial, listening on one frequency after another. They had the situation well in hand, and there didn't seem to be any reason for me to stick around any longer.

"I'm going to find Susan and take a walk over to South Butte," I said. "I hate to move everything that far away from camp, but if by tomorrow, we aren't talking to someone, we should try a move. I'll scout around awhile, see if I can find any likely spots that might serve well as a radio site. Right now, I'm going to get some supper and you two should do the same. See you for the 8 a.m. calls."

They both wanted to stay with the radio for awhile, then go to the kitchens.

My trip to South Butte was cancelled. By the time Susan and I had finished supper and gotten dressed in boots and packs, it was starting to rain. I couldn't see any sense in stumbling around over there in the wet and muck, especially when the river might come up and trap us there overnight. We retreated back to the house, built a warming fire, and took life easy.

The rain had fallen off and on all night, and there was not a hint of a let-up. I shaved, dressed, and told Susan that I would meet her at the kitchens for breakfast. First, I wanted to see if Jefferson was at the radio site.

He was there with Ruth. They had arrived only minutes before I had.

"What do you think?" Jefferson said. "Are we going to fire up the radio today?"

"No, I don't think it'd do any good. Getting wet running back and forth to the generator or changing antennas won't help our health, if this rain keeps up. If you and Ruth want to stay and dial around, stay on 11.775 for awhile. That'll be about all we can do."

I had started to add something, when the two of them became blurry right before my eyes and, all at once, I couldn't stand. Then I heard the large-freight-train sound below my feet. I fell to the ground immediately. I knew what it was, now. Earthquake.

*Oh no, not again*, I thought.

Quickly, everything went quiet again. I looked over at Jefferson and Ruth, who were both on the ground. The radio had shifted on the small bench it had been sitting on, but had not fallen. Jefferson reached up and pushed it back in place.

I heard loud yelling from down below, then people talking in loud and fast voices. All three of us started down the hill to see what had happened. By the time we reached the first row of houses, many people were gathering around the kitchen. Susan was already there, and I asked her what was going on. One of the cooks had been burned badly by scalding water, but Thelma and another person had already arrived and were treating the woman. George came up with a couple of the people who were designated to help in situations like that, and he was asking everyone to go back to work or home, so that Thelma could take care of her patient and the kitchen could be put back in order.

He saw me and gave a wink. "Did you think we were in for it, again?" he asked.

"To be truthful, yes. Let me tell you, I was really scared, really fast."

He leaned over close to me. "I sure am glad we wear long pants; at least no one can see my knees clanking together."

I gave him a big frown. "Come on, George. You're as steady as a rock."

"Steady as the world we live on," he said.

I told Jefferson to forget the radio for awhile. It was still raining, and I didn't want those two stuck up on that hill if we had more quakes. He said he wanted to go back and put everything down on the floor, especially the transmitter and receiver, then he would call it a day.

We all started to disperse, as George had told us to do. He was our law and order, now. No one called him "Sheriff," but that's what he was, in effect.

Susan and I went to the house and made a pot of coffee. It took off the chill of the day. I was wondering what was going on up at Fort Darby and Highland. Since I'd come back and turned in my hand-held radio, it was hard to keep track of the happenings within the community, and we hadn't left a radio with Sam at Highland.

There was a knock on the door. It was Jefferson, letting me know that all was well with the radio equipment. I told him and Ruth to come in, have a cup of coffee, and rest for awhile.

While we were all seated around the hearth, myself and Susan in our chairs and the two youngsters sitting by the fire, the second tremor of the day struck. Both Susan and I froze in the chairs, while the room danced before our eyes. I could have sworn the walls of that little house moved in and out. The two on the floor went flat, and their coffee cups went flying across the room. Within seconds, it was over. No damage done—not in our immediate area, anyway.

"I don't know how much more of this I can take," Susan said. "I'm still shaking like a leaf."

I reached over, took her hands, and held them. She was cold as ice, and trembling.

"I'm sure they won't last," I said. "Everything's settling down from the big one."

Jefferson and Ruth looked pale and shaken. I got up and was going to pour them another cup of coffee, but the pot had bounced off the table and spread its contents all over the floor. I was starting to feel somewhat jumpy myself, and stood for several seconds, staring at the fallen coffee pot.

"Susan, where is your rain suit?" I asked.

"In the closet. Why?"

"Get it on. We're going to get out of here. Sitting around will drive us all up the wall. Jefferson, do you have a rain suit?"

"Yes."

"How about you, Ruth?"

"Yes."

"Okay, let's all get dressed. Susan, you and Ruth head for Steve's house. He may be there, but if he isn't, Beth will be dying for some company, and in her condition she shouldn't be alone. Jefferson, I'll meet you at the old schoolhouse. George might be looking for volunteers, if something's fallen apart around here."

The two youngsters departed. Susan and I got dressed. We kissed goodbye at the door, and she left for the Adams's house. I made my way through the rain, past the meeting hall, which was now the new school and infirmary, and down to the old schoolhouse. There were a few people there before me, and Jefferson arrived about the same time I did. I saw George inside the door, giving orders to two men. He handed them a radio, and they brushed past Jefferson and me as they went out.

"George, is there anything I can do?"

"Yeah, would you stay by the radio in Steve's office until I can get there? I sent two men over to see if everything's okay at the farming area. Mrs. Donley has a dozen or so people over there with her, and if the river comes up any higher, they'll be stuck."

"Where's Steve?"

"Up at Fort Darby. There's been a mud slide. Don't know how bad, yet. Arthur called on the radio. He was pretty excited; someone may be buried, but we aren't sure. Steve's going to call us back."

"Don't you think we should send someone up there to help with the digging?" I asked.

"No. Steve said there are plenty of people there, and we could have an emergency here before this is over."

"What about me?" Jefferson said. "There's nothing I can do up at the radio site."

"Round up all the able-bodied people you can find, and have them stand by in the meeting hall, in case they're needed. Tell Thelma we may have some patients pretty soon. Don't get any of the cooks or anyone who may be working with John, over at the workshops. We'll leave those people alone, unless we really have a catastrophe."

Jefferson indicated that he understood, put up his rain hood, zipped up his jacket, and left. The rest of the day was unbelievably hectic. I thought the day before had been bad, but it was nothing compared to what we were going through that day. Susan came down once to see if I needed anything. I told her no, and asked about Beth.

"She's fine. Scared to death, like the rest of us, but doing okay. She asked about Steve. Is there any news from Fort Darby?"

I'd been on the radio since I'd come down to the headquarters, but hadn't heard from anyone, and told her so.

"If you don't think there is any reason for me to stay," she said, "I'm going back up to the kitchens to stay with Ruth and Beth."

"What are they doing at the kitchens?"

"It was better than sitting in the house. The cook that was burned is going to be fine. She was more scared than she was burned, but she couldn't stay away from the kitchen and is busy making a huge batch of soup."

"That sounds really good. George, you want to take a few minutes and go have some soup?" I asked.

"Better not. Too many irons in the fire to leave, right now."

Susan stood up. "I'll tell you what," she said. "There are a whole lot of people looking for something to do. I'll send someone back with soup and crackers."

"Thanks. Be careful climbing back up that hill."

"I will, J.J. See you both later."

Not long after she'd left, two young men came down from the kitchen with a huge pot of hot soup and a tin of crackers. They stayed and ate with us.

After dark, things started to liven up on the radio. First, I received a call from the farm. The man George had sent across the river didn't know much about radio procedure, but he got his point across, nevertheless.

"Hey, George, you there?" he said.

That was the first call I received. George Foxworth was the only George in the whole valley who would be receiving a radio call, so I answered.

"This is J.J., at the command post. Who is this? Over."

"J.J., this is Scott Allen. George sent us over to see if Mrs. Donley was alright."

"I can take the message. How's it going over there?"

"Everything's just fine. The river's up real high, now. That's why we're late calling; almost lost my partner when he stepped in a deep hole. Some of the fields nearest the river are underwater, but other than that, everything's fine. Mrs. Donley says thanks for thinking about her."

There was a long, silent pause on the radio. "Anything else we can do?" he asked.

"Wait a minute. I'll get back to you."

I thought I'd look up George and see if he had anything for them, but before I left the set, Steve came up on the radio.

"J.J., this is Steve. Over."

"This is J.J. Over."

"I heard that last transmission. Scott Allen, can you hear me? Over."

"Loud and clear, Steve."

"I'd appreciate you two staying over there for the time being, at least until the rain stops and we seem to be out of danger of tremors or earthquakes."

"Sure thing. The river's so high, we were going to wait until morning, anyway."

"Okay, Scott. J.J., are you still there? Over."

"I'm still here."

"I'm going to tell Scott to close down his radio, to save the battery. How about you and George staying there and monitoring for the rest of the night?"

"Ten-four."

"Scott, did you hear my last transmission?"

"Sure did. We'll turn the radio off. See you tomorrow."

The circuit was silent. I was sure Steve would come back with some kind of a report on Fort Darby. When five minutes had passed and he hadn't come up, I called him.

"Steve, this is J.J. Over."

No answer. Either he'd turned his set off or his radio had gone dead.

"J.J., this is Rich. Steve is outside, right now. Can I help?"

"Yes, Rich. I was wondering how things are going up there."

"About half the fort was covered in a slide. They've rescued three people, so far. We are still trying to get a count, but so many people have been coming and going for the past few days that no one's really sure who was here. Wait, here comes Steve now."

It seemed like a very long time before Steve finally came back on the radio. "J.J., Steve here. Sorry to keep you waiting. We've confirmed that everyone is accounted for, now. Most of the fort is gone and some of the tents were carried away, but all of the occupants are safe. The emergency seems to be over, but I'm going to spend the night up here and come back in the morning, if the weather turns better. Have you seen Beth?"

"Not to worry; both Susan and Ruth are staying with her."

"Good. Tell her not to worry about me. I'm going to shut this radio off. I'll come up if we have some emergency. The river's very high, but I don't think it'll flood. Will give you a call first thing in the morning."

"Roger, Steve. J.J. out."

George had come in during Steve's call, and I brought him up to date.

"Seems like there's no sense in keeping everyone waiting around the meeting hall," he said. "I'm going to go up there and send everyone home. You want me to bring back some more soup?"

"Soup and a big jug of coffee. One of us is going to have to keep an ear glued to the radio all night."

"Be back in a little while," he said.

"If you see Jefferson, bring him back with you. He can spell us and take a watch during the night. And tell Susan I'll be stuck here for the rest of the night." As I finished my statement, George was going out the door, waving as he went to indicate that he had heard me.

Before long, George returned with soup, sandwiches, and between him and Jefferson was a huge jug of hot coffee. We would need it before that night was over. He said Susan and the rest of the women had already gone home, anticipating that we would be up all night; said they would be sleeping on the floor, fearing another tremor or quake during the night.

None of us could sleep, so we stood or sat near the front door, eating, drinking, and watching the torrents of rain come down and flood by, in front of the building. It was well after midnight when we finally set a watch, and the other two put chairs together or stretched out on a table to get a few hours sleep.

Morning brought no change in the weather. The rain did let up somewhat, but if it followed the pattern set while we were up at Highland, we could expect rain all day and most of the next.

No work was accomplished that day. Even John Syminski told his helpers to stay home. Everybody was too wet and miserable to get anything accomplished. All of the people who were living in tents had vacated and moved into one of the houses for the duration. Susan said we had eight guests for the next two days.

During that time, George, Jefferson, and I stayed close to the radio at the command post. Steve didn't come back the next morning, but stayed up at Fort Darby until the rain stopped. We had one more tremor on the second day, larger than the ones before, but the shock was not so violent. All of the amateur geologists predicted that we were out of danger, for awhile at least.

After two full days of rain, we finally had a break in the weather around early evening. The sun was very visible before it went down. The cook fired up the kitchen stoves and fed everyone a good, hot, evening meal.

Around 7 p.m., Steve came up on the radio. "J. J., this is Steve. Over."

The call caught me by surprise. I jumped three feet when the radio came to life. I ran to the radio.

"This is J.J. Go ahead."

"We'll be needing some transportation here, tomorrow morning. I have three people who need to be brought back there, and they won't be able to walk. I'm not sure, but the road seems to be impassable for the old van. Would like either you or George to bring a Jeep and trailer up here. Over."

"Understand. Will be up there shortly after daybreak. Anything further? Over."

"No, that'll about do it. This place is a mess, and we might bring more people up to help with the cleanup, but not for several more days. See you tomorrow. Out."

The rest of the night was uneventful. Beth, Ruth, Nancy, and Susan came down to see how we were doing. Beth was very concerned about Steve. We set the watch about 10 p.m., and all had a fairly restful night.

George had enough to do, so I volunteered to take my Jeep up to Fort Darby. Our gas supply was down to only a few hundred gallons, so the vehicles were used only when absolutely necessary. The small generators consumed most of what was being used. Steve wouldn't have called for the Jeep and trailer unless it was absolutely necessary.

I left the command post at dawn. It looked like it was going to be a good day; only small patches of clouds were crossing the sky, and it looked like they would be gone before noon.

The drive up was uneventful. I could see the houses and fields on the other side of the river. Someone was working around the barns as I passed, and waved. I returned the greeting, and proceeded on my way.

Steve had been right about the road. The rain had turned the surface into a soft mush. I had to use four-wheel drive all the way up. Pulling the empty trailer was enough to make the Jeep slip to one side of the road, every now and then.

Fort Darby looked like it had been dipped in the ocean for forty-eight hours, and then returned to the land to dry. There were flattened tents everywhere, and even the wooden structures looked soaked through. The stone building was covered in mud that had come down from the hill west of the structure.

Steve was waiting by the flagpole with the three people to be taken back to Goldston. Everyone was very solemn, as we loaded the injured onto the trailer. Steve walked over and said a few words to Mr. Tibbs, and returned with Rich Arthur. We then left immediately.

The trip back was very silent. Steve mentioned how tired he was, and Rich Arthur made some remark about hoping he never saw the place again. I drove straight to the hospital, where the injured were taken off by many willing hands that had been waiting for our arrival.

One man had had both legs broken when a beam had fallen across him. His daughter had sustained head injuries; and the third person had been punctured by splintering wood, in several places, and was undoubtedly our worst case.

People spent the day taking care of themselves. Drying out clothes, tents, and other equipment that had been wet for days was the order of the day. Jefferson, who was something of a free spirit, had only his small tent to take care of, so he took it up to the radio site, draped it over the observation post, and proceeded to clean and dry out the radio equipment.

Susan and I had been very fortunate. The little house had sustained no damage, and except for a few small water leaks in the thatched roof, we were in excellent shape. We spent the remainder of the day helping others in any way we could.

The two men George had dispatched over the river returned. One barn roof had been lost to wind and water, and some of the planted acreage down near the river was irreclaimable.

By nightfall, Goldston was almost back to normal. I went to see how Jefferson was doing on the radio. He had the receiver on, but said that no one had been transmitting in the hour he'd been listening.

"Do you think we can get back on the air tomorrow?"

"I don't see why not," I said. "We'll start our standard calls at 8 a.m. Where's Ruth?"

"She was up for a couple of hours, today. I told her we'd more than likely start transmitting tomorrow, so she'll be here at 8:00 also. I almost forgot, Steve wants to see you. I guess he went by your house and you weren't there."

Susan and I both had been running around most of the day, and hadn't been home except once, when we'd checked for leaks and I had shaved.

Jefferson told me that he was going to pitch his tent next to the observation post, since he'd be spending most of his time working with the radio. I told him good night, and walked back down the hill. Susan was coming up from the house, so we detoured over to the kitchens for supper, then walked down to the command post to find Steve.

We found him sitting with several other people, on the benches in back of the building. There were Tim Engles, Johnny Burnside, Jack Fost, George and Nancy Foxworth, Ranger Goodman, and Beth, Steve's wife. There was no formal meeting; it seemed that everyone had drifted together, one at a time. It was like a class reunion or the old neighborhood gang getting together again.

For the next few hours, we drifted from one conversation to another, laughter from this group and a joke coming from that. It was nearly midnight before people started drifting off, saying good night, and disappearing into the dark. Susan and I were getting tired, so we got up to say goodbye to everyone. Steve came over before we left.

"I was looking for you earlier, to tell you I'm trying to set the meeting for a week from today. That should give everyone time to get everything done and get down here." Steve paused for a second. "Any problem with you or Susan making it?"

"None whatsoever," I said.

Strange that Steve should ask me such a question. He had probably been given so many excuses by so many people that the question had become standard.

"One more thing, before you go," he said. "If you think Jefferson can handle the radio by himself, I'd like you and Goodman to make a short trip to Highland, to check on Sam and everyone else up there. Ask Sam and the Lancasters to be here. We'll call it a 'festival,' from now on."

"'The Festival.' That sounds good. Anything else?"

"Not that I can think of, at the moment. See if the tremors did any damage that they might need help repairing. Susan, you might want to go with him."

"I don't think so," she said. "With all due respect to my husband, that's one trip that he's welcome to make by himself."

"Good enough, you two. See you early in the morning, before you leave. Good night."

"Good night."

By the time we'd reached home, there was no way we could have stayed awake any longer. We washed up in the small basin and hit the sack.

The next morning, I said goodbye to Susan, and climbed up to the radio site to tell Jefferson I'd be gone for a day or two. I knew there wouldn't be any problems. I only hoped he could establish contact before I returned, and save us a move over the river.

Steve and Goodman were both waiting, when I reached the command post. I shook hands with Goodman; we hadn't seen each other since we had been at Highland, with the exception of the meeting the night before. After a cup of coffee and some small talk, Steve came up with one of the hand-held radios. He wanted me to leave it up at Highland with Sam, in case they got into trouble and needed help.

Both Goodman and I had brought a pack, extra boots, socks, and food for at least three meals, in case we were stranded anywhere along the road. We would never be more than ten miles from either Fort Darby or Highland, but we had already found out that one mile away was as good as a thousand.

We left the command post shortly after 8 a.m. The going wasn't really tough; we were on a well worn trail. But in some places, the mud and mud puddles were an obstacle. We came to Fort Darby about 10 a.m. The whole population seemed to be busy with a variety of projects.

We stopped for a few minutes to talk with some of the people around the stone building, as we passed. They were going to uncover it and build a retaining wall on the west side, just in case. Mr. Tibbs wanted to go to Butte City and take a look, but there was too much going on at Fort Darby.

"I'm not sure I could take seeing the place burned to the ground," he said. "Not just yet, anyway."

After a short stay, we told Mr. Tibbs and the others goodbye, and proceeded up the trail. We thought a good place to stop for lunch would be the old observation post overlooking Butte City. There was nothing left there, but we did have a good view of the country to the north and Butte City below us. Much of the burned wood and debris had been washed away by the rains. The old pavilion had been on piles, with no concrete foundation, and there was absolutely nothing left of it.

We reached Highland Village in the early afternoon. Sam, the Lancasters, the Whites, and Jimmy Wills were all there to meet us. They were delighted, for as much as we had wondered about their fate, so had they been thinking about us.

The tremors had not damaged any of the dwellings, although a few of the older trees down the draw had fallen over. Other than that, nothing had happened. The rain had been no trouble; they were plenty high enough, well away from the river, and drainage was excellent. Sam invited us to spend the night, and we were both happy to do so.

Not much had happened since we were there. Sam was sure that someone had been over in the old town, the night before, but it might have been an animal just as well as a human. He hadn't been over to investigate, because the creek was running so high. He figured two days for it to go down enough for an expedition, and he asked us to stay a few days before returning to Goldston.

I told Sam we'd be delighted, but that we had to get back and get ready for the Festival. I gave him the radio, and told him not to worry about what he said on the air. We had someone close to the radio at all times, and if he needed help, to press the transmit button, say "Help," say his name a few times, and we'd get the message.

The next morning, Mrs. Lancaster fed us a big breakfast of eggs, jam, biscuits, and coffee before we left on the return trip. Sam said to give his regards to Susan, and that he would see everyone the next week, at the Festival.

The trip was without incident, although we did manage to flush out a small herd of deer just after we left the plateau above Sam's valley. I made a note to tell him about that, just in case he didn't know they were there, which was very unlikely. We didn't stop for lunch, and with the exception of a ten-minute break, walked back to Fort Darby without stopping.

Everyone there was busy, as usual. The stone fort was cleared of mud, and bucket after bucket of water was being carried over from the river, to be used in cleaning the walls. I did manage to have a few minutes to talk with Mr. Tibbs, and asked him if there had been any trouble with people not being satisfied with the way things were going. He looked at me as if I had divulged a secret known only to him, then with a grin, assured me things were fine. He said I'd have an answer when Steve talked to us at the Festival. We stayed there for over an hour, then proceeded on our way.

Upon arrival, I went to the command post, as usual. I told Steve about the talk with Tibbs, and that everything was all right up at Highland. He told me that Jefferson had made contact with Fred that morning, and that everything there was as well as could be expected. Fred had been in an accident while driving one of his golf carts.

It had happened during a driving rain and wind storm. He was transporting people to higher ground, to get away from rising water, when his cart had gone off the road, crashed into a tree, and rolled over. He'd sustained some cuts and bruises and a possible concussion.

"Jefferson can tell you more about it, when you see him."

Steve was busy, as usual. It seemed someone was always waiting out in the hall to see him, so I said goodbye to him and Goodman, and started up the hill to the radio site.

Susan saw me coming. She'd been working with some other people, cleaning furniture that had been salvaged from South Butte. After a big, welcome-home hug and kiss, she asked me if I'd seen Steve, and did I know about the radio contact with Fred. I told her I did, and if she weren't too busy, that she should walk up there with me. She agreed, and waved to the others that she would be gone for awhile.

Jefferson was busy writing, when we arrived at the radio site. He seemed to be very excited. Ruth was looking at some papers and writing, also.

"Hey, you two. I hear we're back in business," I said.

"Good to see you. Fred's back up. We just finished talking to him." Jefferson passed me the piece of paper he had been writing on, when we'd arrived.

THE STATION I HEARD WAS VERY WEAK. HE WAS TALKING TO SOMEONE IN BRUSSELS. DON'T KNOW WHERE HE WAS LOCATED. HE WAS HARD TO UNDERSTAND BECAUSE OF STATIC, AND MY FRENCH IS NOT THE BEST, BUT SEEMS THAT HE NEEDS HELP. I COULD NOT HEAR OTHER STATIONS TRANSMISSION, BUT HE ANSWERED. THE FRENCH STATION ACKNOWLEDGED, THEN THEY BOTH WENT OFF AIR. SECOND TIME I HAVE HEARD THEM.

I looked up at Jefferson. "Is this all that you received from Fred?"

"No, Ruth is recopying the first part of the message. Let's see, it says he's glad to be able to transmit again. They're sure that they have the battery problem fixed. Did Steve tell you about Fred's accident?"

"Yes, he did."

"What happened was that, when Fred was laid up, one of the other fellows moved the radio. When the guy put everything back together, one of the batteries was hooked to the radio in reverse polarity and blew something. They don't know what, but they searched around and replaced some tubes and modules, and finally got it working again this morning."

He anticipated my next question. "I've already asked if they've heard from Jerry. They said no; no CW since they've been back up."

He looked down at his messages. "The first time they heard the French station was yesterday, but they couldn't transmit, just receive. They heard me calling over and over."

"I'm glad to hear we have contact," I said. "When you finish with the message, I want to run it down to Steve. I'm tired and could use some good chow. You and Ruth want to come down with us for supper?"

"Sure. Let me finish rewriting the message. Steve could never read the scratch I take down when receiving."

Susan and I waited until the message had been rewritten. Jefferson gave me a copy for Steve, and we all went to supper.

Things at Goldston seemed, at last, to be returning to some kind of orderly pattern. The weather was clearing nicely, we had radio contact again, and everyone was settled in, doing one thing or another. In a few days would be the Festival, and we were all excited about that.

# Chapter 16

‹⁓›

# FESTIVAL

The week leading up to the Festival was busy for everyone. Steve had a speaker's platform built on the meeting grounds, by the old schoolhouse. Benches and chairs were filling up the yard.

Eleven more people joined our group, but only temporarily. There were two ranch families, who had been living some miles east of us on Little River. The latest bad weather and earthquakes had wiped out the farm they'd rebuilt after the major destruction. Not being able to go east because of the rough terrain, they'd headed west until they'd come to Goldston. They couldn't believe their eyes, when they'd come upon our farm. After the festival, they planned to go back and rebuild. Steve had promised to help with manpower, tools, seed, and food to last until they could grow a crop.

Jefferson was now solely in charge of the radio. He was qualified, and I told him there was no sense in my coming up and looking over his shoulder every day. I did like to know what happened on the circuit from day to day, and usually in the afternoons, before supper, I'd walk up and we'd talk for awhile.

George stopped sending a lookout up there. Jefferson was now living on-site, and Ruth was with him every day, so between the two, they acted as both lookout and radio operator.

I felt that I had worked my way out of a job, and asked Steve where I could be placed to help out the community. He had only said to take it easy for a few days, that he was making plans, and that it would take awhile to get everything in place. So for the time being, I helped where I seemed to be needed most. I worked on the houses for one day, spent a morning in the blacksmith shop with Syminski, and finally had the time to cross the river and visit with Mrs. Donley and the folks over there.

On the morning before the Festival, while I was in the process of finishing some notes I wanted to use in my presentation, we finally reestablished contact with Jerry in Connecticut. Ruth came running down the hill, saying Jefferson wanted to see me immediately. Naturally, I dropped my notes on the table, and took off after her for the radio site. By the time we arrived, Jerry had already shut down.

"I'm sorry," Jefferson said. "I couldn't keep him on the air any longer."

I was more excited than Jefferson seemed to be, at that moment. "What did he have to say? Where has he been for so long?"

Jefferson was shaking his head. "I'm not sure. I was caught by surprise when he started sending. He asked for a readability check, and I have him at three by three. There was plenty of static, and he was hard to read. Then he came back with this."

Jefferson was holding up some notes he'd taken, but they were jumbled. I looked them over for a minute.

"Can you decipher this?" I asked.

He started to write another copy.

"I don't think that'll be necessary, if there wasn't any substance in the traffic," I said.

"Well, all he really told me was that he'd been having a lot of trouble, but he didn't elaborate. He also asked if we knew if his people had reached Canada. Then he stopped. I don't know what happened; possibly his transmitter gave out."

"Did you answer him? I mean, tell him that his people had reached Canada?"

"Yep, sent it three times."

He handed me the message. YOUR PEOPLE ARRIVED SAFELY. FRED AND GROUP SEND THANKS AND BEST REGARDS. YOUR PEOPLE SHOULD BE ON WAY BACK NOW. WILL LISTEN ON THIS FREQUENCY UNTIL YOU CAN TRANSMIT AGAIN. GOLDSTON OUT.

"Well, at least we know he's still there. Do you want me to stick around and help copy, in case he comes back up?" I asked.

"No, I guess not. I sent Ruth after you because I thought for sure he'd have miles and miles of copy, after not being on the air for so long, but whatever trouble he's experiencing, he hasn't found the source, or so it would seem."

"Okay, I'm going down the hill for now. I'll be back about 3:00 and stay awhile, in case he comes up again. Now, don't forget to close down everything and be down at the command post early tomorrow, for the holiday. Don't make any commitments to Fred or Jerry."

"Wouldn't a contact be more important than a party?"

"It might be the last time we have all of the valley together, in one place and at one time, ever again."

Jefferson looked a little puzzled. "Why would that be?" he said. "I'd think, if this works out right, we might do it again next year."

"I agree. But now that the big disaster is over and people are starting to split off and go their own way, I don't think we'll be able to do it again."

"Too bad."

"Well, I'm going to head back down the hill. Don't make any message delivery of the last contact with Fred; just put it in the log, so that we have a record."

"Okay, see you later."

I returned to the house and gathered up my papers. Susan was working in the gardens that day, so I went down to the command post to see how George was doing on his presentation. He was out, as usual.

I think he made work for himself just so he wouldn't have to sit around the radio. If there was anything George didn't like to do, it was radio watch. As he would say, all you could do was sit by the silly thing and hope someone would call, but they never did, unless they had an emergency. Then you had to leave the radio to go and help them.

The woman on duty said she thought he was up at the workshop, talking with John Syminski. I looked in on Steve. He was up to his eyebrows in paperwork. He saw me at the door and waved for me to come in.

"Glad you came down. Have you got a minute?"

"Lately, I've had all kind of minutes," I said. "Not that I'm complaining. I've enjoyed being able to walk around and get acquainted with some of the new folks."

"But you've had enough of the good life."

"I'm ready to go back to work whenever you say."

He leaned back in his chair and closed his eyes, as if in deep thought. Finally, he opened his eyes and stared at the ceiling. Then he looked straight at me.

"I've been thinking about what you said about leaving the valley."

I was sure he was about to give me the date we were going to pack up and head out. But he had another idea.

"I'd like for you to make some preliminary excursions around the local area. See how many people are around. You might want to take some notes on what you find—animals, what species, how many. Same with birds, plants, and something about the terrain, so that there'll be a record to keep here."

"Then, what you're saying is that you plan on settling in this valley."

"Not at all; you didn't let me finish. Once that's completed, I want you to look for the best possible route out of the mountains, either east or south. I wouldn't recommend north, because we never traveled extensively in that direction before the disaster and I don't see any reason to go that way now. We'd be lost after the first few days out. As for west, I would rule against that, because I don't think you'll find much in that direction. What do you think?"

"I'm all for it. Then, you do eventually plan on leaving Goldston?"

"Yes, indeed. I can't walk away from here right now, but given enough time and planning, say six to eight months, then I'll be ready to go. How about you?"

"You've known me for a long time, Steve. I'm always ready to see what's over the next hill."

"Then it's agreed. You'll be ready to leave after the Festival?"

"A few hours to pack some chow and a dry change of clothes. How big of a party do you want me to take?"

"I'll leave that to you."

"Small outfit, travel light, three people at most. I'd like to take Goodman and one other man."

"What about Susan? She's going to want to go with you."

"I know, but not this trip. I'd like to go north first—make sure your decision of going either east or south is correct, and it might be dangerous up that way. She'll be mad at me, but she's a practical woman and knows that she's better off here and can be of more use to the community."

"Suppose you're wrong?"

I laughed. "Then she'll be my third member in the team," I said.

He stood up, shook my hand. "Then it's agreed. I hate to hustle you off, but as you can see, my desk is covered with paperwork I have to complete before tomorrow."

I understood his predicament. Seemed everyone in the community looked to him to provide answers to all of the questions that plagued us, those days. From the look of his desk, he was working on a lot of answers.

When I returned to the cabin, Susan was there. I asked her to take a seat at the table so that we could discuss a few things. She promptly said no.

"No?" I said.

"You have that little boy look that says, 'I want to do something, but first I have to have your approval.'"

"Are you sure of that?"

"Positive. Either Steve has asked you to do something dangerous, or you've asked to do something dangerous."

"Well, not exactly."

I explained to her what Steve had said about exploring the countryside. I saved the part about her staying in Goldston until last, because I thought that would be the toughest part of the discussion, and I was right. She thought we had been separated enough during the previous months and wanted to go along. I agreed, but I was also worried about what we would find out there. Sleeping on the ground every night, for weeks on end, wasn't very rewarding, and I worried for her safety if we did run into trouble, whether it be with humans or animals.

In the end, we compromised, as we did on many occasions. She would stay in Goldston while I went north. She would go on the trip west, where we knew there were people to talk to and interview, and a lot of paperwork would be required. Although Jason and his group had disappeared somewhere to the west, the last two rangers who had shadowed them had returned telling us that his group was so demoralized and unorganized that we would never have trouble about them again.

She also would make the trip back through Ioda and south, because we thought there might be more people down in that area that Tim had not discovered. As for the trip east, I was determined to have her stay in Goldston.

The trip that way would be filled with days and days of trying to find a way over the mountains and down the other side. We already knew from the two ranching families that many changes had taken place in the terrain, and that where there had been a pass or valley none now existed. The mountains to the east had actually pushed even higher, and there was still the threat of earthquakes and mud slides. The rocks were jagged and unstable for miles, and according to the ranchers, would start moving at times, as if they were floating on a river.

She finally agreed not to make that trip. But there was one small compromise on my part. If the families that were now in Goldston were back in the eastern valleys by the time I went in that direction, then she would go that far with us and stay there until we returned.

With that settled, we spent the rest of the afternoon at the radio site with Jefferson and Ruth. Nothing had been heard from Jerry by nightfall, so we all left. The next day was going to be a busy day for us all.

We were up bright and early, the next morning, but not as early as the rest of Goldston. Seemed everyone was anxious to get an early start on the day. The kitchens were crowded with people, by the time Susan and I arrived. The cooks wanted to get breakfast over, so that they could start on the big afternoon meal that had been planned. There were to be no lunch and dinner, just one huge meal, lasting from about 3 p.m. until everything was eaten. With everyone arriving from Fort Darby, Highland, and the farms across the river, there would be quite a crowd by early afternoon.

After breakfast, I went to find Goodman and tell him that he'd been selected to come with me on yet another trek across country. I didn't really know how he'd like that. I thought perhaps we should have talked it over before I'd volunteered him. I didn't find him in his tent, and no one seemed to know where he was, at that moment. Susan joined me, and together we headed for the command post. I could always talk with Goodman later.

Mrs. Donley and her farmers had arrived. They'd brought the baked goods, and pots of coffee were already waiting on long wooden tables constructed specially for this day. People who I had seen at the kitchens not long before started eating again.

Sam and the Lancasters came down shortly after 9:00, followed by Dave White and his wife. Their children were already there. People could be seen coming down from Fort Darby, but I didn't see Mr. Tibbs among them. The area around the old schoolhouse was very jovial. People were greeting each other, shouting hellos. People who hadn't seen each other in a long time were shaking hands and hugging. Conversations were going hot and heavy all over the place.

I finally spotted Goodman, and took him aside and asked him if he would like to make a few short trips around the neighborhood. He was all for it. Mr. Syminski had him working on house flooring, and that wasn't one of his favorite jobs. I asked if he knew of anyone else who might join our crew, but he couldn't think of anyone offhand.

As it turned out, Johnny Burnside jumped at the chance to go, the minute he found out about the expeditions. Traveling around, looking over the territory, was right up his alley. The more he saw of the land, the more he seemed to want to find out about it.

The talking and visiting lasted until eleven o'clock, then Steve and Tibbs walked out of the command post and climbed up on the speaker's platform. Steve asked that everyone take a seat. That took a few minutes to accomplish; no agenda had been presented for that day, and more than a few folks had to be rounded up from around the town. When everyone had grouped around the platform in a rough semicircle, Steve made a short welcoming speech.

"I would like to welcome you, one and all, to this gathering, today. I hope that you will have an enjoyable day, and by the time you go home tonight, we'll have a better understanding of what we have to do for the foreseeable future. First, before we get down to business, I'd like to introduce Mr. Joe Tibbs to those whom he hasn't met. Mr. Tibbs is a very religious man, and will be establishing a nondenominational church up at Fort Darby. I will ask him, now, to lead us in a prayer. Mr. Tibbs?"

Tibbs walked slowly to the speaker's rostrum. He looked to be in heavy thought, as if choosing words. He stood there for a moment, looking over the audience, before finally speaking.

"As I look out over those gathered," he said, "I wonder why we were all brought to this place at this time. I can only wonder, for I have no answers. I would ask that you all have faith in each other, in the difficult times that are sure to come. In that regard, I will not offer up a prayer for us all, but ask that you bow your heads and pray, each in his own way, for a better world in the days to come."

He bowed his head, as did almost everyone in the crowd. Some looked skyward, as if asking for guidance. There was a low murmur; then, as the prayers ended one by one and silence was once again the order, Mr. Tibbs stepped away from the podium.

Steve came forward. "We'll have several speakers, today, and I ask that you listen to each and every one during this next part of the presentation."

He stopped looked the audience over, and waited until the talking between neighbors stopped. "I'm going to ask that the men who had a hand in bringing different groups into Goldston come forward. These talks will let you all know where your new friends and neighbors have come from, and what they had to go through to get here today."

Steve looked at a card in his hand. "Tim Engles, Johnny Burnside, and Adrian Mayor, would you please come up to the platform?"

There was a smattering of applause as they came forward. Steve shook their hands and introduced them to the audience.

"For those of you who do not know these three men, they were part of my group, an archaeological dig out on the reservoir near the small village of Ioda. After the destruction, I asked them to go south and see what they could find, and they had quite an adventure. I've asked Tim to tell you about his trip." Steve indicated that he wanted Tim to come forward and take over the speaker's position.

"Good morning. For those who don't know me, I'm Tim Engles. On my right is Johnny Burnside, and to his right is Adrian Mayor. Adrian is, or was, a park ranger. I think Steve would've liked to have had him on the dig, but unfortunately, he was working for Uncle Sam at the time of the disaster."

He looked around at Steve with a smile. Steve shrugged. We all knew it had been hard to separate the two groups, ours and the rangers. We had been together since this thing had happened.

Tim looked at the notes he had in his hand. "Shortly after the big earthquakes, Steve sent us south to see what we could find. We were gone for a total of twenty-four days, not counting the time we spent at Ioda, before we proceeded from there to Goldston.

"I think our biggest surprise, or maybe our first big surprise, was to find that Lakewood City didn't exist anymore. The road we traveled on our way there disappeared several times, due to changes in the terrain, land slides, and so forth.

"When we first arrived at what should have been the town, we checked our map several times, because we thought we had to be wrong. We finally realized that the town was buried under a quarter-mile of earth. The people who lived there probably never knew what happened. The valley where the town was located is no more."

Tim paused for a minute, and looked out over the crowd. "We weren't sure what to do next, our first objective having been so completely destroyed. Finally, we decided to go west—it was the path of least resistance, at the time. We traveled in that direction for two days; we estimated a distance of eighteen miles.

"We stopped when we came to a large river, where there should have been no river. To the north lay a large flood plain, which appeared ever larger to the north. We knew Jack Fost was up that way, so we crossed the river and followed it in a more-or-less easterly direction."

Tim paused, shuffled some of his papers around. "We took our time, stopping frequently to check a small valley or to cross a river and look around. We had been following the river for three days when we came across human footprints. It seemed, at first, that people had crossed and headed north, but with some checking, we found they had, in fact, looked around and then again proceeded south. We followed for no more than half a day, and ran across twelve of the people we brought back with us. Would you please stand, wherever you are in the audience." Several people stood and the rest applauded.

"Thank you. These people had come from Ala Vista, and were making their way north to Lakewood, but were low on food. We informed them that the town didn't exist anymore.

"We stayed in camp, there, for two days while they gained enough strength to proceed. The best thing to do, we thought, was to head east and try to find Santa Vista." Tim stopped again and looked through his notes.

"After two more days of travel, and way short of Santa Vista, we came to the water—our next big surprise. We came over a rise and there was the ocean. No one could believe it. We all stared for what seemed like hours, which in reality was probably no more than a couple minutes. There before us, where there should have been a huge valley between two mountain ranges, was an ocean. Off in the distance were the tops of the next range of mountains, but now they were a group of islands.

"After we'd composed ourselves and started north, working our way slowly back toward Ioda, we came across another small group of people. They were refugees from Santa Vista, which was now covered by several hundred feet of water. Their escape had been a miracle in itself. When we found them, they were living off some berries they had found and an occasional fish they could catch. I believe I see them back there. Would you stand, please?"

After another round of applause, Tim continued. "I wanted to reach the river by nightfall, so we gathered up our newest acquaintances and moved on. While searching for firewood, after we reached the river, Johnny found nine more people camped about a quarter-mile north. That family had been on a camping trip. They'd stayed put, living off fish in the nearby shallow water while waiting for rescue. I don't believe we were exactly what they'd expected, but they were glad to see us anyway.

"By this time, our food was gone and we had collected thirty-five people. I was ready to panic. Everyone was worn out, and the trip north was out of the question—the terrain was too rugged in that direction. So I sent Johnny and Adrian back to Ioda for supplies and any other help they could round up. I didn't know, at that time, about Steve's move to Goldston. But it all worked out. I kept everyone at the mouth of the river for a week, while we gathered strength. The mouth of the river is very shallow, and reeds were growing thickly everywhere. We lived off fish and berries, until they returned with the supplies from Ioda.

"Our trip back was made easier because of Johnny and Adrian. They had found the best and easiest route, while going up to Ioda for the supplies. We were there, at Ioda, when Jack Fost returned from his trip west."

Tim paused once again, looked over his notes, then looked around at Steve. "I believe that's all I have, unless you have some questions."

He then looked toward the audience. "Does anyone have any questions, out there?"

"No questions, Timothy," a man said, "but thanks a whole heap for bringing me and my family back here."

A big round of applause followed. Tim waved, and the three men left the platform. Steve again stepped up to the podium.

"Now, I'd like to have Jack Fost come forward."

It took a few minutes for him to work his way through the crowd. While we waited, Steve said a few words.

"I won't make the same mistake twice. Mr. Fost didn't work for me at the Ioda site, but was maintenance chief for the National Park out on the lake. Tim caught me on my last presentation, but I believe I have this one right."

Jack Fost arrived on the stage, with the two men who had accompanied him on his trip.

"I'm going to turn the stage over to you, Jack. Go ahead."

"Thank you, Steve. I'd like, first, to introduce the two people who made the trip from Ioda with me. First, Ranger White, here on my right, and on my left, Ranger Allen. We were Park Service employees before the destruction."

Jack cleared his throat then continued. "We left on our trip at the request of Stephen Adams, just a few days after the disaster. Somewhat like Tim Engles, we were gone for a total of twenty-six days; I believe that's a few days longer than Tim was out.

"We followed the south side of the old reservoir upon leaving Ioda. We did cross to the north shore and look around the visitor center, housing area, and workshops, where the park headquarters had been located. I can truly say that was the most emotional thing I have ever done in my life."

Fost stopped there to take a couple of deep breaths. It was still hard to talk about the park. He had lost his wife there, and Scott Allen had lost his wife and two small children.

"Forgive me. Let's see, I need to check my notes. Oh, yes. After leaving the park, we continued on west for two days. That brought us to the vicinity of Rosemont. We climbed a small series of hills west of there, to see if we could find any of the personnel who had been stationed at another federal park, called Valley of the Dark Angels, but the area had changed so radically that we couldn't tell for sure where the park headquarters had been located. It had been perched on the south side of a high cliff, but all of that was gone. We could tell from our vantage point that Rosemont was not there anymore. There was, in its place, a huge river wash. At the point where Rosemont should have been, we estimated the wash at between three-quarters and a mile wide.

"Our plan was to proceed south for a day, cross the wash, and head back north until we reached Junction City. We did proceed south as planned, but when we crossed, there were many human footprints going off in the direction of Silverton. We followed these tracks for a day and a half, before finding Mr. Tibbs and his group. Not knowing the trouble they'd been through at Butte City, we were quite surprised when the group split up and ran in three directions, as we approached. More surprising was the attack on us that followed. Luckily, I kept yelling that we had come from Ioda to help, and no one was hurt seriously. Once we had all of the facts straightened out, we all became friends rather quickly." Jack looked around the crowd and found Tibbs, then nodded in his direction a confirmation of their friendship.

"The Tibbs group had very little food and water, and our supply was in no way adequate for that number of people. So we thought the best thing to do would be to send one or two men back to Ioda for help, exactly as Tim did. While Scott and John went for help, I led the Tibbs group back to a point slightly south of where Rosemont should have been.

"There we found, along the east bank of the wash, a total of eighteen people who had come together over the previous week or so. Some were from Rosemont, some from smaller towns, and some from ranches in the vicinity. Somehow, we had missed each other when we'd passed that way the week before."

Jack was interrupted there, when a man stood up in his chair in the audience, and yelled, "And a good thing for us all, you came along when you did, Mr. Fost." He started clapping, and the crowd joined in with him.

"Thank you, sir. I'm glad we made contact that time, and didn't miss each other twice. Now let's see, you have me all rattled and I can't find my place."

Laughter came up from the crowd.

"Here we are. Mr. Tibbs will agree with me when I say that we were all drained, physically and emotionally, by the time we reached Rosemont. We all took it easy until my two friends here returned with provisions. We were a happy bunch that day.

"While everyone was regaining their strength, the two lads and I proceeded up to Junction City, as planned. We followed along the east side of the wash until it closed in, about two miles east of our destination. There was a small stream flowing there, from northwest to southeast, but when it emptied into the wash, it disappeared into the sand. It's my guess that the water was flowing under the large wash—an underground river, if you will. It had taken us four days to get that far, so we camped for the night at the mouth of the stream, before we turned around to head back.

"It was our turn to be surprised, the next morning, when we were joined by a group of people—I believe there were nine—who had been on a hunting trip farther up the valley. They were from Junction City, and were heading back that way. We packed quickly, and joined them on the return trip.

"The city we found in no way resembled what any of you may remember, if you visited there in the past. The survivors had built a log cabin city on a large grassy knoll, west of the old town site by a good mile. It was surrounded by trees and was a very picturesque spot, as I remember.

"From what they told me, on the day of the destruction, the whole countryside— town and all—collapsed. This is hard to imagine, but from the way I understand it, everything fell perhaps hundreds of feet—no one knows how far; but when it all landed—humans, animals, buildings, streets, cars, trucks—everything disintegrated, blew up. Many people were crushed by falling buildings, boulders, and tons of earth.

"Everyone there was in shock for days. To give you some idea of how devastating it was, out of a population of over nine thousand, there were only forty-one people left. They believe some are still wondering around dazed, if they haven't died by now, and they're looking every day for more people."

The audience was hushed, now. Even the small whispers that are always present at a gathering like that were absent. Fost paused, to let what he'd said sink in a little deeper.

"To wrap up, let me say that there are a good bunch of people trying to make a go of it, there. I hope they fare as well as we do. Before we left, they gave us fresh meat to take back to the group we had left at Rosemont.

"The only other incident, besides the long walk back from Junction City through Rosemont and finally to Ioda, was the finding of six persons who had been trapped on the top of Observatory Peak. They joined us, and are in the audience today.

"I would like to say one other thing, before I leave the platform. We were thrilled to reach Ioda and find Tim and his group there. The feeling of friendship was overwhelming then and continues to this day. The provisions left behind by Steve and his crew were a life saver; we were definitely on our last legs when we arrived."

The audience arose as one, and there was a lot of whistling, clapping, and yelling as Jack left the stage, followed by Scott and John. Steve again took over the podium. He waited for the crowd to settle down before he spoke.

"I have an idea," he said. He stopped and raised his hands in the air for quiet. "I was under the impression that these presentations would be short and would not generate the response I have heard so far. What I would like to propose is that, instead of a one-day Festival, we stretch this into two days."

The crowd was again on its feet, yelling, clapping, and having a good time in general. Steve again raised his hands for quiet.

"It seems that we are all agreed. I'd like for J.J. Darby and George Foxworth to give their presentation on Butte City and Highland Village, and then we can all relax, get something to eat, visit, and have a good time for the rest of the day. We will continue our presentations at 11 a.m., tomorrow."

George and I took the platform, and for an hour, we described what had taken place up there. It was amazing how the audience reacted to those talks. As George was speaking, I was able to study them and see the intensity with which they were listening. They were learning what had happened to themselves and the others in the group. When we finished, they were again on their feet, applauding. Steve called a halt to the talks, and asked again that everyone gather at eleven o'clock, the next day, for the wrap up.

By then, everyone was hungry. It was way past everyone's usual mealtime. The kitchens were the first stop, and after that, it was visit and talk. The children found balls and bats for various games, and the adults joined them in many cases. Someone had found cards, and three or four card games were going by the afternoon. Various instruments that had been found and rehabilitated were put to good use. Jefferson had taken a group up to the radio site, to explain about the contacts and to demonstrate the equipment. He got stuck there, because as he would finish one demonstration, more people would show up and he would have to start all over again.

There was a small scuffle down by the river in the early afternoon. Two or three very opinionated people had gotten into a discussion that had eventually exploded into hand-to-hand combat. George and some of his guard were on the scene in a short time and calmed tempers.

The evening passed rather quietly, after that. People who were not now residents of Goldston were found places to bunk for the night, and many of the youngsters slept out under the stars with thin blankets over them. Susan and I had Sam and the Lancasters for guests, and we talked the night away, each telling the other our dreams for the future and what we thought might happen.

I didn't mention to Sam that, within a year, myself, Susan, and many of the people who had worked with Steve on the dig would be leaving Goldston, possibly for good. Sam was sure that eventually Susan and I would move up to Highland. It was a very enjoyable night with friends and I couldn't spoil it.

The next morning was as bright and clear as the day before. Sam, Ronald, and I left the cabin early. The women said they would meet us at the kitchens later, for breakfast. We spent some time at the radio site with Jefferson and Ruth. They had made the preliminary calls before we arrived, and were awaiting a reply from Fred, but no reply came.

We passed the time in light conversation, until we saw Susan and Miriam leave the cabin and proceed toward the kitchens. I helped Jefferson secure the radio equipment, and we left the site to join the ladies for breakfast.

Shortly after 10 a.m., the people who had been visiting over at the farm started coming back. Some of the residents of Fort Darby had even ventured a trip home through the dark night, and were coming back down the trail. Once again, the long wooden table was piled high with baked goods and large urns of coffee. Everyone seemed to be enjoying the two-day respite from their labors.

Precisely at 11 a.m., Steve climbed the few steps up to the platform and came before the assembled crowd. "I'm glad to see that there was enough interest for you all to return, today. I hope everyone is having a good time and that we can do this again next year, providing of course we get through this one."

There was a smattering of laughter in the crowd. I don't think anyone was sure if Steve's comment was to be taken lightly or not.

"I think you will enjoy the next speaker. He was a member of the archaeology team at Ioda, and has prepared what I think is the best estimate we have of what happened on the day our world suddenly flew apart. He has put many hours into this project, and even though he tells me he isn't entirely sure of his findings, I see no other alternative, at the present. Johnny, would you come up?"

Johnny was all the way in the back of the audience when Steve called to him, and getting through the crowd while keeping all of his papers from flying away was a chore in itself. Steve left the stage as soon as Johnny got there. Johnny put his papers on the podium and looked over the crowd. He had never liked to speak before large audiences, and he took his time in gathering his thoughts, so as not to make a mistake.

"Good morning. I'm Johnny Burnside, and as Steve just said, I have a theory as to what happened to put us all in the spot we find ourselves in, now. I am not a professional geologist, nor am I a professional astronomer. What understanding I have comes from courses I attended in college and my amateur standing as a stargazer and rock hound. I'm not saying this is correct, and all of what I am going to say is open to interpretation."

"I never went to college, and don't know one star from the other," someone said. "I'll believe anything you tell me; just tell me, and stop all the talk."

That seemed to make him all the more determined, rather than rattle him. "If it's facts you want, then it's facts I'll give you. My opinion is that we've undergone a plate or continental shift, or even a polar shift, and I wouldn't rule out both happening at the same time. I would say that this disaster is worldwide and encompasses the entire planet. It was a chain reaction. One incident triggered another, and so forth, until it worked itself all the way around the world."

"You saying somebody dropped a bomb on someone else?"

"Not at all. I'm saying this had nothing to do with man, directly. I would say a continental plate shifted. The shift would have the impact of the San Andreas fault in California slipping, magnified by a million times. That in turn caused another shift, until the poles, especially the south pole, covered with millions and millions of tons of ice, couldn't take the strain any longer and moved. To put it in one word, we tilted. We physically moved on the face of this planet."

No one interrupted Johnny then. What he was saying was beyond belief, but something had happened to us, and that made what he was saying believable.

"Do you have any questions, before I continue?"

Someone in the audience raised his hand. Johnny looked in his direction.

"How many people could have survived?"

"I don't have any idea about that. But it's not how many survived the shocks or the tilt. The important thing is how many were able to find food and shelter, as we did. How many had uncontaminated water to drink."

Johnny waited for more questions, but there were none.

"I know most of you don't follow the stars or groupings of stars, but I'm basing my next theory on the stars in the night sky. Before, a certain arrangement of stars would cross the heavens every night, depending upon one's location and the time of year. I have no sky charts to help me, but I would say we are definitely below or near the equator. All of the constellations that were associated with that latitude line are now showing up in our night sky.

"The next thing I would like for you to consider is the marked increase in vegetation in the area. Trees are growing faster, taller. Ferns that never grew here are sprouting up everywhere, probably from spores brought in on the air currents. And I know you all have noticed we've had more rain in the last month than we had in any two-year period before. We are, without a doubt, going to live from now on in a tropical climate." Johnny stopped for a moment, to let what he was saying be thought over by his audience.

"When things settle down a little more, we should be able to figure out the rainy season, the best growing season. All you farmers, you'll be able to grow anything you can think of, with the exception of plants that need freezing or prolonged cold weather. We will definitely not have cold weather or snow ever again. Whatever cool and unsettled weather we have should last from late May, about now, through August. The opposite to what we have been accustomed to."

Johnny stopped talking, and unfolded a map that he had lying on the podium. He held it so that the audience could see it.

"Now that I have you thoroughly confused, let me add one more thing. If any of you are traveling, using the present maps we have, I would suggest shifting your north arrow about forty degrees west. Use this when planning trips. Tim and I did, and we came out very close."

A hand in the audience shot skyward. Johnny nodded in that direction, and a young lady stood up.

"If, as you say, the poles have moved and we're below the equator, where are you placing the poles now?"

"Good question. I've placed the north pole somewhere off the southern coast of Korea; I would say, in the strait between Korea and the Japanese island of Kyushu. As for the south pole, I'd say it lies in the Atlantic, off the South American continent, near what would have been Uruguay, possible at or near Montevideo."

Some in the audience understood what Johnny had just said, some others did not, but they all knew that those two places were a long way from where the poles were located in the world atlases they had studied in school.

Johnny looked over the crowd. "Do I have any further questions on this subject?"

Not seeing any hands raised or hearing any questions being shouted at him, he picked up his papers, looked toward Steve, and started to walk away. The audience, although skeptical of his findings, nevertheless rose as one and gave him a standing ovation. He waved acknowledgement as he went down the steps.

Steve came to the podium. He had a whole stack of papers with him. His turn to speak had come.

"Before I get started, I want to make sure there are no other persons that want to have the floor before I begin my presentation. Sam Burns, where are you?"

Sam held up his hand. "Right here, Steve. Over here."

"There you are. Do you have anything you'd like to say to this crowd, while we have them all in one group?"

"Not that I can think of at present, Steve."

"Okay. Mrs. Donley?"

Mrs. Donley stood. "Right here. Nothing at this time, Steve."

"Alright. Mr. Syminski?"

"Yeah, I want to see everyone back to work bright and early, tomorrow morning. Talking will be over; now it's time to do."

Laughter rippled through the crowd. Stephen waited for the laughs to stop, then continued.

"Mr. Tibbs, anything to add?"

"Just that I think we are all grateful to be where we are today, in light of everything that has happened to us. We all have come out on top."

Applause from the group, loud and long.

"Then, if there are no other speakers, I'll get down to business. I have not asked Mr. Yates or Mr. Arthur to speak, as they both declined beforehand. As you all know, these two gentlemen and I have tried as best we can to run things around here since we got together, shortly after the destruction. We've grown much stronger since that time, both in physical strength and sheer numbers."

Steve thumbed through some of the sheets of paper before him. He finally found what he was looking for.

"We are, as of today, one hundred and ninety-nine strong. That's every man, woman, and child in our group, which includes the people living in Goldston, the farms across the river, Fort Darby, and Highland Village.

"We have been joined by two families, the Pratts and Whittneys, from east of us, down the Little River. They were wiped out in the last floods. We would like for them to join us permanently, but they would rather return and rebuild their farms, sometime in the future.

"We have supplies and personnel to sustain ourselves and anyone else who may come our way in the future. And make no mistake, more people will turn up from time to time, or we will find more on our own.

"But simply taking care of ourselves isn't the issue, anymore. We are going to move on; we cannot stay with the status quo. I hope you all realize by now that we are not going to be rescued; there is no one out there with the power and resources to do that. We are on our own. We must assume we are alone." He let that statement sink in for a minute.

"Therefore, I am proposing today that we establish our own form of city and county government and law, and that we redistribute lands. It will be a big job, and we need to get started right away."

One of the young men from the fight the day before stood up. "Who are you going to give this land to, your friends?"

"I think if you hear me out, we'll come up with an equitable solution," Steve said.

"An equitable solution for you or me?" the young man said.

Three or four voices were raised in Steve's defense.

"Shut up, kid. You don't have any idea what he's talking about, yet," someone yelled.

"He's gotten us this far, and we want to hear him out," someone else hollered.

"Sit down and shut up," George yelled at the guy.

Steve waited for more responses; none came. He continued.

"Holding elections and voting aren't possible yet, so I am proposing that, to get us started, we appoint a board of commissioners—persons in our group who have helped in one way or another to help us reach this point."

Steve again studied some of his papers. "The recommendation I have here, and which has been discussed, is a board of five commissioners to head a government for six months. We would hope that at the end of that period everyone would be self-sufficient.

"After that time, the next board will be elected from among the public at large. To head this board, we'll need someone who can concentrate completely on the job and is willing to work much longer than the rest of us. The nomination I have here is for Mr. Tibbs."

There was a smattering of applause and some very notable *no's* from the audience. Mr. Tibbs stood up; he was one of the people yelling no.

"It's not that I'm not flattered," he said, "and I will be glad to serve on the board, but I would nominate you as head commissioner. You hold the position now, and are doing the best job that can be expected of any man."

Someone in the audience seconded the motion, and everyone followed suit. Finally, Steve held up his hands for quiet.

"All right. I'll be more than happy to serve for the first six-month period, but I want the right to choose my own board."

"You got it," someone said. "Name them, and we'll bring them to you."

"Mr. Tibbs, Sam Burns, Mr. Yates, and Thelma Brown. These are fine people, and represent a good cross-section of the community. Any objections to these selections?"

Nothing was said. There was a little rumbling from the young man who didn't seem to be satisfied with anything, but everyone ignored him.

"I've named four people who I want to help run things for the next six months. As for the fifth member, I would like a volunteer."

No one came forward, no one held up his hand. Steve waited, looking over the people before and all around him.

"Surely someone wants to help make the decisions that concern us all. How about someone brought back by either Tim Engles or Jack Fost?" Again, Steve looked over the group, but no volunteer was forthcoming.

"One more time. The young man who was asking all the questions. Yes, you. What about volunteering for duty? There's no pay, but you seem to have the community at heart and want to see that all decisions are on the up and up."

The young man stood up, somewhat bewildered by Steve's having picked him out of the crowd. "I don't know anything about government or how to run things," he said. "I have my own opinions, that's all."

He was nervous, his hands moved around from his pockets to behind him, then to the front, where he folded his arms, then began all over again. All the time, he was looking around him as if surely someone would come to his aid.

Steve wasn't going to let him off lightly. "Tell us something about yourself," he said. "Where you came from, how old you are, things like that."

"My name is Harold Savor. I came back to this place with Tim Engles. I was living with my parents in Ala Vista, but I haven't seen them since the world exploded. I'm nineteen, which makes me too young to serve on any committee."

"We won't know that until we make a law which states the age requirements. You may be the only nineteen-year-old to ever serve, but you aren't disqualified yet."

There was mild laughter from the audience, which seemed to ease the tense moment. Someone near Harold stood up.

"Go ahead, kid; give it a try. All they can do is kick you off, if you become too much of a headache."

There were several more yells for him to go ahead, accept the job.

"I'll do it," he said, finally. "Where do I sign up?"

There was applause from all around.

"Be here at the old schoolhouse first thing in the morning. Eight o'clock will be fine."

Steve waited for the frivolity of the moment to subside. There was a sternness in his voice when he continued.

"One of the big issues we must come to grips with will be making sure we have an adequate water supply, once the rains stop and summer comes—and it will, according to Johnny. I suggest a dam above Fort Darby, with a grain mill nearby to make use of the power that can be generated by the water.

"Mr. John Syminski has been acting as our overall building engineer, and I'd like to see him stay in that job and build this community in the months to come. He's told me that there's always room for anyone wanting to learn the building or blacksmith trades, and he'll be looking for a lot of help."

Steve studied his notes for a moment. He looked up and continued.

"I think everyone here knows Mrs. Donley. She's taken on the responsibility of starting our farm and animal husbandry programs. I would ask for her cooperation in the months to come, to train more farmers.

"Mr. Tibbs wants to rebuild Butte City, but I've asked him to stay at Fort Darby for the foreseeable future and put off that project for awhile. He has agreed, and I thank him for that.

"Now, to get down to a very touchy subject. That is, where everyone will work and live within the community. I've heard reports of dissatisfaction with the job some have been assigned, who they work with, where they live, and so forth. My suggestion is that, for the next six months, everyone should stay right where he or she is now. Then we'll be more organized and changes can be made.

"I am aware that being told what to do is alien to most of us. We are from a free society and have not been drafted to perform any given task. This is not, and will not be, a totalitarian state, and if anyone here is not satisfied, he can walk out at any time. But at present, it is impossible for everyone to work where he will. Our community is still building."

Someone in the audience stood up. "If I want to leave tomorrow and stake my claim, say, down the Little River, will you give me the provisions I need to live, until I can get on my own two feet?"

"No, definitely not. I'm saying, if you want to leave the group and set up on your own, you have the right. We don't have the people, time, or provisions to have everyone split up and go his way. The community will fall apart if we try to do that, and we'd come to a point where there would be no organization at all. Let me ask you this, where are you working now?"

"Over at the farms, with Mrs. Donley. It's not that I don't like her. I want to go out on my own. Do you see anything wrong with that?"

"No, I don't. And after a couple of growing seasons, when we have more seed and animals, then I'll back your desire to make a go of it on your own. That's what the commission can accomplish. Would you agree that only the best farmers, people who prove they can do the job and have the will to continue farming year after year, should be given help first?"

The man looked around the crowd for help. None was forthcoming. Most looked right back at him.

"You have a point," he said. "I'm willing to abide by whatever rules you establish about help, when the time comes."

"I'm glad you asked the question," Steve said. "Others may have been thinking the same thing. You also said something about staking a claim. We will have to respect anyone who was a landowner before the destruction, especially here in Goldston, at Butte City when we move up there, and with regards to the land up at Highland. These are all things that will have to be worked out in the coming months. Before I leave the subject of land, do we have anyone in the audience who has any background in survey work?"

Four or five men held up their hands. Steve questioned them for a few minutes, then picked the two he thought most qualified.

"If you two will be here tomorrow morning, Mr. Yates has agreed to be our land commissioner. He doesn't like the title, but he'll be in charge of all the land we need to survey, and when it's taken by anyone, he'll be the one to record the transaction. You might have to wait around for awhile. He's also our school principal, and may be a few minutes late."

An older gentleman in the audience stood up. "I have a question, Mr. Adams."

"Yes, sir, what is it?"

"What are we going to use for money? I've seen a few dollars in a few pockets, around here, but there isn't enough money in this crowd to buy a good steak dinner."

"We've talked that over, and we have enough expertise in the area of money and how goods should be priced. We'll have to work out a system of script, or something of that nature. Does that answer your question?"

"Not really, but it'll do for now."

"There's one more thing I think we should discuss before leaving today, and that is law and order."

There were a lot of moans and groans from the audience.

"No one may want to talk about it, but I think we have to discuss the matter before we leave today. We have no laws to break, at the moment, no courts, and no police force, but one has to be put into effect. Until then, we must take care of ourselves.

"Right now, George Foxworth has a few people, mostly rangers from the park service, who have been acting as sentries and look-outs in several different locations. We can keep this unit intact and build off that. I would appreciate any of you who has law or court experience to come to the command post, if you think you can help us set up a working judicial system."

Steve was silent for a few moments. He shuffled his papers, picked up the stack, and walked to the front of the stage.

"I know there are many things to be worked out, but we have a good start, now. We can build and grow from what we have accomplished. There are several things I would like to discuss, but as I look over this crowd, I can see you are as tired of listening as I am of talking." He waited for some kind of reaction from the crowd before him, but no one said anything.

"All I ask is that everyone be patient. We have a lot of decisions to make in the months to come and many items to work out. Everyone be patient. There is literally no place to go."

"Stephen?" someone yelled.

"Yes."

"Make a motion to adjourn and go get something to eat. I'm starved."

"The motion is made."

There were almost two hundred seconds. Everyone applauded Steve as he left the stage. I believe they were applauding themselves as much as they were him.

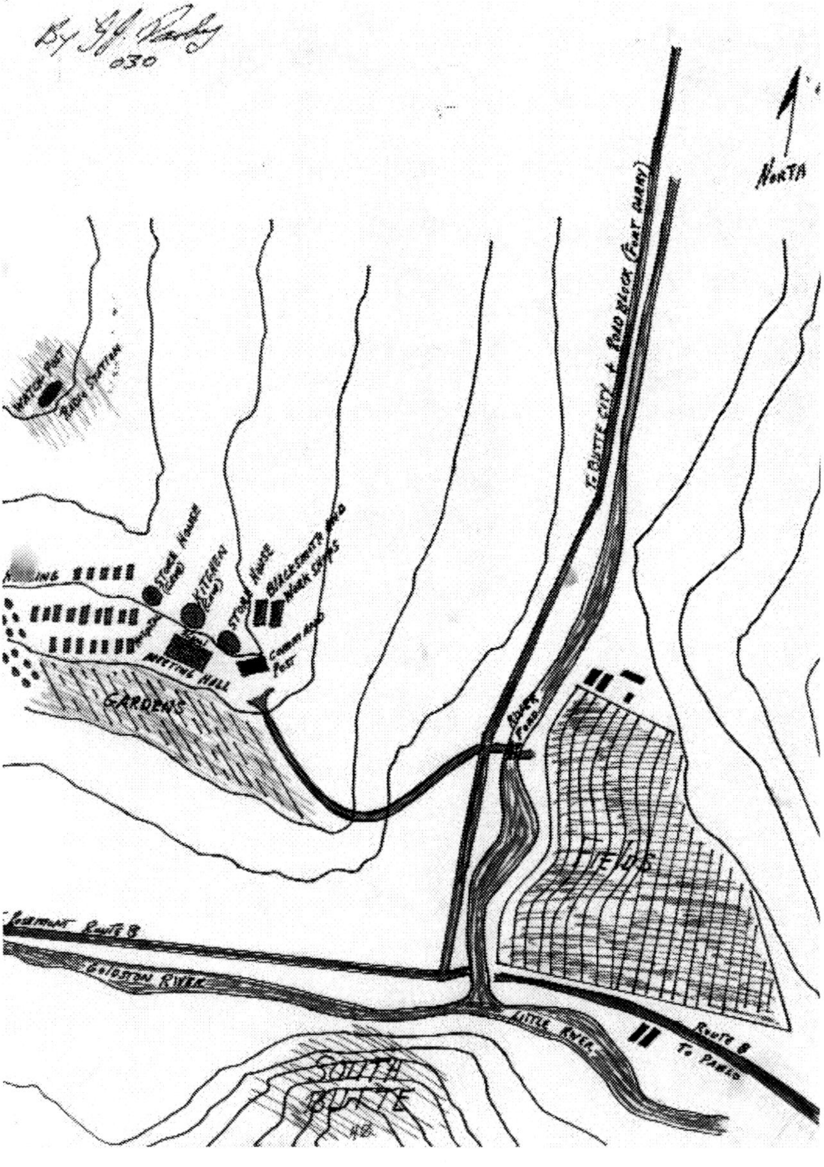

By G.J. Harley
030

NORTH

(ROUTE CITY & BAD ROCK (FORT GARRY)

Water Pit
RADIO STATION

STORE HOUSE
KITCHEN
STORE HOUSE
BLACKSMITH AND
NAIL SHOP
HORSE SHED

BARRACKS

MEETING HALL
GARDENS

WELL

GERM AND
POST

RIVER FORD

GIRLS

JACKSON ROUTE 8

EGLOSTON RIVER

LITTLE RIVER

ROUTE 8
TO RIVER

SOUTH
BUTTE
AZ

..... Route of Tim Ingals

------ Route of Jack Post

## Chapter 17

⟨❧⟩

# LIFE ON THE PENINSULA/ THE BOAT

The next six months were filled with more activity in and around Goldston than I have even seen before or since. After the Festival, things seemed to go along somewhat smoothly. There were trying times, of course, and not everyone was satisfied with his lot. A few people couldn't or wouldn't adapt to the life in our community, and left. Where they went, we don't know. They could have died, found another community they liked better, or remained on their own. We did find out later that the land to the north stretched many hundreds of miles, so they could have been lost there forever, if they wanted to be left completely alone.

A week after Steve had asked me to lead the expedition, we were on our way: Jim Goodman, Johnny Burnside, and myself. We found the going fairly easy for the first few days, and we were thankful for that. Our packs were crammed with food, survival equipment, emergency water, paper and pencils for recording our journey, maps to use and to change as needed, and we took turns carrying our one and only tent. We had agreed on that one piece of luxury equipment, in case we were stuck for a few days in one of our monsoon-like storms. Sitting in the rain for three or four days didn't appeal to us, and the strain of carrying the tent seemed well worth the effort.

Our trip took us north, through Fort Darby, Butte City, and beyond. The country was beautiful. Trees were growing in great abundance from Butte City northward, and animals seemed to be more plentiful than down where we had settled.

We had traveled for approximately seventy to seventy-five miles, when we came across a large river. By our maps, there was no river. In fact, our maps indicated that we were on a very high and relatively flat plateau. The mountains we had passed through the previous week were now giving way to slow, rolling terrain. Instead of the large valleys being covered with sagebrush and semi-arid plants, we encountered thick, rich, hearty grasses.

We camped for two days at the river's edge, but saw no one and heard nothing that would indicate to us that humans were anywhere in the vicinity. We searched both sides of the river for signs of human habitation, but found none. There were ample signs of animals, and the riverbank appeared to be one of their favorite travel paths.

The river flowed very rapidly to the east. We followed upstream for two days. The river didn't get any smaller, the farther we traveled; in fact, it became larger as we proceeded on our journey. After four days and forty-eight to fifty miles without detecting any sign of human life, we gained the north bank and started back. The north side of the river was much different from the south bank. The cliffs were higher, and the soil was sandy and covered with more scrub plants than the south.

When we again reached the place where we had first come upon the river, we pitched camp and rested for two days. The plan was to continue on to the mouth of the river; but first, we did some local exploring and found, a mile north of the river, a large, flat plateau between two ranges of hills. The hills were no more than two hundred feet high, and the flat area, two miles wide, stretched many miles north of our position. What made that place unique was that hardly anything grew there. The ground was so warm that we could feel the heat coming through our shoes.

There were cracks on the ground, running north and south. They were ten yards wide in some places, and some ran for up to a quarter-mile. We spent the better part of a day there, looking around and writing notes. We dropped rocks and pebbles down into the crevasses, but couldn't tell how deep they were. As Goodman said, that was one place you wouldn't want to be lost in, at night.

After our two-day break, we were ready to tackle the trip down the river. On the next leg of the journey, we tried rafting, but found the going was actually slower than walking, if we wanted to keep track of what might be only a couple of hundred yards away from the river. The thick vegetation we were encountering made it difficult, in some places, to see the river bank and impossible to see beyond. We walked for four days, making frequent trips away from the river.

The terrain became very flat two days before we reached the mouth, and we rafted again. We were on a large, marshy plain;. The river was running rapidly, and with an absence of sand bars and snags, we made excellent time.

When we did come to the mouth of what we now referred to as the New River, it was early afternoon. On the north shore where we stood, there were large reeds growing up on the bank and for many yards into the water. There was a huge sandbar in the middle of the channel, where it emptied into the larger body of water, which looked for all the world like an ocean to us.

We were making camp when Johnny stopped, noticing something across the river, and stared for a long time. I turned and looked over at the south bank, but didn't see anything unusual—some birds on the sandbar, but nothing else. Johnny shaded his eyes and continued to stare.

"Do you want the binoculars?" I asked.

"I don't need binoculars. I see a boat dock, over there."

Jim and I both were on our feet really fast.

"Where?" I couldn't see a thing.

"Look straight over the bar, on the far bank. There's a duck swimming around the piling."

I thought they were just some old tree stumps in the water, slightly off the bank. I said so to Johnny.

"I don't think so," he said. "Why would there be a thick board running parallel to all those stumps, held up there with a rope?"

Jim had the binoculars by now. "By God, you're right. Let's go take a look."

"Not all three of us," I said. "Johnny and I will go. Jim, you keep watch on us with the binoculars, and break out the rifle in case we get into some kind of scrape. I'm not sure what we might find back in those trees."

We worked our way back up-river a ways and swam across. We slowly crept downstream, hugging the south bank of the river for cover and protection. When we were only a few yards from the dock, we stopped to look things over.

The dock was only about three feet wide and about eight feet long. There was a narrow walkway, made out of planks, leading from the dock back to the bank. We approached slowly, climbed up on the dock, and followed the plank walk to shore. There had been someone there, and not too long ago. A beaten path led from the bank back into the trees, and there were pieces of wood spread along the path. I looked over at the other side of the river, and saw Jim standing there, watching us with the binoculars. I waved and indicated that we were going to follow the path. He waved back, and we proceeded down the trail.

We followed the path until we reached the trees, then stopped to listen. The air smelled of freshly cut timber. As we proceeded farther down the trail, we passed downed trees and places where other trees had been felled. Stacks of branches were all that remained of the trees that had been cut up and hauled away.

Five hundred yards from the beach, we came to a clearing. There were stacks and stacks of wood there. Also a lean-to, and whoever lived there had built an elaborate rock-and-mud stove and oven, a short distance from the lean-to. I thought I could detect the faint odor of fresh bread.

Other than the lean-to and oven, there was nothing of a personal nature there. Whoever lived there used a lot of wood and had a boat. We retraced our steps, and left the place exactly the way we'd found it. We crossed the river again, and joined Jim at our encampment.

He was highly enthusiastic about what we told him was across the river. "What do you think?" he said. "Big Group, small group?"

"I don't know, Jim. Not many people, but all that cut wood intrigues me. It's not used for building, or they'd at least have something more than a lean-to. But they could never use that much wood in the oven we saw, unless they were cooking for an army."

"You don't think that we have ran across a forward base for an army?" Jim said.

"Nope, not enough people," I said.

Johnny stood up and looked over the river. "I've got it. The boat, it's a wood burner. There has to be a shortage of fuel, oil, gasoline, so we have a wood burner. Has to be."

He had the best idea we could come up with, but where were they now? We unpacked and relaxed, resigned to wait a few days to see if anyone showed up. If no one did, we would leave a letter telling them who we were and where we could be found.

We didn't have a very long wait at all. The next day, we made a short trip up the coast, looking for survivors and mapping the coastline. We were back in camp, working on lighting a cooking fire, when we all heard the distinctive sound of a engine. At first, there was a faint chugging, then the wheezing of escaping air. We scrambled to the shore.

We saw a large, white boat, trimmed in black, needing a paint job very badly. One man was standing on the bow, giving arm and hand directions to the pilot in the wheelhouse. They were navigating around the north side of the large sandbar just off the mouth of the river. Their course would take them very close to our position before they turned and headed for the boat dock on the other side of the river.

We started waving our arms wildly and yelling to them. The man on the bow saw us and pointed, yelling back to the captain. He immediately threw the engine in reverse, and the big boat came to a stop and started backwards ever so slowly. Another man appeared from below deck with a rifle and took a position next to the first man, on the bow. The boat was no more than one hundred yards from us. The pilot shut down the engine and peered out of the wheelhouse. The man on the bow with the rifle was the first to speak.

"Where you fellows coming from?" he yelled.

"A town called Goldston, about a hundred miles south of here," I answered.

He looked around at the man standing next to him. His partner shrugged his shoulders.

"Never heard of it. How'd you survive the floods?"

"We weren't in any floods," I said.

It appeared they weren't any more trusting of us than we were of them.

"We mean you no harm," I said. "You see our entire crew, three people, armed with one rifle. We've been here two days now, waiting for you. The town we told you about has a population of about two hundred, now, and we're out trying to find other survivors."

The captain yelled something at the two men on the bow. The man with the rifle relayed the message to us.

"The captain says we'll take a chance you're telling the truth. Meet us across the river, as soon as we dock. But leave your rifle at home."

Jim was holding the rifle, and looked at me as though he didn't think it was a good idea.

"Let's leave the weapon here," I said. "They have the boat to protect. We can protect ourselves without the rifle."

"I don't know," Jim said. "They may be making a living jumping other people and taking what they can find."

"I don't think so, but you're beginning to worry me. You stay here. Johnny and I will go over and talk to them."

Once across the river and in the company of the three older men, there seemed to be no danger whatsoever. After handshakes all around, we called for Jim Goodman to join us. As soon as he was there, we all boarded the boat, and spent the afternoon telling each other as much as we knew of what had happened to our planet. Johnny explained his theory, and all three of our new acquaintances were, as everyone else had been, quite skeptical.

The captain of the Wind River was named Hannibal "Big Nose" Dushea—it was easy to see where he had acquired his nickname. He had been a logger most of his life, working the woods of Minnesota, but his brother was a big boat man and had built several during his lifetime, and Big Nose had been out on the lakes many times with him. His story of the disaster was quite different from any we had heard up to that time.

The morning of the destruction, he had been leaving for work, and was no more than two blocks from home when a powerful earthquake struck. The earth was moving so much and with such great violence that his car was flipped completely over. He'd managed to break a window and drag himself out, but the world was in such turmoil that he couldn't even determine the direction back to his home. As the violent shaking had stopped, he'd had the sensation that the earth under his feet was moving away from him at a great speed, both vertically and laterally. He was thrown into a tree and stunned or knocked out, he wasn't sure which, but when he awoke, he was on the roof of a house with another man, who had apparently dragged him there.

He had been lying across the ridge of the house, face down, and as he'd looked up, he'd seen that they were literally at sea. There was debris everywhere. People were yelling for help, and even though he hadn't been fully awake, he swore that the roof of that house was being propelled through the water at a great speed. Again, he'd passed out, only to waken and find that the sun had gone down. It was pitch black, not a star in the sky could be seen.

"I knew I was dead," he said, "and traveling somewhere between heaven or hell. I slept most of that night and the next day. When I did finally open my eyes, my head hurt so bad, I wanted to take it off my shoulders and get a new one. The man who'd been on the roof with me was gone, nowhere to be seen. There was debris in the water, and I saw some other people clinging to objects, but everyone was quiet—the yelling had given way to despair. I never did find out what happened to the man who saved me.

"I floated on that roof several days, until Bob Johnston here came along. He found me drifting down a sand spit, a couple hundred miles north of here, and brought me ashore." He indicated the man who had been on the bow of the boat when we had first seen them.

"I'll always be grateful for that, and Bob knows it. He could have left me alone to drift until I starved to death."

Bob didn't say much during our stay there. He was very shy of people, and according to Big Nose Dushea, had been that way since they'd met. Bob Johnston had worked on a huge ranch in eastern North Dakota. His principal job there had been caretaker of the ranch. The owners had closed the ranch, and were trying to sell off acreage. No one was there when the earthquakes struck but Bob, his dog, a horse, and a dozen or so cattle that were left there to graze and give the place the look of a ranch, or so the owners had told him. Every building on the ranch had been flattened. His dog had been killed when the house had come down on him, and the horse and cattle had scattered.

He told of lying on the ground for an hour, while the ground heaved and buckled under him. The next day, he'd gone looking for the horse, but had never found him. He had found some of the neighbors. A dozen or so had banded together, and the last time he'd seen them, they were going to stay there, build a house, and salvage as much food, grain, and animals as they could, until help arrived.

For his part, he'd kept going south; he didn't really know why. He'd followed along the new shoreline, finding food from time to time. Once, he'd run across thousands of canned goods—tomatoes, corn, peas, and the like. He'd eaten his fill, taken along as much as he could, and continued south, until he had seen the house roof floating just offshore, where it had grounded. He'd taken Big Nose ashore, and had fed and taken care of him until he'd recovered enough to go back north, where Bob had seen all of the canned goods. They'd stopped there and started a salvage operation.

They estimated that, at one time, they'd had 30,000 cans of vegetables, juices, and canned fruit of all kinds. No one knew where they all came from, some warehouse somewhere. The strong winds and tide may have carried the cases of food hundreds of miles.

They shared their stores with the people they had met not far away. Another group of ranchers and farmers had banded together, the same as they had done up where Bob had been caretaker. A small town was slowly growing, where only a short while before there had only been open prairie.

They were making a trip over there, one day, when they'd seen smoke coming from the direction of the ranch. By the time they'd reached there, everything was in flames. Cattle and horses lay where they had been slaughtered, and the worst thing was seeing the people, dead, everywhere, draped over animals, lying on the ground. Big Nose wasn't sure, but he thought there had been about fifty people there.

They'd finally found one man alive. He'd been shot several times and was covered in blood. He'd told them that, the night before, seven people had come in looking for food. They'd fed them and put them up for the night in one of the barns. The next morning, the seven had become seventy, and they had been taking everything in sight. They'd started by shooting the cows, good milk cows; they'd cut out the hindquarters and left the rest to rot.

The fighting had started when the ranchers had brought out weapons and demanded that they stop. They'd come at the ranchers like locusts; they'd been everywhere, the man had said. When the ranchers had said they'd had enough, they'd continued to kill. They'd taken some of the younger children.

After they'd ransacked the whole place, they'd set the barns and the houses ablaze, and had made a bonfire of all that remained. Then they'd left.

The dying man had advised Big Nose and Bob not to go home, because they knew of the large cache of canned goods at their place. The old man had died shortly after. They had taken his advice and not returned. After burying him and everyone else they could find, they'd struck out north, away from what they referred to as the "Locust People."

Big Nose and Bob had met John "Fat Man Scared of the Horse" Dupree a few days later. He had been hunting when they'd run into each other. He'd asked the two to join him around his campfire for venison and potatoes.

After talking for awhile and finding out that Big Nose was familiar with boats, Fat Man had said that he knew of a boat that would float. They'd marched farther north and found the Wind River, right where he'd said it would be. It had taken some work to right the big boat, and even more work to slide her down into the water. She had been a coal-fired tug that had pushed supply barges along the lakes in southern Canada; also a passenger boat. Most of her cargo had gone to the Indian reservation where Fat Man had been raised. He had remembered the boat, even though it had been out of service for many years.

The three of us were curious about Fat Man's name, and finally, Johnny asked him why he had such a name, when in fact he was tall, slender, and not fat at all. All three of our new friends got a big laugh out of that, and Fat Man told us the story behind his name.

When he was just a lad of three, he'd been very chubby. His father had referred to him as his "little fat man." His brother was a teenager and owned a pony, but he would never let his little brother ride. One holiday, when all of his aunts, uncles, cousins, and other relatives were over to celebrate, he'd thrown a fit to ride the pony. Finally, the brother had given in, brought the pony around, and put him on it. Once there, he hadn't liked the view at all. The pony was much taller than he'd imagined, and he'd started to cry. A young cousin, slightly older then himself, yelled out, "Look, Fat

Man is scared of the horse," and the name had stuck. Even after he had grown into a man, had lost all of the baby fat, and become a very good horseman, the name had stuck.

When John Fat Man had finished his story, I asked Big Nose why they had been so leery of us when we'd first met, and he said it had been because of the Locust People. After they'd finally found out how to run the boat and had enough wood and food aboard, they'd headed south. When they were offshore of where they had stored the canned goods, they'd run into the Locust People.

"We lay about two hundred yards offshore and observed them for an hour or so," Big Nose said. "They seemed peaceful enough, and they'd put a big dent in the mountain of goods we'd stacked up. Bob had sounded the bottom and said we had about fifteen feet of water under us, so I thought to go a little closer. As we neared the beach, they became curious and started gathering near the shore. As soon as Bob said we were down to ten feet, I stopped the old girl and let her drift a bit. I yelled to the beach that those rations were mine, and said we wanted to come ashore and take them back.

"Boy, you want to see a bunch of people go completely crazy. Of course, I had no intention of going ashore. They started throwing rocks, shells, empty cans, and mud at us, but they weren't even reaching the boat. They brought out a couple rifles, some they more than likely stole when they killed the ranch people. Well, that was a big mistake. Johnny Fat Man, here, is about the best shot I've seen, so after we took a couple rounds, he fires back three shots; three fall. People scattered in all directions. Then I saw swimmers in the water, not more than ten feet from the boat.

"I threw Wind River in reverse, spun the wheel, and we started out for deeper water. A couple made the sideboards, but we beat them off with the rifle butt and a boat hook. Looking at those devils close up gave me goose bumps." As the captain talked, he was indicating with gestures how he had been handling the boat and helping beat off the boarders at the same time.

"There was no use in hanging around there," he said, "so we went south, then farther south, until we ended up here. We use this and two more spots for fuel and watering. We've run into some better people on the beaches we've passed. The reality is, you have to be cautious when you first run across anyone you haven't met before somewhere."

We assured him that we understood completely, and told them about the time we'd had with Jason.

I asked Big Nose about the oven. He explained that if we'd taken the time to look under the lean-to, we'd have found a small, natural cavern, which held their supply of flour, lard, and salt. They had chosen that clearing to make bread, because up to the time we'd arrived, they'd been completely isolated from other people. The other two stops farther north held other supplies, so that if some-one should move in on them and discovered one stash, they always had another.

They invited us to stay aboard and have supper with them, so we did. After we had eaten, I asked Big Nose if he had ever crossed the large body of water to the east and seen what was on the other side. He said no, that the three put together made only about half of a good seaman, and they'd been traveling the shoreline between that spot and as far north as where they had found the boat. Eventually, they wanted to make a long voyage, when they had a lit-tle more experience in navigation and were more sure of them-selves when operating the boat. That's when I formulated what I thought would be a good plan for us both.

"Tell me, how many passengers will this boat carry?"

"I don't really know," Big Nose said. He turned to Fat Man and asked him the same question.

"Well, there were rails and benches at one time, around the stern," Fat Man said. "I remember many people going to the main-land on her, with all kinds of packages and boxes. I know she could carry twenty-five, maybe more."

Big Nose looked around at me. "Why do you ask?" he smiled. "You have a passenger route for us?"

"I was just thinking. We eventually want to leave Goldston and go either to Mexico or the East Coast, and with so much water, it seems that the only transportation would be a boat. What do you think? We could support each other, and check out some of this world together."

Big Nose looked around at his two companions. "What do you two think?" he asked.

Bob seemed to be the most reluctant of the trio. "When? How many people are we talking about?"

I had to think for a minute. "I'd say roughly fifteen to twenty people."

"That's too much of a load," he said. "Sick children, hysterical women, and it would take too much to keep that many people fed on a long voyage. We don't even know if there's anything on the other side."

"Come on," Fat Man said. "If the white man had never wanted to see what was on the other side of the ocean, you'd've never been a caretaker in North Dakota."

Fat Man continued with a wink and a nudge at Bob. "And who knows, maybe I'd have been a land baron. What else have you got to do with the rest of your life but sail up and down the coast with Big Nose and me. Big Nose, you for going?"

"I'm going to wait and see what Bob says first," he said.

Bob was on the spot and he knew it. He had raised the objection, and it was up to him to either approve or disapprove the adventure. I had a feeling the other two would go along with whatever he agreed to do. They had taken care of each other up to that point, and we were hardly more than strangers.

Bob sipped his coffee, looked over at Big Nose and me, then smiled. "Why the hell not? It's going to get pretty boring around here, after awhile. I hope I can stand all those screaming kids."

Big Nose had the last word on the subject. "Looks like you have a crew, if you want to cross the ocean. But we aren't the best sailors, and we could get lost out there and all end up dead."

"Chance we all have to take," I said. "Johnny knows all about the stars, and I'm sure he can help you out on navigation. We won't be ready to go for awhile yet, anyway. Would you be ready to sail in about a year, give or take a few days?"

"Why so long?" Big Nose asked. He seemed a little let down, as if I'd been talking about leaving the next week.

"Well, we have a lot to do back at Goldston to get prepared, and the three of us are committed to two more trips—one west and one south. The man we worked for before the destruction has been helping form the government at the town we're living in, and it'll be at least six months before he'd leave. You still for making the trip? Of course, you can go by yourselves, but there's safety in numbers, and we do have a good navigator here."

"We'll get the boat ready to carry passengers. Where will we meet?"

"I'll tell you what. Give us a ride south, and we'll find a place you can drop us off. We can plan a meeting back there in about a year."

With the matter of sailing settled, we enjoyed the rest of the evening talking. Fat Man and Johnny went fishing for awhile, and returned with quite a catch.

The next morning, we packed up our camp and returned to the boat for a ride south. I enjoyed that boat ride. She wasn't the fastest craft in the water, but she was very sturdy, and the chugging of the engine was somehow strong and reassuring. Big Nose had been experimenting with different sails. The one thing the old engine loved was wood, and plenty of it. As long as he sailed the coast there would be an ample supply, but a voyage away from that supply might require alternative power sources.

We checked several spots where I thought we would be directly east of Goldston. Finally, we came across a small bay that was very deep and ran northwest, away from the open sea, a good mile. We parted company with the boat crew, with the understanding that we'd all meet there in one year.

Before we left, we spent a full day helping in the construction of a landing site for the boat and establishing the place as a base camp. We wanted to stay and help with wood cutting, but they told us to get on our way. They figured the sooner we left the sooner we'd be back.

The trip from the boat site took eight days, the first two being the hardest. The mountains were highest and the most rugged near the water. We spent many hours searching for the best route for the return trip we hoped to be making in one year.

Once we'd gained the valley of the Little River, the trip was just a matter of time. We passed the place where the ranch families who were in Goldston had lived, and took an assessment of the area for their benefit.

When we arrived home, everyone wanted to know about the contact with the people on the boat. We told the story time after time. In fact, Steve called a work stoppage one morning, so that everyone could gather around, listen to our story, and ask questions. It was at that meeting that Steve told everyone of his desire to one day leave the valley.

We were saddened to hear that we had suffered our first death since the big disaster. The man who had been hurt during the bad rains and mud slides at Fort Darby had passed away while we were gone. Steve had called a work halt for half a day. Everyone had gone up to Fort Darby and attended the ceremony for him, conducted by Mr. Tibbs. He had been buried on the east bank of the Goldston River, directly across from Fort Darby.

Johnny Burnside, Jim Goodman, and I spent the next week writing an account of the trip north and making maps that could be used in the future. On one of the maps, I plotted the location where we had seen seven to twelve head of cattle, which could be a major supply of beef in the future. Also, we'd seen some horses in the same vicinity. The remainder of the week, we planned for the next trip, west to Junction City. Susan was going with us, and was a great part of the preparations.

Johnny was very enthusiastic about making sky charts and constructing a sextant, to be used when we crossed the ocean, and he asked to be left out of the next trip. Scott Allen, who had been working closely with George on law and order and had been on the first trip west with Jack Fost, took his place.

We left Goldston exactly two weeks after returning from the first trip north. We stayed north of the Goldston River, and hadn't planned any stops until we reached the great flood plain where Rosemont had been. But we had to make one slight change to those plans and stop in at Ioda.

The supply trailer was still there. It had been restocked with canned goods, crackers, blankets wrapped in plastic, and a few sleeping bags from the sports store in Goldston. Susan wondered what was going to become of those supplies; would we leave them there indefinitely?

"I don't know," I said. "It's a good idea. Tim and Fost couldn't say enough about being able to rest and get food and water, when they were here. Speaking of that, does anyone see any water cans?"

We all looked, but none were found. At first, I thought that strange. I would have thought water would have been the first thing to be replaced when the trailer was restocked. Then I remembered that a small spring north of there had been reported by Tim, and plenty of water was available. A note describing its location was posted inside the trailer.

Susan wanted to walk over to the dig site before we left. As we stood looking over the site, Susan began to cry. I couldn't help but cry myself, and taking her by the arm, motioned to the other two that it was time to leave. We left Ioda and the dig site for the last time.

Scott Allen has been on this journey before; therefore, he was the logical one to be our guide. We made Rosemont in four days, pitched camp, and rested. We made short trips around, but found nothing to indicate any humans had been there since Fost had brought the Tibbs group through, on the way to Ioda and Goldston.

In three more days, we were in Junction City. Those people had not been as fortunate as we were. They had started over from scratch; no buildings had remained, very little food, and no organization for rebuilding. We were not surprised to find that they hadn't come as far as we had.

They hadn't started what could be called any kind of farming, depending mainly on what animals could be hunted for food. Their diet was supplemented by a variety of greens and roots that grew wild in the vicinity. They had no school system for the children's education, and seemed not to care when we mentioned it to them. They were living in small huts made of logs, mud, grass, and in some cases, animal hides. There were even a couple of fairly well-made teepees, but no structure that would stand up to any really heavy weather.

They had grown in population since Fost had been there, and now had more than sixty people in their group. The present inhabitants didn't refer to where they were living as Junction City, but simply called it "the Place."

We explained what we had accomplished in Goldston, and that we were there to see what help we could give to each other. When I said that we'd like to take a census, count everyone, and get information on who they were, they became somewhat skeptical.

"What you need that for?" an old man said. "There ain't no government, anymore. You plan on writing D.C. and getting assistance for all of us?"

His companions burst out in laughter.

"Not really," I said. "But it wouldn't be a bad idea to start a self-help program. You help us, we help you. We've been very fortunate, considering, and would be glad to send people over to give you a hand getting organized."

"What makes you think we want to get organized?" he asked. "We've been doing quite well for ourselves. No complications, no headaches, getting by very nicely, thank you."

I couldn't help but look at him and shake my head from side to side. *The usual way of the world*, I thought.

"What you do is fine with me," I said. "Do you mind if we ask a few questions, take down your names, get some idea of the ages of the children, things like that?"

"I personally don't care. Got no children; my wife disappeared in the flood. You can ask the rest what you like."

We did just that. They were a loosely knit group of people, and it took a week for us to find everyone. Some of the men were out on hunting trips, and people wandered in and out of the town from time to time.

Susan did the best job she could, under the circumstances. One person told Susan during one of the interviews that we were considered as being from the government, and government always wanted to know things that didn't amount to a hill of beans, so if they lied to her, it wasn't going to hurt anything, anyway.

Once we'd accomplished all that we could, we packed up and started west, to complete our journey. We had company for that part of the trip. A few of the men had traveled all the way to the ocean, to the west of us, and went along to show the way.

Our new guides were always in a hurry, and would become impatient when we wanted to make side trips to check out the land we were passing through or write down what plants or animals we found. At one point, I became a little hostile, and told our guides that if they were in such a rush to reach the coast, to please go on ahead. They didn't want to do that, and settled down to some extent.

We reached the coast three days after leaving "the Place," Junction City, turned south, and proceeded in that direction for another day and a half, before coming to the end of our new landmass, which seemed to be nothing more than a very large island. It was a strange feeling for all of us to stand on a high point of ground, which was somewhere in the vicinity of the Utah and Colorado state lines, and look over an ocean of water. We wondered where we'd find the next landfall.

We had a good idea of what our new island looked like, from the mountains in the east to the slow-rolling hills in the west. We estimated the peninsula we were on to be about 155 miles wide and anywhere from a few hundred to a thousand or more miles long.

We left the guides from the Place there, to continue their hunting trip, while we cut across country in what would have been a northeasterly trip, according to our old maps, but was due east according to Johnny's reckoning. We took our time on the return trip, and reached Goldston exactly one month from the day we had departed.

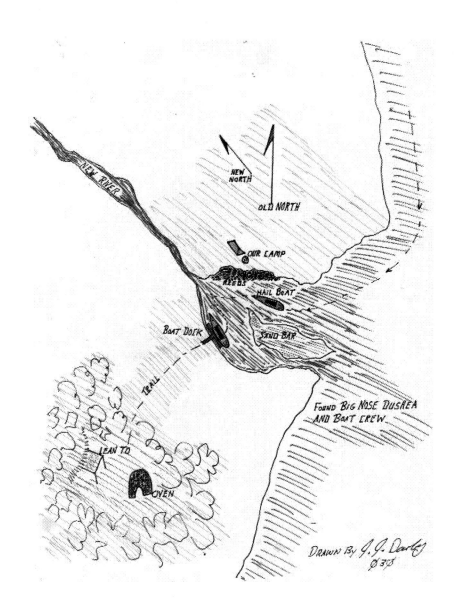

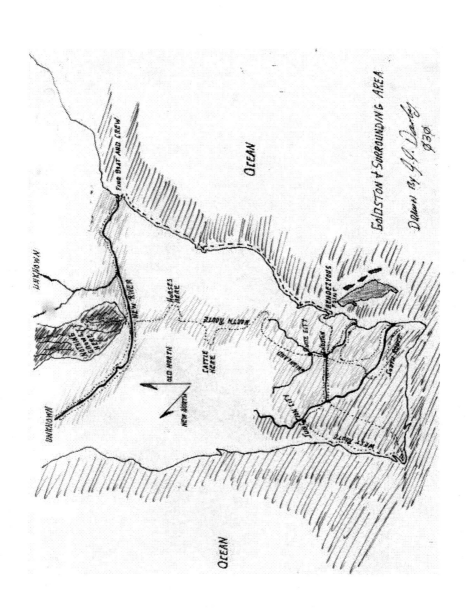

GOLDSTON & SURROUNDING AREA

Drawn by A.A. Darby
1930

## Chapter 18

*૭૭)*

# HAVE I GOT A STORY FOR YOU

It was late Sunday afternoon. Rodney and I had talked the weekend away. I thought it was time to finish off the cookies Susan had baked, so I went to the kitchen, retrieved the last batch, made a fresh pot of coffee, and returned to the gazebo.

"Let's see, Rodney, where were we?"

"You were telling me about the trip," Rodney said. "You were back in Goldston a month after you left."

"Oh yeah, we had a good time on that trip. No pressures, plenty to eat, no timetable. Exploring, looking, smelling, and glad to be alive."

"Did you and the rest leave Goldston soon after you returned from that trip?"

"Oh no. There was still a lot to do. Your dad had promised those people six months of government, and he stayed true to his word.

"We started to cancel the trip south. Tim had covered a good bit of that territory, and if anyone else was down there and still alive, they were making it on their own. But your dad had planned for a trip south, so I gathered up Jim Goodman and Johnny Burnside, and we made a trip roughly on the same line as Tim had done, some months before. Tim wanted to make that trip really badly, but he had contracted a bad foot problem from too much time in the water, from the previous trip, and had to sit that one out.

"We had the maps he and his crew had used, but were unable to locate any more people. We saw human tracks on a couple of occasions, but could never make contact with anyone. Either they did-n't want us to find them or we weren't looking in the right places.

"We made camp at the place where the river and the ocean met. About, we thought, where Tim had stayed while he waited for his people to return from Ioda with supplies. We searched around there for a week, but found nothing. Before leaving, we left notes all around that we were in Goldston, with directions on how to find us. We returned home empty-handed, after four weeks of search-ing, but we'd tried. After we returned from that trip, the trailer at Ioda was dismantled and taken to Fort Darby, to be used as hous-ing."

Rodney was ready with his next question as soon as I stopped talking.

"Tell me what happened between that time and when you all finally left Goldston for good."

"Well, let me see. You were born, of course. But you weren't the first baby born after the destruction; I believe you were the third. But your mom and dad didn't care about that; you were their hope for the future. I do believe your dad worked even harder after you were born.

"We eventually closed the radio station. Jefferson married Ruth, and they took a piece of land up at Highland Village. Sam made sure they were put right on the place where the old ranch house had once stood."

Rodney looked puzzled. "Why did you close the station?" he asked.

"Eventually, Fred, up in Canada, ran out of batteries. Jerry came up every so often, but his equipment was so unreliable that he, one day, said he hoped to meet up with us and shut down. We tried fur-ther contact; Jefferson tried and tried until it was no use anymore. He took the equipment back to Highland with him, and would lis-ten from time to time, but so far as I know, he never did have a real-ly firm contact with anyone.

"But I mentioned the marriage of Ruth and Jefferson. Johnny Burnside and Judy were married at the same time as the Jeffersons. Tibbs had a double ceremony, that day. He turned out to be one heck of a preacher. Built a really nice log church."

"What did you do until you left?" Rodney asked.

"Me, personally?"

"Well, yeah."

"Many odd jobs. Susan was tied up with paperwork. She went around and recorded everyone's name, age, and whatever they could remember about other members of their families who hadn't survived the destruction. She helped when it was time to write up the laws and ordinances that the council came up with, and helped with the registration of deeds, births, deaths, and so forth. She was one busy lady. Oh, but you asked about me.

"A group of us went back north, rounded up the small herd of cattle we had seen earlier, and took them back to Highland to join Sam's herd. I helped build some of the houses up there; in fact, Jefferson's house was the first one I worked on.

"I drew many of the maps that were used for reference, when it was time to lay out the township. And we went back to Ioda and the old park headquarters, and put markers and placards at both places in memory of our friends and family members who had died there."

Thinking about the friends we had left at Ioda brought tears to my eyes, even though it had been thirty years since the event. I cleared my throat and continued.

"I remember your dad sending Johnny and me back out to where we were going to meet old Big Nose Dushea. We made maps of the trail we wanted to follow. Johnny brought along his sextant and stayed with the boat crew, making several runs out to sea with them, making sure he knew what he was doing and that they understood how to use it.

"They'd done an awful lot of work since the last time we'd seen them. A big fancy boat dock, two huge log cabins, and enough cut wood to steam around the world four or five times.

"We weren't able to make the year rendezvous as we had planned, but the extra months gave the boat crew more time to get proficient at traveling away from the sight of land."

"Whatever happened to Captain Dushea and his crew?"

"We stayed together for awhile. They took us to several spots, looking for a way back to the east coast. Once we struck out overland, we parted company. They may still be out there somewhere, steaming from one place to another."

"What about Goldston? Do you think it's still there?"

"You can bet on that," I said. "Your dad worked hard to get a good, solid community started there. When the first elections came around, he could have had the job of head commissioner, hands down, but he said over and over that he was going with a party that would be leaving soon, and couldn't serve."

"What about Junction City, or 'the Place,' as it was called? You think they survived?"

"Some people from there came over, took a look, and didn't believe what we had accomplished. A few brought their kids over for schooling. I don't know about Junction City, but do I believe Goldston is there? I do.

"I planned many times to go back and see how much the place had changed. I can still remember Susan and myself climbing up on South Butte before we left, to look the place over. Never have forgotten that sight. But now, I do believe I've waited too long. These old bones could never make that long trip."

I took a long sip on my coffee, as I waited for Rodney to catch up on some of his notes. Then a thought came to me.

"You seem like the adventuresome type, Rodney. Why not talk yourself into a trip west, and go see what it was like for all us old folks."

"That's something to think about. Now, what about the trip away from Goldston?"

I looked at Rodney for a long time. He began to get uneasy. Finally, I took a deep breath and spoke.

"Son, that's a long story, and this old man has told you twice what he thought he could remember. In a way, I'm thankful for that. You've made me recall events long forgotten to me. But for now, I need a break, need to do some gardening and think about what I've told you already. Susan's going to be home tomorrow, and to tell you the truth, I'm going to tell her some of the things I've told you, and we're going to relive them together."

Rodney said that he understood, made some more notes, then put his notebook away. We enjoyed a steaming cup of coffee, while talking and looking down on the town below, in the valley.

Later, I helped him pack all of the papers, books, maps, and notes that he wanted to take with him. I gave him Susan's diary, which she had offered to him.

He made me promise that, from time to time, I would come down to the valley and help him with his history. I assured him that I would change my ways for his sake, and come down and see him and the rest of the family. It had been a very long time since Steve and I had talked. Then we shook hands, and he left.

I spent a quiet evening by myself. That was the first time in a good while that I could remember being absolutely alone.

I was up early, the next morning. Fixed breakfast, then straightened up the house; did a little gardening work, then sat down in the gazebo to enjoy the cool, quiet day and wait for Susan.

About noon, I saw and heard some of the children, as they came around the exposed corner of the trail. About twenty minutes later, they came into view. I walked out to meet them and welcome Susan home.

We gave each other a big hug and kiss. I had missed her those past days. She saw the great, big smile on my face, and asked me about it. I told her that my next big project would be to straighten out that crooked trail, so she wouldn't have such a tough time climbing.

She looked at me, surprised. She turned to the children, and told them to take all the packages to the house and wait for her there. She told them they could have cookies and milk until she arrived. Then she turned back to me. I took her hand, and we walked to the gazebo.

"Susan," I said. "I am going to tell you the most wonderful story about the past."

Printed in the United States
25169LVS00004B/52-57

9 781587 364495